Blackthorn Winter

Blackthorn Winter

KATHRYN REISS

Harcourt, Inc.

Orlando   Austin   New York   San Diego   Toronto   London

www.HarcourtBooks.com

Library of Congress Cataloging-in-Publication Data
Reiss, Kathryn.
Blackthorn winter/Kathryn Reiss.
p. cm.
Summary: An idyllic seaside artists' colony in England is the scene
of murder, and fifteen-year-old American-born Juliana Martin-Drake
attempts to solve the crime while unraveling the mystery of her own past.
[1. Adoption—Fiction. 2. Artists—Fiction. 3. Family life—England—Fiction.
4. England—Fiction. 5. Mystery and detective stories.] I. Title.
PZ7.R2776Bla 2006
[Fic]—dc22 2005003645
ISBN-13: 978-0-15-205479-3 ISBN-10: 0-15-205479-0

Text set in Minion and MrsEaves
Designed by Cathy Riggs

C E G H F D B

Printed in the United States of America

*This is a work of fiction. All the names, characters, organizations, and events
portrayed in this book are products of the author's imagination. Any resemblance
to any organization, event, or actual person, living or dead, is unintentional.*

For Stanley Hooper—
and in memory of his wife, Audrey—

two dear friends
whose early-blooming blackthorn bush
in a lovely English garden
inspired this mystery

Blackthorn Winter

PART 1

*"Other sins only speak;
Murder shrieks out."*

—John Webster, 1623
The Duchess of Malfi, ACT 4, SCENE 2

M om glanced over at me impatiently and said, "Come on, Juliana, what's with all the doom and gloom?" As if she didn't know.

We were driving on a highway in England (a *motorway*, Mom called it). We were whizzing along—on the wrong side of the road, as far as I was concerned—through a chilly, windy afternoon, with rain from the wet road and the cars ahead sluicing over us in sheets. The wipers' rhythmic *swoosh-swoosh* had lulled me into a kind of trance as I sat there in the front passenger seat, staring out at the drizzly English day. How could I be filled with anything other than doom and gloom when I'd been dragged away from sunny California (and from *Dad*) to move to England like this in the middle of the school year? How else was I supposed to feel?

I didn't want to be here in the first place, away from Dad, away from friends, away from everything. In the second place, I felt tricked. Like, where were the little thatched cottages with roses around the doors and diamond panes of glass in every window? Where were the romantic castle ruins and sun-dappled stately homes featured on the "Visions of England" calendar Mom had given me for Christmas? Everything felt wrong. Nothing was the way it *should* be.

"Faulty advertising," I muttered. We'd landed at Heathrow Airport that morning after an eleven-hour flight, whizzed through passport control and customs, collected our luggage pretty fast, but then had to stand in line for another hour to get our rental car. Finally we'd crammed ourselves and our stuff into the car and set off, driving away from London. We'd been traveling a couple of hours already, and all I'd seen were clusters of dreary brick houses huddling together as if for warmth and wet fields dripping with sheep and cows.

"Fifteen years old, and you've never experienced an English winter," Mom said to me. She didn't even take her eyes off the road, which was probably a good thing, with all those cars driving on the wrong side and everything. "We're going to fix that!" Her voice was maddeningly cheerful.

"It's March, Mom. That's spring," I told her.

"Spring in California," Mom agreed. "But not here. This is still winter."

Our one family trip to England had been years ago, and in summer. We had visited Mom's father. I had a vague memory of Grandad's little house in a big city. It had been hard to fit us all around the kitchen table. After our one visit, Grandad always came to visit us in California instead.

In the backseat my nine-year-old sister and brother woke up. They had been dozing on and off, probably still on California time, ever since we left the airport. Now Ivy and Edmund, also known as the Goops because of their perpetually sticky fingers and dirt-streaked T-shirts, started clamoring about how they wished they could see Grandad Martin again, and more especially *Dad*—since he wasn't even dead—and it wasn't *fair*.

"I wish we could see Grandad again, too," Mom said, picking out the one thing we could all agree on. He had lived in the house where Mom grew up until he died three years ago. It had seemed strange not to have him come to us in California for Christmas. And it seemed very strange to be in England now and to know he wasn't here. Somehow that made everything feel even more dreary.

Mom circled our little car off the motorway. "We're almost there. Now you kids are going to love Blackthorn." And then she launched yet again into the irritatingly enthusiastic description of the place where we were going to be living. We'd already heard it a million times.

Mom's voice sounded dreamy. "It's a bustling little village right on the sea, and it's full of artists, Liza says. Just the sort of place where I can really get some work done. Where people *respect* art." Her voice hardened a little when she said "respect," and I knew she was thinking of Dad back in California. Mom and Dad were having a trial separation. Mom felt that Dad was too busy being a big-shot architect to notice that she wasn't happy anymore. She was homesick for England, she said, and decided that she needed to live there again, and start painting again, and be near other artists.

"People respect art in California, Mom," I said, although I knew it was pointless. We had already had this particular argument over and over.

"The point is that it's time for a change," Mom said firmly. "It's going to be great in Blackthorn. We're starting our new life."

I slumped in my seat and shut my eyes to hold back the sudden prick of tears. I had liked our old life.

"Hey look, the dog is driving that car!" Edmund

shouted, and of course my eyes flew open to check it out. It looked so weird. In what should be the driver's seat of the car passing us sat a huge shaggy dog. As the car pulled ahead, the dog hung his head out the side window—open despite the miserable drizzle—and looked back at us, panting. *Surreal,* I thought. But what else was new these days? My whole life had been feeling as surreal as one of Mom's paintings ever since her decision to leave Dad. On a trial basis, of course.

"Keep your eyes on the road, Dog!" Ivy yelled out her window.

"And look there," added Edmund, "that other car doesn't even *have* a driver!"

"It's a ghost driver," declared Ivy, and both Goops broke out in tandem, ghostly *whoooo-ooooos.*

Our car followed the winding exit road to a narrower lane, where a sign announced: BLACKTHORN, 3. The lane, lined on both sides by high green hedgerows, bordered green fields dotted with white sheep and stands of gnarled trees. Almost like one of the calendar pictures, except for the constant patter of rain and the darkening sky.

"It's like night already," Edmund piped up. "And so foggy. Must be a storm coming."

"A *huge, torrential* storm," Ivy added with relish. "With thunder and lightning and floods."

"I don't think so," Mom replied in a mild voice, switching the headlights to low to help her see through the fog. "Remember, England is pretty far north. It just gets dark early here in the winter—and stays light long into the night in the summer. Remember how it stayed light till nearly ten o'clock when we visited Grandad?"

I didn't remember that, but—speaking of light—in the distance I could just make out other headlights approaching us. As the car neared, I could see that it was a long, low sports car, and a teenage boy was driving. He had bright red hair. But wait—of course he couldn't be the driver; the left-hand seat was the passenger side in England. The driver sat on the right. It was a man wearing a leather cap like somebody in an Italian movie. Twigs and leaves flew against my window as Mom veered hard against the hedges, trying to give the passing vehicle as much room as possible. The driver in the leather cap raised his hand to wave as he zoomed past, disappearing into the fog.

"Hey!" protested Edmund. "He nearly hit us, Mom!"

And Ivy declared, "He nearly ran us off the road!"

I was thinking the same thing. I was also thinking that the boy in the car had been very cute. I had told myself I was going to be surly and sour and not get the least bit interested in anything to do with this move to England, but a cute boy was something I hadn't expected. Did he live around here, or was he just passing through on his way to somewhere else?

"You'll get used to these narrow lanes," Mom was saying calmly. "They crisscross the whole country. Take a good look at the hedges, kids—they were planted hundreds of years ago as fences to divide property and to keep animals in the fields. The roads can't be widened without ripping out the old hedges. And they're home to all sorts of animals. Badgers and foxes . . ." Mom's voice trailed off as we rounded a bend in the lane and the fog lifted. A village that must be Blackthorn suddenly came into view.

"*Whoa*," I murmured.

"Whoa is right," said Ivy excitedly.

"*Major* whoa!" yelled Edmund right in my ear. "I can smell the ocean!"

I could, too, with the usual sick jolt to my stomach and a flutter of panic. I pushed the flutter away resolutely as I always did. I was just not a seaside sort of person.

Mom glanced over at me. "Our cottage isn't particularly near the water at all. Don't worry, honey. And you'll get used to the ocean air in no time. It's good and fresh and healthy."

I pressed my hands against my stomach and nodded. I couldn't help but look out the window now with interest. After all the weeks of talking about it, all the upsets and troubles, all the packing and arranging, all the good-byes to friends and promises to stay in touch . . . it was really happening. We were here.

Not a thatched roof in sight. Not a single rose trellis framing a doorway. No brilliant-hued gardens of flowers at all. Only one color had been used for this painting: gray. Or *grey*, as Mom said you'd write it in England. Gray stone buildings, two and three stories tall, marched downhill along both sides of the narrow street. The road split to allow for an island of dense, leafless shrubs, whose bare branches made a darker gray silhouette against all the other gray. They were planted thickly and had twined together to form what looked like an impenetrable, thorny thicket.

"Those bushes are called blackthorn," Mom said as we passed. "They're where the village got its name. They can look like trees, too, and grow to be something like nine or ten feet tall."

"It's like a movie set," Edmund exclaimed, "for a ghost story!"

"Or a mystery," shuddered Ivy. "All this foggy fog."

"A murder mystery . . . ," I added. I cracked my window and sniffed the air experimentally. My stomach clenched again at the fresh blast of sea air overlaid with wood-smoke—and something else. I breathed through my mouth.

We drove on. The paved road was gray and the sky above it was gray, and the seawall at the bottom of the street was gray, with gray water churning beyond. I decided I could tough it out. I rolled my window down further and felt the damp, cold fog on my face, and I smelled salt. And . . . there it was again. Something else besides. A smell—or was it just a feeling?—of something *wrong*.

What was I smelling that made me feel suddenly quite desolate and lost in this gray place? I'd been joking about the murder mystery, but what was I smelling that made me think of . . . *death*?

And where had I smelled it before?

2

"Don't be silly," Mom said briskly through the fog that now seemed to be in my head. It seemed to me that Mom's voice sounded suddenly much more English than it usually did after all her years of living in California. Soon she'd probably be asking us to call her *Mum* the way kids in England said it. I rubbed my eyes and squeezed my nose to try to clear my head of the weirdness I'd felt.

"The village will look gorgeous as soon as the sun comes out," continued Mom. "It's a vibrant place, from what Liza tells me, with plenty of art galleries—look, we're passing some now. It's not the least bit spooky. It's going to be heaven for me, kids!"

I tried to focus on her chatter as I rolled up my window to get the uncomfortable, strange smell out of my head. I was imagining things, I told myself. It was just the salt and the sea, and the fog. Different countries had different smells. That was all.

Mom was slowing the car. She pulled a sheet of paper out of her purse and passed it to me. "Here, Jule. Liza sent this. Can you navigate?"

Glad to be distracted from my uncomfortable thoughts, I squinted in the waning light at the e-mail printout. "Enter the village on the main road, called Castle Street," I read obediently as we passed a row of shops and a bank. I saw no sign of any castle. "Then take the first left past the ironmonger onto Dark Lane, then left again onto Water Street."

"What castle?" demanded Edmund predictably.

"What's a monger?" queried Ivy.

Our car veered left and bumped along a narrow, cobbled road. "There's no castle anymore," Mom explained. "Liza told me it fell down hundreds of years ago, and the villagers used some of the big stones to build their homes. And an ironmonger is a hardware store, Ivy."

"Hey, Mom, maybe your side of the family once lived in that castle—back before it fell down!" Ivy bounced excitedly in the backseat.

"I'm fairly sure we're descended from good hardy peasant stock," Mom replied with a little laugh. "The closest we'd have got to this castle would be to clean out the moat."

"Well—maybe Juliana has ancestors who lived in the castle before it fell down."

Ivy was persistent, you had to hand it to her.

"Now hold on," said Mom, slowing the car. "Where are we? Navigator?"

"That sign says Water Street," I said, pointing.

"Okay, kids—this should be it! Water Street. Now look for Old Mill House Cottage."

"Well, is it a house or a cottage?" asked Edmund as Mom pulled up in front of a gray stone wall and cut the engine. From the light of the streetlamp we could read the plaque on the wall announcing that this was the Old Mill House, circa 1664. A wooden door in the gray stone wall was painted bright, shiny red—the only spot of color I'd seen so far in the whole village.

"That's so old," said Ivy in awe. "That's like during Pilgrim times in America!"

"You're right," Mom said. "The American colonies still belonged to England."

"And we're going to live here!" sighed Ivy rapturously. She adored old things—funny little kid. I preferred things new and bright. Even though Ivy hated leaving Dad as much as Edmund and I did, she was excited about having the chance to live in an old house in a little village. I would have preferred someplace trendy and cool in London.

"That must be the main house—I wonder where the cottage is?" Mom's voice was eager. "We're so lucky Liza found it for us." She opened the car door and stepped out into the cold, with Edmund and Ivy tumbling after her. I sat alone in the car for a long moment, looking at that bright red door, welcoming the silence. I was bone-tired after the long flight from San Francisco, and after this long drive south and west to the coast, all the time in the rain and murk. . . . I stared at that red door and thought of my dad back in sunny California, and I just wanted to curl up somewhere and go to sleep for a million years.

Then the red door opened and the silence was shattered. "Hedda, darling!" someone shrieked, and a figure dashed over to our car, black hair streaming.

"It's a witch!" I heard Ivy pronounce with relish, and she and Edmund started laughing. I resisted the impulse to lock my door. It *did* look like a witch.

The woman was about Mom's age, I guessed. Early forties. But there the similarity ended. Mom was tall and comfortably round, while this woman was very short and very skinny, with straggly black hair and a long thin nose. Her glittering dark eyes were wild with excitement. She wore a long, black caftan. Pipe-cleaner arms reached out to grab Mom.

"Hedda Martin!" screeched the witch. There were two bright circles of color in her cheeks. "Has it really been twenty-two years? Let me see you!" Her English accent was much stronger than Mom's.

"Liza!" Mom hugged the woman. Okay, so not really a witch . . . I knew this must be Liza Pethering, Mom's friend from her art-school years, with whom she had once shared a small student apartment (a *flat,* Mom called it) in London. Back then Mom was Hedda Martin. Dad's name was David Drake. After they married, they became the Martin-Drakes, and so we kids all had the double last name, too. I liked it.

Slowly I emerged from the car and stood there with Edmund and Ivy. The drizzle had stopped, but a brisk, salty wind blew along the road. Even though you couldn't see the ocean from here, you could tell it wasn't far away.

"Hello, hello, little American people!" caroled Liza Pethering, peering at us one by one. "Two little people, and one middle-sized one!" She thrust out her bony hand and shook ours. "Come over here and let Aunty Liza get a good look at you." She turned back to Mom. "What luscious little people. I could just eat them up!"

Maybe a witch after all. I tried to smile in a friendly manner at Mom's old friend, though I wasn't really feeling friendly. This was the woman responsible for finding us our cottage in this village, for persuading Mom that her painting career would flourish if she took a break from her marriage to move here.

"So tell me," gushed Liza, "which babies did you find in the cabbage patch and which are your very own?"

I knew how much questions like this annoyed Mom.

But she spoke calmly. "They're all my own, Liza, of course. But Juliana and Edmund were adopted, if that's what you mean."

Edmund elbowed me in the side and rolled his eyes. I rolled mine back. We were united. The Adopted Ones. Next to me, Ivy harrumphed; she always felt left out.

"Twins, eh?" The woman was grinning down at Ivy and Edmund, revealing uneven rows of very white teeth. "Peas in a pod, eh? You're the ones from—where was it? Poland or someplace? Romania? I know you sent me an announcement, but it was years ago. And they all three of them look alike—blonds, just like you, Hedda. They could really be your own!"

"Edmund was born in Russia," Mom clarified briskly, "and Juliana was born in California—although we were told that her birth mother may have come from England originally. In any case, Juliana's our eldest—she's fifteen. And Edmund and Ivy are both nine. I know they look like twins, but they aren't really."

"Sure we are," protested Edmund, grinning.

The Goops were both very blond, and Ivy's hair was curly like Mom's. My own hair was a darker shade, and straight. I wore it long, usually tied back in a single braid.

"We have the same exact birthday, after all," said Ivy, linking her arm through Edmund's. "And we have the same parents now and we live in the same family now, and so that makes us twins, no matter where we were born."

Liza-the-witch blinked, looking confused. The Goops often had that effect on people. Of course, we were all used to people needing explanations about how our family was formed, but Mom always resented having to explain anything. "We're a *family*," she always said. "Families come together in all sorts of ways. What difference does it make?"

"People are just interested, Hedda," Dad would always reply. "It doesn't matter."

"Well, it's none of their business, that's all," said Mom.

"So, tell me the story of *this* one, then," said Liza Pethering now, pointing at Ivy. "Is this one the *real* daughter?"

I gritted my teeth and looked at that red door, wondering if we'd ever get inside or if we'd have to stand out here in the cold, explaining ourselves, forever.

Mom frowned. "All three children are as real as can be, Liza! But yes, Ivy is our birth daughter. It just so happened that we were planning to adopt from an orphanage in Russia when I found out I was pregnant. And then when we went to Russia several months later to get our baby boy, we discovered he had been born on the very same day as Ivy. A special coincidence."

"Makes you believe in fate, eh?" chuckled Liza.

Mom looked at her more kindly. "Exactly."

"Sort of how it was fate that made me find your e-mail address when I was sending out announcements for my new gallery, and fate that had me contacting you at the very same time you were over there in California deciding you just had to come back to England!" Liza flashed her snaggle-toothed grin. "I wrote to you after—how many years? And there you were, needing to reconnect with old art-school chums because you wanted to get back to your own painting. 'No, don't go to London,' I told you. 'Come to Blackthorn instead. That's where the real action is in the art world these days. Not to mention we've got a fabulous drama society with yours truly as the new president, and a brilliant historical association with yours truly as fearless leader, and so there will be tons for you to do and lots of ways for you to connect . . .' And look—here you are! Wait till you see your new home. Let's not just stand around— let's pop the boot and bring in your luggage."

The Goops sniggered. "I'll pop your boot," Edmund threatened under his breath.

At last. I opened the trunk of the rental car and started pulling out our suitcases. Edmund hurried to help. Ivy grabbed Polar, the dingy white stuffed polar bear who always traveled with her.

"And didn't I tell you I'd help find you a place to live?" continued Liza excitedly, leading us inside that red door. "Didn't I tell you that I'm special chums with Quentin Carrington, the famous sculptor, and that he has a huge place with a cottage out back? Oh, my ducks, you're going to enjoy living in such a place. It's fabulous!"

"And where is Mr. Carrington?" asked Mom. "I had only one e-mail from him, saying he would rent us the cottage, but he didn't return my phone call or write again."

"He's a busy man, is our Quent," laughed Liza. "Anyway, he's had to go out this afternoon—something about another sale. He's doing so well these days with his pieces based on his trip to Iceland. He's setting up an important London show now. Sculpture with sort of a Viking look, and very good if you like that sort of thing. Seems tons of people do! Anyway, he rang me to ask if I could be here when you arrived, and give you your key, and show you around. He'll be back later tonight, him and the boy."

"Yessss!" Edmund punched his arm up in the air for victory. "There's another boy around here?"

Liza eyed him doubtfully. "Don't get your hopes up,

ducky. He's a much bigger boy than you—a really great strapping sort of lad. Looks to be about as old as your big sister here."

Edmund slanted a look over at me. "Sooo, maybe a boyfriend for you, Jule."

"You shut up," I mouthed. But it wasn't as if anything had worked out at home with Tim, so of course I'd be interested. Never mind a boyfriend—any old friend would do. Someone my own age living nearby could be a good thing.

My head was buzzing with tiredness as I followed Liza and my mom through the red door in the wall into a large garden. A graveled path led straight ahead to a huge, imposing house of (what else?) gray stone. Another path led around the left side of the massive building, and it was along this path that Liza took us. I looked up at the windows of the big house as we passed. In one I could see a gaily painted carousel horse, complete with gilded pole.

"Quent will give you a full house tour, I'm sure," Liza said, leading us around the back of the Old Mill House. The gray wall enclosed a vast garden with several smaller buildings shaded by black-branched, leafless trees. "Look, over there are the ruins of the old grist mill," Liza said, pointing. "The old millstone is still there, but it doesn't work anymore, of course." She wheeled around and pointed to the right. "And there you go. The gardener's cottage."

We approached the small stone house covered in vines. The windows were arched. No thatched roof, but this was getting closer to what I'd been imagining. My big suitcase bumped against my legs with every step. The place looked ancient, and intriguing. The Goops were making soft, ghostly *whoooos* behind my back, giggling.

Liza handed Mom a large, ornate key. "Quent gave me the key ages ago, so I could get the cottage all ready for you. But it's yours now. Here you go, Hedda—and welcome! I think you'll find it's a lot cozier than the place we all shared back in those London days."

Mom turned the key in the lock and pushed open the door. "Come on, kids," she said. "Home sweet home!"

This could never be home without Dad, but I was interested in seeing it, just the same. I brushed past Liza into the little stone house—and stopped. I smelled it again: that smell of salt wind and fog—and something more, something that made me back up a few steps, my heart starting to pound hard.

Wake up, please wake up—oh no—help! Help! Come quick!

I knew no one had spoken—not really—but why was there this sudden voice in my head? It seemed to be a child's voice, high-pitched and frightened. It was somehow a familiar voice, but not one I could place. . . . I rubbed my nose—hard—and coughed, trying to rid myself of the strangeness. The smell disappeared along with the voice as Liza darted ahead of us, switching on lamps. I blinked in surprise—and pleasure—and was happy to push the weirdness out of my mind.

We were in a simple whitewashed room furnished with a cushiony couch and matching armchairs in rose-patterned fabric. There was a built-in bookcase along one wall—filled with books—and a large, old-fashioned sort of cupboard that stood open to reveal a very modern television. There was a large stone fireplace with a wood-burning stove set inside, topped by a carved wooden mantel. The cold flagstone floor was mostly covered by a thick rug in an oriental pattern of dark reds and blues. The fading light came through diamond-paned windows that looked out into the dusk of the dripping garden. This, at last, was worthy of my Christmas calendar.

"Your sitting room," Liza announced proudly, as if she herself were responsible for its charm. "Now through this door is the kitchen and eating area. And there's the bath, converted from what used to be the larder, I think. No shower, I'm sorry to say! I know Americans like their long showers. Half of the villagers still use woodstoves to heat their homes, but Quent has recently had central heating installed in here, plus a brand-new water heater. So there should be plenty of hot water . . ."

Well, I was relieved to hear *that,* because the only thing I hadn't liked at Grandad's was how there was never enough hot water for a really good bath. And right now the thought of a good long soak in a really hot bath was just what I wanted. But Liza's next words made me sigh.

"I bet you can get two full tubs a day. I'd make the kiddies share, Hedda, that's what I'd do, and save the other for yourself! You can keep warm and snug with the woodstove, too—and look here, outside the back door there's a pile of wood already stacked and ready. Now, bedrooms are upstairs—four little ones. They're practically cupboards, but at least you'll each get your own."

"This is just wonderful," said Mom, wandering into the kitchen. She turned back to beam at Liza. "And *you* are wonderful for finding the cottage for us, Liza. I can't thank you enough. It has everything we need."

"It doesn't have a computer, does it?" I asked Liza. I hadn't seen one yet, but maybe upstairs . . .

"No—" She sounded surprised. "I would have thought you'd bring your own."

"I would have thought that, too," I said, giving Mom what she and Dad called my "dagger" look. "But Mom said we didn't need one here."

"I just wanted to keep everything simple," Mom said. "My old laptop was on its last legs, so I didn't bother to bring it. Anyway, I want the kids to make friends here— not just e-mail their friends back in California all the time or play computer games. We'll get a new setup eventually. But I don't see the rush."

"No fair," complained Edmund, the computer game addict.

This was a sore subject with me. It was bad enough to take us away from Dad, but that we couldn't e-mail him and would have to rely on phone calls and old-fashioned letters seemed unfair—not to mention ridiculously dark age. It felt like Mom was deliberately cutting us off from Dad. She insisted that wasn't the case at all, but she was the one who kept throwing around phrases like "need to find myself again" and "must immerse myself in the artistic community," both of which made me want to puke. Plus, I loved instant-messaging my friends Jazzy and Rosy, and of course Tim every day. Without e-mail, I would be totally out of the loop.

"Well, I know Quent's got several computers, Juliana," Liza told me cheerfully, as if she could read my mind. She pronounced my name JuliAWna. "I imagine he'll let you e-mail your chums whenever the need arises."

"Thanks, Liza," said Mom, giving me a *look*. "Now, what about the upstairs?"

"I get first pick of bedrooms!" Ivy yelled, heading for the narrow flight of stairs.

"No fair!" Edmund dashed up right behind her. I lugged my suitcase up after him, thinking morosely that I would *not* share bathwater with the Goops. Not unless I got to go in first.

At the top of the steps I stopped and rested. I was standing in a small hallway with two bedrooms on either side and another room at the end. "Hey, Jule, come check this out!" Edmund's voice called to me from the room at the end of the hallway. I left my suitcase and joined him and Ivy inside a sunroom full of windows. Stacked along the wall by the door were the large boxes I remembered seeing last in our own living room at home; they were Mom's canvases and paints that she'd sent on ahead. Mr. Carrington must have put them up here. And that meant this would be Mom's studio. I crossed the room and peered out the windows onto the side lawn where, in the fading light, I could see the bulk of the Old Mill House. On a sunny day the light in this sunroom would be gorgeous, I'd bet, because even on this gray afternoon, the room felt airy and *ready*. Ready for *Art* to happen. Art with a capital *A*.

With a sinking heart, I knew Mom would love this space, and would think it was much nicer than the studio she had at home over the garage. This was probably the perfect place for her to *find* herself again—not that I'd ever noticed we'd *lost* her in the first place.

"I call this room," said Ivy.

"No way, I saw it first!" shouted Edmund.

"Listen, you Goops," I said sternly. "Mom's boxes are

already in here, so get over it. This place is already reserved. It's claimed. It's NFG—Not For Goops."

They grumbled, but I ignored them and they stampeded out of the room. I wandered around the sunroom, enjoying the sudden quiet. The room was furnished with a simple wooden table, two easels, a cupboard to store supplies, and a deep, comfortable-looking armchair of worn leather. Along the window ledges were interesting pieces of the sort of things Mom always called "found art." She had collections at home of things from nature that might inspire a painting. These things weren't hers, though. I wondered if our new landlord had set them out to inspire his new tenant. There was a large conch shell. Pinecones in several sizes. A heavy, softball-sized beach rock, with thick white veins branching through it like a spider's web. A bouquet of feathers, large and small, held in a vase made from a gourd.

A large square basket held several smaller boxes. I reached in and opened them one by one: Collections of dried pods and flowers, tied with twine. Red autumn leaves that had been pressed flat. Tiny seashells.

The last box was a small one, the sort that might hold jewelry. I opened it eagerly and lifted off the square of cotton. Sure enough—a necklace. I dangled it from my finger. Curious—and enchanting. Immediately I wanted one like it. Silvery blue embroidery floss had been threaded through delicate, white pressed blossoms and tiny silver beads. A polished pink quartz stone, nearly as round and smooth as a marble, hung from it.

"Where did you find *that*?" asked a sharp voice at my side, and I looked up with a start to find Liza Pethering standing next to me. I had been so engrossed by the flowery thing, I hadn't heard her come upstairs.

"Here in this little box—at the bottom of this basket," I explained. "Isn't it beautiful?"

"It is positively *glorious*." Liza Pethering's voice was uncharacteristically soft. She reached for it. "I'm just surprised to see it—after all this time. It was Nora's good luck talisman. My friend Nora, who died. She used to make necklaces for her special friends. It wasn't her art, of course—that was painting. But she made jewelry when she felt like it, when she found a special good luck charm. No two were alike."

At the thought of a good luck necklace I felt my stomach clench—much in the unfathomable way it always had at the sight of a stretch of sandy beach or the sounds of waves lapping the shore. "I think it's pretty," I said after a moment's hesitation. "I'd love to have one like it."

"No two were alike," repeated Liza, rubbing her finger meditatively over the quartz. "She made one for me, too—just before I opened my gallery. With a lovely dangling seedpod to rub for luck. She wore hers and rubbed the quartz just before any big event, and I always wear mine and rub the seedpod. And I always will!" She held the necklace to her own throat, then gently laid it back in the box. "Only death would keep us from wearing our lucky charms!"

I laughed a little at this.

"No, really, it's too bad Nora wasn't wearing her talisman the night of the accident—or she might still be with us. Odd, really—that she *wasn't* wearing it . . ." Liza broke off and stared out the window in silence for a moment. I wanted to ask what accident and who this friend was, when Liza turned back to me with her loud, trilling laugh. "What I came up to tell you is that your mum is making a pot of tea downstairs. She says to choose your bedrooms quickly and come down and have some."

"Okay, thanks," I said, rubbing my finger over the smooth pink quartz before carefully fitting the lid back onto the little box. I stowed the box back into the big square basket. "I'll do that." I wasn't really a tea drinker, but maybe it would help settle my stomach—or at least help ward off jet lag with a jolt of caffeine. Yet after Liza left the sunroom, I still stood there, looking around.

There was a peaceful feel to the place. All too well, I could imagine Mom sitting at an easel, or sitting in the armchair, to sketch a new idea.

I left the sunroom to go in search of my bedroom. I found a small corner bedroom only about as big as my bathroom at home in California, but clean and pleasant, with sponged yellow walls, floorboards painted light blue. There was a narrow bed along the far wall, with a huge, puffy white quilt (a *duvet*, Mom called such things) folded on top of it. A low white bookshelf stood at the foot of the bed, waiting to be filled. A small dresser was tucked into an alcove. Since I *had* to be in England, this room would suit me just fine.

I crossed to the window and leaned into the deep windowsill. The stone walls of this little cottage were nearly two feet thick. I unlatched the casement window and pushed it open. Cold air gusted inside. The March afternoon had darkened further, and the chill rain had started to fall again. I heard Ivy and Edmund chattering out in the hall. I heard Mom and Liza downstairs, laughing in the kitchen. I thought I could even smell the tea they were brewing, pungent and spicy. Or was that the salt wind from the sea? And then—there!—that other smell again.

Wake up, oh, please, please—wake up!

Again, the frightened child's voice in my head. And a sense of danger—close by. What was going on? I stood staring out the window, trying to capture whatever it was that seemed just beyond my understanding; it was like straining to see around corners, or through a dark, smoky glass.

Was there danger—here and now?

Or only the memory of danger?

3

You see, there was something weird about me, something that set me apart from other people. Everybody in my family was *normal*—even, yes, even the obnoxious Goops—and I wasn't. My friends at school were all *normal*—even the amazing, fabulous Tim Raglan, who was a mathematical genius and won all the competitions at state level . . . and Jazzy and Rosy, my two best friends, who were part of a set of triplets and the most popular girls in school. I was the only different one, the only *not* normal person I knew. But I kept quiet about it.

It was a memory problem. A major one. And though it did make me feel weird—set apart from other people—it had never included hearing voices or smelling smells. So what was happening here? Was it part of my general odd-girl-out brand of weirdness, or was it something to do with this place? Were all the people living in this village smelling things and hearing voices and not telling? Was the voice in my head some ghost of a long-ago child who had once lived in this cottage? Was this demon possession? Or was it just weird little old me, cracking up completely?

Give me a break, I thought angrily, and it felt way better to be angry than scared. *No more weirdness!* I didn't need any more oddball stuff in my life. My memory problem was bad enough. No one knew how much it bothered me. It wasn't something I could talk about, not to friends, not to family. Even my parents didn't really know how much it bugged me.

The rumble of a deep voice down in the sitting room made my musings vanish. For one thrilling moment I thought it was Dad down there, somehow transported to England. Then I heard the peal of Mom's laughter, and knew it couldn't be Dad. Mom never laughed anymore when Dad was around. I closed my bedroom windows and started unpacking my suitcase into the small dresser, throwing the clothes into the drawers *hard*.

Then Edmund and Ivy were at my door. "Hear that downstairs?" Edmund hissed. "It's the new landlord, the famous sculptor."

"With his son," Ivy whispered, wiggling her eyebrows at me. Then the two of them stifled their giggles and snapped their fingers under my nose. "Bet he's cuuuuute!"

"Hey hey hey!" my very annoying little brother tried to chortle suggestively. Not that he knew what he was suggesting.

"Out of my way, Goops." I pushed past them.

Mom was at the foot of the stairs, talking to a tall, dark-haired man. She smiled at me. "Come down and meet our new landlord, Juliana. Mr. Carrington, this is my eldest, Juliana."

Our new landlord's hand enveloped mine. He was a large man with a shock of dark, unruly hair and a booming laugh, and I was surprised, because somehow I'd pictured the famous sculptor as an old, stooped, white-haired guy. "Juliana," he said warmly, pronouncing it the way Liza had—*JuliAWna.* "Lovely to meet you, young lady. And please, both of you, call me Quent. It's going to be very nice having you here. Don't you think so, Dunk-o?"

I looked around for the son who had such an unfortunate name, and there, coming out of the kitchen with Liza behind him, was the red-haired boy I'd seen racing by in the sports car!

"Hullo," he said, ducking his head rather than shaking hands. He was tall and lanky—gangly, my dad would have said—but I liked gangly. And I liked his red hair. He looked about my age—fifteen—or maybe a little older. He didn't look much like his dad. Must have gotten the red hair from his mom. Or maybe he was adopted. Some of the best people are.

"Hi," I said brightly, thinking that maybe Edmund was right with his hey hey heys.

He gave me a shy smile, then shuffled across the room and started looking at the books in the shelves. Okay . . . so the Dunk-o was not a great conversationalist, obviously, as well as the possessor of a totally crazy name. "So Liza's shown you all around, has she? And everything is to your satisfaction?" Mr. Carrington—Quent—was asking Mom.

"I haven't been upstairs yet," Mom said. "But it already feels like home."

"Wait till you see your sunroom studio," I told her. "You'll die."

"The conservatory?" The red-haired cutie spun away from the bookshelf, his voice sharp. He was frowning at Quent. "You're letting *her* have it?"

"It's a perfect place to work, Dunk," Quent said mildly. "You know that."

"I know Mum certainly thought so!" His voice rose.

Quent walked over and rested a hand on Dunk-o's shoulder. "And your mum did some of her best work in it, didn't she?" he said soothingly. "I'm hoping that Hedda will find it just as inspiring for her own work." He turned back to Mom. "It'll be good to have the sunroom in use again."

I wasn't so sure that Dunk-o agreed, but at least he'd stopped glowering. I wanted to say something to him, but the only thing that came to mind just then was "I love your accent." I caught myself in time, thankfully, because *I* was the one with the accent here, not him.

Now he was just looking fixedly out the window. I glanced at the window to see what was so fascinating, but it was dark. I didn't know what the story was about his mum, but my mom obviously did because she spoke gently to him. "Your mum's death came as very sad news to me, Duncan," she said. "I knew your mum back when Liza and I were art students in London, you know, years ago. Nora was such a sweetheart. And such a vibrant person. We just knew that she would be the one of us to hit the big time first."

Duncan, I thought, glad to know his name wasn't really Dunk-o. I gave him a sympathetic glance, but he wouldn't look over at me, just kept his eyes fixed on the window.

"And she did," Quent said. "Nora was really moving up in the art world before the accident. Getting a real name for herself. We were so proud of her, weren't we, Dunk?"

Duncan nodded, looking away. I wondered if he was trying not to cry.

"Such a tragedy," Liza said, moving over to slip her arm through Quent's. "Cut down in her prime. Hard to believe it's already been two years . . . But that's always the way it is with death, isn't it? You never know when your number's up."

"We shared a flat back in the old days," Mom said hastily, smiling over at Duncan. "We were like three eccentric artists in our garret."

He spoke up shyly, warming to Mom as people always did, eventually. "She showed me where that flat was once, when we were in London together."

"Not that we were in our garret all that much, Hedda," Liza corrected her with a giggle. "We had our classes, of course, and studio work, but don't forget our home away from home . . . the Dark Horse!"

"Our little pub on the corner!" Mom was giggling, too. Edmund and Ivy were hanging over the banister, all ears.

"I can imagine," said Quentin, smiling at Mom. "Now, speaking of pubs, Hedda, I'd like to invite you and your children to dinner at the Old Ship. They do a very good meal—not just your basic pies and chips but a really good roast as well. My treat, of course, to celebrate your first night in Blackthorn."

"Why, thank you so much," said Mom. "But you really don't need to—"

"I want to. Duncan and I both do, eh lad?"

"Right," said Duncan. He slanted his shy smile at me then looked quickly away.

So he wasn't entirely hopeless! And he had such a sweet smile, and such a nice, warm English accent—plus all that lovely red hair! I slanted a glance back at him, but he wasn't looking.

Ivy and Edmund cheered from the stairs. *Food and plenty of it* was their motto. They came clattering down and then had to be introduced.

After Quent had shaken hands with the Goops, Liza linked her arms through his. "I think a meal at the Ship sounds lovely," she trilled.

But Quent unlinked his arm from hers. "I saw Oliver at the Emporium and he told me to tell you to hurry on home if you were still here when I got back. Said he hadn't seen you all day and he could use you in the shop now that Veronica isn't working there anymore."

"Oh, bother." Liza wrinkled her brow. "He can run the shop much better on his own, especially since I sacked the little thief! And he is capable of making his own tea, too, you know. He likes to play helpless about anything more complicated than cheese on toast, but it's just a ruse to cover up that he's bone-lazy." She turned to Mom with a toss of her head. "Husbands!"

Mom rolled her eyes as if she agreed, which I thought was being totally unfair and disloyal to Dad. "We'll have to make this a quick meal, though, I'm afraid," Mom said. "The jet lag is really starting to get to me, and the kids must be ready to collapse."

"No we're not!" cried Edmund and Ivy.

I felt pretty near to collapsing, just as Mom had said, and not really a bit hungry. But Duncan was suddenly chattering away to the Goops as if he were their long-lost friend. And yet he'd said barely two words to me! What did they have that I didn't?

"To the Old Ship then," said Quent, ushering us toward the door.

Liza pouted for a moment, then brightened. "Well, I'll walk that way with you," she said cheerfully, "and then be off for home. It's for the best really. I've got a Drama Society meeting later tonight . . . I've been elected president of the society—did I tell you already? And we've just finished tryouts for our new three-act play, *Voyage of the Jumblies*! I've phoned all the cast members to announce their parts, but we're meeting tonight to hand out the scripts. Too bad all characters have been assigned, Hedda, or I'd be asking you to join us!" Liza spoke rapidly, never giving Mom a chance to say that she wouldn't want to be in a play, that she always had stage fright, that even having to approach gallery owners about exhibiting her paintings was an ordeal for her. "But, never mind," Liza was saying, "I'll pop round here again in the morning, Hedda, darling, to take you and your kiddies on a tour of the village. And then, of course, I'll be seeing you tomorrow night at the party as well." She quirked an eyebrow at Quent. "Or wasn't I supposed to tell her about the party yet?"

"Good thing it wasn't meant to be a surprise," he told Mom with a warm smile, shaking his head at Liza. "Yes, I'm hosting a little gathering of the Blackthorn art scene at the house tomorrow. Very informal. Everyone's coming around seven. They're eager to meet you. They've looked at your website and read the reviews, and there's a lot of interest. In fact, the local Art Collective is putting on an exhibition at the end of April—it's a yearly springtime extravaganza— and we've all agreed we'd like to have several of your pieces in it. If you'll agree."

"How kind of you!" exclaimed Mom. "Of course I agree. And won't a party be fun, kids? Juliana, you'll enjoy a party!"

Liza's trilling laugh filled the room again. "Oh, I don't suppose Quent meant it to be a *children's* party, Hedda, darling!"

But Quent quelled her with another impatient shake of his head. "Of course Juliana's most welcome, and Ivy and

Edmund, too. Duncan will be there, won't you, Dunk-o? And I've no doubt Celia Glendenning will be bringing Kate along."

I wasn't sure he'd meant for the party to include kids after all, but at least he'd covered it up gracefully. I wondered who Kate would turn out to be. I liked parties, and going to one at Duncan's house sounded fun to me. Maybe *then* I'd manage to get him to talk to me.

It didn't hurt to dream, I told myself, grabbing my coat off the row of hooks by the door and following my little brother and sister and their cute-but-shy (or possibly indifferent) redheaded pal out into the rainy evening. Maybe if I were very lucky I could get out of going on the village tour with Liza Pethering in the morning, and Duncan would show me around instead. However, it was more likely, I had to admit to myself from the look of things, Duncan would offer to show the Goops around, and I would just end up tagging behind.

WE HURRIED ALONG the wet streets, huddling together under Quent's and Liza's large, black umbrellas (*brollies,* Quent called them), and soon came to the center of town and the pub called the Old Ship. The Old Ship was built back in 1615 as an inn for travelers along the coast road, Quent informed us, and it was even older than his Old Mill House. It was a gray stone building directly across from the bush-filled traffic island in the middle of the main street. We entered through an archway into a low-ceilinged dining room. "Watch your heads," cautioned Quent. "People were shorter in those days!"

"This place was here even *before* the Pilgrims came to America!" Ivy whispered to me, awed. "King Henry the

Eighth might have come here to eat—or wait, was he dead by then?" She was a bookworm who knew more about history than people twice her age—or at least that's what Dad always said. She danced her way inside the Old Ship now. "Hey, maybe *Shakespeare* ate here!"

The room inside was dimly lit, with a bar lined with stools at one end, and tables at the other end. The air smelled of old oak and smoke—though no one was smoking at the tables. Maybe it was the residue left from centuries of cook fires. The smoky smell mingled with the smells of meat and onions, creating a warm fog, and I was glad because it would mask any other, weirder smell that might try to find me.

Liza Pethering had walked with us as far as the Old Ship. She came inside, but was now saying further goodbyes and arranging with Mom what time she'd come over in the morning. While they were talking, a girl about my age turned from the bar and walked over to us with a smile that faded away. I thought at first she was mad because she thought I was with Duncan or something—but then I saw she was glaring at Liza. The girl's eyes were made up with heavy dark liner, and her hair was a deep royal purple. Very cool—though not my style. She had loads of earrings dangling from her ears, and over her very tight jeans she wore a neat white apron with a picture of a ship on it. "How many for dinner, then?" she asked Quent sullenly. Her voice was high and clipped. She gathered our coats and umbrellas and tossed them onto the coatrack in the corner.

"Just six, Veronica," Quent told her. "Mrs. Pethering won't be eating with us."

"Good," replied the girl, turning back and making a face. "Because I couldn't promise not to slip some poison into her beer if she sat herself in here." Quent chuckled at that, as if Veronica had made a joke, but I noticed the girl with the purple hair wasn't laughing.

"Well, good evening to you, too, Veronica, dear," gushed Liza. "So you're employed again, are you? How long do you think it will last this time, hmmm?" She laughed heartily and turned to Mom, adding in a confiding tone, "Our little Miss Pimms isn't exactly the most reliable of employees, shall we say? But she's old friends with Duncan, so when Quent suggested we hire her at the Emporium, we wanted to oblige. Bad move in the end, though. Isn't that right, dear?"

The girl shot her a killer look, but Liza remained undaunted.

"Hullo, Ronnie." To my surprise, it was Duncan who spoke up affably. But he left it to Quent to introduce us. Mom, always tactful, shook Veronica Pimms's hand and tried to find something to chat with her about.

"So you're in school with Duncan, Veronica? Well, I hope you'll get to know Juliana, too, even though she'll still be doing homeschool, for a while at least. Maybe you can interest her in going to your school, and show her around a bit—"

But Liza Pethering broke in again with a little derisive laugh before Veronica could reply. "Veronica Pimms at school?" Liza snorted. "Now there's a concept! She left ages ago, didn't you, dear? Or did they kick you out?" She gave Veronica a withering glance, then waved good-bye to the rest of us and left through the archway. "Ta-ra! See you tomorrow!"

Veronica tossed her purple hair and led us over to a long table by the windows. "Someone ought to kill that bitch," she muttered darkly. "If you want my humble, *uneducated* opinion."

4

While we ate, Quentin Carrington chatted with Mom about Blackthorn's art scene and all the people she'd be meeting the next night at his party. Ivy and Edmund played hangman with Duncan, who wrote letters on the paper place mat as they tried to guess the word he was thinking. I sat watching everyone, my head buzzing with tiredness, actually sort of glad that Duncan was too shy or too uninterested to talk to me. The way I was feeling, I doubted I could hold a sensible conversation. Everybody ordered fish and chips or chicken pie and chips or roast pork with chips—but I just asked for the chips on their own. They turned out not even to be potato chips at all but big, greasy, yummy, salty fries. Not the best diet choice, but I felt I deserved some comfort food after this very long day. Ivy pretended her drink was mead instead of Coke. Edmund was shocked that there weren't free refills.

Just before we left, two guys stumbled into the Old Ship. They were a little older than me, maybe late teens or early twenties, and they were loud and demanding. They sat at the bar and the older one called for beer, pounding on the wooden surface. "Two pints of lager and make it quick, luv, if you know what's good for ya." His accent was entirely different from any I'd heard so far. I was getting the idea that there were as many different kinds of English spoken around here as there were people.

Veronica Pimms scowled at them but hurriedly set two tall glasses on the bar. One by one she filled them from the tap. The younger guy, who looked about eighteen, sipped at the head of foam, watching the other guy intently with a fixed, silly sort of grin on his face. That other one, who might have been his brother because they shared the same stocky build, same sandy crew cut, and pale watery blue eyes, had a fierce frown. He sucked his foam right off the top in one gulp, drained the glass in seconds, and pounded on the bar for more.

"Keep your shirt on, Simon," snapped Veronica. "I've got other customers, haven't I?"

His reply was a low growl.

Quent Carrington chuckled. "Well, there you have them: Blackthorn's criminal element. Simon and Henry Jukes. On-the-dole layabouts and lager louts if ever there were any. I suppose, to be fair, we should say it's really only Simon who's the bad 'un. Henry is far too simple to plan a break and entry or postal scam. But Simon uses his poor brother as a cover whenever he can. They're both going to land in prison if they're not careful. That Simon—he's already done a stint, thanks to our Liza."

"Thanks to Liza?" Mom asked in surprise.

"She was sharp-eyed, and angry enough to go to the police with what she saw. Which was Simon Jukes shoplifting from the Emporium. A couple bottles of wine, some packets of crisps and cakes, and a pork pie from the delicatessen section. When she and Oliver shouted out to stop, old Simon raced for the door, trying to get away, knocking over several customers. Elderly Mrs. Parker broke a hip, thanks to Simon—and from what I hear, it never did heal properly. Anyway, Liza and Oliver caught him, with help from their customers. Oliver might have let him off with a warning, but Liza insisted on pressing charges. She said it wasn't the first time and wouldn't be the last if she didn't see him stopped. Simon ended up doing six months in jail, which he richly deserved, to my mind. But now he's just out, and he's plenty mad."

"What did the other brother do?" I asked. "Did he straighten up and get a job?" I watched the pair at the bar, now well on their third beer, and doubted it somehow.

"Poor Henry wandered the village like a lost soul for the whole time his brother was away," said Quent. "He's a slow sort of bloke. A dim bulb, if you get my meaning. But he wouldn't be so bad, I think, if he didn't hero-worship his awful older brother."

"I guess Simon's the only family Henry's got, though," said Duncan quietly. "Sometimes you've got to just stick with what you have."

Quent winked at him. "Like you're sticking with me, eh, Dunk-o? Well, I'm the lucky one, I'll say that much. Anyway, I don't know if there's any other Jukes relations around town, do you? I think the two of them live alone in a squalid council flat over by the Fields."

"I heard they ditched their parents years ago and moved here from London," Duncan said.

"Or maybe their parents ditched them first, and who could blame them?" Quent laughed.

We finished our dinners and left before the surly Jukes brothers did. I could hear Simon, the older one, shouting for another lager as we left the Old Ship and started our walk back. I walked slowly, trailing behind everybody. My body ached with tiredness.

But then, even though I was totally exhausted, it took me a long time to get to sleep that night. I was used to the sounds of the city outside my window at home, and the unfamiliar quiet here roared more loudly than any traffic noise. The bed in my new little bedroom was much narrower than my big bed at home, too. Every time I turned over, my arm either hit the wall or flopped off the side of the mattress. I heard Mom come upstairs and go into the bedroom across the hall from mine. When I finally fell asleep, I dreamed that Liza Pethering, witchy black hair streaming, was standing by the stove in our little kitchen, stirring a big pot with a wooden spoon and asking Mom over and over again: "So, which are your *real* children? Which are the *real* ones?"

IN THE MORNING, a wavery gray sunlight filtered through my bedroom window. A drizzly rain was falling outside. I slid out of bed, shivering in the chilly room, and pulled on my warmest sweatpants, sweatshirt, and fleecy socks. I could hear the Goops arguing about burned toast as I walked in for breakfast.

I sat at the small round table in the kitchen, braiding my hair, and Mom set a mug of steaming tea in front of me. I didn't usually drink tea, but on this cold morning England's national drink seemed just right. "Put in plenty of milk," Mom advised, setting a glass bottle in front of me. "That's how they drink it here." But I kept mine black and strong and it tasted good that way.

Ivy and Edmund drank their tea so white it might as well have been plain milk, but they felt they were being authentically English. They talked in silly, fake English accents as they ate, and Mom laughed at them. There wasn't a toaster, but she made us toast the way Grandad had, by laying slices of bread under the broiler—the *grill*, Mom called it—which accounted for the many burned pieces. Just as we were getting the process down to a science, and turning out perfect toast with lots of butter and marmalade, Liza Pethering tapped on our door. I remembered my dream as she pushed it open and stepped inside. "Which are your *real* children?" I half expected her to ask, but "Ready for your tour?" she trilled instead, shaking her streaming umbrella all over the rug.

"In this weather?" Mom shook her head. "Why don't you sit down and have some toast and tea with us, and we'll wait it out."

"Nonsense, there's no time like the present, as my grandmother used to say," Liza said firmly. "She was a painter, too, in her time. Landscapes, mostly. Some pretty good. Artistic genes must run in the family! Anyway, if we sit and wait out the rain we might well be waiting six months, Hedda. Have you forgotten *everything* you know about England while you've been over there in sunny California? Besides, I want to get some painting done this afternoon, and I've had to promise my lazy husband to help him out in the shop today—we own the Emporium now, did you know? Best place to buy all your groceries, and no need to go rushing off to the markets in Lower Dillingham or Portsmouth, thanks to me for keeping the upscale items in stock. Oliver is so deathly old-fashioned and such a stick-in-the-mud that it's all up to me. Left on his own, I daresay Oliver would have us bankrupt and out on the streets. He managed to get up enough money to buy the place, but at heart he's really still just the butcher, like he was for years. All I can say is that it's a good thing we've had all the sales I've been getting for my paintings." She lowered her voice and spoke confidentially, "I don't mean to brag, Hedda, but I do a wonderful likeness and the market for my portraits has been excellent." She tossed back her head, preening herself like some famous film star or something. "Oliver resents my success, though. Always on at me to stay home or help out in the shop. And a lot of artists around this town are jealous, I can tell you that! And who can blame them?" Her trilling, self-satisfied laugh made me wince, but Mom smiled.

"I'd like to see your work very much," she told Liza. "Why don't we do a quick tour of the village and end up at your gallery?"

Liza agreed this was a good plan, so off we went along the path through the Carringtons' wet garden, through the red door in the stone wall, and out into the gray streets of Blackthorn, with Edmund, Ivy, and me trailing along like ducklings behind our mother duck.

I stopped at the entrance to Dark Lane and stood there, just looking, sniffing the air and taking in the feeling of the place. Ivy stood next to me and reached for my hand. "Isn't it wonderful?" she whispered. "Everything here is *so old.*"

I shrugged, but she was right. The village *was* so old. So much older than anywhere I'd been in California. The high walls rising on both sides of me were ancient, built of damp gray stone. And what was on the other side of these high walls? What secrets, what hidden lives? The back of my neck prickled a little as if someone were watching me from a chink in the stone. The path under my feet was gray stone. How many feet had worn it smooth over how many centuries? The sky above was all heavy gray clouds, weighted further with the woodsmoke that spilled, as Liza had said, from half the village homes. And nearby, though I could not see it from where I stood, churned the sea—no doubt also cold and gray. I was struck by how right now could have been any time at all, any year, almost any century. Did things ever change in Blackthorn?

"Can you feel it, too?" asked my little historian sister, and for a second I thought she'd also felt a prickle of unease. "Isn't this place totally awesome?"

I squeezed Ivy's hand. I didn't know about totally awesome, but it was something totally different from what I was used to. *I'm going to remember this moment forever,* I thought, and shivered.

To get up to the main street we took a shortcut through Dark Lane, then crossed a little footbridge across a stream called Shreenwater, which Liza also referred to as the "Shreen" for short. We passed the newsagent's, which also housed the village post office, then stopped briefly at the ironmonger's to have the cottage key copied so that I would have one, too. There was no use getting keys for the Goops, Mom and I both knew from experience. They always lost keys.

We passed the bank and some stores (*shops,* Mom reminded us they were called here): two antique shops, another called Seaside Treasures that had a very unseasonable display of beach balls and brightly colored, plastic sand pails and shovels (*buckets and spades,* Mom informed us) in the window, and a shop Liza called a fishmonger, which kept Ivy giggling for at least half a block. We passed the chemist's (which was a drugstore, I hated to inform Edmund, and *not* a mad scientist's chemistry lab), and then finally stopped at the Emporium, the large grocery store on the main street, owned by Oliver and Liza Pethering. It was bustling with shoppers.

Liza strode in like a film star, bestowing greetings on everyone she passed and introducing Mom but not us kids. When we got to the back of the shop, Liza pointed out her husband, Oliver, a bulky, balding man who was working behind the "Quality Meats and Cheeses" counter. His smile was big and yellow-toothed. She waved energetically at him, then turned back to Mom with a sigh. "See?" she murmured to Mom. "A butcher at heart, that's all he is. Just a butcher in his soul."

"There's nothing wrong with butchers," Mom said mildly. She didn't like when people put other people down, and she never let us kids get away with doing it. I was sort of glad to see she didn't let her old friend get away with it, either.

Liza rolled her eyes. "I'm a vegetarian," she said wiltingly. "Yet he comes home with a bloodstained apron still wrapped around him, and I'm supposed to be happy to see him? Not bloody likely!" She giggled at her own wit.

We set off again, and she darted here and there, showing us the plant nursery, the bakery, the fish and chip shop, the Chinese takeaway, and St. Michael's, the ancient church.

The drizzle had stopped for the moment, and it seemed the sun was trying hard to shine out from behind the heavy cloud cover. We all closed our umbrellas and pulled off our hats. Ivy wanted to stay and explore the graveyard behind the church, and Edmund was clamoring to go down to the beach, and I would have liked to climb Castle Hill, the high green hill rising above the village, even knowing there wasn't a castle up there anymore, and even though the path might be muddy. But Liza turned left off the main road. She led us up to the top of a hilly side street and stopped outside a gray stone rowhouse (*terraced cottage*, Mom told us such houses were called).

"Just a quick stop here," Liza said, fishing in her coat pocket. "I need to drop something off here for a gentleman who couldn't make it to our drama meeting yesterday evening."

Her brisk knock on the black-painted door was acknowledged by a beady blue eye peering out the little glass window set into the door, and then the door slowly opened. An elderly, rather stooped man stood there, wearing brown pants and a buttoned-up brown cardigan, and brown bedroom slippers on his feet. His thinning hair was gray, but still held a trace of ginger. "Well, well," he said dourly, "it's the Grand Lady President herself, is it? But—out in the rain? Now how can that be? I thought wicked witches melted when they got wet." He let out a cackle.

"Oh, Dudley, don't take on," snapped Liza, holding out a booklet to him. "Here's your script. Since you, ah, couldn't make it to the meeting last night, I've been kind enough to bring it to you. Door service! What more could you ask for?"

"I could ask to be given the part I tried out for," the old man snapped right back, not taking the script. "I could ask for a little respect!"

"Please, I beg you, do *not* confuse drama with melodrama," Liza returned witheringly. "I assigned you the part for which you are best suited. A part that won't be too taxing on you. You know how your health has suffered this past year. I don't want you overstressing, Dudley. Trust me on this, can't you?"

"*Trust* you? And I suppose I should be thanking you for your thoughtfulness as well?" He laughed bitterly. He seemed only then to become aware of the rest of us shifting uncomfortably on the sidewalk behind Liza. "Who've you got out there with you? More newcomers you're going to hand out lead roles to, just like you did the other night?" His angry gaze met my eyes, and he blinked. I guess I blinked, too. *What a geezer,* I was thinking.

"Nonsense, Dudley. Now you're being quite rude," Liza chided the old man. "This is Hedda Martin-Drake, a famous painter, and her children, just arrived yesterday afternoon from America. Hedda, this rude person is Mr. Dudley Cooper. Hedda's living in Quent Carrington's garden cottage, Dudley. In fact, Duncan met them last night."

As if her speaking his name had made him appear, Duncan himself stepped out of the room on the old man's right. I was totally surprised, and felt a stupid flush start in my cheeks.

"What is it?" Duncan asked. "Who's here? Oh—Liza!"

"Hello, lad. Yes, I've just come to give your old curmudgeon of a grandfather his script."

Ivy and Edmund surged forward and were grinning and talking to Duncan a mile a minute, while I just tried to look cool and casual. He fended the Goops off good-naturedly, peering around Liza to where Mom and I stood on the pavement. "Um, good morning," he said to us. "Are you out on your village tour?"

"Yes," I said. "What are you doing here?"

"Visiting with Granny and Grandad," he said. "I'm often here."

I could see now that the gingery tint to the old man's hair might once have been a fiery red like Duncan's.

"It's his home away from home," Mr. Cooper said in a friendlier tone, opening the door a bit wider. "Now, come in, come in. Hazel would never forgive me if I didn't ask you to come in for a cuppa, Mrs. Drake. Anybody who's a friend of our Duncan is always welcome here."

"Why, thank you—," began Mom, but Liza cut her off.

"It's *Martin*-Drake," Liza interrupted, "and I'm afraid we don't have time for tea just now, Dudley. I must get to my gallery. I'm setting up a new exhibit. Local portraits."

"I wasn't inviting *you*, Madame President," said Mr. Cooper cuttingly. "I was speaking to our American visitors."

Liza tossed her head in annoyance. Duncan looked embarrassed. Mom came to the rescue in her usual tactful way. "Thank you so much, Mr. Cooper. My children and I would love to stop in for a cup of tea with you and your wife—if you'll give us a rain check on the invitation. I'm afraid we need to get back to our new little cottage and finish our unpacking. We were so tired from the long journey yesterday, we didn't get to it last night."

"A rain check, you say?" chuckled Mr. Cooper, peering outside. It was starting to rain again and we all fumbled to open our umbrellas. "All right, very well, if you're certain. We'll keep the kettle on for another day, then. Duncan, you see that you bring these Americans back soon. Granny will make them her famous scones!"

"I'll do that, Grandad," said Duncan. He reached out and plucked the script from Liza's hand. "And I'll take this, shall I? Maybe you'll decide you want to be in the play after all . . ."

"Enough, boy!" shouted the old man, glowering at Duncan. "I won't be in any play run by that woman. Hanging's too good for her, if you ask me. I admit she can paint a fair likeness, and she ought to stick to *that,* thank you very much, and not try to meddle in what she has no talent for!"

"*Er*—good-bye!" Duncan said desperately to Liza and to us. "*Er*—see you tonight!" And he closed the door quickly. But I could still hear Mr. Cooper ranting on the other side.

"Poor Dunk," said Liza, shaking her head as she led us back down the street. "The Coopers are his mum's parents. Both of them are batty old dears, but he tries to help out with them. Goes over to the house a lot to look in on them and do errands and suchlike."

"Why is Mr. Cooper so mad about your play?" I asked.

The wind blew her black hair across her face and she raked it back impatiently, her wild eyes flashing annoyance—at the rain, I wondered, or at the old man? "He's a fool, that's all! A jealous old fool. Used to be president of the Drama Society himself for years, he was, and always creamed the best parts for himself. Now I've been elected and I've made sure people get the parts they deserve. He's lucky I didn't put him on the backstage props committee! But props is run by the chemist, Mr. Browning, and I wouldn't want to do that to him. He's brilliant, he is." She strode ahead of us.

"Such drama in Blackthorn!" Mom murmured to me from under her umbrella.

"Please, I beg you," I replied pertly, "do *not* confuse drama with melodrama."

"*Shhh!*" hissed Mom, glancing down the street at Liza's indignant figure.

We all stopped to have a cup of tea at the Angel Cafe on the corner. The Goops had a sticky bun apiece.

"Ah, this is good tea," Mom said. "At home it seems I'm always drinking coffee—just because David drinks coffee, I guess. This is much nicer." She smiled at her old art-school friend.

"Well, you're English. Tea is in your blood," Liza said with a grin. "Starts out there, and stays there."

Mom smiled. "Remember how Nora always said a good strong cuppa tea could save your life? I think I need to start drinking tea again, Liza. Wash away all my troubles and cares!"

Liza leaned across the table. "Now, you tell Auntie Liza about those troubles, luv. It's that husband of yours, isn't it? I always do say that husbands are more trouble than they're worth—and I can speak from experience, let me tell you! But, go ahead, what's the scoop on old David? Still got a stick up his bottom?"

"Liza!" admonished Mom, glancing over at me and the Goops. "*Shhh!*" But she giggled. "Actually, I've been think-ing of dropping Drake from my name and going back to being just Hedda Martin. But my paintings are all signed 'Martin-Drake.' What do you think, Liza?"

I glared at Mom and Liza both, then drained my cup of tea and turned my attention to the Goops, who were qui-etly engaged in drawing mazes on their place mats. *Fine, just fine. Let Mom change her name. Let them sit there and drag Dad through the mud.* I'd heard it all already from Mom. How Dad was a workaholic, how ever since he'd been promoted to partner in the architectural firm, he couldn't stop thinking about business long enough to have fun anymore. He had become an old stick-in-the-mud, Mom said, and all his late nights and conferences and busi-ness trips kept him so much away from home that she might as well be a single mother. They never went out to the opera, which they both had loved, or to art shows, and worst of all, Mom never had time for her painting anymore, thanks to him. I'd heard it, and heard it, and *heard* it until I thought I would scream if Mom complained anymore about "How Hard It Is to Live Without Art." And if she was gearing up now for a long chin-wag with Liza about Dad, then I wasn't about to sit here and listen. I'd leave, and go . . . somewhere. Anywhere.

But maybe Mom was more thoughtful of us kids than I was giving her credit for being, because instead of talking about Dad in front of me and the Goops, she turned the talk to the upcoming Springtime Art show in the village. Liza reported that much of the local talent was a crock, but some of it was truly good, and that was why the London art collectors liked to come to the show. Both Quent and Nora had been asked to exhibit in London galleries after being discovered in Springtime Art shows, and Liza herself had sold a painting to a London gallery last year. It all seemed very exciting to Mom. Liza and Mom finished their tea and went off to see the Pethering Portrait Gallery. I opted to go down to the rocky beach with the Goops. Beaches are rarely my first choice, but the Goops could not go alone yet, Mom said. Plus, the sun had come out, and I'd had enough of a tour of Blackthorn, and I definitely needed some time away from Liza. She was the sort of person my dad described as "enervating." Someone who sort of sucked the life out of a room with her energy. I felt exhausted now, though it was still morning, and even the thought of seeing Duncan at Quent Carrington's party tonight didn't perk me up.

Or maybe it was just jet lag.

5

As long as I could remember, walking on beaches brought on a strange, lost feeling. Especially at night—or on foggy days—standing on a beach could make my stomach churn in a sick sort of way. Even on sunny days, I often felt a little dizzy as I approached a beach. It wasn't that I was afraid of water. In fact, I was a really good swimmer— Mom and Dad had seen to it that all three of us kids had lessons from a young age, and we were all adept at both swimming and diving. My uneasiness was more to do with the atmosphere of the beach—the expanse of open sky and stretch of sand, and the sense I always had of being very small and vulnerable. But once I forced myself to go to a beach, the sound of the surf made me feel better and after a while I forgot the weirdness. Maybe it was something to do with all those negative ions bouncing around in the waves—at least that's what Tim Raglan had told me was responsible for the improved mood I got at the water's edge. He was a brainy sort of almost boyfriend. He said my good mood came from the energy generated by the waves. Whatever. Maybe he would also have come up with a theory about my stomach-churning reaction to beaches on overcast days—or in darkness. But I'd never told him about my problems.

All I know is that after the Goops and I said good-bye to Liza Pethering, and promised Mom we'd be back at the cottage in forty-five minutes, we walked to the end of the main road, where Blackthorn met the sea. I was so tired I was dragging my feet. As we approached the seawall, the dizziness started, and I felt tiny and unprotected. But I kept walking, and when we had climbed down the steep, stone steps from the sea wall to the rocky beach, and when I was standing at the edge of the sea with Ivy and Edmund, the cold salty spray swept my tiredness and dizziness away. In no time the three of us were hurling those round, smooth beach rocks into the water, trying to see who could throw the farthest. All of us were pretty good at tossing a baseball around, thanks to Saturday afternoons in the backyard with Dad, back in the days before his big promotion, when he wasn't always so busy with his job.

"Hey, did you see *that* one?" crowed Edmund. "That one went almost all the way to that ship out there!"

"Pretty good," conceded Ivy. "But watch this one!" She let fly a round, smooth stone. "I bet mine goes all the way to *Russia*!"

"Mine went to Russia, too!" Edmund shouted back. Then he pointed. "Hey—I bet that ship is going to Russia."

"Russia," I informed them, "is totally in the other direction." But it was the nature of Goops never to listen to big sisters, and so in two seconds they had completely forgotten our rock-throwing contest and were off into a game, pretending to be on board the big ship we could just see out on the horizon . . . pretending that they were docking in Moscow (though from what I recalled of my geography, Moscow wasn't even on the ocean, anyway) . . . pretending they were taking a train to the orphanage where we'd first seen Edmund nine years ago . . .

"Hey, let's adopt some babies and take them home on the ship with us," Ivy said, and Edmund, who wasn't really into babies, agreed, because he *did* like adoption games.

"Okay," he said readily. "Now we're getting off the train and going to meet the director of the orphanage. Her name is . . . Mrs. Bobblehead. *Yes,* Ivy!" he shouted when she started to protest. "It really is! That's what the director was called when I lived there. I remember—"

"Edmund, can you really remember anything?" I asked him suddenly. "I mean, really remember?"

"He was only a baby," Ivy said severely. "I don't remember anything before I was about two and a half. Why should he?"

I sighed, and the brisk wind carried my sigh out to sea. "Oh, never mind."

"My first memory is of Ivy taking my bottle," Edmund yelled over the crash of waves. "Stole it right out of our double stroller and threw it in the road."

"I never did that—," protested Ivy.

"Oh, yes you did," I told her. "Because I was pushing that stroller, and I remember."

"There, you see?" said Edmund comfortingly. "You do remember *some* things."

"Not much, but a few things," I concurred.

"Maybe the reason you don't remember more is because you got hit on the head and have amnesia," Edmund suggested helpfully. "Or—maybe you got taken by space aliens who did weird experiments on you, and it was so nasty you don't want to remember. I saw a TV show like that once. Hey!—" He broke off, bending down to dig in the sand at the edge of the rock line. "Hey! Look at this, you guys. A bottle! Maybe there's a message inside!"

Ivy ran to help him rinse the beer bottle in the waves. "Empty," Edmund said, disappointed. But Ivy took the bottle and held it up to the sunlight.

I watched them, bemused, thinking about amnesia and aliens.

"Maybe it's really old, Edmund," Ivy said. "Maybe it's an empty bottle of *mead*. And it was last held by King Henry the Eighth as he . . ."

"As he sailed past this beach in his royal yacht—"

"They didn't have yachts then, I bet," I said dourly, but nothing would shut the Goops up once they got into a story.

"Maybe he was on his royal *barge*, sailing to Russia to visit Mrs. Bobblehead, and he drank his mead from this very bottle—"

"And then a huge wave nearly capsized the barge! And the bottle fell overboard . . ."

"Maybe it fell down, down into the sea, and it conked a mermaid on the head! And she put a *curse* on it—"

"Yeah—a *curse!*"

And the Goops were off again as the clouds rolled in and obscured the sun. I shivered on the cold beach. My brother and sister were perfect playmates for each other. It was always like that with them. I could just as well have gone to the Pethering Portrait Gallery or be back at the cottage for all they needed me there, or noticed me. But I knew Mom wouldn't want the nine-year-olds left alone at the ocean's edge. They were good swimmers, true, but that was in California, where the sky was as blue as the water. This English ocean was as gray as the English sky above it had become, and I didn't trust it. I was glad to turn away from the wind blowing off the water and zip my raincoat and walk up the deserted beach a bit. Glad, too, to get away from the Goops and their ancient bottle, and Mrs. Bobblehead, and all of Edmund's dumb, fake memories.

They had to be fake. Of course he couldn't remember anything about his adoption or what life was like before *us*; he had been only a few months old when we brought him home to California. It wasn't as if he'd been older, as I had been when Mom and Dad adopted me. I had been, after all, fully five years old and ready for kindergarten when I joined this family. And kindergartners were old enough to remember all sorts of things.

So why *didn't* I?

The waves crashed over the concrete pier with a vengeance, spraying me. I jumped back, then tripped on a loose stone and sat down hard on another one. "Ouch!"

"Are you all right?" called a concerned voice out of nowhere, and I jerked my head up to see a girl about my age and my height (which is pretty tall), striding down the beach from the stone stairway. She wore a bright red jacket and had a large camera slung around her neck. The wind blew her short mouse-brown hair into spikes, then flat again. Her gray eyes looked worried. I stood up slowly, rubbing my bruised backside (*bum,* Mom said it was called here).

"Yes, I'm okay," I called back.

"I saw you fall," the girl said, coming to stand next to me, and then we both just stood there awkwardly for a moment. Then she added, "You sound American."

"I am American!" I laughed. "My name's Juliana Martin-Drake. We just moved here." I pointed to the Goops, who by now had taken off their shoes and started piling stones into a big tower--by the water's edge. "And *those* strange, half-frozen creatures are my brother and sister."

"Oh—you must be the people living in the Old Mill House Cottage," the girl said. "Everybody's talking about the new artist and her three kids. That must be you."

"We're big news?" I was surprised.

"Well, it's a small village. Any new thing is big news." Her voice was a little defensive, as if I had somehow insulted Blackthorn.

"Anyway, what's your name?" I asked hastily.

"Oh! Sorry! Mother always goes on at me about my atrocious manners, and I guess she's right . . . I'm Kate Glendenning. It's nice that I'm meeting you now, because we were going to meet tonight at Quent Carrington's party, and I was a bit nervous."

"Nervous? How come?"

Kate ran one hand through her wind-tossed hair. Her eyes still held that worried look. "Well, I don't know. Meeting new people . . . well, it's hard. I never know what to say, and I always make a fool out of myself somehow. Mother says I'm highly strung."

So it seemed I wasn't the only one with problems. But at least I didn't go around *announcing* mine to people I'd just met. "Well," I said encouragingly, "we've met now, so you don't have to be worried anymore, and you've said all the right things—and I'm the one looking like a fool, tripping over my own feet and falling on my . . . my *bum*. So now when you come to the party, we'll have each other to talk to, and that's good because I don't know anybody here except Duncan Carrington, and he's not very talkative. At least not to me."

Kate nodded. "Duncan's shy at first," she agreed. "But he'll loosen up, and once he starts talking—watch out. And by the way," she added, "his last name isn't Carrington actually; it's MacBennet. Quent Carrington is his stepfather."

Had I already been told that? I couldn't remember. "So, why are you coming to the party tonight?" I queried. "I mean, I'm glad you are coming . . . but it must mean your parents are artists, right? Because isn't this party about introducing my mom to the artists of Blackthorn?"

"Neither of my parents is an artist," Kate said, "but *I* want to be. I mean, I am—rather. I'm quite interested in photography, you see, and I've been taking and developing my own pictures for about a year now. Oh, I know it's not really *art*—or at least that's what Mother says. It's just dabbling, I know that. But I saved up and bought myself this really good camera, and it's brilliant."

"I think lots of people consider photography to be art," I countered, not much liking the sound of Kate's mother. "Loads of museums have exhibits of photographs. And there are tons of famous photographers—"

"Dabbling, that's all it is," repeated Kate sadly, running her fingers over her camera. "Mother says. And she knows. She knows everything there is to know about art. That's why she's invited to this party—she likes to buy original artwork, and she especially loves discovering some new artist whose work isn't known. She's got several Carrington pieces, and she was especially excited about Nora Cooper— that was Duncan's mum—who was absolutely fabulous."

"What about Liza Pethering?" I asked. "The one who has the portrait gallery—"

"Oh her." Kate grimaced. "Don't even mention that woman's name around Mother! Mother is absolutely *furious* about a portrait she commissioned from Liza Pethering that turned out to be sort of—well, rather unflattering. Mother hates it. She says that's *it* for Liza Pethering. Mother says she's going to boycott the gallery and won't buy any more of Liza's work, and she'll tell other people not to."

"Your mother feels betrayed?" I asked.

"Exactly. Mother says, how *dare* Liza Pethering paint such a thing after all she has done for her?" Kate shook her head. "I hope Liza won't be at that party tonight."

"Oh, but she will be," I told her, wondering daringly if maybe Liza had just painted Mother as she really looked, but Mother imagined herself some incredible beauty. "She'll be there. Guaranteed."

"Oh dear," said Kate, the worried expression firmly back in place. "It may mean fireworks. And I do hate Mother's scenes . . . "

She broke off as the Goops came running over, bleating that they were *freeeeezing* cold and *staaaaarving* hungry. I introduced them to Kate, then said we'd better hurry home, but we'd see her that night. She walked with us back to the main road, then we said good-bye and set off in different directions. Edmund insisted on carrying home the glass bottle he had found, now filled with sand, seaweed, and water. A souvenir, he said it was, of their trip to Russia.

"It's an ancient potion," Ivy informed me loftily. "Mrs. Bobblehead gave it to King Henry the Eighth."

❦ 6 ❦

"You're the guest of honor, so why do *I* have to dress up for this party, too?" I sulked after dinner. Mom was standing in the doorway of my little bedroom, stunning in a slinky black number, high heels, a velvet jacket, silver earrings—the works. I was wearing jeans as usual, and the thick fleecy sweatshirt my friends Jazzy and Rosy had given me as a going-away-to-a-cold-land present, and I wanted to keep it that way. Our cottage was chilly, and the central heating that Liza had raved about didn't really do the job very well. The fire in the woodstove blazed cheerfully, but you had to stand close to feel its warmth. All afternoon I'd been wandering around, trying to help unpack things while cupping mug after mug of hot tea in my hands. It was hard to get much done with my hands full, but the warm mug kept the shivers away. Plus, I figured the nice strong fragrance of tea would mask any salty whiffs of weirdness, and maybe even keep the creepy child's voice out of my head, too. It seemed to work because there had been no repeat of yesterday's strangeness so far. Still, I felt wary.

"I want you kids to look presentable," Mom was saying now. "I want all the artists of Blackthorn to be impressed by my three charming children. Wear a dress."

"But I don't have anything warm enough!" I wailed. "It's freezing around here!"

"Then wear a skirt," Mom suggested, "with that fleecy top you've got on."

Giving up without much of a fight, I exchanged my jeans for a longish denim skirt, rebraided my wind-tangled hair, dabbed on some lip gloss, and then I was ready. I never had been much of a glamour girl.

I wondered if Duncan liked glamour girls.

The Goops were ready, too, their yellow hair still damp from the baths Mom had insisted they take after their tower-building on the beach. They complained bitterly that the bathwater was no warmer than the sea had been. I hadn't tried the bath in our cottage yet, and I wasn't looking forward to it.

We ran through the dark, rainy garden to the Old Mill House. Quent Carrington opened the door even before we had a chance to knock. "The guests of honor have arrived!" he announced with a flourish. Looking past him into the large hall, we could see it was already full of people. The carved wooden wall panels gleamed in the light from chandeliers overhead. Candles flickered in sconces along the walls. There was a little balcony at one end of the long room (*the minstrels' gallery,* Mom whispered to me), hung with red velvet curtains.

"I love this," breathed Ivy.

It was an impressive room—and for a moment I felt like my sister must, imagining how the same room might have looked in the long-ago past, with a formal ball taking place here, and musicians playing dance music up in the minstrels' gallery.

Liza Pethering, looking less like a witch than she had the day before, wore a sequined red sheath and had her black hair pulled back into an elegant bun. She came gliding over to link her arm through Mom's. "Hedda, darling, let me take you around and introduce you to everybody!"

Her husband, Oliver, bobbed at her side, smiling genially. "Hello, Hedda. Hello, little children. Wonderful spread in the dining room. Liza's been here much of the afternoon. Helping to get everything ready, you know." He winked at Edmund and continued, all his sentences coming out in short, staccato bursts. "No doubt sampling the wine, too! But now, come and look, lad. There's quiches and ham. Sausage rolls and all sorts of cheeses! Ought to do for a hungry boy like you! Or do you prefer cakes and trifles, lad? I bet you do! And we've got all the best sorts from our Emporium. Laid right out on the table in there. Better hurry! Can't let these starving artists get it all."

"This way, duckies!" caroled Liza, and we all followed as, tottering slightly in ultrahigh heeled pumps, she headed for the dining room. In seconds we were surrounded by guests eager to meet Mom. Mom introduced us as her Life and her Inspiration, and chattered brightly to everyone, immediately seeming right at home. I smiled a lot and shook their hands, but it was hard to keep the names straight.

One large, imposing woman with very short, mannish hair and long, dangling earrings pumped my arm. "I'm Celia Glendenning," she boomed. "And you're Juliana!" I was getting used to hearing it pronounced the English way—JuliAWna—by now, but this woman said it with a special emphasis, almost gleeful. "How fabulous to meet you! My Kate told me she'd found you at the beach today, and I am so glad she did. The poor girl needs to socialize more, I always tell her, and make an effort! But, no, she'd rather wander around the village with that camera of hers. A shocking waste of time, I try to tell her, but will she listen? No, indeed not, but that's teenagers for you. Ah, well, it's a hobby, I suppose." She peered closer at me. "Heavens—you do put me in mind of someone. Or have we met before? No, of course not; you've only just arrived! But you're tall, and with that long fair plait down your back— it's very striking—I'll bet you resemble some Hollywood star, do you think that could be? Or one of those awful, bare-midriffed pop singers?"

"Um, I don't think so," I said hesitantly. This woman was alarming.

"In any case, I wish my Kate would take a good look at your hair, dear. I do wish she wouldn't chop hers off in such a boyish style. Most unbecoming, don't you think, in someone so young? Of course, mine is short, but that's entirely different."

"Well, no—I thought Kate's hair looked nice . . ."

"No, it *most definitely* does not look nice!"

This woman was *most definitely* a royal pain. But I just smiled. "Kate told me she's into photography. I guess it's easier to take pictures out in the wind if you don't have long hair blowing into your face and getting in the way of the lens . . ."

Mrs. Glendenning cut me off sharply. "No, indeed not. Long hair properly cared for—tightly dressed in a classic plait like yours, for instance—would not get in the way! You do put me in mind of someone . . . someone who also wore her hair in just such a way. And as for Kate's being, as you say, into photography, all *I* can say is that it is nothing I would consider an art form. Now, young lady, tell me what do *you* do?"

"Well, I love to read—," I said cautiously, but she cut me off again.

"I mean in the way of artistic pursuits! Are you a painter like your talented mother?"

"Oh, no . . . not at all . . ."

"Perhaps you would like to learn the art of glassblowing," said a tall, thin man wearing his fair hair pulled back in a curly ponytail. He winked at me. "You're welcome to come by our studio any time you want to," he said. "Juliana, isn't it? I think that's what your lovely mummy said you're called."

"Yes," I said, eagerly turning to him. It would be a relief not to have to chat anymore with Mrs. Glendenning. "And thanks. I'd like to see glassblowing."

"This is Rodney Whitsun," said Mrs. Glendenning with a big toothy smile at him. "He's brilliant. I have several of his pieces on display in my own home, and I always buy new ones to give as gifts. He and his partner, Andrew Parker, have just opened a new studio over by the Shreenwater. They offer classes for children, don't you, Rod, dear?"

"Andrew will, starting next month," Rodney said. He frowned. "It's just so hard to find space in the new property. Since we want to hold classes in glassblowing technique as well as have a separate display room, we really needed something larger, and it makes me just *furious* that we didn't get—" He broke off and glanced around the crowded room. "Well," he said with a little shrug, "you know the story. I've bored everyone with it for months now."

"Indeed I do know that story," said Mrs. Glendenning, nodding vigorously. "And I have every sympathy. The woman is a positive menace to this village!"

"Who is?" I asked, confused and intrigued by this mean-spirited gossip.

"Liza Pethering, that's who! Your mother's old school chum!" Mrs. Glendenning's face grew red. She pointed. "Right over there, causing who-knows-what trouble!"

We all looked across the dining room to where Liza was standing in a circle of guests, her head thrown back, laughing wildly. Her face looked flushed to me. Feverish, even. Nearly matched her sequined dress. I wondered if she were drunk already.

"Manners, manners," chided Rodney Whitsun, taking Mrs. Glendenning's elbow and turning her away from the circle of party guests that included the Petherings, Quent Carrington, and my mom.

"You're right, Rodney, dear, of course," said Mrs. Glendenning with a little laugh. "I mustn't forget myself. But you have to admit she's become more and more unpleasant and grasping with every sale she makes and every drink she takes. Really fancies herself. She's a terrible portrait painter, actually. And a terrible person altogether." She put a confiding hand on my arm. "Rodney and Andrew are too gentlemanly to spread the tale, dear, but I don't mind telling it. You see, they were angling to buy a new studio— needed more space. And the corner building where the Emporium is now was for sale last year. Liza knew—everyone in town knew!—how delighted Rodney and his partner were with the chance to buy it. They were working out the finances, when all of a sudden, Liza Pethering decided it would be perfect for her husband's shop. Their Emporium used to be in a teeny alley off Dark Lane—just a small shop, where Oliver was the butcher. But then he bought the shop, and then Liza decided they needed to expand, and so she convinced him to buy the very property that Rodney and Andrew wanted! The Petherings swooped in with the ready money, and the sale went through quickly—and in the end there was nothing for Rodney and Andrew to do but buy the old shop building that the Petherings were selling! Galling, wasn't it, Rodney? And it's not nearly as desirable a location, I'm sorry to say." She shook her head and glared over at Liza in her bright red dress. "That woman is poison. I don't know why Quent Carrington tolerates her at his parties."

"Come on now, Celia," chuckled Rodney Whitsun, but the chuckle sounded a little uncomfortable. "Let it go, luv. That's all water under the bridge." He nudged me and pointed to Duncan and Kate. "It seems those young people want your attention, Juliana, my duck. And I see Andrew wants mine." He waved at another tall, elegant, ponytailed man across the room. "It was lovely to meet you, and I must say your mummy seems a dear. Nice to have some new faces in town. Now, remember—if you and your brother and sister would like to learn about glassblowing, do come along to our new classes."

"Thanks," I said. "I'll tell them."

"Perhaps your Kate would enjoy learning, too, Celia," he added to Mrs. Glendenning. "I know you'd rather she weren't spending so much time with her camera . . . And now, will you both excuse me?"

As he wandered off, I made my getaway, too. Mrs. Glendenning, with a sour expression on her round face, bulldozed through the crowd, heading out of the room.

I took a plate as I passed the table and helped myself to a slice of ham, a sliver of quiche, and a couple little sausages wrapped in pastry. I noticed that the Goops, in true Goop fashion, had piled their plates with masses of

everything and were now sitting together in a corner, looking around and giggling.

Before I could head over to Kate and Duncan, my mom
came up and put her arm around my shoulders. "Here's my
daughter Juliana," she said, turning me to face the couple
at her side. "And those two munchkins in the corner with
their dinners are also mine."

A short, round, middle-aged couple smiled at me. The
woman had soft dark curls that bobbed on her shoulders.
The man had graying fair hair. He wore black-rimmed
glasses that made him look like an aging Harry Potter.
Both reached out and shook my hand eagerly, and the
woman exclaimed brightly to my mom, "She's just lovely,
Hedda. How lucky you are! I wish we could get one just
like her . . ."

At my baffled expression, Mom smiled a little. "This is
Jane and Leo Thurber, honey," she told me. She glanced up
at the couple. "Do I have your names right?"

"It's Jean, actually," corrected the woman. "But you're
doing very well, considering how many new people you're
meeting tonight."

"Sorry," said Mom. "*Jean* and Leo Thurber," she said to
me. "Mr. Thurber is a potter, and Mrs. Thurber is a
stained-glass artist—"

"And we were very interested in meeting the new talent
in town," Mr. Thurber said, "and all the more so once we
learned that Hedda's children—or some of them—are
adopted." He beamed at me.

I nodded, then glanced at Mom for clarification.

"I was asking Jean about commissioning a little
stained-glass window for Ivy's bedroom," Mom explained.

"Maybe for her birthday—something with a fairy theme; you know our Ivy! And then somehow the talk turned to a window that Jean is making with an angel theme, and she said it was for the child they hope to adopt soon. So then talk turned to adoption. The Thurbers are very interested in hearing other families' adoption stories."

"Yes," added Mr. Thurber eagerly, taking off his black glasses and peering at me earnestly. "We were thinking of adopting an infant, but now are considering an older child instead."

"We've been married twenty-five years already," Mrs. Thurber said, with a sweet smile at her husband. "Twenty-five years of happiness—but no little ones ever came our way. It's the one thing missing from perfect bliss."

"Um—I, I'm sorry," I said, thinking how funny that this little round couple felt they'd nearly obtained perfect bliss! Anyway, I never really knew what to say when people wanted to talk about adopting kids. Of course I think it's a fine idea! But I hate when people think I somehow represent adopted children everywhere and look on me as a shining poster child for adoption. Mom knows this, and pretty much feels the same. I wished she'd go over and introduce the Thurbers to Ivy and Edmund instead—but probably one look at their loaded platters of food and goopy chops would put the Thurbers off the idea of any kids, period.

Mom squeezed my shoulder affectionately. "So," she said to me, "have you eaten yet? I see Duncan over there—"

Before I could tell her that's where I was heading when she stopped me, Mrs. Thurber reached for my hand. "We wished and wished and *wished* for a child," she confided urgently. "Right from the start—from our honeymoon! But month after month passed, then year after year, and no baby! I used to wish on the first star I saw each and every night . . ."

"I had a special ring made for Jeannie on our tenth anniversary," added her husband. "A diamond ring in the shape of a star. Sort of a lucky charm, for wishing on."

His wife released my hand and patted his arm instead, gazing up at him adoringly. "He made it into the shape of a star so I didn't have to wait till dark to make my wishes!" She held out her right hand to me. "See?" she asked, wiggling her fingers. "Isn't it glorious?" A star-shaped arrangement of diamonds glittered. "And then—even better!— this past year, once we started our adoption search, lovely Leo outdid himself and had *these* made!"

She shook back her curls to reveal extravagantly large diamond earrings, star-shaped, of course, that flashed in the lamplight. "Aren't they to *die* for?"

Mom and I agreed they were. "So now you've got good luck charms all over," Mom observed drily.

Both Thurbers beamed. "Nothing short of death would keep me from wearing my stars!" Mrs. Thurber declared dramatically, and we all laughed. I was thinking this couple was a bit odd, but artists tended to be that way. At least they seemed sweetly eccentric instead of just plain weird.

"I hope you get your child soon," I said politely, looking over their heads to where Duncan was still standing with Kate.

"Sweet girl!" Mrs. Thurber's eyes got all misty.

"We're thinking our agency will find our special match before the summer," said Mr. Thurber, putting an arm around his wife. "It's all very exciting. I am making a special series of glazed garden pots to commemorate this time of our life, and to symbolize growth."

"I'm thinking of this time as my *pregnancy*," giggled Mrs. Thurber, wiping her eyes with brisk fingers. "And I'm working on a brilliant new stained-glass window—the angels I mentioned to your mum." She reached for my hand again, and leaned in close. "Now, Julie, dear, tell me how it *feels* to be adopted. From the *child's* point of view, I mean—not that you're a child anymore, really. Clearly a young lady now, isn't she, Leo?"

Give me a break! But Mom squeezed my arm, so I took a deep breath and smiled winningly. "It feels great to be adopted."

Mom patted my back. "Now," she said, "let me introduce you to Edmund. We adopted him from Russia as an infant . . ."

The Thurbers brightened even more and pressed my hand and waved good-bye as Mom led them across to the Goops. I hurried over to Duncan and Kate. My stomach was growling now.

"We meet again." Kate greeted me with a shy smile. "But out of the wind this time."

"Er—hullo," Duncan said, slanting a glance at me. "Er—I was just suggesting a house tour. Are you interested?"

"Sure," I said, munching on one of the little sausage and pastry things. "That sounds fun—," I broke off as raised voices burst out in the hall. Liza's wild laughter, and then the sound of a slap—and silence.

We stared at each other. Then Celia Glendenning stormed back into the dining room and headed our way. She grabbed her daughter's arm.

"Kate, get your coat. We are leaving this instant! I will not stay and be insulted by that—that viper! That snake in the grass who has not one ounce of talent to her name! Somebody should take a hoe to that snake—"

"*Mother,*" Kate hissed, her face flaming with embarrassment.

Liza Pethering tittered from the doorway. There was a red handprint on her left cheek. "I was just saying to dear Celia before things got rather out of *hand*—," she said in a slightly slurred voice that nonetheless carried across the room, "—just saying that perhaps she'd like to commission *another* portrait, one I could copy from a photograph of her in her younger, *slimmer* days."

Some of the guests were mean enough to laugh at this, but most of them just stared at Liza disapprovingly.

"It didn't look a thing like me!" screeched Celia. "You made it ugly out of spite."

"It would take a good bit of magic," laughed Liza shrilly, "to turn out a portrait you'd be happy with. You'd need some sort of lucky charm to be the beauty you imagine yourself to be! I only paint what I see—"

Oliver Pethering rolled his eyes, probably totally humiliated by his drunken wife.

"Now Liza," he said helplessly. "Mind your manners, luv."

"Mind your own!" trilled Liza. "I'd say they need minding just as much as mine do, if not more so! This conversation doesn't concern you. Celia and I are just talking business."

"You'll need a magic charm to stay in business at all, if you keep painting the way you did me in my portrait." Celia turned away disgustedly. "You'll need a magic charm— or you're dead to the art world, lady."

"Oh yeah?" screeched Liza.

"Think we ought to leave now, darling," Oliver said evenly to Liza. "Get on home."

Liza laughed loudly, and sounded once again like her brittle, angry self. "*You* get on home, little bald man. This party is just getting started!"

Oliver scowled and wiped a hand across his round face. He looked exhausted. "Time maybe I *will* be getting on home, Quent," he said. Then he looked back at his wife and shrugged. "Send her home when she gets on your nerves. Shouldn't take long."

"Are you saying I'm drunk?" sneered Liza. "I'm not the least bit drunk. I just can't toady up to that Glendenning witch the way all the rest of you do, and I'm not afraid to say so! Just because she buys your work, you let her think she's a respected art critic—but she's not. She's *nobody*."

"Why, you nasty cow!" cried Celia Glendenning, whirling around by the door.

"Oh, dear," Jean Thurber murmured. Her husband, Leo, put his arm around her shoulders.

Quent Carrington calmly walked over and did the same to Liza—put his arm right around Liza's shoulders—but gave her a little shake. "Come along, old girl," he said tersely. "Let's get you a nice cup of coffee right now." He steered her toward the kitchen. Over his shoulder he asked, "Oliver?"

Oliver Pethering plucked his overcoat off the coatrack in the corner. "I really should take her off home," he said, glancing around at the assembled party guests. "She's just making a spectacle of herself. And I've got some, er, book-keeping to see to. But . . . all right. We'll pour some coffee into the old girl first. Sober her up." He followed Quent and Liza out of the room.

"But I don't want coffee," they could hear Liza protesting. "Bring out more wine!"

"That's the spirit!" called Andrew Parker, raising his wineglass to the empty doorway. "Cheers."

The guests laughed and raised their glasses and shook their heads. Then they turned back to party chitchat, which after such theatrics was quite a buzz. Jean and Leo Thurber wandered over toward us, cocktail glasses in hand.

"Really," said Mrs. Thurber, tossing her curls in disdain. "Such theatrics. It's a good thing Liza and Oliver don't have any children, that's what I say. And no one would ever let *her* adopt a child—that's for certain! She would make a perfectly *dreadful* mother."

Liza's wild laughter drifted out from the kitchen. "Go home alone, little man," we all heard her shout. "I'll come when I'm good and ready!"

"Dreadful *wife* as well," asserted Mr. Thurber. "She's a disgrace." He scowled.

"Well, *we're* good and ready to head off home right now," said Mrs. Glendenning. "I've been insulted quite enough for one evening. Come along, Kate." She turned to Duncan. "Do give your stepfather our thanks for the invitation."

Kate sighed and rolled her eyes a bit, but meekly said her good-byes. Then she and her mother got their coats from the hall stand and left the house. I wondered if there was a Mr. Glendenning in the picture. When I asked Duncan, he shook his head. "Nope," he said. "Kate's dad ran off at the same time mine did. Kate and I were both about nine, I think."

I was confused. "Your dad ran off with Mr. Glendenning?"

Duncan laughed. "No, though that would have been only slightly more scandalous, I guess." His face flushed a little bit, and he looked down at his feet, then back at me. "No, the true and sordid story of my life is that my dad ran off with a Brazilian dancer—that's code for a stripper, I'm fairly certain. At least in her case."

We stood there, just looking at each other, and I was aware that this was our first time alone together. It felt awkward.

"I'm sorry about your dad," I mumbled.

Would conversation be this awkward the whole time? I worried? What if I couldn't think of anything to say on the house tour? Or what if Duncan grew as silent and shy as he'd been at the Old Ship?

Duncan was looking at me with a worried expression, so I smiled. He smiled back, and his cheeks blushed as red as his hair. I felt better immediately, and then suddenly it wasn't so awkward anymore. "Before we do the house tour," he said, his bright color subsiding, "I could show you the grounds. Have you seen the old mill? Or Quent's studio?" He led me toward the kitchen. "Let's go tell them we're out of here."

Through the kitchen doorway we could see Liza slumped on a stool at the high, polished counter. Quent was spooning instant coffee into a mug. "I'm going to show Juliana around," Duncan told Quent. "All right? We'll be back later."

He looked up with a smile. "Fine, fine," he said distractedly. "Tell her all the history of the place. Show her the ancestral portrait gallery!"

Liza lifted her head. "Portraits!" she snarled. "That's *my* talent, and I'm damned good, y'know. I don't need any damned charm to paint well—I have magic in my fingers!"

"Yes, yes," Quent was saying soothingly as we started walking away. "No one doubts that, Liza."

"That Glendenning woman does!" flared Liza.

"Forget her," said Quent sensibly. He poured water from the kettle into Liza's mug and stirred briskly with a spoon. "Here you go."

"I have my own strength," Liza mumbled drunkenly, ignoring the coffee. "I'm not like those people who need charms to be successful! Not like your Nora. She would never do *anything* without consulting her tea leaves or wearing that lucky necklace—" She broke off suddenly and stared at Quent as if she weren't seeing him anymore, but something else in his place. Then she blinked, and the baffled look was gone, replaced once more by drunken laughter.

"Drink your coffee, Liza," said Quent wearily. "You're hopeless."

Her laughter grew fainter as Duncan and I headed out the back door. "Let's start with the grounds," he suggested. "Get away from the lunatics."

I wiggled my eyebrows and laughed, trying to imitate Liza's cackle, and he chuckled. We set off side by side into the hallway and out the back door into the garden.

We wandered along the garden path, illuminated by the occasional light strategically planted among bushes or flower beds. He pointed out the old mill wheel, a large stone wheel lying on its side in a tumbledown stone outbuilding. "Wheat was ground here a hundred years back," Duncan explained. "It was big business for the village and employed most of the villagers who weren't farmers or local fishermen. But now the main business is tourism—and art."

"You mean there aren't any more farms around here?" I asked. "And no fishermen?"

"Not as many farmers," he replied, "with the farmland getting developed for council houses. There are still the fishing boats, of course, but not as many people grow up wanting to make fishing their livelihood anymore. It's not where the money is."

"Catching tourists is more profitable than catching fish?" I giggled.

He glanced down at me with a grin. "They stink less, anyway." He directed me back along the path to the next outbuilding—less ramshackle than the mill, with modern windows and a stout wooden door. "This is Quent's studio. It's locked, but you can see through the windows. Ask him for a tour one day—I'm sure he'd love to show you the newest project."

I stepped up to the long windows and peered inside. The large room was in near darkness, but the light from the path allowed me to make out mysterious humps— sculptures-in-progress covered over with blue plastic sheeting. There was a stack of wood in one corner, and long sheets of metal leaning against the far wall. A long table held cannisters of tools; I could see hammers and chisels and files. There were machines, too: probably drills and saws for the metal and wood. "He's working on some sort of Viking project, isn't he?" I asked. "Liza mentioned it."

"Right. Sculpture inspired by the ancient boats and artifacts," Duncan explained. "Last year Quent went on a trip to Scandinavia and Iceland. He came back full of ideas. He whipped up a few smaller pieces and exhibited them in London, and the orders have been flowing in ever since. Now he's setting up a huge exhibit at the Millennium Dome for a show this summer."

"Wow," I said. "Impressive!" I thought I'd like to come back in daylight sometime and see the pieces close-up and uncovered.

We walked back to the main house for the rest of the tour, passing our cottage. I noticed how camouflaged it seemed, surrounded by trees, a shadowy bulk in the surrounding darkness. We entered the Old Mill House, skirting around the huge hall room where the party guests were still eating and laughing, and went into a smaller—though still very large—luxurious living room, then through a well-appointed study and then into a dark-paneled, book-lined library. Here was the carousel horse I had seen through the window when we arrived. Duncan sank onto the window seat and patted the place next to him. I sat down, feeling happy to be with him and hoping he'd keep talking.

Since we'd been alone, curiously, Duncan seemed much less shy and much more relaxed. "Yes," he said musingly, "a stripper. Her name was Eliana, and she was somebody Liza Pethering had met at a London club or someplace."

"Liza Pethering—again!" I said. "The woman gets around."

"She's got a great knack for making trouble," he agreed. "She invited this Eliana to come to Blackthorn for a visit— you know, to see something of the English countryside instead of just touring all the usual spots around London—and Eliana came. She stayed with Liza and Oliver a couple weeks after Liza decided to have her sit for a series of portraits. My dad met her at the pub, and the rest is history."

"They went off together—to Brazil?"

"That's right. Well, not straight away. My dad spent a lot of time with Eliana while she was here, having dinners at the pub and keeping her company during the portrait sittings. And when the paintings were done, he followed her back to London, and then on to Brazil. And they haven't been back since. Oh, my dad sends me the odd birthday card and such, but I haven't seen him for years and don't expect to. Then, after my mum died two years back, he wrote to say I could come live with them in Rio de Janeiro if I wanted, but Granny put her foot down. She said I was to stay right here in Blackthorn and live with her and Grandad, or else stay with Quent. They're my legal guardians now, since Mum died. I mean, I live with Quent, but it's not like he ever adopted me or anything official."

It was on the tip of my tongue to tell him I was adopted—but then I figured he'd probably already have heard that detail from Liza.

"Anyway," he continued, "Granny's never forgiven my dad for leaving my mum—which is rather funny, really, because Mum herself never was all that upset, I don't think. She and Dad weren't terribly well suited to start with—at least that's how it seemed to me. There were always tons of rows. Granny is still furious at Liza Pethering because she blames Liza for introducing Eliana to my dad."

"Liza's got loads of enemies," I observed. "Does she have any friends? Besides my mom, I mean?"

"My stepfather likes her, and my mum did," he replied,

shrugging. "It's all madness. But just melodrama rather than tragedy, really. I mean, Mum soon enough took up with Quent, and we moved here. They got married the following year and lived happily ever after, each one growing more famous every month with her painting and his sculpting." He looked at me and his eyes grew dark. "Well, happily ever after until the car crash that killed her."

"I'm so sorry," I said, and I truly was. Something twisted inside me at the very thought of dead moms.

"No, I'm sorry. Sorry to be running off at the mouth this way."

"Don't be sorry!" I said quickly. "I asked because I wanted to know."

"I was supposed to go with her that night. The night of the crash. She was going to London to be on a program on telly about amazing new artists—and she'd promised I could come and watch the filming."

"But in the end you didn't go?"

"Well, she left without me. Something must have come up, so she had to leave earlier than planned—I don't know what it was. But, whatever, it probably saved my life."

"So that's good," I said with a smile. But the bleakness in his face touched me. We were both without our birth mothers and our birth fathers; it was a bond between us. "You must have loved your mother very much," I said quietly.

"Yeah." Duncan sighed, then smiled at me. "Well, now that you've heard my tale of woe, don't you have to get revenge and tell me yours?"

"You don't know what you're asking," I teased, but really he *didn't* know, and I wasn't sure I should mention my unusual history. "Let's get on with this house tour."

We stood up and left the library and wandered on through the whole, amazing house. It was huge and elegant, but still felt comfortable. "Thirty-two rooms," Duncan told me. "I counted 'em myself once, just to make sure."

"Your stepfather must be a *hugely* successful sculptor," I said, impressed.

"He is," Duncan agreed. "But he actually inherited this place from his great-uncle. I think it takes most of the money Quent makes just keeping it up. There's always something springing a leak or breaking down or getting woodworm. My mum was glad when her own work started winning awards and stuff so she had extra money to add to the house fund." He stopped in the doorway of another room. "She loved this place," he said. "The whole house. In fact, she's the one who redecorated it and made it a real home instead of a museum. This room here was her special retreat—her parlor, she called it. I think her parlor was her favorite place—next to the studio out in your cottage, of course."

I stepped into the parlor and looked around. It was painted in a soft rose, lined with low bookshelves, and furnished with deep, soft couches, the sort you just want to sink into with a book in your hand. The windows looked out to the garden, and through the darkness I could see a light on upstairs in our cottage, in the sunroom. Maybe Duncan's mum had sat here, looking over at the cottage, thinking about a project and then walking over to her studio to paint it. This room had some of the same found art touches that I'd seen up in the sunroom: pinecones lined up on the window ledges, and a bare branch in a pot, hung with tiny crystals, tied with thin slivers of colored ribbons. "I'd like a room like this one," I murmured.

"Mum often sat in here to read," Duncan said softly. "And it's where she would sit when she was making jewelry, rather than up in her painting studio."

"I saw some of her jewelry," I told him. "Or—one piece, anyway. Up in her studio in our cottage—a really pretty necklace made of flowers and beads."

He nodded. "One of her talisman necklaces, I'll bet. She made them for friends, and no two were alike. I still have the one she made for me, and I always wear it before a big test at school. It has a big brown nut attached, and Mum said I should rub it before I started the test. That's what she did with hers—before a big exhibition or interview. Mum was terrified of audiences the way I'm scared of essay questions. She would rub her lucky pink quartz like I rubbed the nut. She made her necklace from dried black-thorn blossoms because the blackthorn branches used to be burned in the olden days to ward off evil spirits. Mum half believed in magic, I think. I never did, really—but I wanted to! It used to feel magical, just watching her work. I would sit up in her studio in the cottage—just watching while she painted . . ."

I wanted to reach over and smooth that pained expression off his face, but I just sat there. It was sometimes good, not having memories. Memories could make you sad.

"I guess that's why the thought of another family moving into the cottage and using that studio bothered me," he said, glancing sideways at me. "I didn't mean to sound angry yesterday."

After a short silence, I asked, "I hope you don't mind very much that we're living in the cottage now."

"Well," he acknowledged, glancing at me, "Quent and I had a row when he first told me he planned to rent it to your mum. But now that I've met you, I'm glad you're there."

"Me, too," I said slowly. "I mean, I'm getting gladder. But it's hard being away from my dad. It doesn't feel right. I miss him."

"Are your parents divorced?" Duncan asked gently.

"No," I said, "not yet anyway." I spun away from him because I really didn't feel like talking about Dad. "It still feels magical in this room, somehow, don't you think?" I asked, as much to change the subject as because it was true. "As if your mother left behind a good feeling—" Then I broke off because there was suddenly something else in the room besides a good feeling.

That sweetly sickening smell.

I remembered—

Wake up! Oh, please, please wake up!

I dashed out of the parlor. *No!* I remembered *nothing.*

7

"Juliana?" Duncan's voice was insistent. "What's wrong? Are you all right?"

I looked up at him in a daze. I put my hands up to my head and scrubbed my fingers into my hair, massaging my scalp as if I could rub the voice away and banish the smell. . . .

"What's wrong?"

Dizzily I stood up. I needed to leave, I needed to leave right now. "I feel so . . . strange. I have to go—"

"Wait—come with me," Duncan said, and he put his arm around me and walked with me out of the room and up a staircase—not the main, curving, dramatic staircase in the front hall but a smaller, narrower staircase.

Maybe the servants' staircase, I mused foggily. I liked the feel of Duncan's arm around my shoulders, and I leaned against him as we walked. Quickly I felt fine again.

"Better now?" he asked worriedly, looking down at me.

"Yes," I said. "Sorry about that. I was just—dizzy for a minute."

"Oh, good. I thought you'd seen a ghost or something!"

"Are there ghosts in this house?" I asked teasingly, knowing fully well that if what I'd smelled and heard were ghosts, they were my own ghosts. But—something had triggered them here. What had it been?

I couldn't think what, and I felt completely better with Duncan's arm around me, so we continued the house tour, shyly touching shoulders as we walked. The place was incredible. Huge. There was a games room with a huge pool table in the center of the floor, and a conservatory with glass walls and a glass ceiling and a zillion blooming plants, and even a ballroom on the third floor, where I whirled around, arms out—imagining dancing someday with Duncan in our own personal version of a waltz. I spun the frightened child's voice right out of my head.

"And now I'll show you my lair," said Duncan when I'd finished dancing. With my head still spinning, I followed him down the stairs. As we were heading down another corridor, we saw Quent ahead of us, carrying someone— Liza Pethering!

He stopped when he saw us and smiled ruefully. "I'm afraid she's had a drop too much," he said in a low voice. He pushed open a door with his foot.

"Need help?" asked Duncan.

Quent shook his head as he moved into the shadows. "Nothing to do," he said over his shoulder. "She's totally soused. We'll let her sleep it off in the guest bedroom till Oliver can come back for her."

"Stupid woman," Duncan muttered to me as he and I continued along the corridor. At the end was another flight of stairs. At the top of the stairs we walked down another hallway and came to a closed door that had a poster of Mount Everest taped to it. Duncan reached out and twisted the doorknob. The door swung open.

His bedroom. Duncan stepped away from me and I felt a stab of sadness to be standing alone. But at least the only smell around was his nice boy smell, and the only sound was his friendly voice saying, "Welcome to my lair."

We sat on his bed. My head was clear now. I looked around with interest at the crowded bookcases, the over-flowing dresser drawers, the piles of CDs and stacks of mountain-climbing magazines. I smiled at the big brown teddy bear perched on his pillow.

"Want to tell me what happened?" Duncan asked after a few minutes.

I nodded slowly, deciding suddenly that I *would* tell him. I reached out for the bear and sat cuddling it. "You want to hear *my* tale of woe?" I asked the bear. I looked over at Duncan. "I'm not sure he's old enough."

"Oh, he's plenty old enough," Duncan said. "'Normous is sixteen, same as me."

"Norman?"

"No, it's 'Normous. Short for Enormous. Which he is. My dad gave him to me when I was born, or so I'm told. Anyway, he's definitely old enough for whatever secrets you want to tell us."

I lay back on his bed with 'Normous in my arms and took a deep breath. Where to start with my story? Probably at the beginning—or, at least, what was all the beginning I knew about. I told Duncan how I was five when my parents adopted me. "Five *years* old, that is," I clarified. "Not five months, like Edmund was when we got him from Russia."

I told him how my parents had thought even before they got married that adoption was as good a way to build a family as any other way, and so they decided to adopt after they'd been married for two years. They went through the process to adopt a child from the foster care system in California. The way it worked, I explained to Duncan as it had been explained to me, was that kids got taken into foster care when their birth families couldn't take care of them for whatever reason. Sometimes the birth parents died, and there were no relatives to take the kid. Or sometimes the birth parents just couldn't handle raising kids. Some of the kids in the foster care system had been abused or neglected by their parents, and nobody else in their family was able to take them in, or do any better raising them, or whatever. Kids in foster care either moved back with their birth families eventually—if the troubles got ironed out—or else they were put up for adoption. I had been living in foster care for about six months when my parents adopted me.

I stopped. That was the easy part to tell. After a moment of silence, Duncan reached out and touched my hand, which was still clutching his teddy bear. "'Normous suspects there's more to the story," he said. "And he wants to hear it."

I remembered those foster parents, I told him—an elderly couple in a tidy little trailer park. They were very sweet and gentle and always spoke to me in soft, encouraging voices. I could remember sitting at their table doing puzzles with the lady. I could remember watching a football game on TV with the man, both of us sitting together in his huge reclining chair, and him yelling his head off when his team made a touchdown.

"Oh," said Duncan, "you mean American football. Here we say football when we mean what you call soccer."

"It was football," I said. "Regular American football.

Big guys with huge, padded shoulders tackling each other to get the ball. I remember it."

"Okay," he said. "Sorry to interrupt. Go on."

I remembered football, I continued, but the thing was, I didn't remember anything *before* football. I didn't remember how I came to be living with those foster parents. It bothered me terribly, because the official records my mom and dad were given just said that I had been found wandering on the beach, all alone. A little waif of a five-year-old, hungry and tattered. Apparently I was able to tell the people who found me my name and age and even my birth date, but I didn't seem to know where I lived or why I was on the beach or how I'd gotten there. They took me to the police, of course, and Child Protective Services found me the foster home.

I didn't remember my birth father at all, and I had a vague sense that he had died—something to do with a motorcycle crash. My birth mother later also died . . . and that's why I had to go into foster care. Apparently someone who remembered her from living on the streets was questioned by the police, and this guy said that my mom was a drug addict who had overdosed. The guy said she had an accent, maybe British or maybe something else. He didn't know her name or any more about her—he'd always just called her "Majesty" or "Your Highness" for a joke when he saw her, which wasn't often. But beyond my hazy memory of being little and playing with a yellow plastic duck in a warm bath, with someone sitting nearby—someone I loved who was laughing with me while I splashed—I couldn't picture anything from that previous life. The next memories were of sitting at the table in the foster home doing puzzles, or sitting in the big chair shouting for touchdowns. Edmund and Ivy, not to mention all of my friends, could remember *lots* of things that had happened when they were much younger than five. So why couldn't I?

I felt like I had a hole in my head.

"And so that's my tale of woe, 'Normous," I said, lying back against Duncan's pillows and holding the big bear up in front of my face. "What do you think of that?"

"You win the Tale of Woe contest," Duncan said gently. "It must be scary for you."

"Well, it's weird," I said, sitting up and handing him his bear. "But it was never particularly scary before. It's only turned scary since I've been here in Blackthorn, and I keep getting a whiff of—I don't know how to explain it. Some sort of smell that reminds me . . . of something. I don't know what! And I keep hearing a voice in my head—yes, that *is* scary."

He was silent for a long moment. "Scary . . . because maybe you're beginning to remember. Maybe something happened to you then—something that you're blocking out. And something here, now, is reminding you."

His words shook me. Edmund had said the same thing at the beach. I had to take a deep breath because I had this gut feeling what they said must have some grain of truth to it. *Something* had caused this stupid amnesia—or else I just had the worst memory in the history of the world. I looked up and met Duncan's wide green eyes and was glad I'd told him as much as I had. But what could have happened *then* that would link the smell and the urgent voice to *now*?

"You could be right," I murmured, reaching out to stroke his big teddy bear's head, trying now for humor. "Something happened that I can't *bear* to remember. It must be something I can *bearly* bear to think about, in fact!"

"Thank you beary much for telling me, though," he said, straight-faced. And although we were lightening the mood with our puns, I knew we both knew that a line had been crossed. We had each shared something important about ourselves, and now the two of us were on the way to being more than just new acquaintances. "Seriously, though. It might have been some sort of trauma that made you forget stuff. Maybe you need to go through some other sort of trauma to remember again."

"Oh goody!" I said heartily. "Something to look forward to!"

We rolled off the bed and started acting silly, goofing around with 'Normous, making him dance to Duncan's favorite CDs. Duncan showed me his electric guitar and played a riff. He showed me his collection of detective novels, and his mountain-climbing magazines. "I want to scale Everest someday," he told me. "*And* be a rock star when I grow up. *And* maybe a famous detective." I laughed and said I'd be a detective, too, when I grew up. Or maybe a famous scientist. "A *mad* scientist, I hope," teased Duncan.

"Of course! My little brother would tell you those are the best kind. He's in training to be one himself, I think."

"Trained by the master herself?" Duncan wiggled his eyebrows at me.

"You're the one who's mad," I countered. "As in loony tunes!"

"Mad about *you*," he murmured, "or at least getting there." He blushed—bright red cheeks clashing with his orangey red hair, and I just sat there staring at him because I was so surprised—and thrilled—that he'd said such a thing. Nobody had ever said anything like that to me before. And this wasn't just anybody—it was a really cute Brit with very cool red hair. Forget old Tim Raglan—who was *he* when there was Duncan MacBennet? For a minute I felt a little bit of magic in the room. Or sparks between us. Or *something*.

But then he broke the spell by jumping up and suggesting we go down and get some food. So we took 'Normous along to the kitchen. Mom was working with Quent Carrington in the kitchen to replenish the food offerings. From the sound of the guests still gabbing away out in the Great Hall, the party was in full swing.

"Liza was so good to arrange all this food for the party," Mom said, sliding little salmon puffs off the baking sheets onto serving plates. "But I do wish she'd stuck around to help serve it instead of going off someplace. I suppose she's out there somewhere, but I haven't seen her. I thought she was with you."

"Nope. She was so out of it when I stuck her in the guest bedroom, I told her to stay put until Oliver could come back and get her. But it looks like she got up and went off home on her own. Or else she's wandering somewhere around here, in search of more to drink." Quent shrugged. "She can be one determined woman. That's what I was talking to Oliver about. He was very put out because Liza never spends time with him anymore, and is so focused on her own painting that she won't help out in the shop. He was hoping that tonight, at least, they could attend the party as a couple. She basically ignores him whenever they're out in public, and she was doing it again tonight. So he went home." Quent shrugged again. "I'm surprised she left, really. It isn't like her not to stay till the party's last gasp!" He arranged little cakes onto another platter and slid it into the microwave oven. "Oh well, in the words of Duncan's granny, Hazel Cooper, 'if you want something done you have to do it yourself,' right, Dunk-o? Good thing we're equipped here with all the modern conveniences we could want."

"For such an old house," Mom commented, "the kitchen looks pretty up-to-date. I love the countertops!"

"Nora had this room remodeled about two or three years ago," he answered. "Isn't that right, Dunk-o? Just before she died, in fact. But the house itself is ancient."

"Duncan gave me the whole tour," I said. "He told me some parts of the house are over four hundred years old. Nothing is that old in America."

"I'm impressed," Mom said.

"Can I impress you with a cup of coffee?" asked Quent with a laugh. "I made some for Liza, but after Oliver left she had only a few sips before heading back out into the fray to see who else among our guests she could piss off tonight. Or I can make tea."

"Yes, thanks, I'd rather have tea," said Mom.

The water boiled and Quent poured it into a fat brown teapot, swirled it around, then dumped the water out into the sink. "Must warm the pot first," he said to me when he saw me watching. "I hope your mum has taught you to make a proper cuppa over there in America! As Duncan's granny always says, 'A cuppa tea can save your life!'"

"Mum always said that, too," Duncan said.

"Yes, I remember." Mom nodded. "She made a fine cup of tea, your mum did."

Quent scooped tea leaves from a tin and dumped them into the pot, then poured the hot water. He set out milk and sugar. At home Mom didn't really drink tea much. Since Dad preferred coffee, they both seemed to drink coffee. But after only twenty-four hours in England, tea was clearly once again her beverage of choice. Quent handed around cups of freshly steeped tea, then suggested we get back to the party.

The guests stayed late, and Duncan took me as well as Edmund and Ivy back up to his bedroom to listen to music and play with his bear. I was often impatient with the Goops, but I really did appreciate it when someone was good with them, and Duncan was *great*. Duncan acted as if he really *liked* them. Maybe he got lonely sometimes being an only child.

I was about to fall asleep on Duncan's bed when Mom came up to say we were going home. The last of the guests had departed, and she and Quent had cleared all the things from the dining room table. She had offered to stay and help with the last of the dishwashing, but Quent said it wouldn't be necessary. We went out the kitchen door—the quickest route back to our cottage—and for a second I thought Duncan was going to hug me good-bye. Instead, he and Quent stood in the doorway, waving, and Duncan, since Ivy had carried his bear downstairs, made 'Normous wave, too. "See you tomorrow!" we all said. It took only seconds to walk back across the lawn and along the flagstone path to the door of our dark little cottage.

It had drizzled most of the time we were gone, and although the rain had stopped now, the bare branches of the trees were dripping on us while Mom fished in her purse for the key. It was hard in the dark to see anything, and she had to find it by touch. Finally she did, but then looked surprised when she discovered the door already unlocked. "I guess I forgot to lock it," she said vaguely.

I couldn't see that it mattered, really. "This isn't the Bay Area, remember," I said, as if anyone would ever mistake sleepy Blackthorn for San Francisco or Oakland or Berkeley. "It isn't as if we're living in a high-crime area, you know."

All I knew was that I was totally ready for a good night's sleep. We came inside and brushed our teeth, and hauled ourselves up the stairs to our little bedrooms. I was ready to drop in my tracks, but while Mom tucked Ivy and Edmund into their beds, I was sent on a mission to search for Ivy's polar bear, which I finally found under Edmund's bed ("*No* idea how it got there," Edmund maintained with a sly grin). I kissed Mom good night and was *finally* able to stretch out in my own bed. I was lying there, thinking about Duncan and musing dreamily over the whole evening we'd just spent together and reflecting that, although I was looking forward to getting to know Kate Glendenning, I wasn't at all sorry she'd had to leave so early... when the phone rang and Mom answered it in her room, and I heard her cry out. It was a sound in between a shriek and a groan.

Exhaustion forgotten, I jumped out of bed, my heart in my throat because when a phone rings at midnight it's never good news. My heart started thudding hard, and I could smell that smell again, that salty, sweet smell... *Dad?* I thought. *Oh, no, not Dad.*

I hurried into Mom's room. I ran to her bed and sat on the edge, listening. "Oh dear," she was saying into the phone, staring at me with wide, disbelieving eyes. "Oh no, that's awful! Poor thing—how did it happen?" She listened, her face flushed. "Is there anything I can do? No, no, I suppose not. Not tonight . . ."

She spoke a moment longer in a hushed, tense voice, then hung up the phone. "No," she said, reading my expression. "It's nothing to do with your dad . . ."

No, the phone call was from Quent Carrington. He was calling to say that almost as soon as we'd left his house, Oliver Pethering rang with the shocking news that there had been an accident—and Liza Pethering was dead.

PART 2

"Beware of false prophets,
which come to you in sheep's clothing,
but inwardly they are ravening wolves."

—MATTHEW 7:15

8

"Dead?" I couldn't quite grasp this news. "Liza—dead? But we just saw her! I mean, she was there at the party. How—oh, wait. Did she drink too much?"

"No—she woke up and decided to take herself home." Mom rubbed her eyes. "Quent didn't know all the details yet. Just said that Oliver had rung, sobbing that he'd stumbled upon Liza's body by the footbridge. He called the police right away. It looks like she must have tripped while walking home, and knocked herself out when she fell . . . or maybe it was a heart attack? In any case, bad luck would have it that she fell into the Shreen."

I thought of the little bridge we'd crossed that morning, that little bridge over that shallow stream. "She *drowned,* you mean?"

"That's what Oliver told Quent. Oh, Juliana—what a shock. I can't quite believe it . . ."

I put my arms around Mom and she was trembling. "Let's go downstairs and make a cup of tea," I suggested after a while.

"You're an English girl at heart, I think," Mom said shakily with a little laugh.

"Well, you told me you and Dad heard that my birth mother maybe came from England, right?" I said as we wrapped up in our fleecy bathrobes and headed down the stairs. "Maybe that's where I get it from. Of course, she could have been from Australia or New Zealand—or other places. Americans aren't very good at pinpointing foreign accents, are they? And the guy who maybe knew my birth mother said she was an addict, so maybe that means he was, too, so maybe his entire report wasn't reliable in the first place. Anyway, people drink lots of tea in Australia and New Zealand, too, don't they? And tea gets in your blood, Liza said . . ."

I knew I was blabbering nonsense, but somehow the words were just flowing out and I knew if I stopped them and tried to speak sensibly, we would have to speak about Liza Pethering, and neither of us was ready to do that. Liza was dead? Liza—*dead*? That black-haired, energetic, in-your-face, witchy woman I had met only yesterday—*dead*?

People died all the time, of course, but it was so hard to imagine this had happened to such a lively person, someone who only an hour or two ago had been loudly full of life and obnoxious vigor.

"In the midst of life we are in death," Mom murmured. "That's in the Bible, I think."

I made the tea the way I'd seen Quent do it. I boiled the water; I warmed the pot; I measured out the fresh, loose tea leaves. Mom and I sat at the little table, sipping silently. I had run out of chatter, and Mom didn't seem to want to talk. Liza was dead, and everything felt different.

Wake up, wake up! Oh, please wake up!

I shook my head to dislodge the sudden, strident little voice. I saw that Mom had tears on her cheeks. "Liza was always rushing about," Mom whispered. "Heedless. Careless. Tactless, too, but always, always full of life. And such a talented portrait artist, Juliana—you've never even seen her work! And now . . . a stupid fall and she's gone."

"Her work isn't gone, though," I said, trying to comfort Mom. I had known Liza Pethering not quite two days, and I'd found her irritating, but Mom had known her more than twenty years, had lived with her and studied with her. I was shocked at the suddenness of the accident, of course, and I'd be sorry in a general way for *anyone's* death—but for Mom this was a personal loss.

"Poor Oliver," Mom murmured. "He'll be shattered. Now he's all alone . . ."

"They didn't have children, did they?" I asked.

Mom shook her head and reached for a tissue. She blew her nose. "No, they never did. Liza wasn't the mothering type, it always seemed to me. She was too busy to slow down for a child, I think. Too involved in her own life. Or maybe her painting was her child. Opening that gallery was her biggest goal and most glorious achievement."

It was another hour before we went back to bed. The Goops had slept through all the excitement. I had thought I was tired when we'd first come home from the party, but now I lay in bed for a long time, unable to fall asleep. I kept seeing Liza Pethering in her clingy red dress, kept remembering how she flitted around at the party, chatting all the time, watching everything with her bright, sharp eyes . . . and then I pictured her walking home, probably still more than a little drunk, tripping in those impractical high heels, falling into the stream. When I closed my eyes I saw her face underwater, the inky black hair floating out like seaweed.

IT WAS TAPPING that woke me the next morning. No, not tapping—heavy knocking. Then as I realized someone was at our door, the knocking changed to peremptory banging. *All right, already, all right!* I thought, as I grabbed my bathrobe and stumbled out of the room for the stairs. *Keep your shirt on!* I unlocked the front door—and started with surprise.

Um—let me rephrase that. Keep your uniform *on . . .*

Two police officers stood there, a man and a woman. The man wore a uniform—the uniform was different from that of police officers in America—but a cop's a cop. The woman wore regular clothes: a gray skirt and jacket. They both flashed badges at me.

"Sorry to wake you, young lady," said the older, gray-haired man. "I'm Constable Petersen of the Blackthorn police, and this is Detective Inspector Link, from Lower Dillingham. We'd like a word with your parents."

Constable Petersen reminded me of Grandad. Detective Inspector Link was younger, but also gray-haired. Despite her sort of cozy, grandmotherly appearance (she looked to me like she ought to be serving tea and scones or something), she had an air of stern authority. You wouldn't want to get on her bad side, I decided.

"Um—my mother isn't awake," I told them. "But just a minute—"

"Who is it, Juliana?" Mom called down the stairs.

"Police, Mom!"

"Goodness! I'll be right down. Ask them to come in."

"Would you like to come in?" I asked, though why else would they be here?

They both stepped inside. Detective Inspector Link smiled at me. "Sorry to bother you so early." But she didn't say why they'd come.

Mom came downstairs, dressed in jeans and a sweatshirt and thick socks. She had taken time to brush her hair, which was short and always neatened up easily. My long hair must be a mess. Self-consciously I put my hand to my head. Yes—a rat's nest. Ivy and Edmund, sensing excitement, barreled down after Mom, still in their pajamas.

"What can I do for you?" asked Mom, smiling uncertainly at the officers.

"We'd like to offer our sympathy, ma'am," said Constable Petersen. "We understand you were a friend of Liza Pethering's, and one of the last to see her at Mr. Carrington's party. Is that correct?"

Mom glanced pointedly over at Ivy and Edmund, and I realized the Goops didn't know what had happened last night. The officer looked abashed.

"Kids," Mom said to them gently, "a very sad thing happened last night after Liza left the party. Juliana and I heard about it once you two were asleep, and we didn't want to wake you. But she was walking home, and she tripped in the dark and hit her head—and fell into the stream."

"Brrr," shivered Ivy. "I bet she was mad about that!"

"Well," said Mom slowly, looking to the police officers for help, "I think she was knocked unconscious when she fell. So she didn't know . . ."

"Couldn't she swim?" demanded Edmund.

"Not if she was unconscious," Ivy said, rolling her eyes. Then she stared at Mom. "So what are you saying? What happened? Is she in the hospital?"

Mom put her hands to her face. She took a deep, shuddering breath. "She died last night," Mom whispered.

The Goops gasped.

"I'm sorry," said the policewoman. "Perhaps it's of some comfort to know that it seems she was unconscious and didn't suffer."

Ivy's and Edmund's voices merged in a tangle of shrieks: "But we just saw her!"

"She was wearing that slinky red dress!"

"She was wearing the coolest highest heels in the world!"

"She invited us to see her art gallery today!"

"We were just talking to her at dinner!"

Mom asked the police officers to sit down while she calmed Ivy and Edmund. Then she delegated me to take the Goops upstairs and supervise while they unpacked their clothes into their dressers. I knew she wanted us all out of the way before the police said anything else, but I was intrigued and wanted to stay. It isn't every day that we have two cops, especially English cops (*bobbies,* Mom said they were sometimes called) on our doorstep, much less sitting in our living room. But Mom signaled me with her eyes to get going.

Reluctantly I climbed upstairs after Ivy and Edmund. They ran down the hall to their rooms, jabbering a mile a minute in excited, horrified voices. I lingered at the top of the stairs, listening, wondering what this visit was about. I had a sick sort of feeling in the pit of my stomach—as if I could guess. As if I almost knew . . .

"We're investigating the death of Liza Pethering," I heard the male officer say gravely.

"You're *investigating*—?" Mom's voice rang with surprise. Let the Goops deal with their own suitcases! I ran back downstairs and stood next to Mom, linking my arm with hers.

"Yes ma'am," rumbled the deep voice. "Because it turns out that Liza Pethering's death was not an accident after all. I'm sorry to have to tell you that Liza Pethering was *murdered.*"

9

Mom gasped. I squeezed her arm tighter as we listened to the officers' explanation. Liza had been found last night by her husband who, Detective Inspector Link told us, had been waiting at home because his wife had not left the party when he had. After about an hour, Oliver rang her cell phone to tell her to come home on the double, but there was no answer. He rang Quent's house, too, but there was only an answering machine. So, annoyed now, he decided to go back and fetch her. As he crossed the little bridge over the Shreen, he saw a body lying across the footpath, half in the stream, half out. He'd run to see if he could help, and was horrified to discover that the body was his own wife's. He dragged Liza out, but it was too late. Apparently she had been coming home to him, but had tripped in her high heels and fallen, hitting her head on the pavement. She must have lain there unconscious, breathing in stream water until she drowned.

Oliver had snatched up Liza's purse from where it lay on the path nearby. He noticed right away that the wallet was gone. But at least the cell phone was there, and he grabbed it and punched in the emergency number.

"That's 9-9-9 in England," Mom muttered to me urgently, interrupting this account. Her face was very pale.

"*Not* 9-1-1 like in America. Juliana—remember that! 9-9-9. Promise me!"

"Nine-nine-nine," I repeated. "I'll remember, Mom."

"The ambulance and police van came quickly, but there was nothing we could do," Constable Petersen said, continuing the account. "Mr. Pethering spent the night at his mother's house in the next village, calling various friends to tell them the dreadful news."

"But what the police learned early this morning," added Detective Inspector Link, "—once the coroner had Liza's body moved to the morgue, that is—was that Liza's head wound was inconsistent with a fall onto the pavement. Further investigation revealed she'd been coshed on the head, I'm sorry to tell you, and knocked unconscious."

I winced. Mom's face tightened.

Detective Inspector Link hurried on. "We suspect that Mrs. Pethering was knocked out first and then laid in the stream to make the death appear to be an accidental drowning. As indeed it did appear—at first."

The detective and the older constable met each other's eyes and each had a satisfied expression. I realized that to them, solving murder was a puzzle. And as much as they no doubt loathed the nature of the crime, they enjoyed putting the puzzle pieces together.

The older officer nodded. "A bad business all around," he said to Mom. "And now we need to speak with all the people who last saw Mrs. Pethering. You and your children were the guests of honor at the party Mrs. Pethering attended last night, were you not? So we'd like to know your impressions of the events of the evening."

Mom wrapped her arms around herself. She was shivering. "I just can't believe it," she whispered. "Murder?"

"A very clever setup, ma'am," said Constable Petersen. "Should I make a pot of tea, Mom?" I asked. She didn't answer, but Detective Inspector Link nodded. I escaped gratefully into the small kitchen.

Boil the water. Warm the pot. Measure out the tea leaves. Leave them to steep. *A cuppa tea will save your life.* But all the cups of tea that Liza Pethering had drunk had not saved her from the nameless, faceless person who'd snuck up from behind and bashed in her head and stolen the wallet from her sequined red handbag—and then left her in the Shreen to drown.

I SAT AROUND all day, feeling as if I should be *doing* something. A person had died, and now everything felt different—and yet everything was already feeling totally different to me anyway, since we'd only been in Blackthorn a couple of days. I'd barely recovered from jet lag. I didn't have a regular routine. Even so, everything felt disrupted.

Kate Glendenning and Duncan knocked on our door after lunch. I invited them in and they sat at the table with us, talking about Liza Pethering. The Goops had finished their soup and pushed the bowls aside to make room for their sketchpads and markers. "We're making portraits just like Liza did," Ivy announced.

"In her honor," Edmund added solemnly. "Hold still, Duncan. I'm doing you first."

"I'll do Kate," said Ivy. "Can you turn your head a little to the left, Kate?"

I didn't have much to say. I left the table and started unpacking one of the several boxes left in the corner of the sitting room. Photo albums and framed school pictures, a scrapbook the Goops had made of our vacation to Hawaii last summer, various candleholders and votives, a clock that had been Grandad's that had stood on our living room mantel at home. I listened to the talk while I found new homes for these things now.

Mom told a funny story about when they were students in London and had gotten themselves locked out of their flat one night. "Liza was the bold one," Mom said with a little laugh. "She just took down somebody's laundry line in back of the flats and used it as a lasso—and looped it around the iron railing to the second-story balcony. Then she and Nora and I all shinnied up the wall of the building, using the rope to help us. We felt like Spiderman. It was all very exciting. When we all climbed onto the balcony, Liza untied the rope and threw it back down into the garden— covering our traces, she called it. But then we found that our balcony door was locked, too, and we were still stuck!"

"What did you do?" Ivy asked.

"What we could have done from the start," Mom admitted. "Pounded on the door and yelled for the landlord, and he woke up and let us in." She laughed. "He was fairly puzzled as to how three young women could be locked out on their balcony with the key on the *inside* of the door.

"'Let him wonder,' I remember Liza said. She said, 'It's good to have a bit of mystery in life.' And later she painted a portrait of the landlord from memory—with this wonderfully baffled look on his face, just the way he looked that night when he rescued us. She titled the painting, *Unsettled.* It was the first piece she sold when she held her first show."

Mom laughed reminiscently, and Duncan and Kate and the Goops laughed a little with her. But I was thinking about how Liza's death was providing "a bit of mystery in life" for all of us, and it didn't feel good at all. Someone had killed her, and that someone was out there somewhere. Talk about *unsettled.*

Edmund started drawing a picture of three girls stuck on a balcony. I set Grandad's clock in the center of our mantel and surrounded it with framed family photographs. There came a tapping on our door, and Ivy leaped up to open it.

Quent stood there, with Celia Glendenning at his side. "Hello," Quent said. "Celia came knocking at my door looking for her daughter, and I figured we'd find her here."

"Come in," Mom invited them warmly. She moved to the kitchen and refilled the electric teakettle.

"I was just out doing my shopping," said Celia. "And thought I'd stop by rather than ring. You've got a dentist appointment, Kate, remember. So you'll need to come along now." She looked around the cottage appraisingly. "A nice little place you have here. Rather small for a family, but sweet."

"Thank you," said Mom. "We're delighted to be able to rent it. It's perfect for us."

"Shocking news about Liza Pethering," said Celia. "Crime in Blackthorn is nearly unheard of. And *murder?* Abominable."

We all agreed it was.

"The police came round my house!" Celia announced. "And not just our local bobby, either. They'd brought in a special detective from Lower Dillingham. To interview me, can you believe it?" She wandered around the sitting room, stopping to look at the photos I'd just set out. "They'd heard I'd had a little disagreement with Liza last night. A little altercation."

"They came here, too," said Mom.

"And to me, of course," said Quent. "I think they'll be interviewing everyone who saw her last night."

"Well, I don't like it." Celia picked up my school photo from this year. It was one of my better ones, because my smile didn't look fake, and my hair wasn't frizzy.

"This is you," she said to me, as if that was news.

"Yes," I said.

She replaced the photo, then picked up another one— a picture of me with the Goops, all of us holding boogie boards on the beach on Oahu.

"You do put me in mind of someone I once knew," she said musingly. "A striking resemblance—"

"Look, Mother," said Kate. "Ivy has drawn my portrait."

Celia Glendenning turned to look. "Remarkable," she said approvingly to my sister. "You did a good job, and already display a lot more talent than that Pethering woman ever showed."

"*Mother,*" hissed Kate.

"Now, Kate, I'm not speaking ill of the dead. I'm just stating a fact." Celia looked at her watch. "Really, now, we must hurry. You'll miss your appointment." She replaced the framed photo on the mantel, giving me another piercing look before turning to the door.

Mom showed them out, but Quent stayed and had a cup of tea with us. He and Mom talked about Liza in hushed voices. Duncan invited me and the Goops to go over to his house and watch a video.

"Something funny," I said.

"No murder mysteries or anything," Edmund added, surprising me. He usually goes for blood and guts.

"Something historical," begged Ivy. "Something that happened a long time ago and isn't sad anymore."

OVER THE NEXT couple of days, everyone who had been at Quent's party the night Liza died was questioned by the police. So were all the members of the Drama Society. So were all the employees of the Emporium. So were all the neighbors who lived in The Mews—the lane where the Petherings lived. The village was buzzing over the murder of Liza Pethering. Rehearsals for *Voyage of the Jumblies* were canceled until further notice. Parents kept their children indoors. There had not been a murder in Blackthorn for more than one hundred years—and that had been a case of a pub brawl turning deadly. It turned out there was a pub connection to this murder, too; everyone was relieved when Simon Jukes ("that lager lout," Quent called him) was arrested.

"I never done nuffink!" he shouted when the police arrested him outside the Old Ship two days after Liza's death. Quent Carrington was there and reported the whole thing to us later that night. Witnesses had seen Simon at the Old Ship on the night of Quent's party, mouthing off about how much he hated Liza Pethering for sending him to prison, and how she'd better be watching her back now that he was free again.

Quent screwed up his face into a disagreeable leer. "'Sure I said that, Officers,'" he said ingratiatingly, imitating Simon Jukes talking to the police. "'I said it, but it were just *talking*, you know, it were just a joke! I didn't *mean* none of it. It were just talking!'"

We laughed, but then Quent grew serious again. "He protested his innocence, but then the police informed him they'd found Liza Pethering's credit cards right on the Jukeses' kitchen table! The officers had stopped at the house while searching for Simon, and his brother Henry let them come in—to prove to them that Simon wasn't there."

"That berk, Henry," Simon had fumed, using the derogatory word I'd learned from Mom that meant "fool." "I never stole them cards from her! I just found them in the bushes. Found the whole wallet tossed there, I did! Just took what might be useful—and who wouldn't? Who can blame me for that, I'd like to know? Anyways, it was only about twenty quid. *Jeez.*" He scowled at the police. "You lot better not've got our Henry upset now, I hope."

"At least he cares about his brother," Mom observed.

"He does," affirmed Quent. "I guess that's something."

Simon Jukes was taken off to jail to await a hearing, and it seemed to me everybody we talked to after that was sighing with relief. A saleslady at the Emporium told me that no one liked him, anyway, and he'd always been a trouble-maker, even as a child. The fisherman on the pier assured me Simon was the first person you'd suspect when your garden shed had been broken into, or your new bicycle had gone missing . . . and you'd be right. Celia Glendenning, standing in line behind us at the bank, declared that Simon had always been a ruffian, and had once shot an air rifle at all her milk bottles, breaking them to bits right on the doorstep. "It was wanton mischief when he was younger," she said, "but now he's turned truly dangerous."

"You feel safer with him locked up," agreed the bank clerk.

THE DAY OF Liza's funeral dawned warm and balmy. A soft sea breeze blew up Mill Lane and along Castle Street.

Overnight the blackthorn buds opened, and the white blossoms scented the air and decorated the village. This unexpected and totally gorgeous spring day lifted my heart as we walked over to St. Michael's Church with Quent Carrington and Duncan. It felt almost as if the weather was paying tribute to Liza Pethering.

"This weather makes me feel like I'll be able to paint again," Mom told me, and I was glad. She had not gone near her studio since we'd learned of Liza's death. "I just keep thinking of her," Mom had confided the day before when I'd asked why she was sitting at the kitchen table to sketch rather than up in her sunroom. "How we were in art school together . . . and now . . ." Her voice trailed off.

The pews in the church were narrow and hard, despite the thin cushion on the bench. Mom whispered to me that the church had been built in the fifteenth century—which was mind-boggling to me—but people were shorter then, so I guess the pews weren't quite as uncomfortable to them. Then Quent whispered that people weren't supposed to get too comfortable, because sermons were long and they might fall asleep. If people were fidgeting on their hard seats, at least they were awake.

There were flowers all over the altar, and there was a small table in front of the altar, with a simple wooden box in the center, flanked by candles in tall silver candlesticks. Liza had been cremated, and her ashes were in that box, I knew. I felt tears prick behind my eyes at the thought of that vibrant woman reduced to ashes. Then the minister (the *vicar,* Mom whispered) started droning on about how good Liza was, and how beloved she had been, and what a driving force in the community, and a dear neighbor to many. It all seemed the sort of thing you *should* say at funerals, but somehow it rang false to me. I looked around at the other people in the pews, and I saw a few raised eyebrows and even heard a snicker.

I realized with a shock that most of these people weren't even particularly sorry that Liza Pethering was dead. All those simmering angers had alienated Liza from her neighbors. I saw Jean and Leo Thurber sitting together in a front pew, and I remembered Leo's disdainful pronouncement at the party: *She's a disgrace.* I caught sight of Veronica Pimms seated between two heavyset people who were probably her parents. I bet she hadn't wanted to come to the funeral but her parents had made her. In my memory I heard the echo of her furious statement at the Old Ship on our first night in Blackthorn: *Someone ought to kill that bitch, if you want my humble, uneducated opinion.* I heard in my mind Duncan's grandfather, Dudley Cooper's verdict: *Hanging's too good for her, if you ask me.*

I felt someone looking at me and turned my head to meet the self-righteous, penetrating gaze of Mrs. Glendenning. Kate, looking shy and mopey, slumped at her side. Celia Glendenning nodded at me, and I remembered her declaration at the party: *Somebody should take a hoe to that snake—*

Oliver Pethering's face was in shadow. But I noticed him checking his watch once as the vicar's solemn prayers for the dead continued. The Goops fidgeted. Only Mom and Quent Carrington seemed truly sad. Next to me, Mom was crying audibly. Sitting on her other side, Quent's face looked stricken. He patted Mom's hand a few times, and finally put his arm around her. She buried her face against his broad, jacketed shoulder.

I shivered in the cold, ancient church as the vicar led the prayers for Liza's soul.

Afterward in the church hall, the mourners (if that's what they could be called) sipped cups of tea and nibbled at biscuits and pastry puffs (from the Emporium, probably), and murmured to Oliver Pethering how sorry they were. Ivy and Edmund, unaccustomedly solemn, hovered near me. Kate Glendenning came over to us, cup of tea in hand. She looked pleased to be free of her mother for the moment. I spotted Celia on the other side of the room, seemingly deep in conversation with the vicar, but looking over his shoulder at me while she spoke. Or more likely she was keeping an eye on Kate.

"I hate death," Kate said tersely. "Isn't it just too grim for words?"

"Yes, it is," I replied. "My mom is really upset. She's known Liza a really long time. And I keep thinking of Liza's husband. What a shock for him—finding her like that."

"Poor Mr. Pethering—," began Kate, but she was cut off suddenly by Dudley Cooper, who bore down on us like a tank, Duncan trailing along behind him.

"Did I hear you say *poor* Oliver, young lady? My girl, don't waste even another second pitying that henpecked husband." Dudley Cooper had an excited gleam in his eyes as he reached us. "I'm sure he'll be dancing a jig on her grave soon as they get those ashes properly buried in the churchyard. She treated him very shabbily, I always thought. Finding fault in everything he did! And all her flirtations with other men! If the police hadn't arrested that Jukes boy, I would have thought they'd be looking very carefully at Oliver Pethering. People can take only so much, you know, before they snap. Nobody wished the poor woman dead, of course, but I know I myself would have quite cheerfully wrung her neck on many occasions." His eyes narrowed. "The lead role in the play should have been mine by rights and she knew it."

"*Grandad!*" hissed Duncan, but the old man just shrugged. Duncan glanced at me in embarrassment.

Across the room I saw Celia Glendenning pouring out a cup of tea and carrying it over to where Oliver Pethering stood by the door. His head was down, but he looked up when she handed him the cup, and a little smile turned up the corner of his mouth.

An elderly lady, her snow-white hair worn in a bun at the nape of her neck, walked up to us and linked her hand through the crook of Mr. Cooper's arm. "Now, Dudley," she said. "Are you minding your manners with Duncan's new friend?"

"I was just saying what nice weather we're having," the old man lied gleefully.

But I was glad to talk about something besides death. "Yes," I said with a smile for the woman Duncan introduced as Hazel Cooper, his grandmother. "It's nice that spring has come early. The village seemed so gray when we first got here, but now the blossoms everywhere have totally changed that!"

Mrs. Cooper chuckled. "You think spring has sprung? Maybe in California, but not in England, my duck. No, this'll prove to be a blackthorn winter, mark my words."

"'Blackthorn winter?'" I asked. "What's that?"

Dudley Cooper spun me around and pointed to the windows. "Ah, the blackthorn! The leaves make a pleasing tea. The fruit is delicious. It even has medicinal properties, my girl, and can cure you of all sorts of things—nose-bleeds, constipation, whatever. But you see those blackthorn blossoms? Lovely to look at and a sure sign of spring, you think—right? Aha—think again! It's all a ruse. It's Mother Nature's trick, my girl. When the blackthorns bloom this early, and spring seems to be in the air—you can't trust it. In another couple of days those blossoms will all have fallen to the ground, and it'll look like snow everywhere, like winter. A blackthorn winter, that's what we call it. Cold winter weather will be back, in full force!"

"Oh," I said faintly, trying to take in this onslaught of information. "But, well, maybe *this* year there really *will* be an early spring." I truly hoped so; the sunshine and fresh blossoms lifted my spirits higher than they'd been since we'd come to England.

"Gotta love an optimist." Duncan grinned at me.

"A positive attitude is nice to see in a young girl," agreed Mr. Cooper. "Eh, Hazel?"

"Certainly—however misguided," the old woman agreed mildly. But then her pleasant expression changed. The blue eyes darkened. "But I always say that the black-thorn has messages for us. My old granny used to tell me that if you were traveling and came upon three blackthorn trees growing together, you should give them a wide berth. It's a sign that nothing good will happen to those who come near. And she told me the blackthorn winter came as a message to us: a reminder that you can't be too trusting, my duck. That what you think is true might actually be false. Take heed."

"Oh, Granny," Duncan rebuked her gently. "You sound like a prophet of doom."

"Do I? Well, my old granny certainly was! But look

here, lad, a woman has been reduced to ashes. Reduced to ashes before her time, just as your own mum was. And that's a gloomy thought if anything is, don't you agree? Our own lovely Nora! So I say it's very sad indeed about Liza Pethering, Lord rest her soul, even if she was a meddlesome and unpleasant sort who was responsible for your father's running off with that Argentinian woman—"

"Oh, Granny!" Duncan's cheeks were crimson. "Anyway," he mumbled, "Eliana is from Brazil."

"Well, wherever," said the feisty old lady. "The Lord— or Fate—makes certain that justice is done in the end, at least that's the way I see it."

"The justice is that Simon Jukes is in police custody, Granny. He'll pay for what he did to Liza and—"

"That remains to be seen," interrupted the old man. Then he took his wife's arm and the two of them moved off toward the food table. "Just you remember this blackthorn winter."

I stared after them, puzzled . . . and felt again the nudge of memory. *Wake up, wake up!*

The church hall was unusually warm on this winter day. Someone pushed the casement windows open, and the scent of the blackthorn blossoms was very strong. I thought about the beautiful talisman necklace made of those pressed flowers. Had Nora gathered them during a false spring like this one? If Liza had been wearing her own lucky necklace, the one Nora had made for her with the dangling seedpod, would she be alive now? In fact, if Nora had worn her own necklace with the pink quartz stone, would she be alive now, too?

I sucked in my breath, as a memory played around the edges of my unconscious. My heart seemed to beat faster. . . .

*See, see? I told you she wouldn't have gone away! I knew
she wouldn't! Look, look . . . here she is! Oh, wake up, wake
up—please wake up . . .*

A shiver prickled between my shoulder blades. The
voices around me rose in a great wave of sound until they
were a cacophony. The sympathetic smiles of the mourners who had gathered after the funeral seemed painted on.
Across the room Celia Glendenning was staring openly at
me. I stared back until she turned away. What was her
problem, anyway?

A shout from the doorway jerked me out of my daze.
Henry Jukes, Simon's younger brother, stood at the door
with his hands on his hips. "You're all celebrating that my
bruvver's locked in jail!" he shouted, his words slurred.
"And it's wrong! It's all wrong!"

"Now, Henry," said the vicar gently, hurrying to him,
"this is just a gathering after Mrs. Pethering's funeral service. It's nothing to do with Simon—"

Henry shook off the older man's comforting arm. He
took a step and stumbled against the wall. "He didn't do it!
He didn't do . . . nuffink! You're always after him, you lot."
Henry's face was red with fury.

"Go home and sleep it off," called someone from the
crowd.

"One of you lot killed her and you're trying to blame it
on me bruvver!" Henry shrieked at them. "I'll find you out,
I will! You'll not get away with it!"

"Oh, do shut him up, somebody," ordered Celia Glendenning. She strode across the room toward Henry. "Come
along, Henry, it's time for you to go home."

Several men, Quent Carrington and Oliver Pethering
included, moved to the door to take Henry by the arms and

escort him outside. "Maybe it's that Yank what did it!"
Henry shrugged out of the men's grasp and pointed across
the room at my mom. "*She's* the newcomer, in't she? *She's*
the one what comes to town, claiming to be an old friend,
and look what happens! First murder in a hunnert years."

I saw Mom's expression grow pained. She turned away.
I started over to comfort her, but both Thurbers got to her
first. Jean Thurber put her arm around Mom's shoulders. I
turned back to Henry as the men grabbed him again.

"And if it weren't that Yank, it were the Yank's daughter!" he howled, staring at me in fury. I stared back, shocked.
His eyes were wide and pale. There was something child-
like in his expression, something of a little boy as he strained
against his captors. His shouts of protest grew fainter as the
door closed behind them.

I made a sudden decision and slipped out the door
after Henry.

The men left him slumped against the side of the
building. "Leave him alone, missy," said Oliver Pethering.

"He's nobody to tangle with, Juliana," Quent affirmed.

"I won't—I just want some fresh air," I said, standing
on the steps. "I'll be right in."

The men returned to the gathering, shutting the heavy
wooden door. Cautiously I stepped down to the path and
walked a little closer to Henry. I could hear him making
weird snuffling noises, and then realized that he was crying.

"Henry?" I said.

He whirled around, wiping his sleeve across his face. I
jumped back a few steps. He reminded me of a large, fair-
haired bear. Wild and unpredictable. "You Yanks!" he
yelled. "It had to be you! Nobody was killing nobody till
you came here!"

"I didn't kill Liza, and my mother didn't, either," I said firmly. I glanced back at the steps leading to the door. I could run back inside fast if Henry came near me.

"Nor did Simon," he declared, glaring at me. "He's not a killer. He's a good bruvver, he is!"

The tension was broken as the big wooden door of the church hall opened and Duncan stepped outside. Slowly he came down the steps to stand beside me on the path. I was glad of his presence. "Your brother wanted revenge on Liza Pethering," I reminded Henry. "People heard him say so."

"We was at the Ship that night," he muttered, scowling at Duncan. "Then we went home, walking right over the Shreen. We didn't see nuffink, nowhere. Then later we heard that a body'd been found! So we went back, and Simon found them credit cards tossed right in the bushes. He's no fool, our Simon! We brung them straight home. Who wouldn't? But stealing don't amount to murder." He crossed his arms and leaned back against the stone building.

"You really didn't run into Liza that night?"

He shook his shaggy head, reminding me again of a bear. "I swear on me muvver's grave." His sad, pale eyes gleamed.

And—perhaps strangely, because I was still afraid of him—I found myself wanting to believe him. "Well, somebody ran into her," I said.

"Will you help?" he rasped out. "If you Yanks didn't do it, then find out who did and get me bruvver out!"

"Well, I—," I hesitated. "I don't know—"

"Oh, you're useless!" Savagely Henry kicked the stone wall and swore. "A whole pack of useless gits in this town, that's what you are. Artists and toffs, and now you Yanks. Yanks are the worst!" Snuffling again, he strode away from us, around the side of the building and through the arched canopy of yew trees into the graveyard.

I almost ran after Henry, but stopped. I looked over at Duncan, helplessly. The mild springlike breeze fluttered the white blossoms on the blackthorn bushes by the door.

"He's a lout and a drunk," said Duncan, putting one hand on my shoulder, "and that's dead certain."

"But . . . I wonder," I said softly. "I wonder."

10

He linked his arm with mine. "What do you wonder?" I was relieved that Henry was gone, and I liked that Duncan and I could be so casual, touching each other. I hadn't ever known another boy I felt so comfortable with so quickly. "I wonder if he's right. I think I believe Henry," I said. "I mean, I know he's . . . strange, and a drunk, but I believe him. And if his brother is innocent, someone else killed Liza."

Duncan shrugged. "Who knows? I suppose it's possible. But not very likely." Then he smiled at me. "When I grow up to be a detective, I'll investigate this sort of thing."

I steered him back up the steps. "We were just kidding around the other night, about being detectives someday, I mean. But someone should look into this. Maybe we should."

"You mean you don't trust Britain's finest to ferret out the truth? I don't know. We could offer our services, maybe."

"Really? Duncan, I think we should." I was serious. But Duncan's next words let me know he was teasing me.

"It would be interesting. Ferreting out the truth." He twirled an imaginary mustache. "Uncovering the lies, the falsehoods . . . we would be the superheroes of Black-thorn!" He opened the door and the two of us stepped back into the church hall. The room was still buzzing with chatter as Liza's family and friends and acquaintances mingled. The food trays were nearly empty now.

There—again—I felt a nudge of memory. *Something was hidden. Someone had lied.* Then the feeling of being just about to remember something receded. "You know," I said slowly, "I'm serious about believing Henry. When I was talking to him I was getting a feeling . . . a feeling that things aren't quite adding up. I mean, everybody's *acting* so sad about Liza—but a lot of them aren't sad, not really. And what your grandparents were just saying about the blackthorn blossoms, and a false spring, and well—Duncan, look around!"

"You mean the secret sighs of relief?" He shook his head. "Liza made a lot of people really mad. That doesn't mean any one of them killed her."

I frowned at him. "I read somewhere that when a woman is killed, her husband is usually the main suspect."

"*Prime* suspect, the police call it." Duncan looked down at me thoughtfully. "And in the murder mysteries I read, it's the person who finds the body who is usually considered a prime suspect by the police. They also look at who profits by a death. Who stands to inherit."

"Oliver Pethering fits those categories." I lowered my voice to a whisper because Oliver was walking past us toward the food table. "They didn't have children, so he'd get all her money. And don't forget—," I reminded Duncan darkly. "He was trained as a butcher."

"Liza was bashed over the head, though. Not chopped with a meat cleaver."

"Still." To Duncan it was a game, to me a serious consideration. The men who had taken Henry Jukes outside were mingling with the crowd. They were smiling and chatting. People shook their heads and laughed about Henry Jukes. Covertly I watched Oliver Pethering help himself to another scone and bite into it with gusto.

THE NEXT MORNING after Liza's funeral, Mom and I walked the Goops to the village school for their first day. The weather was still springlike, sunny and mild. The air was scented with the blackthorn blossoms. The Goops looked unusually sweet in their new school uniforms of dark gray pants for Edmund and dark gray skirt for Ivy, both topped with red sweatshirts with the school crest and the words Blackthorn First School. Duncan also was at school, but his was in the next village of Lower Dillingham. I saw him waiting with Kate Glendenning at the bus stop outside the newsagent's when we walked past with the Goops. The two of them were laughing together.

I had been so sure I didn't want to go to a new school in England that I had insisted my parents arrange a semester of home study for me. I would be doing assigned work on my own and sending it via e-mail attachments to my teachers when we got our new computer. That way I would still be on track for graduation and wouldn't have to change schools. Homeschool had seemed to me the only way moving to England would be tolerable. But after we waved good-bye to Ivy and Edmund, who had been welcomed warmly into the Year 5 classroom (*same as fourth grade,* Mom said) and had met their teacher, Mrs. Bundy, it felt strange and lonely to come home and sit at the kitchen table with my history textbook, and a mug of tea at my elbow. I almost wished I were at school in Lower Dillingham with Duncan and Kate. Almost—but not quite.

On the way home, Mom and I had passed the police station. I wondered if Simon Jukes were in there, locked in a cell. I remembered his brother Henry's outburst after the funeral. People said Henry was strange, not quite right in the head. But . . . what if he were right? What if his brother were innocent? How horrible to be locked away for something you didn't do while the real murderer got away with murder.

When I finished the history assignments, I moved outside to sit on the warm stone step of our cottage and read my science textbook. It felt so much like a true spring that I decided the Coopers were wrong this time about its being false. The long morning ticked slowly past. Mom didn't go upstairs to her sunroom studio even though she'd said the day before that she thought she could work again now. Instead, she puttered in the sitting room, unpacking one of our remaining boxes. Then she went out again, carrying canvas tote bags, to buy groceries at the Emporium. I went inside and watched the clock and began a descriptive essay for English about my arrival in Blackthorn. At lunchtime I made a sandwich for myself and poured a tall glass of milk. The Goops always complained that English milk tasted different, and they fussed when Mom wanted them to drink it. But I liked the taste, and I'd drunk more than enough tea lately.

As I finished eating, the sky darkened and the rain started again, but it was a soft rain and still held that wonderful scent of spring. Mom came home, juggling her umbrella and two tote bags of food. I unpacked them for her: fruit and veg from the greengrocer's (I loved that name almost as much as *ironmonger*) and packets of pasta and cereal and cans of soup (*tins* of soup, they were called here) from the Emporium. Mom spent the rest of the afternoon on the phone, arranging to lease our rental car long-term. She didn't go near the sunroom. I worked on my assigned chapter of algebra until the Goops came barreling home from school with dripping raincoats and damp book bags. They were full of stories about their first day, and again I felt a twinge of regret that I'd refused to consider going to school here. Half an hour later Duncan was home from school, too. He came over and casually invited me out for a walk.

"Maybe we'll stop somewhere for a coffee," he added. That sounded so classy and . . . European. At home my friends drank mostly soda. Mom said I could go, but to be back in time for dinner.

I grabbed an umbrella and my hooded jacket, and we set off down the path and around to the wall with the shiny red door. "I've been stuck at home all day," I said. "Thank you for coming to rescue me."

"At your service, madam," he said gallantly, then slanted a shy glance at me. "Actually I've been, er, sort of thinking about you all day. Sitting home while I slave at school . . . I've been dying to get home and be with you."

"Dying?" I asked, wincing.

"Okay, wrong word," he said. "I was longing to *hang* with you. To *chill* with you. To impress you with my use of American slang!" I laughed, and we headed for the Angel Cafe on the corner of Castle Street and The Mews.

"That's where Liza Pethering lived," Duncan said, pointing down the narrow lane. "Where Oliver lives."

"All alone now," I said softly. Then I wondered how sad he really was about that.

"Should we call on him?" asked Duncan, as if he had read my mind. "Have a little chat with our prime suspect?"

"He isn't really that," I objected. "Oh, I don't know. Let's wait."

"Let's eat while we wait," Duncan said, and he opened the door to the Angel Cafe. Inside, the cafe was brightly lit and cheerful. The small room held about twelve tables, and half of them were taken. Most of the customers seemed to be kids about our age. Duncan waved to a few people he knew as the waitress led us to a table by the window.

"What would you like?" she asked us, smoothing her apron and pulling a notepad out of the pocket.

Duncan ordered coffee, but I opted for hot chocolate. We both ordered scones as well. They came quickly, warm and fresh, and we piled on the strawberry jam and fresh clotted cream, yellow and thick.

We began talking in low voices about whether to approach Oliver Pethering, but we were soon interrupted by a group of teenagers, some still in school uniforms, who ambled into the cafe, laughing. "Hey, MacBennet!" one boy hailed Duncan.

"Cor—look at him!" another bellowed. "This is serious, man!"

"Did she say she'd marry you?" a third boy called out. He winked at me.

"I wouldn't recommend it," the first boy said to me, shaking his head mournfully. "MacBennet snores something fierce. I had to share a bunk bed with him on a school trip to London and he kept me awake all night long. Sounded like a donkey!"

The boys started braying—*hee-haw, hee-haw!*—and the girls laughed. I saw suddenly that one of them was Veronica Pimms, with her purple hair tucked back inside a hood. I hadn't recognized her at first.

"Sod off," Duncan said, but he smiled at the kids and then introduced me. "Everybody, this is Juliana. Juliana, this is the lot you're cleverly avoiding by staying out of school. You can see you've made the right decision." Then he pointed to each kid in turn: "Brian Harkins, Harry and Will Brooks, Alina Sinclair, and you know Veronica already."

"I'm on a break from work," she said. "Thought I'd have a drink with the schoolchildren."

"Hi everybody," I said.

They pulled up chairs at the table next to ours and ordered tea and coffee and fizzy drinks. The waitress frowned when one of the boys—Brian, I thought it was—propped his feet on an empty chair, but generally she seemed happy that the little cafe was such a popular hangout on this wet afternoon.

"So how do you like Blackthorn?" the girl named Alina asked me. She had short, dark curls that hugged her head like a cap. Her hair was damp from the rain, and her red jacket was spattered with wet spots.

"I do like it," I said.

"You're American," commented the boy called Will. "Listen to that accent!"

I felt my cheeks color self-consciously. "From California," I said.

They started imitating an American accent (badly) and asking questions about California, and I sat there for about fifteen minutes laughing and trying to dispel the notion that I knew movie stars personally, went surfing every morning before school, and got rocked in earthquakes every couple of days. I remembered how I'd looked for the rose-covered, thatched-roof cottages on the day we'd arrived in

Blackthorn. *Stereotypes,* I thought. At least the kids weren't asking if I only ever ate hamburgers and fries.

"Why did you want to come here, that's what I don't get," said Alina.

"I didn't want to, really," I admitted. "My mom did."

"I know, but I mean, why would she—when you were living in *California,* for chrissake! I mean, that place is everybody's dream destination!"

"The Golden Dream," Will added.

The boy named Harry snorted, sinking low in his chair. "Anything would be more golden than *this* dump." He pointed out the window at the dark, rainy street.

I shrugged, looking out. "I don't think it's a dump! And even though it wasn't my idea to come here, I can see what my mom likes about England—especially about a small village like this one. It's so . . . so *old,* somehow. There's an atmosphere. And there's—"

"Rain," said Harry dolorously.

"Well, true. The weather in California is definitely better. But, I don't know, there's something really *nice* about this village. It's beautiful . . . with all those narrow streets and tall stone walls and cobblestone lanes and hidden gardens. And the smell of woodsmoke everywhere—"

"Pollution," grunted Harry.

"I'd rather live in California," Alina maintained staunchly.

"Okay, okay." I finally gave in. "But enough about California. What about Blackthorn? What do you do here for fun?"

The kids looked at each other, perplexed. "Well," Duncan said after a moment, "there's the church fete in June— that's always good fun."

"And Carnival—in September," said Alina. "I was voted the Baby Queen in Year Two!"

Veronica smirked. "I was one of the Carnival Queen's Ladies-in-Waiting two years in a row."

"That was back when you were a looker," Brian teased. "Back when your hair was normal."

She flipped her purple mane over her shoulders. "Ladies-in-Waiting grow up. That's what they're waiting for."

"There's not that much to do in Blackthorn, not for teenagers," conceded Duncan. "There's the youth club on Thursday nights, but not much goes on there, and I've got too much homework, usually, to go over. There's the snooker club—I used to go with my grandad. It was fun to hang out with the old men and play."

"You can join the Drama Society, I suppose," said Will. "My mum and dad are always at me to try out for a play. But it's not really my scene."

"There are clubs in Lower Dillingham," said Veronica. "Dancing and drinking and some good bands. I've been escaping to Lower Dillingham for years."

"Yes, but you're supposed to be eighteen to get in those!" Alina raised her brows.

Veronica raised hers back and said mockingly, "Oh, no, *really*? Oh dear me!" Then she shrugged. "Anyway, I'm eighteen now. I'm older than you lot. You forget."

Duncan rolled his eyes. "Blackthorn was a great place to be a little kid, though, you have to admit it. Lots going on for the small fry."

"When we were babies it seemed a sleepy sort of fishing village, with a lot of artists setting up easels on the pier," Harry said musingly. "I remember that every time I came to the sand with my bucket and spade, some artist type would come by and start sketching me!"

"But there weren't tourists in summer then, not like there are now," Alina added. "I think it was really *your* parents who changed that, Dunk-o. Your mum and Quent, I mean."

"How?" I asked. "What did they do?"

"They became famous! They put Blackthorn on the map as a brilliant place for artists. People from London started coming here on the weekends, and loads more people in the summers. It used to feel like a small village. Now we're practically a *city*!"

I had to laugh. "You should see the Bay Area—in northern California where I come from. Believe me, this is a very, very *tiny* village!"

"You haven't been here in summer yet," Will declared. "It gets positively overrun with tourists and day-trippers."

"But even then it's really still a small village," I insisted.

"I suppose so. It's all relative." Will grinned at me. "Anyway, that's what we were saying. It's boring for teenagers, but great for little kids. Most kids get to run around and have a lot more freedom here than they would if they lived in a city."

"Yeah, because it's so safe," agreed Alina. "Everybody knows everybody."

"Need I remind you we've just had a murder in this village?" Veronica asked icily. "And it's probably someone we all know? That's hardly 'so safe,' is it? You might as well be living in America!"

"But, Ronnie, Simon Jukes is locked up," Alina pointed out comfortingly. "He always was a terror. I'm glad he'll be going to prison for the rest of his life."

Veronica snorted. "Everybody wants to think we're so safe with Simon Jukes locked up, but I don't know about that. His brother Henry swears they were together the night Liza Pethering died. He swears Simon didn't have anything to do with it. What if he's right?" Veronica pushed back her chair. "Anyway, I'd better get back to work or I'll be sacked again." She grinned at Duncan. "Good thing it's only just down the road! Who knows what evil stalker might reach out and grab me from a dark lane?"

She paid for her drink and left. I sat there thinking about what she'd said about Simon Jukes, while the other kids started chattering about films and how that was something Blackthorn sorely needed: a cinema. They were sick of having to take the bus or beg a ride to Lower Dillingham each time they wanted to see a film.

I listened idly. Alina, Brian, Will, and Harry all seemed like nice kids. I felt comfortable with them, and they seemed to accept me, American accent and all. I hoped I'd see them again. Veronica was something else.

After a while they said they had to leave. Duncan shoved back his chair, too. "Shall we go?" he asked, and I nodded. He paid for our drinks and scones, and we stepped out of the warm room into the cool, misty evening. At least it had stopped raining. We said good-bye to the others, and waved as they set off up the street. Alina called back to me that she'd ring me soon, and I had the warm feeling I'd made another friend. Across Castle Street the figure of Henry Jukes lurched through the archway of the Old Ship.

"So what do you think?" I asked Duncan.

"Think about what?"

"About what Veronica said. About Henry's brother.

About Simon Jukes. Do we have a prime suspect? Is Simon really it?"

We stood on the corner outside the cafe. "You mean you're wondering about Oliver again? Well, should we call in and say hello? Check on how he's doing, at least—even if we can't exactly accuse him of murder! We still have time before you have to be home, and he lives right here—in The Mews."

The rain started again, a gentle mist. We started walking into The Mews, a narrow, cobbled lane with terraced stone houses rising straight from the street on both sides. "What would we say to him?" I asked.

"We'll just say how sorry we are, and see where the conversation goes." Duncan knocked on the door of number 3.

"We can say I never got to see Liza's gallery, and I wondered if he'd mind . . ."

Duncan and I huddled together in the drizzle, but no one answered the door. "Stupid me," Duncan said after another minute. "Of course Oliver will still be at work."

"The day after his wife's funeral?"

"Lots of people lose themselves in work when they're grieving," Duncan said, frowning at me. "It doesn't mean anything."

I didn't argue the point. I wondered if Duncan's frown meant he had coped that way himself after his mother died—immersed himself in schoolwork, or something. We walked back to Castle Street and over the footbridge to the Emporium. The stream, already swollen from the rain, rushed under the bridge and surged against the riverbank. The paved walkway was puddled. There was no sign that anything had happened here recently; there was no mark on the pavement, no yellow crime scene tape from the police investigation, no marks of struggle or distress. But we both fell silent and stood staring down at the dark water. The stream flowed swiftly. Pieces of sticks were carried downstream, and I could see underwater reeds and, in the streetlight, a flash of rock, white and gleaming, beneath the surface.

Duncan slowly reached for my hand. His hand was big, and totally covered mine, and I liked the feeling. His clasp was warm and strong, and banished that sense of loss I knew we'd both felt.

We walked on through the dark evening to the Emporium. Bright pools of light spilled out of the building to illumine the puddled darkness of Castle Street. There was no sign of Oliver anywhere, but the shop was bustling with housewives snapping up late-afternoon dinner possibilities. We were surprised to see Veronica Pimms there in all her purple-haired glory, presiding over the "Quality Meats and Cheeses" counter. She had tied a dark green Emporium apron over her tight, faded jeans. A thick ring of keys dangled importantly off her belt loop. She tossed her hair when she saw us.

"What happened to your job at the Ship?" asked Duncan.

"I've still got it," she said smugly. "*And* got this, too. Ollie gave me my job back, didn't he? I asked him at the funeral. He knew I never should've been sacked in the first place. We get along fine, me and old Ollie, and now that *she's* gone, I can work here in the daytime and down at the Ship in the evenings. I'm saving up for a car, you see, and it won't take long at this rate. Ollie said I can fix my own hours here, to make it work at the Ship, too."

"Great," Duncan told her. "That's brilliant, Ronnie."

"So—how can I serve you, kind sir? Cheddar's on special." With a glance at me she added, "What do California girls like in the way of cheese?"

"Cheddar," I told her. "But we haven't really come to get cheese . . ."

"We're looking for Oliver, actually," said Duncan.

Veronica laughed, and her many earrings danced along her cheek. "He's over at his wife's gallery. His *dead* wife's gallery. Dismantling it, I hope. I was there this morning, pulling everything out of the storage cupboards before he got there, to make it easy for him to decide what to keep and what to throw. I'd throw all of it myself, if it were up to me."

"So Oliver's given you his keys, eh?" asked Duncan with a little smile, glancing pointedly down at the ring dangling from her belt loop. "You look very much in charge, Ronnie, and it suits you."

"I can tell you it's a relief not to have her breathing down my neck all the time, checking up on me. But as for the keys, I've had 'em for ages. Liza's keys, they are! I copied 'em, didn't I, over at the ironmonger's, first time she left them out on her desk. Silly cow."

Her voice was so venomous, I stared at her. How much had Veronica hated Liza Pethering? I was realizing that although Veronica had not been at Quent's party that night, she might have been able to leave the Old Ship on a break. She might have run into Liza stumbling drunkenly along the footpath, and maybe Liza would have insulted her again . . . and Veronica could have knocked her down and then dragged her to lie facedown in the Shreenwater. Veronica was thin but looked wiry and strong. And Liza had not been very big.

I felt a prickle of unease between my shoulder blades.

"So you work at the Old Ship every night?" I asked casually, but moving the conversation deliberately around to where I wanted it.

"I'm at the Ship Mondays through Saturdays," Veronica said airily. "They need me at the bar *and* in the kitchens. Haven't missed a night yet."

"Were you working on the night Liza died?" I pressed.

"Every night means every night," said Veronica. She took a wet cloth and started polishing the glass countertop.

"Did you see Simon Jukes come in that night—the night Liza died?"

"Oh, yeah, I saw him," she said, tossing the cloth down and wiping her hands on her apron. "For my sins. The Ship is too high quality to attract the lager lout crowd, but Simon and Henry can't be bothered to go to Lower Dillingham where their sort usually hang out at the Bib and Tucker. And now Henry's been coming in alone, poor thick bloke."

She leaned toward us over the counter. "I heard Simon talking that night," she confided in a low voice. "The night of the murder, I mean. He was going on something fierce about how he hated Liza." Her eyes widened—possibly in admiration. "I heard him talking about getting even someday . . . and then he left. When the police came round asking later, that's what I told them."

"How did you find out Liza was dead?" Duncan asked. "Did someone ring you?"

"No—I saw her."

"You saw Liza!" My voice squeaked. "You saw her—dead?"

Veronica rolled her eyes at me. "I was walking home

from the Ship, wasn't I?" she said to Duncan. "Could hardly miss seeing all the coppers and the emergency van and everything, there by the Shreen. The body was covered, though. With a plastic sheet sort of thing. I didn't know who was under there, not till later."

"You were walking home alone?" I asked.

She raised a thin, disdainful eyebrow. "Blackthorn's not like America."

Still, a woman we knew had been murdered *here*. But I didn't say anything. Duncan waved good-bye and we moved away from the cheese counter.

Out in the street, I grabbed Duncan's arm. "I'm starting to wonder if maybe it was *Veronica*. She hated Liza, you know. You can hear it in her voice. She *says* she was at the Old Ship the night of the murder, working the whole time, and came upon the scene later, but that could be a lie."

"You suspect *Ronnie* of killing Liza?" Duncan's voice was incredulous.

"Well, she did say 'someone ought to kill that bitch,' remember?"

"Yes, but she was just talking. She didn't really mean anything by it, I'm sure."

"It would be stupid, I suppose, to say something like that right out and then go do it," I admitted. "But I think we should check if she really did stay at work that night. Let's stop in at the Old Ship and ask before we go to the gallery. If they say she was there the whole time, then we can cross her off the list."

"List?"

"Of suspects," I said.

"You really have a list of suspects?"

"Well, not a real list. I just keep thinking—if it wasn't Simon, who was it?"

He stood staring at me for a long moment. "What I think is that you've been watching too many cops-and-robbers shows on the telly."

"I have not!" I sputtered.

"Or maybe it's because you live so close to Holly-wood . . ." He frowned at me.

"I do not!" I protested hotly.

He shrugged. "All right, but now we'd better hurry. Your mum said to be back in time for your supper."

We started walking again. I used the automated bank machine on the corner while Duncan went into the Old Ship. It seemed so strange that I could push my bank card from my own bank in California into the slot, tell the machine I'd like to withdraw fifty dollars in cash, and then have the money slide out—converted into British pounds. I peered at the unfamiliar, brightly colored bills under the glare of a streetlamp before stashing the money in my wallet. Duncan came out and told me that the owner of the Old Ship corroborated Veronica's account of the night Liza had died. The owner would have noticed if she'd taken time off from her duties, he'd said. And why did Duncan want to know? Was there some problem?

"What did you tell him?" I asked. "Did you say we're investigating a murder?"

"I just said there wasn't a problem, and thanked him. But I hope he doesn't tell Veronica we were checking up on her story. She'll be upset with me."

I was a little upset to realize he cared what Veronica thought.

We set off for the gallery on Castle Hill Lane. The narrow stone building had been a house once, I imagined. But now it had a wooden sign on the door: PETHERING PORTRAITS. A large bow window at the front displayed some flower arrangements and two portraits on easels. One was of Oliver Pethering, looking quite a lot more handsome in oils than he did in real life, and one was Liza herself, with her fluff of black hair and her wide smile. I winced; the picture was so lifelike.

A bell tinkled as I pushed open the door and we walked inside. I looked around with interest. There was no sign of Oliver, so we wandered around two downstairs rooms, studying the paintings and sketches. I recognized a few people I had seen at the party, as well as the lady who worked behind the counter at the newsagent's. I saw a few more that I might have passed in the Emporium. Many sketches were of children, and quite a few were of people's pets. There was even one of a much younger Veronica Pimms without purple hair. A special wall exhibit showed the process Liza must have gone through when painting: First a photograph of her subject. Then pencil or charcoal sketches. Then a rough painting, mostly just blocks of color. Then a much larger painting, this time detailed and shaded and textured.

Liza was *good,* I thought, surprised. *Really good.*

"Look, Juliana," Duncan said behind me. "Here's my mum."

I whirled around to find him standing next to the fireplace, where a painting of a very beautiful woman was hung. The ornate oval golden frame complemented the delicate red gold of her hair and the shape of her oval face. Her smiling mouth was generous and tender. In her arms she held a sleeping baby wrapped in a blue blanket. A tuft of reddish hair peeked out from the blue. Her eyes, instead of looking out at the portrait painter, were cast downward, as if she were studying her baby. Her expression was radiant.

"That baby must be you," I whispered.

"I know," he said softly. "I've never seen this picture!"

"I'm surprised you don't *own* it. It's fantastic. Don't you want it?"

"Yes," he said. "Or my grandparents would want it. Let's ask how much it costs."

"Maybe Oliver's upstairs," I suggested, noticing for the first time a narrow stairway in the back corner of the gallery. The steps were stacked with boxes.

We headed over and started up. But after we'd taken only two or three steps, Oliver himself came hurrying down. "Oh! Heavens!" said Oliver. "I suddenly heard footsteps! You gave me a fright!"

"Sorry," Duncan said. "We were just looking around."

"Liza had said I should see her portraits," I explained. Why did Oliver look so nervous?

"Take your time, take your time," he said genially, shooting a worried glance up the stairs. "She was a genius, was my Liza. She could paint anybody. Made you look the way you saw yourself. She had a knack, she did. Talent." He shooed us in front of him, back down the stairs to the gallery.

"Oh, she had the knack, all right. The knack of stabbing you in the back," boomed Celia Glendenning's voice. And then Mrs. Glendenning herself started down the stairs. She frowned at us. "What are you children doing here? Is school out already? Goodness, it is! I must be dashing home to make Kate her tea."

Her cheeks were pink and her hair was uncombed. She sidled around Oliver Pethering and headed for the door. "Oh! It's so mild out, I nearly forgot my jacket! Oliver, would you . . . ?"

Oliver went back upstairs and came down with her coat over his arm. He helped her into it in true gentlemanly fashion. "There you go," he said heartily. "Thanks for stopping in."

"Yes, indeed," she said gaily. "I'll see you again sometime. Cheerio!" And she was gone, with Oliver staring after her. Was the expression on his face *longing*? I narrowed my eyes, wondering.

Duncan looked at me and raised his eyebrows expressively. Then he turned back to Oliver Pethering. "I was wondering how much that portrait of my mum costs." He pointed to the fireplace.

Oliver tried to drag his attention away from the door through which Celia Glendenning had exited. "Lovely one, isn't it, lad?" he said jovially. "Your mum was a beauty, yes she was for a fact. I'd have to find Liza's books and look that one up before I could tell you a price. She wrote down how much each one was to sell for, she did. But I can check. Let you know soon."

"Thanks," said Duncan. He started heading for the door, but I put out my arm to stop him.

"Umm, Mr. Pethering," I began, and again Oliver had to drag his attention away from the door. "We were wondering if we could see the portrait Liza did of Mrs. Glendenning. The one she's told everyone she hates so much?"

Oliver Pethering blinked at us. Then he started chattering in his staccato manner. "What? Oh—oh, no, sorry. Sorry! Don't have that one on display. Celia absolutely refused. Said it was ghastly. Unflattering. And indeed it is! Doesn't do her justice in the least. Certainly wasn't up to Liza's usual standards. No, not at all. Didn't capture Celia's energy. Or charm! In fact—in fact, *that's* why she was here just now, Celia. If you were wondering, I mean. Returning the painting and getting her money back." His gaze sharpened. "Now, is there anything else I can do for you young people?"

He seemed eager to have us gone, but I had to try again. I spoke in a sincere and admiring voice: "Everything Liza did is *so* good! I guess you were her muse! It's hard to imagine she could paint anything that wasn't beautiful. I just can't imagine that she could paint a terrible portrait. Please won't you let us see the one Mrs. Glendenning doesn't like?"

He hesitated. "It's in the back room."

"Oh, please?" I wheedled. "It wouldn't take long to bring out, would it?"

He frowned at me, then shrugged. "All right, just a quick peek, then."

We waited while he went to get it. Duncan winked at me. I wasn't sure why I needed to see the portrait. But when Oliver returned and pulled the cloth covering off the canvas, I could see what might have driven Celia to murder.

The other portraits ranged around the gallery were of various villagers, each presented in a flattering light, as if they'd been sitting in their garden on a sunny afternoon. Each face was painted with bright, clean colors, a friendly smile, and a sense of happiness and goodness shining forth from the eyes. The portraits presented people you'd want to meet, and you just knew you'd like them. But this portrait of Celia Glendenning was different.

The background was a gloomy purply brown, as if rather than a garden, Celia had been sitting in a closet. Her face had been painted in muddy oranges, blotchy grays, and sickly greenish browns. The eyes were puffy, the expression unpleasantly sly. The mouth was tight and ungenerous. The overall expression on Celia's painted face was one of arrogance, but also stupidity. I thought again that Liza Pethering had been a greater painter than I'd expected.

"I can see why Mrs. Glendenning hated it," I said slowly. "But it's actually . . . very good, isn't it? I mean— not pretty, but . . ."

"It's horrible," Oliver snapped. "Terrible insult to Celia. Can't imagine what Liza was thinking. Of course it's technically brilliant. Liza *was* a gifted artist. But she had a nasty streak, I'm afraid. No getting around that."

I gazed at the painting's hooded, shadowed, spiteful eyes. When I moved away, I thought I could feel them watching me.

"We did want to ask you about the night of the party—," began Duncan, but I cut him off.

"No, let's go now, Duncan," I said urgently. "I've got to get home."

He raised his brows, then shrugged. We said good-bye and left the gallery. The drizzle had stopped and the air was mild and damp. By the low stone wall around St. Michael's Church, in the yellow light of a streetlamp, I stopped and turned to Duncan.

"What was the rush to leave?" he asked. "I thought you *wanted* to keep him talking. Try to figure whether he's still our prime suspect."

"He's definitely my prime suspect—either him or Mrs.

Glendenning. Or both! What if they're in love, and Liza was standing in the way of their happiness?"

"But why not just ask for a divorce then?"

"I don't know," I admitted. "I just get a weird feeling about that woman. And she's always watching me. Even her portrait was watching me."

Duncan laughed. "Lunatic American."

He was teasing, but I was serious. Somebody out here in the streets of this little village was a murderer. That person wouldn't be wearing a sign saying I'M THE BAD GUY, but if I was clever, I might be able to figure out who had killed Liza. Duncan and I might figure it out together. "I am not a lunatic," I said. "Just listen to me! It could be anyone. *Anyone*, Duncan. A person no one would suspect."

"Like—who?"

"Someone who hated her."

"Yeah—but can you name names?" he challenged.

I could—but he liked Veronica Pimms. And he *loved* his own grandparents. And they were only *some* of the people who had hated Liza.

"Look, I'm thinking about that fight Mrs. Glendenning had with Liza the night of the party. It was pretty clear she hated Liza's guts. And remember—," I added, "Oliver Pethering wasn't the only one to leave the party early that night. If you'll think back, you'll remember that Celia Glendenning did, too."

"Yes, but she had Kate with her. If you're thinking that Oliver and Celia teamed up to get rid of Liza, how could they do that with Kate right there?"

"That *is* what I'm thinking," I said, and it did make as much sense as any other scenario. "Maybe Kate's in on it, too."

Duncan snorted. "What did I say about lunatic Americans? Kate's all right. You're starting to see criminals under every bush."

I could hear he was annoyed with me now, and I hadn't even told him of all my other suspicions. "Sorry," I said. "I like Kate, too. It's just . . . I think we should talk to her. Ask her about her mother."

"Ask if her mum's having an affair with Oliver Pethering? Ask if her mum killed Liza?" Duncan shook his head. "I don't think so."

"Somebody killed Liza," I stated doggedly. "Somebody in your safe, perfect English village killed her. That isn't my imagination!" I reached out and touched his jacket sleeve, but he pulled away in irritation. "Okay, look—we won't ask Kate anything directly."

Now we had reached the door in the stone wall, and Duncan took out his key to unlock it. "We'll be subtle," I added softly.

Duncan stared down at me for a long moment. "I don't think subtlety is your strong point," he retorted. But then, relenting, he flashed me a smile. "We'll come by tomorrow after school, Kate and I. We have a half day, so we'll be early—and have lots of time to talk."

❧ *11* ❧

After Mom and I walked the Goops to school the next morning, I reluctantly settled in at the kitchen table with my algebra book. Mom bustled around in the small kitchen making a pot of tea to take up to her studio. She made a second pot just for me, covered it with a quilted sort of pot-holder thing she called a tea cozy, and set it on a little trivet with a tealight burning beneath to keep it all warm and snug. I had to laugh at her. "You're really getting into tea, Mom."

"I'm just reclaiming my English heritage," she countered, pausing on her way up the stairs. "And it feels *right*, Jule. I've missed living here, and I hadn't realized how much. If it weren't for Liza's death, I'd be perfectly happy here."

"Even without Dad?" I muttered under my breath.

She heard, and nodded. "For now, yes. I need to be here, Juliana. And it's not just the tea! It's the pace of life, the sounds and smells, the feel of the air, the quality of sunlight—"

I rolled my eyes at her. Mom was an artist, through and through. She laughed and went up to work in her studio for the first time since Liza's death.

I sat alone at the table and looked out the window. The Mill House garden shimmered green through the mist.

Green shoots of flowers were starting to poke through the ground. Crocuses and daffodils everywhere. I got up from the table and opened the front door. The air was damp but warmer than inside the cottage. The old stone walls held the chill, I realized, and I left the door open when I returned to the table.

As I poured out another cup of tea just to warm my hands on the hot mug, I found myself unable to concentrate on my math. Instead, I sat there at the table, sniffing the garden scent that wafted in through the open door. I was quite sure, suddenly, that old Mr. Cooper was wrong this time. It was truly spring. It just didn't feel like winter anymore. Much balmier—like a California spring with hints of dark soil and wet blossoms and salt from the sea. It was the salt smell that always made me try to capture the *other* memory—the elusive threads of memory that flickered tantalizingly just out of reach.

In California we lived about an hour's drive from the ocean, so my memory wasn't stirred up unless we made a special trip to the beach. As a young child, I never really enjoyed having a picnic or building a sand castle because the beach would make me agitated. I didn't want to play or wade; I wanted only to run along the water's edge. I wanted to run until I was exhausted and needed to be carried back to the car—although whether I was running away from something or toward something in my memory, I could not say. Later, when I was older and the Goops begged for a day at the beach, I would come with my family reluctantly. I learned to sit still and enjoy sharing a picnic. I helped Edmund and Ivy build sand castles. But the urge to get up and race across the sand was always with me, as were the tendrils of memory that blew through my mind like ghosts.

Whenever I tried to pin those memories down, tried to think back, back, back—I felt I was looking through murky water or smoked glass.

I felt that same barrier now—but now, here in Blackthorn, I felt a sense of danger, too. I felt as if whatever separated me from my past was not just the usual murky water but fathomless depths in which I could drown; not just the usual dark glass, but a hard, impenetrable surface that would cut me if I broke through it. Whatever I was almost remembering, I suspected, was something about my childhood, about my first five years in another family. It had to be. And I both longed to remember—and dreaded remembering.

I knew the basic story, the one my parents had told me, of how they'd been contacted by a social worker who knew they were looking for a young child to adopt. They were told how I'd been found wandering on the beach in Santa Cruz late one night, drenched with salt spray. The people who found me were two teenagers on a date, sneaking off to the dunes for some private cuddling or a midnight swim. They were shocked to find a little girl there in the inky darkness, all alone. They called the police, and the police didn't even cite them for being on the beach after it had officially closed for the night. Instead, they were heroes.

I wouldn't talk, except to whisper that my name was Jewel Moonbeam and I was five. I knew when my birthday was, but that was all. Some investigation led the police to find the apartment where I'd been living. It wasn't the sort of place where people knew their neighbors. Everybody kept to themselves, and people came and went weekly. But the police learned from one of the tenants that "Her Highness"—a young woman with some sort of accent (maybe British, or Australian, or New Zealand, or something)—had a little girl. She'd told neighbors she once had a husband who got himself killed in a motorcycle wreck. The other tenants didn't know anything else, and the police couldn't find any papers of identification in the apartment. No letters, no bills, no passport or wallet with a driver's license. They had searched all records for anybody with the unlikely surname of Moonbeam and came up with nothing.

Nothing.

My own memories started out of that nothingness and formed a cloudy picture of how I'd sat at a table, the table where I learned to do puzzles with the foster mom, and how a policeman sat across from me, asking about my mother, the one with the accent. Not the woman I knew now as Mom. My *birth* mother.

I remember how I just shook my head, not having any words at all. Not knowing anything at all. It was as if that first day in foster care was the first day of my conscious life. I had no birth certificate. I became Juliana Martin-Drake, beloved first child of Hedda and David, and we celebrated my adoption date as well as my birth date, and as far as I was concerned the adotion date *was* when I had come to life.

All these years later, I still knew nothing. But where, then, were these feelings coming from now, these uneasy glimmers of panic and that voice, a child's voice—*my voice?*—crying out: *wake up, wake up!* Why could I recall nothing of that birth mother, my first mom? I wanted to know and at the same time was afraid to know.

And . . . why did I now feel that the memories were linked to Liza Pethering's murder? That was the strangest thing of all.

I set down the mug of tea and slowly wound my long braid around and around my hand, biting my lip, staring out the window. Through the mist in the garden I could see a light from Quent Carrington's Old Mill House.

I reached for my pencil and tried to work a math problem, but the numbers blurred on the page. I reached up to wipe my eyes and was startled to find tears.

Mom's voice called down to me, asking if I'd mind making some toast for "elevenses" and bringing it up to her. I jumped up gladly, relieved to have something to do besides sit lost in my thoughts.

"What in the world is 'elevenses'?" I yelled up the stairs.

"Late-morning tea break!" she called back.

That figured, this being England. "How many pieces of toast?" I shouted up to her.

"Lots," replied her laughing voice. "And make some for yourself. We'll have a study break together. Then maybe you can help me tackle the last of these boxes up here."

I might as well, I thought morosely. It wasn't as if I was really getting any schoolwork done. I wished again that I hadn't decided to do homeschool. On a balmy springlike day such as this, school with Duncan and Kate—even an unfamiliar school in an unfamiliar land—would be a lot nicer than sitting here with my own muddled thoughts and no computer from which to e-mail my friends back home.

I turned on the broiler (the *grill*) and laid six slices of bread on the metal rack. I had to watch carefully because the bread would crisp and burn quickly. Deftly I turned the slices over with tongs, and then stacked the perfect pieces of toast onto a plate. I turned off the grill, then arranged the plate along with butter, jam, knives, and napkins on a wooden tray. I carried the whole thing up to Mom's studio.

Mom's paintings were colorful, detailed scenes of people going about their lives. Her settings were mostly imaginary, but they sprang to life on the canvas, full of tiny stories. The longer you looked at Mom's paintings, the more you saw. My family still liked to tease me about the painting Mom hung in my bedroom at home—a busy village with a parade down the main street and a carnival in full swing in one of the lush fields bordering the town. The painting had hung on the wall next to my bed for nearly two years before I noticed that the twists and turns in the carnival maze spelled out J-u-l-i-a-n-a. I'd studied that picture every night, marveling at the tiny scenes—the little boy who was afraid of the clown, the little girl eating a huge fluff of cotton candy, the couple daringly setting off in a hot-air balloon—but I'd never noticed my own name, right there.

"Some things are best hidden right in plain sight," Dad had told me, laughing. "So the moral is, always keep your eyes open. If it had been a snake, it would have bitten you!"

In this new little sunroom studio, Mom had unpacked most of her canvases and hung about a dozen. There wasn't enough wall space for more. She had several others stacked by the door. Those, she told me, we would hang down in the sitting room, and in the bedrooms. Someday maybe she'd be able to rent a little studio on Castle Street. The five boxes of books and supplies she had not yet unpacked were over by the windows. Three boxes were stacked in a leaning tower. Two were shoved up against the wall.

"The same rules apply here as at home," Mom said, also eyeing that unstable stack of boxes. "All kids out of my studio unless invited in!"

"I never touched your old boxes," I said indignantly, setting the tray of toast on an unpacked box. "Don't go blaming me if the Goops have messed with your stuff."

"Not messed with, just moved," Mom said. "I don't know why Ivy and Edmund would drag them to the other side of the room and pile them up that way—they're heavy boxes!"

"Maybe they needed a throne for a king or queen," I suggested. The Goops were big on fantasy stories as well as orphanage tales.

We both started slathering the butter and jam onto our toast and gobbling it up. While we ate, my eye fell on a new blank canvas Mom had set on the easel. "So, what are you going to paint?" I asked.

"*Mmm*," mumbled Mom, her mouth full. "Not sure yet. Maybe Ivy and Edmund, throwing stones down at the beach. Interesting light over the water at this time of year. And I love the way all those beach stones are different colors. Have you noticed? They appear to be all gray at first, but when you look closely, they're full of colors. Layers of pinks and greens and purples." She looked thoughtfully out the window.

"Like in Nora's big rock," I said, nodding. "With those bright white quartz veins running all through it. Sort of like a spider's web."

Mom looked at me. "Which rock is this, honey?"

"You know, the one in the found-art collection." I looked around the room. "It was on the window ledge."

"I haven't seen it."

"Really? It was right there in the collection with the other stuff," I said.

"Maybe Ivy or Edmund took it for their game as well," she said, frowning. "Really, I shall have a little talk with them when they get home."

I stood up and went to look through the things Nora had displayed on the ledge: the conch shell, the gourd of feathers. The pinecones. The basket of small boxes . . . but no stone. Probably it had fallen. I knelt to move the stacked boxes out of the way, grunting as I managed to slide the first box. Mom was right; the boxes *were* heavy. "Ivy and Edmund must be a lot stronger than they look," I said to Mom.

"Ah, but the two of them together have the power of ten. You know, strength in numbers?" Mom laughed. "Half of those boxes are full of my art books—"

"Mom, look!" I cut her off. I was staring down at the floor under the box I'd just shifted. "What's this?" Was I aware right then that my pulse quickened? Was I aware that my breath came faster?

A dark stain marred the old floorboards. I tugged the next box away from the window wall, then blinked. "Mom?" Quickly now I started shoving the other boxes out of their lineup. I rubbed my fingers over the large, dark stain they had hidden. Had the stain been here the first time I saw this room? Surely I would have noticed it!

Probably it was just paint leaking out of Mom's boxes. It could so easily, so logically, be exactly that.

Then why . . . why was I so certain that the dark stain was not paint at all? How could I know—as if I'd seen it before—that that faded smear was *blood*?

"Good heavens!" said Mom, standing next to me. "What have those kids done now?"

Yes, I thought. *Let it be the Goops who made this stain somehow. A nosebleed.*

Mom knelt at my side. "They must have put the boxes over here to cover up their mess. Little devils!" She touched her fingers to the stain as I had. Sniffed. "Wait—I don't think this is paint. Could it be—red wine?"

Yes, I thought again, fervently. *Wine!* Maybe the Goops had been playing around in here—little drunks—sneaking sips from a bottle of wine stolen from the kitchen....

"Hey, who left the door open?" called Edmund's voice from downstairs, and Ivy's shrill tones joined his: "Hey! The rain's coming in! Why is it always raining in this country? That's what I want to know." It was the Goops, home early on their half day off from school, trooping into the cottage with wet boots. "Hey, Mom, I drew a really great picture of a pirate ship! It's for Dad! Want to see it?"

And Ivy shouted, "I wrote Dad a letter in a secret code!"

Mom ran down and told them to take off their boots and close the door and not track mud onto the rug. I came down right behind her and demanded that they come upstairs and account for the big mess in the sunroom.

"What big mess?" Ivy demanded, and I noted uneasily how innocent she looked. She could be wild and loud, but she wasn't a liar. Nor was Edmund. Mom led them into the sunroom and asked them not to play in there anymore, and not to touch her things. "Same rules we had at home, kiddos," she reminded them.

"But we didn't touch your things," objected Edmund. "At least I didn't!"

Mom asked them if they had piled her boxes of books over by the windows, and they said no, they hadn't. They inspected the stain and said they'd never seen it before, but they thought it sort of looked like grape Kool-Aid, only thicker.

"We don't have Kool-Aid in England," Mom said. "Grape or otherwise. But maybe it could be some sort of black currant juice. Children often drink black currant juice here—"

"It looks like blood," I interrupted.

Edmund looked at me with interest. "Hey, yeah!" That was a much more intriguing possibility than mere Kool-Aid or black currant juice, or whatever.

Then a knocking on the front door sent me running back downstairs to let Duncan in, and Kate Glendenning, also just home from school. I had forgotten Duncan and I had plans to pump Kate for information about her mother's friendship with Oliver Pethering. I had forgotten everything but the stain.

The Goops called for our visitors to come upstairs and see it. "Juliana thinks it's blood," Ivy announced with relish.

"Whose blood?" asked Kate reasonably. "Anybody hurt around here?"

"How can you tell if it's blood?" Duncan asked, kneeling to look closely at the darkened floorboards.

The answer was on my lips before I could hold it back. "Because I remember," I blurted out. "I remember!"

Mom stared at me. Everyone did. "Tell us, honey," she said softly. "What do you remember?"

"I—I don't know," I whispered, and that was the truth. Whatever flash I'd had was gone already. "I just thought— I mean, for a minute I thought . . . I thought I remembered something about blood on the floor. That I had seen it somehow before. Oh—I don't know."

"Nightmaaaaare city," moaned Edmund in a fake, evil voice. "That's where you saw it!"

"Maybe," I said doubtfully. The flash *had* had the quality of a nightmare.

"Or maybe you saw something like it in a film?" asked Duncan. "Some horror show?"

"Maybe you read something like it in a scary book," suggested Kate.

"I had a bad dream once," Ivy said, practically shouting for attention. "And there was, like, this *river* of blood. No, like, a whole *ocean* of blood!"

I didn't have anything more to say, but I kept looking at that stain. Mom suggested that we all go downstairs and have—what else?—a cup of tea. We all went to the kitchen and everybody was still talking about what the stain might be while I just sat there, the only silent one. Mom filled the electric kettle with water, and opened a packet of cookies (*biscuits,* she called them) for Ivy to arrange on a plate. Then Mom motioned for me to come back upstairs with her. I could feel Duncan's eyes on me as I went up.

"What?" I asked.

"Come back to the sunroom for a minute, honey. I want you to think if there's anything else—anything not quite right. Anything else that's different from what you remember being here."

"Well, I haven't really been up here much, Mom," I said, following her down the hall to the sunroom. "Just that first afternoon, really, when we arrived. I came in here and was just standing around when Liza said—" I broke off.

"Liza was in the sunroom?" prompted Mom. She ushered me ahead of her into the room.

I averted my eyes from the stain. "Yes, Liza was here," I said. "She was showing us the house. I hadn't even chosen my bedroom yet. She came in while I was looking at stuff on the window ledge, and she told me it was Nora's found art. Nora liked to collect things like that, Liza said. Thought they brought good luck or something."

"Yes," mused Mom. "I remember Nora that way— always looking for magic. Magic in nature. Magic in people . . . magic in feathers and rocks."

I crossed the sunroom and stood by the windows, running my hands over the objects on the deep window ledge. Outside, the garden shimmered green in the drizzle. Through the rain I could see the big Old Mill House, its lights shining warmly out into the already darkening afternoon.

I stared at the light, then sat back on my heels, my heart beating hard—as if I had been running.

"The night we came home from the party," I said slowly, remembering perfectly how we'd crossed the wet garden, "the cottage was completely dark. But—" I took a deep breath. "But earlier, when I was with Duncan, and he was giving me a house tour, we were in one of the rooms and I looked out and could see our cottage." I took another deep breath. "And the light was on, Mom. The light was on *in this room.*"

"But when we came home the house was dark," Mom remembered. She turned wide, frightened eyes on me, and I knew she was picturing it. "And the door was unlocked."

That detail had slipped my mind. "You thought you had just forgotten."

"You're *sure* you saw a light on, honey?"

"I'm totally sure."

This time it was Mom who took a deep breath. "Okay, then. Okay. We need to make a phone call, Juliana. We need to call the police—and ask them to test that stain."

"I know," I murmured faintly. "But still—" A prickle at the back of my neck made me move closer to Mom. "There's still a chance, isn't there? That it—it *might* just be paint? Or wine. Or black currant juice, like you said—"

"Or tea?" she suggested wryly, wrapping her arms around me in a hug meant to comfort us both. "Dream on."

Whad's going on?" demanded Quent Carrington in a worried voice just moments after the police van arrived. My mom had shown the two forensics experts as well as Detective Inspector Link up the stairs and into the sunroom, but I had stayed down with Duncan and Kate and the Goops. "Is something wrong? Is someone hurt?" Quent stood at the door, peering anxiously past me.

"No . . . no, not hurt." I opened the door wider so he could come in. "It's just—upstairs." I hesitated; the news was so strange, so odd. "Mom and I found a big mark on the sunroom floor that looked like blood. We don't think it was there when we moved in. So we called the police to come test it."

"Blood!" Quent paled. "Is Hedda all right?" He pushed past me and took the steps two at a time without even asking me if he could go up.

"I'm Mrs. Martin-Drake's landlord," I could hear him saying upstairs. "Show me this blood!"

Down in the sitting room, we all just looked at each other. "It's probably really *old* blood," Kate ventured reasonably. "After all, think how old this cottage is. Somebody in medieval times may have cut himself with his sword or—his dagger—I don't know. Why did your mum call the police about it?"

I shrugged. "She's a high-strung artist. But you're right. Probably we just didn't notice the stain when we first moved in. It's probably *ancient* blood." I didn't mention how the light had been on in our cottage the night of the party but off again when we arrived home. Somehow, I just didn't want to talk about it then—how someone could have come here that night while we were at the Old Mill House. The night Liza had died.

Had Simon Jukes—the official suspect—climbed over the stone wall and broken into our cottage while we were gone? But there had been no sign of forced entry, and Liza had been at the party, not keeping company with Simon. I had been moved by Henry's insistence at the wake that his brother was innocent; there had been something in his eyes that made me believe him. Now I kept picturing how Kate's mother had quarreled with Liza Pethering at the party that night. And then Liza died. Could Celia Glendenning some-how have lured Liza away from the party, here to our cot-tage, and then attacked her—made her bleed on the floor? Celia was a large, strong-looking woman; could she have dragged Liza's unconscious body out to the Shreen to drown? I remembered how Duncan and I had discovered Celia in Liza's gallery with Oliver. With Liza out of the way, Celia Glendenning could marry Oliver Pethering. . . . I re-membered how nervous Oliver had seemed when Duncan and I came to the gallery. Did he know what Celia might have done? Were they in it together?

Obviously I couldn't talk to Kate about any of these questions, so I just kept quiet. Soon the team of police fin-ished gathering evidence and came downstairs, with Mom and Quent following. They would get back to us, they said vaguely. But it was quite likely this stain had nothing at all to do with Liza Pethering's death. That case was going to be irritatingly difficult to take to court. It was full of dead ends, and this stain would most likely be another. It was all very frustrating; they didn't even know yet what the murder weapon had been, and Simon Jukes wasn't talking.

Quent requested that the police keep him informed as well. They replied that of course they would; they said as our landlord he had every right to know what was happening. Quent walked the police out to the road, but then came back to us.

"I'm so sorry, Hedda," he said.

She looked surprised. "None of this is your fault, Quent."

His lips lifted at the corners. "No, of course not. But I'm still sorry you have to deal with any of this. You've been here less than two weeks, and it's been pure chaos rather than the new start to your career that you'd hoped for."

Mom wrapped her arms around herself. "Let's not talk about it. Let's just wait till we know what the forensics team finds before we start worrying. I mean—there might be a perfectly innocent reason for that stain. In the meantime, what can we do?"

We all just looked at each other and everybody knew that an innocent reason for the stain was pretty unlikely. But any other reason was so awful, we couldn't stand thinking about it.

"We can go back to the Old Ship for another meal," Quent said in his hearty way. "That's what we can do. Get our minds off it. My treat! No—I insist. Or we can go somewhere else if you'd rather . . . There's a nice Indian place in Lower Dillingham that does a very tasty curry. We'll *all* go." His genial smile included Kate. "Call it a late lunch or early supper."

"Oh, I don't know," began Mom. But Ivy and Edmund overruled her.

"Curry, Mom!" Edmund wheedled. "You love curry."

"I love curry, too," Ivy stated. "And that yummy Indian bread—*nan*, I think it's called. Let's get some of that. Okay, Quent?"

"Whatever you like, Ivy. If your mum agrees."

Mom shrugged, and her smile was wan. "I'm just not hungry. But I suppose the children do need a meal, and I haven't started cooking anything. What do you think, Jule?"

I wasn't hungry, either, but I didn't want to sit in the cottage all day, just waiting for bedtime to roll around, knowing that stain was up there in the sunroom. "Sure," I said. "Why not? A nice hot curry will be perfect."

Kate phoned her mother to ask if she could go with us. Mrs. Glendenning gave Kate permission to eat with us— but invited herself as well. She would meet us at the restaurant, she said. So we all piled into Quent's other car—not a sports car but a van—for the ride to Lower Dillingham. Mom sat up front with Quent, and I could tell she was making an effort to be cheerful and sociable. I tried for the same lightness with Duncan and Kate.

I couldn't tell about those two. What sort of relationship did they have with each other? Maybe they were just buddies from way back in kindergarten (*reception class,* Mom said it was called here), but maybe they were something more to each other. It seemed to me Kate watched me a lot—sort of like her mother did. But in Kate's case, I wondered if she was watching me to tell me "butt out" or "he's mine." I couldn't tell.

It was a relief to arrive at the Indian restaurant and stop chattering, and just let the smells of pungent spices and fresh bread wash over me. Those smells masked the other smell—the salty, fetid one that had seemed to follow me out of our cottage and into the night.

Kate's mother had arrived before us and secured a large round table in the far corner of the restaurant. We all seated ourselves, and I was not pleased to find myself right next to Celia. Duncan was on my other side, so at least *that* was good.

"What have you been doing today?" Celia asked me briskly.

"I had a lot of algebra to work on," I offered.

"But Kate tells me you aren't in school." Celia looked puzzled.

"I'm doing homeschool for now," I explained, and Mom took over for me and clarified the whole situation. Celia pursed her lips as if she didn't approve of home-schooling, and she was just opening her mouth to tell me, when Edmund spoke up.

"We found a stain at our house," he said. "The police are checking to see if it's blood."

This news had a profound effect on Celia. She let her menu drop out of her hands, and it slid onto the floor. When she and I reached for it at the same time, we bumped heads with an audible crack.

"Ouch!" I clutched my forehead.

"Ooh." She did the same. Her cheeks were drained and pale.

"Oh dear," said Mom, standing up and coming around the table to me. "Are you all right, honey? And—Celia?"

I let Mom rub my forehead.

"Where's the ice?" demanded Edmund. "We can wrap it up in the napkins and make compresses—"

"Drinks in England don't have ice," Quent said. "But I'm sure the kitchen has some. Shall I ask?"

"I'm okay," I said.

"I shall be fine," Celia said, but she was still looking alarmingly pale. "It's nothing."

"It's just that Mum hates blood," Kate informed us. "It always makes her feel faint."

"It's so silly . . . ," said Celia. Color was returning to her face.

"Dad always had to bandage my scrapes," Kate added. "Mum was useless."

"I'm afraid that's true." Celia sounded back to normal now. "Since her dad left us, Kate has had to bandage all her own scrapes. Poor wee child!"

We all settled back down and the waiter arrived and took our orders. When he had gone off to the kitchen, Celia leaned toward Mom. I was surprised to hear her bringing the subject up again: "Now what was this about a . . . a *stain?*"

"It's probably nothing," I said, and at the same time Ivy assured her: "I think it's an old stain. Mead spilled in ancient times!"

Quent and Mom explained about our discovery. Celia listened. Sitting next to her, I could see her hands clenching and unclenching in her lap.

"It sounds dreadful," she said. "I can't imagine what it would be. I'm sure it couldn't be—you know—blood. Perhaps there's some sort of mildew or rising damp. These old houses are prone to such things. In fact, Kate and I had to move out of our place for a whole week last year while we had a damp course done." She then explained in droning detail about damp courses, and what they were—apparently the old plaster had to be removed from the walls and reapplied. Sounded like a messy job, and wasn't really very interesting dinner conversation, but it had the effect I think Celia wanted, which was to get us talking about other things instead of weird stains. Which was fine with me.

The adults talked on and on about home repairs and how costly they could be. Kate rolled her eyes across the table at me, and we were glad when our food arrived. It was delicious, and for a while there was no talking except for requests to "pass the chutney, please," or "I'll take some more of that *raita,* thanks."

Before we finished, Celia Glendenning started asking Mom where she'd been born, and where she'd grown up.

"In Wolverhampton," Mom answered. "In the Midlands."

"Oh! My ex-husband grew up in the Midlands as well—near Birmingham," said Celia. "Same area, basically. I grew up in East Anglia, in Norwich—have you been there?"

Mom said she'd only been once or twice, to the seaside, as a girl. Celia shrugged. "I wondered if maybe you had family there. Relatives?"

"None that I know of," said Mom. "Where is your family from, Quent?"

And the adults were talking ancestors and genealogy. I tuned out and turned to Duncan instead. Genealogy isn't exactly one of the hot topics for most adoptees. I didn't have anything at all to add to a conversation about ancestors. Ivy liked to fantasize that, since my birth mother may have been from England, I was somehow descended from royalty. Secretly a princess! Every girl's dream! But the shadows in my memory were so dark, I didn't think they were hiding anything so romantic and exciting.

Duncan was playing tic-tac-toe (*noughts and crosses,* he called it) on his paper napkin with Edmund. Duncan won easily. I drew a grid on mine and challenged Duncan next. He won, and gloated, and pressed my foot under the table.

The waiter brought another basket of *nan* to our table. It was late when we finally finished our meal and left the restaurant. This time Kate rode with her mother, which was fine with me since it left me to sit alone with Duncan in the middle seat of Quent's van. As the rest of us piled in, Celia called to me, "I hope your forehead feels better, dear." Her voice was normal, quite pleasant, but her gaze was piercing.

Why did she look at me like that—as if she were trying to see through my bumped head, right into my brain?

"Thanks," I said. "I hope yours is okay, too." I sat back and fastened my seat belt.

Celia came to the window on the passenger side where Mom sat. "Let me know what happens," she said in a low, urgent voice. "About the . . . stain." Then her eyes rested on me again, sitting behind Mom.

THE NEXT MORNING, very early, Detective Inspector Link knocked on our door to bring us the terrible news: the stain *was* blood; it was, in fact, Liza Pethering's blood. Now the detective wanted to interview Mom again. Mom invited her in and offered tea, which she declined. She seated herself in our sitting room after breakfast, opened her notebook, and started firing off questions.

I guessed it was obvious that the police would have questions; I had a million questions myself. It was bad enough to know that Liza had been attacked, but to have it confirmed that the attack had happened right here—in our own house—made me feel sick. And I know Mom felt the same way. But I couldn't see where Detective Inspector Link was going with all her questions for Mom—asking for all sorts of details about her relationship over the years with Liza Pethering, about her movements the night of the party, about when she last saw Liza. I didn't think the policewoman really suspected my mom, but she seemed to think Mom would recall some detail that would be useful in proving that Simon Jukes had attacked Liza in our cottage. Mom had been, after all, the one to report the stain, and she had known Liza for years.

The questioning went on and on. Had Simon Jukes *ever* been to our cottage? Mom said he had not, at least not as long as we had been living here. But we had found the door to our house unlocked when we returned after the party, so maybe Simon had entered while we were gone. Was Mom *quite* sure that Simon Jukes had not been at the party? Mom said she hadn't seen him anywhere. Simon wasn't part of Blackthorn's art scene, so he had not been invited. "He's not exactly the sort of company Quent Carrington keeps," Mom added drily.

Detective Inspector Link questioned me again, too. She wanted to know what I had been doing at the party. Had I seen Simon lurking anywhere around the place? No? Was I *entirely certain*? I definitely had not seen him, but I *had* seen a light on in our sunroom when I looked out the window from Quent's house during the party. But the light was off when we came home.

The detective inspector made a note of this. Then she asked what I had done at the party, and with whom, and what had we talked about? She seemed determined to find a link to Simon Jukes.

I didn't have much to tell her, really. I told her that Duncan gave me a house tour, but I didn't mention that we had danced together in the ballroom, and held hands, and I didn't say that we'd talked about our families. Some things were private, after all. What had I eaten? With whom had I chatted? And when, *exactly,* had I last seen Liza, and what had she been doing *exactly?*

I tried to remember. "I saw her last at the Old Mill House, in the dining room," I said. "She was having an argument with Celia Glendenning. She was being sort of—well . . . I think she had already had too much to drink."

"She seemed drunk?" pressed the officer.

"Well, I guess so. I mean, Liza was being loud and rude and wild . . . and her husband wanted to take her home, but she wouldn't go. So Quent and Oliver took her off to the kitchen to make some coffee. I think that was to, you know, sober her up."

"And that was the last time you saw her?"

"Yes," I said. "Wait—no, I guess not. About an hour later, Duncan and I saw Quent carrying her down the hall after she'd passed out from drinking."

"Quent left her sleeping in one of the bedrooms," Mom added.

The detective made a note on her clipboard. "Yes, I've talked to Mr. Carrington. And he said that when he looked in on her later, Mrs. Pethering was gone. Just left the house without saying good-bye."

"So that's when she could have come over here to our house," I murmured, trying to picture Liza walking over from the big house, through the garden, with Simon Jukes at her side—or sneaking in the shadows behind her. "But why would she be coming to our house? She knew we were all at the party. What did she want here? And why bring Simon Jukes? He wouldn't have had a key, would he? But— did Liza? She already had given back our key, Mom."

"She might well have given you back *a* key, but still kept a copy for herself," said Detective Inspector Link. "She might have let Simon Jukes inside."

"It didn't have to be Simon Jukes, anyway," I ventured to suggest. "There were loads of other people who didn't like Liza—"

But the detective shook her head impatiently. "We are quite convinced he is guilty. Our task is to find the proof. And discovering how he and Liza Pethering ended up to- gether in your sunroom is crucial to solving this case."

"But that's what I can't figure out," Mom said. "Simon is the *last* person Liza would bring here—or anywhere. Why in the world would she? She didn't like him in the least."

"In my job," replied Detective Inspector Link sagely, "we are constantly surprised by what people do. But it doesn't mean they didn't do it." She stood up to leave, thanking me and Mom for our help.

MOM DIDN'T GO up to her sunroom that day but instead stayed downstairs, helping me with my algebra chapter. "I know I should be up there, either working on something new or at least selecting the paintings I want to put in the Springtime Art show," she told me. "But, frankly, I doubt I can work up there anymore, knowing that's where Liza was killed."

"No—she *wasn't* killed there, Mom," I corrected her. "Remember? The police report said she drowned. So the worst thing that happened to her here was getting bashed on the head, somehow."

Mom shivered. "Thinking about it makes me feel sick. Head bashing . . ." She curled up on the couch and started sketching the view from our front window. I sat at the kitchen table and put the algebra aside. Instead, I took out a fresh sheet of notebook paper and started writing a letter to my dad. I missed having him around, and I missed having e-mail for quick communication since he wasn't around. I wasn't used to writing letters.

Mom had phoned him already with the news of Liza's death and funeral, and he had called back while we were out. I listened to the message twice, just to hear his voice. Now I wrote him, updating him about the bloodstain in the sunroom. I was getting writer's cramp after about two minutes, but there was still something satisfying about writing to him. It made me feel connected—almost like an Internet link. My words would go from my thoughts through my hand, through the ink, onto the page . . . and then fly across an ocean and a continent, right to my dad's pile of mail. He would sit at our table in the kitchen just as I was sitting here, and he would open my letter. It would be like an umbilical cord of words stretching between us. I told him about the bloodstain, and how scary it was not to know what was going on. I told him the police were sure it was Simon Jukes who had killed Liza, but I wasn't so sure. I told him about Henry Jukes, and his outburst at the wake. Then I tried to write little entertaining cameos about all the people we'd met, and so on—I guess at the back of my mind was the idea that maybe something I wrote would pique Dad's interest so he might decide to come join us here. *P.S. What would it take to make you come see us here, Dad?* I wrote at the end. *We all miss you. I think even Mom misses you. She came here to paint and be a big artist, but now she can't bear to go up to her new studio with the bloodstained floor, and her artist friend is dead, and things are pretty grim. What I really want to know is: why can't you two just work things out?*

I added the picture of the pirate ship that Edmund had drawn for Dad, and the letter in code from Ivy, and asked Mom if she had anything she wanted to send to Dad.

She looked up from her sketch, distracted. "What? Oh—no, nothing, honey."

P.P.S., I wrote. *Mom sends all her love.* I sealed the envelope.

The day stretched out minute by minute. I couldn't settle at anything. I couldn't stand sitting at home with Mom and the stain until school was over and I could talk things over with Duncan, and I certainly couldn't count on writing letters or working algebra problems to divert me from my thoughts. When I tried again with algebra, the numbers swam in front of my eyes. They made as much sense as Liza's death. Which was *no* sense.

Mom decided to walk over to Blackthorn First School to meet the Goops and I shrugged into my coat and started out with her, watching carefully as she locked the door behind us. We crossed the garden and let ourselves out into the road through the red door in the stone wall. There we parted—Mom to the school and I in the other direction, toward the village center. My feet carried me along swiftly through the darkening afternoon, as if I had a plan of action, as if I knew where I was headed. But beyond stopping at the post office to mail (*post*) my letter to Dad, I didn't have a plan. Maybe I would just wander along Castle Street and look in the shop windows. Maybe stop in at the newsagent's and buy a magazine and some chocolate. Maybe see if the tiny library was open. Maybe just head down to the beach to hurl stones in the water until dark . . . Anything to help with this feeling of frustration. Maybe a good dose of those negative ions would banish my bad mood.

I walked down to the beach. It was empty, and the tide was coming in. Gray waves lapped the shore, each new one eating away more of the land. I climbed over the seawall and jumped down onto the sand, then picked my way carefully across the wet, slippery stones until I stood at the water's edge.

Pushing away my usual initial dizziness and concentrating on good form, I heaved beach stones out into the water. It was good to feel my muscles strain, pleasing to have a stone fly really far, satisfying to make a big splash. I reached down for another stone, and another—then stopped, staring at the rock in my hand. It was nearly perfectly round, the size of a baseball. It had thin lines of white quartz running through it, and looked so much like Nora's stone up in the sunroom that it could almost be its twin.

Nora's *missing* beach stone.

With a sudden shock of realization I knew what the murder weapon could have been. The murderer—Simon Jukes or someone else—could have come into our cottage with Liza Pethering and used Nora's beach stone as a weapon, bashing Liza on the head and knocking her out. Okay, then it wouldn't really have been a *murder* weapon, perhaps—not exactly—but using it the murderer could have knocked Liza unconscious and taken her to the stream to drown. I shivered, staring down at the stone in my hand. It wasn't the same one, I could see that, but it was very similar. I dropped it and stepped back.

After a few steps, I couldn't make out which stone I'd been holding; they all looked so alike. *And that's just what the murderer might have done,* I realized. Where better to hide the weapon than on the beach it had come from? One rock among millions—no wonder the police couldn't find it!

But wait—something didn't fit with that theory. It would be bloodstained. A police dog, trained to search, might sniff it out on the beach. So the murderer would have had to throw it into the sea.

No, that didn't make sense—would the murderer, hauling Liza, really have taken her all the way to the Shreen and then walked all the way back across town to the beach? There must be a quicker way to dispose of the weapon. . . .

If my life were a cartoon, a lightbulb would have flashed above my head as I suddenly realized the perfect place to hide the beach stone. I turned and ran to the seawall steps, then made my way as quickly as I could back across the village.

At last I found myself on the footbridge over the Shreen. I stood on the wooden bridge and leaned over the railing, staring down at the water where Liza had been found. The stream was less swollen today, moving more slowly. The blackthorn bushes along the sides of the water were white and fragrant. There was a scattering of blossoms floating on the surface, and—*yes*—a flash of white below. I had seen that flash of white before but not realized its possible importance. Was I right? Was it just the reflection of the blackthorn flowers? Or a tangle of white rope under the water? Or—? The closer I looked, the more I was sure I could see the white, spider-webby lines. . . .

I darted off the bridge, down to the bank of the Shreen. I shrugged out of my jacket and rolled my right sleeve up as high as it would go. Then I knelt on the ground and stretched my arm out, down, down into that cold, dark water. But what I wanted stayed just out of reach.

I sat back, shivering from the chill, and scanned the stream bank. There I saw a long stick that would probably work as a fishing pole. Grabbing the stick, I poked it out and down—stirring up the muddy stream bottom, trying to nudge the white object along. But the stick slipped off the slick rocks. Useless.

I looked furtively to my left and to my right. No one was in sight, thank goodness, and I was determined. I kicked off my shoes, peeled off my socks, and rolled up the legs of my jeans as far as I could. The water was nearly knee-deep and freezing, and I gasped as I waded into it. I strode into the center and leaned down, thrusting my arm into the water almost to my shoulder.

There! My hand closed over the smooth form at last. I needed two hands to pull it up from the sucking mud that held it. I splashed to the bank and laid down my prize: a cold, round beach stone, big as a baseball.

I rubbed off slimy mud with my wet palm and hovered over the rock, certain yet uncertain at the same time. This had to be Nora's special beach stone. I recognized the thick white veins stretching across its surface like a web. I hefted the rock high in triumph—but only for a moment. Then triumph faded fast and I nearly dropped it right back into the Shreen as the thought stabbed me that whoever had held it last—before me—must be the same someone who had used it to bash Liza Pethering on the head.

What should I do with it now?

I heard voices approaching along the path by the water and hurriedly tucked the rock under my jacket. I remembered reading in mystery novels that the murderer often is compelled to return to the scene of the crime. Holding my breath, I scanned the nearby bushes for a hiding place. But too late. Two figures appeared around the bend in the path and shouted my name.

Laughing in relief, I waved at Duncan and Kate. They were walking home from the bus stop, wearing their school uniforms and carrying bulging backpacks. "Hullo there," Kate greeted me shyly. Then her eyes widened. "Juliana— you're soaking wet!"

And Duncan asked, "Are you out fishing? Or *swimming?*"

"Sort of both," I said weakly. Well, wading, anyway. And fishing for clues. But I didn't say that. I just brought the rock out from under my jacket. "Look what I've got here." Quickly I told them where I had last seen the rock, and what I thought Liza's killer had done.

"You mean Simon Jukes," clarified Kate.

It was on the tip of my tongue to assert that I could envision the rock in the hands of Oliver Pethering or Celia Glendenning even more readily than in the hands of Simon Jukes. But Duncan's eyes met mine. Imperceptibly he shook his head.

I could picture Oliver Pethering telling Liza he wanted a divorce. I could picture how Liza would have protested— and how Oliver would have picked up this beach rock from the ledge and smashed her on the head to shut her up. Or maybe it was Celia herself who was with Liza that night, and Liza told Celia to keep her paws off Oliver, and then *Celia* picked up the rock and knocked Liza out cold.

Of course, the one flaw with my vision was that Liza hadn't seemed to care much for her husband. Would she even object if Celia Glendenning wanted him? Again, this wasn't something I could discuss with Duncan until he and I were alone. And why would any of them have been in *our* cottage for this confrontation?

They were both staring at me. "Wow," said Kate. "So that's . . . the murder weapon?"

"Well, technically she died by drowning," I said.

"Technically that's evidence." Duncan shook his head. "Let's take it to the police."

I put on my socks and shoes, rolled down my pant legs, and we headed off together for the police station at the far end of the village.

13

"Now, you say you fished this out of the Shreen, right where Mrs. Pethering was found lying on the stream bank?" Detective Inspector Link looked dubiously at the rock.

"Yes, I did," I told her firmly.

"How did you know what to look for?" another officer asked. This was a man I had not seen before, with a long walrus sort of mustache. We were all standing in the reception area of the police station—yet another old gray stone building, but with a modern addition at one side. Behind a glass partition, an officer was typing something on a computer. It was otherwise quiet. I wondered if Simon Jukes were somewhere in this building, locked in a cell.

I focused on telling my story coherently. "When we moved in, there was a big rock in the sunroom on the window ledge. But then it was missing," I began. "No one in my family knew where it was—and yet I had seen it on the window ledge the day we moved in."

"When did you first notice it was missing?"

"Just yesterday," I admitted. "When I was up in the sunroom with my mom. I moved some boxes and then noticed the stain on the floor. I noticed the rock was missing right before we found the stain and phoned you. I didn't think about it again until today when I was at the beach. I saw all those beach stones, and one of them looked like this one—and it made me realize suddenly that somebody could have used the stone that was missing as a weapon."

I explained how I'd wondered whether a murderer would bother carrying the rock all the way to the beach to discard it, and how I'd remembered that the day after Liza died, Duncan and I had crossed the bridge over the Shreen and looked down at the place where she'd lain. And I remembered I'd seen a flash of white in the water then.

"So I went to the Shreen and started fishing around," I concluded. Detective Inspector Link looked at the other officer and suppressed a smile. What was so funny? Didn't they believe me? "Look," I said. "I know it's the same rock—well, I'm pretty sure—because of these wide white lines. In any case, it's a beach rock, right? I mean, it wouldn't normally be lying in a freshwater stream, right? I mean, it couldn't *naturally* be lying there."

"That is correct, young lady," said the walrus. "But a beach stone *could* be carried up from the beach by anybody, and then dropped into the stream. Which would not be a crime."

"But this is the beach stone from our cottage. I'm sure of it."

"So you say. And in fact, you could have carried it to the Shreen and dropped it in yourself."

"Are you suggesting that Juliana *planted* the rock?" Kate's voice rose shrilly. "She wouldn't do that!"

"Teenagers have been known to lark around." The detective held a quick consultation with the other officer. "But we'll keep the rock," she told us after a moment. "See if it matches the injuries to Mrs. Pethering's head."

"But—she's—I mean, we've already had her funeral," I said, confused.

Detective Inspector Link ran a hand through her short gray curls. "We have photographs to help us there."

I bit my lip, hating the thought of what those photos would look like.

"Can you dust the rock for fingerprints?" Duncan was asking.

"Prints won't stick to a wet surface," the walrus replied. "And I sincerely hope you kids aren't just playing a trick. This is a murder investigation. We don't have time for amateur sleuths, and we have no patience whatsoever with games."

"This is no game," I muttered indignantly. "I'm just trying to help! Why do you think I'd be playing some kind of game?"

"People do strange things, luv. Like to play sleuth, do little pranks. Tricks."

"Well, I'm not playing any sort of *trick*! I'm not trying to be some sort of *sleuth*! I just hate the idea of somebody coming into our house and knocking my mom's friend unconscious."

"Simon Jukes has a violent streak. It's not nice to think about, but it's true," said Detective Inspector Link.

"You leave the investigations to us," said the walrus.

"The situation is very strange," the detective added more gently, "and we just don't want any false clues entering our investigation. The waters are muddied enough, if you'll excuse the pun. But thank you for bringing us the rock. We do appreciate your help. Now . . . haven't you better be heading home? We'll be . . . er . . . getting back to you."

"Eventually," said the walrus.

I glared at them both. I doubted they were ever going to look into any other possibility besides Simon Jukes. It was so frustrating, because there were any number of people who could have gone to our cottage the night of the party. But which person would have attacked Liza in the sunroom, and then carried her to the Shreen? And *why?* That was the biggest question: Why? If I could figure out *why,* then I'd know *who.*

Who else could have a key to our cottage? I wondered about this as Kate, Duncan, and I walked along Castle Street. Quent would have a key because he was our landlord. Duncan probably had a key, too—which meant his grandparents could have gotten hold of it. Liza herself had had a key, of course, since she'd been the one to show us around the day we arrived. She gave back the key—but could have kept a copy. Oliver could easily have had a copy, too.

And he might just as easily have given a copy to Celia Glendenning.

If he had the key with him at the Emporium, Veronica Pimms might have been able to take it and have a copy made on her lunch break.

Another possibility: Liza might have gone to the cottage to let herself in for some reason—and been followed. By whom? My list of suspects was long.

"D'you want to come in for tea?" Kate asked shyly when we reached her house, a freestanding (*detached,* Duncan said it was called) stone house on a rise above the beach. "Mummy usually makes enough to feed an army."

"Do you mean for a cup of tea—or for dinner?" I asked. It was still confusing to me, this liberal use of the word "tea" to mean just about anything: a single cup, a light afternoon snack with scones and cakes and sometimes sandwiches, and an evening meal.

"Dinner is at midday," Kate explained with a laugh. "We ate dinner at school. The evening meal is tea. But you can call it supper, if you like."

I wanted to see Celia Glendenning's reaction to our news about the beach stone. "Sure," I said. "I mean, yes, thanks. I'd love to stay for supper."

"Dunk-o?" Kate grinned at him. I guessed when you'd known someone since nursery school, you could call him by his nickname. I knew I wouldn't dare—at least not yet.

Duncan shook his head and said he had promised his grandparents he would eat with them. "I eat there at least twice a week," he explained, "and especially on the nights when Quent is in London on business. Granny is teaching me to cook, believe it or not. I'll invite you two round there soon so you can sample my mouthwatering shepherd's pie!"

So we said good-bye to Duncan. Then Kate ushered me up the steps and inside her house. I looked around in surprise, immediately feeling stifled. The place was like a junk shop—absolutely and totally *crammed* with stuff. But on closer look, I realized this *stuff* wasn't junk at all. It was *Art*—Art with a capital *A*. The walls were covered with framed paintings, and the tables were covered with sculptures. Larger sculptures stood in corners and in the center of the living room and hallway. I could only imagine that the rest of the rooms were just as crowded. It was hard to walk around without bumping one of the sculptures. They were made of metal, of marble, of stone, of wood. Even plastic and china and blown glass. I remembered having heard at Quent's fateful party what should have been obvious from my first step inside the door: Celia Glendenning was a *major* patron of the arts.

Kate pointed out two sculptures by Quent—a large, flowing form of bronze that reminded me of an ocean wave, and a smaller piece that must be quite recent, from his current Viking phase: a bronze ship, with shapes suggesting oarsmen bent over, rowing hard. There was an amazing mobile hanging from the ceiling in the front hall, handblown glass bubbles from Rodney Whitsun and Andrew Parker. And there was a large portrait of a toddler Kate, grinning out at the viewer so mischievously, you just had to grin back. I recognized Liza's style, and was glad that Celia had not taken that portrait down and thrown it away just because she was mad at Liza herself.

Somehow in all the fascinating clutter of metal and glass and wooden objets d'art, Kate found the phone and handed it to me. Then I realized I didn't know our phone number, so she had to phone directory assistance. I pressed the buttons, trying to memorize our new phone number (which had only six digits), staring all the while out the mullioned windowpanes at the view of the sea and the rocks below the house. Mom answered, and I asked permission to stay for tea.

"Oh, honey, I don't know. Quent was planning on taking me out for dinner," she said. "Just the two of us this time. To a Greek place in Portsmouth."

I didn't mind babysitting, but . . . was this a *date*? Mom shouldn't be going out alone with men when she'd been away from Dad only two weeks.

I opened my mouth to complain, but before I had a chance to speak, Mom's voice was in my ear again. "On the other hand, it's good for you to be making friends here, and being with Kate will take your mind off our troubles. I suppose Quent and I can take Ivy and Edmund along with us. That'll work."

I felt relieved. The Goops would make excellent chaperones. The one time last spring when Tim had come over—officially to copy my science notes after he'd been out with strep throat, but I'd been hopeful of something more and had made us hot chocolate and popcorn—the Goops had been all over him and we didn't get more than three minutes of privacy. "Thanks, Mom," I said.

Then, before we hung up, I told Mom in a hushed voice about how I'd found the beach stone and taken it to the police.

"Goodness!" Mom said. "This is getting creepier and creepier. Maybe you'd better come out to dinner with us after all."

"Why, Mom? That doesn't make sense!"

"None of this makes sense," she said, and sighed. "I guess I just don't want you coming home alone. Being in an empty house."

"I'll ask Duncan to come over," I said. "Or I'll go to his house and hang out there." I figured Duncan would be back from his grandparents' house by the time I was finished eating at Kate's.

"Well, I suppose that will be all right." I could hear the unease in Mom's voice. "I won't be sorry to get out of here myself for an hour or two, that's for sure."

"Ask Quent who else has keys, Mom. Okay?"

"I'll ask. Now Juliana, speaking of keys, do you have yours? Because I want to be able to lock up the cottage when we leave for dinner."

I assured her I did have my key. Then we hung up and I picked my way across the room to Kate to hand back the phone. "Permission granted," I told her. "Now . . . show me around this museum!"

Kate's cheeks flushed. "I guess our house *is* pretty strange, isn't it?"

"I don't know about strange," I said tactfully. "Just unexpected."

"My mother is very, er . . . eccentric," said Kate, with her shy smile. "But harmless."

I wasn't so sure about that.

Celia Glendenning breezed in the door with her arms full of canvases, startling us. "Help me with these, my pet?" she called to Kate, and then, seeing me, added, "Oh, good! Perfect! Juliana, I can use your help. I've got another pile of paintings out in the car. Will you get them? There's a good lass." She shrugged out of her coat and set her purse—an artsy sort of tapestry tote bag—on the hallway table.

We carried Celia Glendenning's newest purchases into the house, though I couldn't think where she'd find places to display them. The walls were full already.

"It's gotten to the point where I have to rotate pieces," she told me, as if she had read my mind. "There isn't enough space. I'd have to live in a place like the Old Mill House if I were to have enough room for every painting and every sculpture. But Quent doesn't even use what he has—not much, anyway. He's gotten too big for us."

"What do you mean, too big?" I asked cautiously.

"He's hit the big time, dear. And now that he has all these galleries in London clamoring for his work, he doesn't have as much time as he used to for mere *local* showings. The last few years—well, since Nora's accident, really—he's spent a lot of time in London. Can't stand Blackthorn for all the memories, maybe. Not that Nora was spending all that much time in Blackthorn herself, right before the accident. She was on her way up, too—and who knows? She might have become an even bigger name in the art world than Quent!"

"My mom said she was talented."

"She was brilliant. Come upstairs with me, dear, while Kate heats the soup. It's just split pea soup and salad for tea, I hope you don't mind. I'll show you some of Nora's work I have on display. She was fabulous! Critics were starting to rave about her—and then there was the accident. She was cut down in her prime—no, she hadn't even reached her prime yet. Very sad. But I like knowing I had some part in helping her career, just as I helped make Quent as famous as he is by purchasing his work back when he wasn't such a star." She started up the steep staircase and I followed behind, telling myself that being alone with her for a few minutes couldn't be dangerous. Not with Kate just down in the kitchen.

The stairwell, too, was lined with paintings. I looked at the framed artwork as we climbed. "So," I said, "do you mean you help new artists start their careers by buying their paintings and sculptures?" I was not asking just to be polite. I hadn't ever known what role an art collector had in the art world other than just getting personal pleasure out of collecting.

"That's right, dear. Any sale is a vote of confidence for an artist. And when collectors start seeking out artists' work, galleries pay attention. And then so do the art critics, and the museums and so on." Her modest smile couldn't conceal the boastful tone in her voice. "I am *rather*

well known in the right circles, dear, as an important collector. Galleries sit up and take notice of my purchases—
the London ones, too."

We were in a square hallway with four doors. She gave
me a quick tour: Kate's bedroom, very neat and austere—
practically bare, compared to the rest of the house. The
desk and dresser were clear, the bed neatly made, and the
only clutter came from the several cameras and a tripod on
the floor in one corner. The next room was Celia's bedroom—an explosion of floral pattern bedcovers, wall-
paper, curtains, and rug. Again, the walls were hung with
paintings. And every surface was covered with sculptures
and stacks of art books. The bedside table was the only ex-
ception; it held simply a lamp, a glass of water, and a
framed photo. I glanced at the photo: Oliver Pethering's
round moon face smiled back at me.

Quickly, Celia Glendenning whirled me around and
steered me toward the third bedroom. Was she trying to
keep me from seeing Oliver's photo? But then why display
it so openly? "Here we go," she said liltingly as we entered
the guest bedroom. "Landscapes and jewelry by Nora
Cooper Carrington."

The guest bedroom was a miniature museum of landscapes, deep hued and richly textured, almost mini-
sculptures themselves. They were paintings of light on
water, light on stone, light on fields and forests, light breaking through clouds. I counted eleven paintings, all framed
in a plain pine. On the wall under the windows there was
a glass display case with four necklaces inside. Each was
similar to the one up in our sunroom—strung with blossoms, beads, shimmery bits of rounded glass, and found
art from nature: an acorn, a seedpod, a feather.

"I had commissioned a special necklace for myself," Celia Glendenning told me. "But Nora died before she had a chance to make it. So I missed out."

"But at least you have these four," I pointed to the case.

"Yes," she pouted. "But these were not made especially for me, to be my special lucky charm. Nora called them that, you know. She believed they would guard against trouble. Against evil. She believed they would bring good luck!" Celia's laugh was indulgent. "They're beautiful pieces, but all that talk of luck and charms is nonsense, of course. If they really held any magic, Nora wouldn't be dead now."

"But she wasn't wearing hers when she died," I said. "It's at our house."

"Oh, I'm sure that isn't her special one, dear. She wouldn't even get into a car without wearing it. She was *that* superstitious. Certainly on a long drive to London she'd have been wearing it. Especially for her big gallery debut!"

I pictured the pink quartz necklace up in the little box in the sunroom. "Maybe Quent and Duncan asked for it back after the funeral—to remember her by."

"No, it's probably just one she was making for a customer and never finished," Celia maintained. "She would definitely have been wearing hers, and so I'm afraid it ended up destroyed in the wreckage, just as she was."

I must have winced because Kate's mother took me by the elbow and steered me back into the upstairs hallway. "Let's go down and have our tea," she said, heading for the staircase. "You're looking a bit rum. And, of course, I want to hear all about the stain."

"We had a call from the police this morning," I said. "It's a bloodstain. It's . . . Liza's blood."

Celia stopped abruptly on the stairs. "Oh my." She turned to look back at me. "Are they sure? I mean, the blood is *proven* to be Liza's?"

"Yes, that's what they said."

"Isn't it awful, Mother?" cried Kate.

Celia continued down the stairs and led the way to the kitchen. "Yes, awful, and exceedingly strange. That's clearly where Simon Jukes knocked her out . . . but why *there*?"

I said I didn't know. I was a little surprised, I guess, that she seemed as puzzled about it as anyone else. Either she was a very fine actor, or she really didn't know. In any case, for all the intensity she'd shown last night, now she didn't seem very interested in talking about the stain.

We sat in the kitchen at a small round table. Above our heads, dangling from a beam in the ceiling, was a glass sculpture that looked like candles dripping wax. Kate's mum saw my gaze and laughed. "That's a chandelier, dear. Handmade by Rodney Whitsun—you met him at Quent's party, I believe. His work is exquisite." She motioned with her hand to a switch on the wall. "Kate, dear, turn on the light so that Juliana gets the full effect."

Kate switched on the chandelier and immediately the dozens of little glass candles lit up and twinkled down on our meal like stars. "It's beautiful," I said. "Has he made more of these? Maybe my mom will buy one." I could imagine it at home in California, hanging over our dining room table. My dad would love it.

"I'm sure he will make one if she orders it," Mrs. Glendenning said. "But they cost quite a bit. I know Nora intended to have one made for your little cottage. Wanted to hang it in the stairwell, I believe. Rodney told me she'd had him come round several times to talk about plans before she commissioned it, but then she died, poor dear, before he ever made it."

I blinked up at the glittering glass chandelier. So Rodney Whitsun had also been in our cottage, I was thinking. He, too, might have been given a key.

Kate served some very tasty pea soup and a salad of spinach and sliced cucumbers. Mrs. Glendenning held forth while Kate and I just listened. She didn't converse so much as lecture. I felt like I was sitting in school, like I should open a notebook and take notes about all the paintings and sculptures she was carrying on about. Like there would be a test before dessert.

I had a few things I'd like to quiz her about, too. Like her relationship with Oliver Pethering, for one.

But she was going on about the Springtime Art show coming up: Did my mum realize that it was also a competition? And Celia herself would be one of the judges—along with several other art collectors and critics from London. "First, second, and third places receive money," she added. "Not a lot, but still an honor. First prize gets to hang in the Tate Gallery for a month! Your mum should be sure to submit her finest pieces," she was telling me. "All the best artists in town will be entering, and there are many different categories—"

"Even photography," murmured Kate.

Her mother snorted. "Let's not get into that discussion again, Kate. But speaking of photography, how about if you take a nice picture of your new friend? Let's have a lovely little photo of Juliana to remember this evening by."

"You're forgetting something, Mother." Kate's voice was cold.

"What is that, dear?"

"My camera is broken."

"Oh, yes—I'd forgotten that it fell. But, you know that was your own fault—"

"I don't know anything of the kind!" Kate's voice was a low muttering. I listened with interest, looking back and forth between Kate and her mother as if I were watching a tennis match.

"You don't look after your things properly. What can you expect? Still, you can get it repaired. But that is, in fact, part of my point, dear. A camera is just a copying machine. *Real* art comes from the artist—through manipulation of a medium like paint or clay. Cameras don't make art."

"If the London critics say there should be a photography category, I don't see how you can still say photography isn't art!" Kate protested, red-cheeked.

"The critics are just pandering to popular sentiment." Celia shook her head disdainfully. I saw Kate's mouth open. I hoped she would say something, something angry, something to defend her own interest in photography. But she just sighed and sat back, defeated.

"Well," I said boldly to Celia, "you must like *some* photos because I noticed the one of you and Oliver Pethering up in your room."

Celia Glendenning shot me a withering glance—as if I'd been caught prying up in her room rather than having been given a tour. "One can like a photo of one's friend, of course," she said coolly. "Especially a photo taken by one's daughter. But that doesn't make it *art*."

One's friend, I was echoing in my thoughts—and skeptically. Had Liza Pethering known that this woman kept a photo of *her* husband by her bed? What if Liza had somehow found out about the photo that night at the party?

Would she have tried to attack Celia? Would Celia have tried to defend herself—with the beach rock? But what would they have been doing upstairs in our cottage?

How much would Liza Pethering have cared that Celia Glendenning had a picture of Oliver, anyway?

I noticed Kate watching me with narrowed eyes, almost as if she could tell what I was thinking. A blush started up my neck and into my face.

Time to change the subject.

"We went to the police station this afternoon," I announced. "Kate and Duncan and I."

"Really?" Celia raised her well-plucked eyebrows roguishly. "Caught in the act, eh?"

"Mother!" Kate sounded embarrassed. "*What* act?"

"Peering in windows?" Celia asked. "Pilfering from the shops?" She laughed gaily. "All right, tell me, then. What did the police want with you?"

"They wanted the beach rock I found in the Shreen," I said evenly, watching her closely. Was she teasing us to divert us from her own guilt? "They said it was evidence."

But Celia just looked intrigued. "Evidence?"

She sounded so innocent, but she'd had time to get her act together, I told myself. The innocent tone could all be good acting. Maybe Celia was part of the Blackthorn Drama Society.

"They think it might be the stone used to knock out Liza Pethering," Kate clarified. "Before she was left in the stream to drown."

"It was stolen from our house," I added. "Probably by the murderer."

"Well, let us hope there are some nice clear prints belonging to Simon Jukes," Celia said. "That'll make convicting him easy." She shook her head. "Your poor mother! It must be hard for her to work now in that room. Perhaps I should offer her a space here . . ." She glanced around at the crammed rooms.

"Maybe Oliver would let her use Liza's gallery," I suggested, just to see what her reaction would be.

"Oh no, that would remind your mum all the more of her dear, departed friend!" Celia shook her head emphatically. "That would never do. I think probably Quent Carrington will offer her a place to paint over at his house. I daresay that would be better, wouldn't it? Closer to home for your mum." She winked at me. "And there's always the chance that Quent might find it highly diverting to have a lovely American artist under his roof. He's all too focused on the London art scene these days, and it wouldn't hurt to have him sticking around Blackthorn a bit more! At least it would make things *interesting*."

The last thing I needed was for Celia Glendenning to start playing matchmaker for my mom. However *interesting* she would find it. "Well, I'd better be getting home," I said, not commenting on her remarks about my mom and Quent. "My mom and my brother and sister are probably back from their dinner now. Thank you for the meal."

"They're not *really* your brother and sister, are they?" Celia asked brightly. "Even though you all look so remarkably alike."

I raised my eyebrows.

"Mother!" hissed Kate.

"Well, you heard from Duncan that Juliana was adopted," Celia declared, "and I think that's very interesting! That's all!" She looked back at me with a big smile. "So all I'm saying is that presumably your sister and brother aren't biologically related—not that it matters, of course," she added hastily, seeing my astonishment. "It's just that you look so much alike, all with that fair hair, I never would have guessed."

"Edmund and I were both adopted," I said evenly. "But I totally consider him and Ivy both to be my *real* siblings— and legally that's just what they are."

"Of course, of course," Celia said hurriedly. "I didn't mean that they weren't, truly. Not at all! I was just thinking about how much you three look alike. How *fascinating* that you're adopted! Where did your real parents come from, do you know? Do you know anything about your background?"

Her voice rang stridently, and I found myself leaning back in my chair as if to get away. Why did she care? Why would I tell her, even if I *did* know my history? The dark clouds obscuring my memory seemed to press closer, as if a storm were gathering.

I had felt strong and in control when I quizzed Celia Glendenning about Oliver Pethering, but now I felt on the defensive. Celia's piercing gaze didn't waver as I muttered my response to her question. "I consider the parents who are raising me to be my *real* parents—I mean, they certainly aren't *fake* parents, are they? And I don't know anything about my background. A lot of adopted people don't."

"Of course they don't," Celia said breezily. "And of course babies couldn't remember anyway! And of course your parents aren't fake—I never meant to imply they were. Well, not to worry! I think it's all just delightful!"

"I'll walk you home, Juliana," Kate said hurriedly, and jumped up to clear our plates.

"It's okay—," I said, but she cut me off.

"I'll walk you."

So we walked through the dark village streets back to Water Street. The night air was brisk and cold, and blew away the usual heavy smell of woodsmoke. The fresh scent of the sea tickled my nose. I was getting used to it; the dizziness came less frequently these days. I was glad for the wind tonight after the stuffy air in the Glendennings' house. Kate strode along at my side, not speaking until we were nearly at the red door in the wall.

"I'm sorry if I wasn't supposed to tell anyone you're adopted—"

"It's not a secret at all!" I replied hotly. "It's just that I don't know much about it. I don't really remember anything . . . I was pretty young, you know."

"That's what Duncan said . . ."

I hated the thought of Duncan and Kate discussing me when I wasn't with them. "I just don't see why your mom is so interested," I said. "Unless bringing it up was just a way to get off the subject of Oliver Pethering!"

"You think my mum had something to do with it," she said flatly.

"Something to do with what?" I hedged.

"I could see it in your eyes, earlier—when you were talking about that photo of Oliver. You were thinking that photo proves something. Well, it *doesn't*. I gave my mum that photo because it was the very first one I developed myself. I'd taken a lot of shots of people all around town, but that one of Oliver turned out best. I framed it because I wanted to show her how a photographed portrait can be every bit as good as a painted one. So you needn't go on thinking that it means anything else at all!"

"Okay, okay," I said soothingly. "I'm *not* thinking anything! It's just . . . *interesting*, that's all. And your mother likes things to be *interesting*, doesn't she?" I was still stung by Celia's blunt remarks.

Kate grabbed my arm and made me stop walking. "Are you trying to say you think my mum killed Liza Pethering because she's in love with Oliver?" cried Kate. "Is that what you're thinking? Well, you're dead wrong. So just keep out of it and don't think you're going to come around our house again, pretending to be so friendly but really just wanting to snoop around in people's bedrooms!"

"Hey—that isn't fair! I didn't snoop—your mom showed me her bedroom of her own free will. And the photo is just *there*, where anybody can see it."

Kate and I reached the red door in the stone wall and stopped. "Right—out in the open, not hiding. She doesn't have anything to hide!" She faced me squarely. "Just listen to me, Juliana," she said in a hard voice with an edge of desperation. "My mum didn't have anything to do with *anything*. I'm completely and absolutely certain of that, and that's *final*, so just stop snooping around and playing detective."

"Fine," I opened the door and stepped through into the Old Mill House garden. "No problem. Good night!" I closed the door and leaned against it. By the desperation in her voice, I knew Kate wasn't really absolutely certain of anything at all.

BACK AT THE cottage, Mom was home from the restaurant, drooping on the sitting room couch, her hands cupping a mug of tea. Dinner with Quent had been very nice, she told me tiredly, but the restaurant had been rather fancy for Edmund and Ivy, and Quent seemed rather annoyed that they ate quickly and wanted to leave instead of sitting and savoring the many elegant courses. He'd wanted Mom to come over to his place afterward, but she told him she had to get the kids into bed first. And now she had a headache. Even the few steps across the garden to the big house seemed too far to go, she was that tired. She asked me if I would please go straight in to supervise the Goops, who were supposed to be getting into the tub, one by one—as if baths would make them any less goopy. I headed for the kitchen, glad that Mom hadn't been especially eager to cozy up with Quent. Mom stayed in the sitting room. I heard the TV (the *telly*, they called it here) come on. Canned laughter.

I phoned the Mill House, wanting to talk to Duncan about what had happened with Kate and her mother. Quent answered and said Duncan wasn't back yet from his grandparents, but would be soon, and he urged me and Mom to come over for a nightcap. I figured he meant a drink. I told him Mom was looking pretty tired and had a headache, but I'd give her the message. Then I said good-bye and rolled up my sleeves to deal with the Goops.

Edmund was sitting at the kitchen table, eating potato chips (*crisps*, the package said they were called), waiting his turn for the tub and complaining because they'd flipped a coin to see who went in the bath first, and he'd lost. "And now the water is going to be all disgusting and soapy from Ivy," he muttered to me resentfully. "And probably cold. I don't see why English people can't take separate baths, like we do at home."

"It's not exactly about English people, Goop," I tried to reason with him. "It's about old houses with small water heaters, that's all. And so we suffer." I ruffled his yellow hair, then tapped politely on the bathroom door. "Come on, Miss Mermaid. Time's up."

At last Ivy emerged from the bathroom, yelling for Mom to untangle her hair and to find her nightgown. Mom called for me to see that Edmund took his turn in the tub, and would I also please comb out Ivy's hair and go upstairs and find the nightgown, because now she had a *splitting* headache and she'd made the tea too weak and was going to have to start over with a fresh pot.

The little cottage reverberated with agitation, and Mom wasn't the only one who had a headache. My own head was starting to pound. After my afternoon with the police and my evening with the Glendennings, I needed peace and quiet and a good book to read in bed. I didn't want to sit and drink tea with Mom, and not with Quent, either. Not even with Duncan, really.

Dad, I thought.

I needed my dad. Somehow he'd always had a way of making me feel snug and safe.

Safe? But I was safe here, wasn't I?

Liza Pethering hadn't been. The thought stabbed through my head as I called to Mom that I'd take care of everything. I pushed thoughts of Liza away, and I shepherded my sister up the stairs, glad to see that the sunroom door at the end of the hall was closed.

Mom seemed totally frazzled. Being a single mother wasn't agreeing with her, obviously. *Good,* I thought unfeelingly as I combed the snarls out of Ivy's hair. Maybe she'd see now that life with Dad wasn't so terrible after all.

Life with Dad was just plain easier. He helped us kids with homework projects and got the Goops ready for bed, and made bowls of popcorn for us all to munch while watching videos on the weekends, and he gave really amazing shoulder massages . . . or at least he used to do all that back before he'd started working such long hours.

Maybe if Dad promised to change his schedule and be home more often, Mom would move us back to California. I pictured her down in the sitting room, sprawled on the couch, eyes closed—and I imagined Dad materializing like a genie at her side, holding out a fresh cup of tea and offering a shoulder rub. Then he'd get the Goops into bed, and finish off my algebra problems. . . . Liza would still be dead, but everything else would be so much better with Dad in the picture again.

From downstairs we heard the slam of the bathroom door. Then a howl of anguish. Then Edmund called up to us that the bathwater was COLD. Ivy and I started searching for her nightgown. "Dad called while you were out," she reported, as I lay on her floor to fish under the bed. It was almost as if she had read my mind. I pulled out the nightgown, along with her polar bear. "Dad said he missed us. I told him we were missing him, too, and the weather here is pretty good, like spring, and he should come to visit."

"Did he say he'd come?" I asked, handing Ivy the nightgown and setting Polar on the dresser.

"He said sometime, but . . . well, he's busy working on a big project right now." She slipped on the nightgown, then reached for her stuffed animal and dusted him off.

Those eternal big projects were what drove Mom away in the first place. I sighed, and Ivy touched my hand.

"Jule?"

I looked down at her thin, troubled face framed in yellow curls. "What?"

"Are they, you know . . . getting divorced?"

"I hope not. But . . . I just don't know."

"They can't!" Ivy hugged her polar bear hard, then stormed out of the room and down the stairs. "Mom!" she yelled at the top of her voice. "You can't get divorced! I know you love Daddy, and I know he loves you, and so why can't you just live together like before and work things out!"

We heard the creak as the bathroom door opened a crack and Edmund's voice shouted out in agreement: "Yeah!" Then the door slammed again. I sank onto Ivy's bed. Downstairs I could hear the murmur of Mom's voice, calming our resident drama queen. Then her voice called up the stairs to me, impatient.

"Juliana, *will* you get these kids into bed?"

Resentfully I trudged downstairs to retrieve Ivy. At least if Mom kept me busy I'd have less chance to think about everything.

At last the Goops were tucked into their beds, reading mystery novels. I kissed each of them good night, and all my irritation with them vanished at their sweet smiles. They were my brother and sister, fully and completely and forever. And it didn't matter one bit if we didn't have the same ancestors. We were family now, and we loved and needed each other, and that was what counted.

Tiredly I made my way downstairs, and Mom made sure I felt loved and needed by asking me to fold laundry and take it upstairs, and then to sweep the kitchen floor and wash the tea things. At last I was on my way up to bed myself, exhausted. Mom's voice stopped me on the stairs, and I braced for the next work order. But this time her voice was gentle.

"So how was dinner with the Glendennings?" she asked.

"*Ugh.* Celia's weird. But you'd like to see her art. The house is like ten museums stuffed into one."

Mom smiled. "Yes, I can imagine it's a bit daunting to navigate. Quent's told me about her collections."

That reminded me. "Mom, did you ask Quent who else has keys to our cottage?" I came back downstairs and sat with Mom at the table.

"I did," Mom replied. "He said he'd been wondering himself. Liza had her own keys, of course, because she often helped him here with housecleaning and parties. And the Coopers, Duncan's grandparents, have a house key, too, but only for the big house."

"But once they were in the Mill House, they could have found the key to our cottage," I pointed out.

"I suppose that's possible," Mom conceded, "but it's hard to imagine that old couple would have any reason to come over here."

"Well, they didn't like Liza. Something about the Drama Society. And about how she introduced Duncan's father to the Brazilian dancer he ran off with."

Mom laughed. "Not really motives for murder, though."

"I guess not. But . . ."

But that stain was still upstairs in our sunroom, testament to someone's motive. "Anyone else have a key?"

"Yes. Celia does, and Duncan, of course—"

"Celia!"

"Apparently Celia was helping Quent move Nora's artwork out of the studio after her death. He gave her a key so she could come while he was working in London. Quent told me Duncan gave his key back already, but I do want to get Celia's back. And there isn't really any reason the Coopers should have a key to this cottage now that we're living in it. I'll ask Quent to talk to them, too."

"Or change our lock!"

Mom reached across the table and squeezed my hand. "Things will sort themselves out, honey. Now, you'd better get off to bed yourself, don't you think? You look like your head's whirling."

My head *was* whirling. "You're not going over to Quent's?"

"No. I'm not very good company tonight, I'm afraid. I'm going to bed and you should, too." She hesitated, then added, "And I'm sorry to be so—whatever—tonight. Just frazzled, I guess, with everything that's been going on. You've been a very big help at a very trying time. What would I do without my sweet, precious Jule?"

I felt better then, and smiled back at her. "You'd be a wreck," I said. "Life would be totally terrible without me."

She laughed, and agreed, and then we said good night, both of us feeling better. But when I lay in my own narrow bed, trying not to think about the stain on the sunroom floor, I kept hearing Mom's voice, over and over again: *What would I do without my sweet, precious Jule?* and there seemed to be an echo, somehow, or a voice-over, like you hear in films: *What would I do without my sweet precious Jule, sweet precious Jule, my little precious Jewel-baby, my little precious Jewel-baby, are you Buzzy's little precious Jewel-baby?*

The loving voices in my head became a sort of song, a lullaby. And I fell asleep humming along and wondering, *Who in the world was Buzzy?*

———

THE DREAM STARTED with a little girl and a young woman—almost still a girl herself from the look of the long legs sticking out from a short, ruffled blue-jean skirt, skinny arms sticking out of the faded pink flamingo T-shirt. They were walking on the beach, gathering shells . . . and then it was me, that little girl, holding the shells in my hot little hands . . . *Look, Buzzy, shells! Pitty shells!*

"*Yeah, Toots, tons of pretty shells. Let's take 'em home and I'll string 'em together. We'll make a pretty necklace for you.*"

"*No, no! Pitty necklace for Buzzy!*"

"*For me? Well, aren't you a sweet Toots . . .*"

And then another scene, with the little girl leaning over an unsteady card table in a gloomy room, with the shells on the table . . . and the shells in her little hands—no, *my* little hands . . .

"*Okay now—hand me another shell, Toots. Look how I'm stringing 'em onto the yarn—oh, careful! That's a sharp needle . . . see how I'm poking the yarn through the little holes in the shells? They're like beads, aren't they? Shell beads . . . Hey, can you do it? You want to try it all by yourself?*"

And then, still later, a necklace of shells held out for display: "*All finished now! Come here, come try it on.*"

"*No, Buzzy wear it. Pitty necklace for Buzzy!*"

Laughter. "*All right, Toots. You win. I'll wear the necklace, and treasure it forever. It'll be my good luck charm because it's a present from my precious little Jewel-baby . . .*"

14

I woke up to wind rattling the diamond panes in my bedroom window. The dream of those shells lingered. That hot beach . . .

Rain slashed hard against the old stone walls outside. The room felt steeped in cold as I slipped out of bed, shivering, and reached for my thickest fleecy sweatshirt. I pulled it on over my nightgown, and tugged on my thickest socks, too. Then, in search of hot tea and buttered toast, I headed downstairs. Mom called to me from the bathroom, "I thought I heard a knock at the door a moment ago, Jule, but I'm in the tub. Will you check if anyone's there?"

"Sure," I said, and went into the sitting room. I unbolted the front door, and pulled it open to only a gust of cold air. I glanced around, but saw nobody—only a white-dusted garden. *Snow!* But wait, not snow, after all . . . just all the white blossoms from the blackthorn trees blown down in the wind.

I started to close the door, calling to Mom, "It was Mr. Nobody—," but then I broke off as I stumbled over something. Looking down, I gasped.

There on the welcome mat lay a large, oval beach rock. Not the same white-veined one I had taken to the police, of course, but another one—quite similar. There were red words on this rock—careful block letters spelling out a message in bright red paint. I leaned down to read it: *STOP. OR BE STOPPED.* Then in smaller letters, *YANKEES GO HOME.*

I blinked a few times, as if blinking would make the words disappear. Then I lifted my head and looked out at the garden again. I shivered, trembling not only with the chill but now real fear because I knew this was a message. To me.

A warning.

Whoever had killed Liza had left this stone to warn me to stop asking questions. To stop figuring things out. To stop doubting that Simon Jukes had murdered Liza Pethering. The person who left this message might still be nearby, even now, watching me. Despite the cold morning air, I felt myself break out in a sweat.

The back door to the Old Mill House slammed and I saw Duncan start across the blossom-strewn lawn toward our cottage. He waved when he saw me in the open doorway.

I waved back, though my heart was pounding. He approached, grinning, his arms wrapped around his torso dramatically to pantomime the cold. "This is the blackthorn winter Grandad was telling you about," he announced as he reached me. "He'll be absolutely gleeful, you wait and see. He loves to have his weather predictions proved true. Missed his true calling as a weatherman on the news, he did. Anyway, I've come to ask you if you'll come with me tonight to have a meal with them. I'm doing the cooking—that shepherd's pie I was telling you and Kate about."

"Sure," I mumbled. "Sounds good ... but, um, Duncan?"

"Hey, what's this?" He saw the stone at my feet and bent down.

"Wait—don't touch it!" I cautioned. "I just found it here. Someone knocked on our door a few minutes ago. Did you see anybody? I mean, in the garden just now?"

He scanned the garden. "No. Did you?"

"Only you."

He peered at me closely. "I hope you're not thinking *I* left this little gift."

"No . . . but I hoped you might have seen who did."

"Sorry." He nudged the rock with his shoe. "I just finished eating breakfast."

"Maybe Quent saw somebody."

"You'll have to wait till tonight to ask him. He left already for London—he's getting ready for a big show, you know."

"Is the door in the wall the only way into the garden?" I asked.

Duncan pointed to the far end of the extensive garden. "There's a back gate, too. But it's kept locked."

I heard Mom's voice behind me. "Juliana! Close the door—it's freezing in here! Oh, good morning, Duncan. Why don't you come in, too?"

"Mom, we've been left a little, um, *gift.*" I pointed to the rock. "Should I bring it in?"

"What is it?" Mom bent down and read the warning aloud. "*Yankees go home* is clear enough, I'm afraid. But *stop or be stopped*? What can that mean, Juliana?"

"I think it means somebody doesn't like that I took Nora's beach rock to the police. I think it means somebody isn't very happy that you found that bloodstain and told the police."

"Oh, I don't think this has to do with Liza's death," Mom protested. "Simon Jukes is in jail."

"Exactly," I said. "So it isn't Simon Jukes who left this message. It was left by the real murderer." I'd already suspected that Simon Jukes might be innocent, ever since Henry Jukes's outburst after the funeral. Now Mom would have to agree.

But she shook her head. "No, honey. It's probably just some sort of prank. There's anti-American feeling in some places, you know. No reason Blackthorn would be immune."

"You mean you think this is *political*?" I couldn't believe Mom didn't understand. I turned to Duncan. "Do *you* think it's just an 'Americans-go-away' thing?"

He shrugged. "It's terribly rude, and I'm sorry. But I think that's all it is."

Mom went to the kitchen for a dish towel. She wrapped the rock up and carried it back inside. "We'll take this to the police," she said over her shoulder. "After breakfast. Maybe they've got other reports of villagers harassing tourists and foreign visitors." Then, as the Goops came hurtling down the stairs, shouting greetings to Duncan, Mom added in a low voice: "Let's not say anything about this to Ivy and Edmund just now. No sense worrying them."

So we all ate breakfast just as if it were any normal Saturday, and Duncan had a bowl of Mom's thick creamy oatmeal, even though he had already eaten at his house. Mom made the oatmeal the way she always did at home in California, seasoned with salt, but Duncan called it *porridge,* and said eating it with salt instead of sugar was the Scottish way. His own dad had come from Scotland, and that's the way he'd cooked porridge, too. Ivy made predictable jokes about Goldilocks and the three bears, and I tried to ignore the rock that lay behind me, hidden in its towel.

After breakfast, we walked through the village, the cold wind whipping the fallen blackthorn blossoms across the footpaths like swirls of snow. All signs of spring had disappeared. It was depressing. Despite the cold weather, the Goops begged to go down to the beach, and this gave Mom and me the perfect chance to slip away to the police station while Duncan, who offered to supervise, went to the water with them.

Because Mom was with me, the police were extra polite. Detective Inspector Link was in a meeting, we were told by the receptionist at the desk. But Constable Petersen was available, and he told us he would see that the detective was given the stone immediately. They said they didn't know of any particular anti-American sentiment in the village, but they would check around, and would contact us if they had any further questions. In the meantime we should just go on home and forget about it; probably the whole thing was an unpleasant joke.

"That's what I think myself," said Mom. "But we thought you should know."

"I think this means you've got to let Simon Jukes out of jail," I announced. "I think this has to do with Liza's murder."

Constable Petersen shook his head as he saw us out the door. "The rock could have been left by anyone," he replied. "I see no link to the Pethering case."

"I think there *is* a link," I said to Mom as we left the police station and headed back through the village. "I can't help it. Liza didn't like Simon, so why would she have gone with him to our cottage?"

"I can't figure why she would have gone with *anyone* to

our cottage," Mom said, frowning. "But perhaps Simon followed her, and tried to mug her." She veered left into a small alley, past a row of red telephone boxes, to a shop where a sign hanging over a doorway announced: BLACK-THORN BAKERY. A bell rang when we opened the door, and a warm rush of delicious, sugary air enveloped us. "Good morning," said a stocky gray-haired woman. I recognized her as the woman Veronica Pimms had sat with at Liza's funeral.

"Good morning," we replied.

The woman nodded. "American accent on this one," she said (pointing at me), "yet not on this one"—pointing at Mom—"I deduce that you are the new people living in Quent Carrington's garden cottage. Am I right?"

"Yes, you're right," I told her. "And I deduce that you're Veronica Pimms's mother."

"That I am," she said with a smile. "For my sins."

"I saw you at the funeral," I told her.

"Ahh, yes. A sad business all around, though Mrs. Pethering was not very kind to my girl. She upset Ronnie something terrible, giving her the sack like that! So unfair! But it's still a sad thing when a person's life is cut short. Criminal."

Mom murmured agreement. Then Mom started chatting with Veronica's mother about the weather while I leaned over the glass counter, inspecting all the yummy offerings. There were cheese pastries and horn-shaped buns with apple filling, glazed donuts, and sugar-dusted cakes.

The bell rang again, and a rush of cold air hit my back. I looked over my shoulder, and stiffened at the sight of Henry Jukes, Simon's younger brother. He wore a thick, grimy, once-white sweater with frayed cuffs. He looked even worse than he had after the funeral; his longish hair looked greasy and unkempt, as if he hadn't been able to find his comb and brush for weeks. He strode into the shop, saw me looking at him, and pointed a finger at me. "You lookin' at me, girl?"

Hastily, I turned back to Mom. She was paying for a box of pastries.

"You Yanks," snarled Henry. "You the ones come to town and started all the trouble!"

"Now, Henry," began Veronica's mother. "You just calm down, and tell me what I can get for you this morning. Another of those apple buns?"

He ignored Mrs. Pimms, looming over Mom and me. "You the Yanks what got Simon locked up." He glared at Mom and me. "I'd say the coppers ought ter be lookin' at *you* lot, not at me bruvver. It's people like you what ought ter be doin' time. People like you oughtn't to be here, anyway. Go back to yer own country!"

"I'm sure if your brother is innocent, he'll soon be set free—," began Mom.

But Henry, towering over us, raised his hand threateningly and slapped it down hard on the glass countertop. "You Yanks better watch your backs, is all," he growled. Then he fixed his eye on me. Behind his sullen expression I caught a glimpse of something else—something that looked like despair. "You're the kid what said you'd help. Fat lot of help you've been!" Then he spun around and strode out of the shop.

I hesitated, torn between wanting to follow him and tell him I was trying—and with wanting to keep far away.

"Oh dear. Now the poor lad's gone without buying his breakfast," sighed Mrs. Pimms.

"'Poor lad?'" Mom asked, incredulously. "He just threatened us, didn't you hear him? And he seems to have something against Americans. Maybe he's the one who left an unpleasant message on our doorstep."

"Oh, dear, did he?" Mrs. Pimms blinked. "Well, he's just that worried about his brother. He's a bit slow, is our Henry. Always has been. You mustn't mind a thing he says. He looks to his big brother for guidance, he does—even when he'd do better to keep his nose clean and out of trouble. Without Simon at home, poor Henry is lost. He's in here twice a day to buy a pork pie or a bun. The rest of the time he haunts the police station, waiting to talk to Simon."

"I'll take two of those pork pies you just mentioned," said Mom brightly. I had a feeling she was just trying to change the subject, but it worked. We said good-bye to Veronica's mother and left the shop.

"Henry gives me the creeps," I said. "The total creeps. But I don't think *he* left that rock. He wants to know who killed Liza, because then his brother will get out of jail. Whoever left it wants me to *stop* asking questions."

Mom sighed and shook her head. She reached into the plastic sack and pulled out an apple pastry. She broke it in half and handed one piece to me. "Have some comfort food, Jule."

We headed for the beach. "Look, there's Kate." I pointed up ahead where Kate Glendenning was coming up the steps at the seawall. She didn't have a camera slung around her neck for a change. "Hi, Kate!"

She did not seem to hear my call. Without looking, she turned and walked up the road quickly, in the opposite direction from our approach. I winced. Mom looked over at me briefly but didn't say anything.

We stopped at the seawall and looked down at the beach. Duncan and the Goops were at the water's edge, throwing rocks. The tide was coming in and only a sliver of beach remained. Far out on the horizon a tanker was silhouetted against the sky. The wind was piercingly cold, and my hair whipped around my face. I had not taken time this morning to wind it into my usual single braid. Gathering it tightly with two hands, I stuffed it into my hood.

"Ivy!" shouted Mom. "Edmund!" She waved both arms to beckon them. "Time to go home. It's cold out here!"

The Goops paid her no notice. Even Duncan did not turn around from the ocean. The sound of the wind and breaking waves mixed with the screeches of seabirds. "They can't hear you. I'll go get them," I offered, and hurried down the steps to the rocky beach. Fine mist sprayed off the sea. The stones were slick underfoot. Had someone come here last night and chosen one of these stones to leave at our door? The chill in my bones was not only from the wind.

"It's time to get back!" I called, reaching out to touch the sleeve of Duncan's jacket. "Hot soup and hot tea— that's what we need."

My brother and sister ignored me, continuing to lob rocks out to sea.

You have to know how to deal with Goops; I used the ace up my sleeve. "Mom stopped at the bakery on our way here—so there will be donuts and pastries and yummy things for people who cooperate and come *right now.*"

"Hooray—cakes!" shouted Ivy, pivoting instantly and hurtling toward Mom.

"Cinnamon buns!" yelled Edmund, racing after her.

"*Bakery* is one of the magic words," I told Duncan confidingly. My hood fell back and my long hair flew out, whipping against his jacket. I struggled against the wind to bundle it back again.

He turned to me but didn't smile. "So you went to the police?"

"Yes. They said they'd look into it. They said it was probably just a joke."

"Predictable, really," he said. The salt spray from a large wave blew into our faces. We turned and started walking together back to the seawall.

"Kate was here," he said.

"Yes, Mom and I saw her, but she didn't see us. Or acted like she didn't."

"Hmmm," he said. "I invited her to the meal at my grandparents' house tonight—but she turned me down."

"Doesn't trust your shepherd's pie?" I teased.

He didn't laugh. When I looked up at him, his expression was stern. "No, that wasn't it. She said she wouldn't come because *you* were going to be there. And she's not speaking to you."

"Ah," I said. "Because she thinks I suspect her mother of killing Liza."

"And you do?"

"I don't know, Duncan. There's just something really weird about that woman. And she's got something going on with Oliver Pethering, I'm almost positive. And she's rude and—I don't know. Something else. She's always staring at me."

"Suspecting people of murder isn't going to win you many friends, you know." His voice was cool. "This isn't some sort of Hollywood film. Why don't you just trust the police to do their jobs?"

Well, what was I supposed to do? Just forget any of this happened? We'd reached the road now, and started trailing home after Mom and the Goops. Ivy and Edmund were already arguing over how to split the goodies in the bakery bag. "Listen, I'm not trying to cause trouble between you and Kate. It's probably better if I don't come for dinner tonight. Then *she* can."

"So now *you're* the one who doesn't trust my shepherd's pie?" This time when I glanced up at him, the smile was back in his eyes.

"I do! But—"

"Please don't cancel. I want you to come."

We turned onto Water Street and walked along to the red door in the stone wall. Someone had smeared something brown all over the door.

"Dog poop! Eww, gross!" screeched the Goops. I groaned.

Mom leaned over to sniff. "No—it's just mud," she said reassuringly. "Probably just a kids' prank. Let's not worry about it."

"Henry Jukes," I muttered under my breath. Mom unlocked the door and ushered the Goops inside. I lingered for a moment with Duncan. "It's another warning, don't you think?"

"Well, Henry has always been a slow-witted troublemaker. He might smear mud on the door, but he wouldn't leave you painted messages on rocks."

"Why not?"

"Can't spell," Duncan said simply. "Writes his own name like a three-year-old, from what I remember of him at school. He'd be more likely to lob the rock through your window to get his message across. Now, stop suspecting everybody!"

Yeah, right. Easy enough for *him* to bark out orders like that since he wasn't the one being threatened. But I invited Duncan to stay for lunch, anyway. I didn't want to be fighting with him. He thanked me, said he had a project for school to work on, and we agreed to meet again at six o'clock to walk together over to his grandparents' house for dinner. I hoped he really did have homework, and wasn't just saying that because he was annoyed with me for upsetting Kate.

Mom opened tins of chicken barley soup and sliced apples and divided the pastries, and we ate lunch. Then the phone rang, and it was two new friends that Ivy and Edmund had met at school, a brother and sister from their class, asking if they could play together up on Castle Hill.

"It's lovely that you're finding chums so quickly," Mom said, adding that they could play on the hill if I went with them.

Why not? I thought. It wasn't as if *my* new "chums" were eager for my company. I might as well hang out with nine-year-olds.

It did me good to be outside again in the brisk, cold air. The site of Blackthorn's ancient castle was a couple of hundred feet high, rising up behind Castle Hill Lane. Edmund and Ivy and their new pals, dark-haired Sophie and Charlie-Tom (who the Goops informed me were *also* twins), raced up the switchback path to the top of Castle Hill. I climbed at a slower pace. Finally we reached the top, a flattened, windswept space. It wasn't hard to believe a castle had once been here. At the far side of the clearing were ancient stone foundations. We climbed on them, and I read aloud from the wooden sign on a post that explained how the castle had been erected between 1237 and 1250 by the Alnwick family. The castle began crumbling a hundred years later. The Alnwick family fortune had dwindled and there were no funds for repairs, so the family left. The castle was pulled down by villagers who then used the stones to build their own homes at the base of the hill. Much of Blackthorn had been built from the ancient castle stone.

Edmund snorted. "Other castles are still standing after zillions of years, but this old thing crumbled after only a hundred!"

"Crumbling Castle! That's what we'll call it," Ivy decided.

"That's a good name," said Sophie. "And let's pretend there's a ghost."

"I suppose they used ghostly mortar to hold it all together," sneered Charlie-Tom. "That's why it tumbled down!"

Edmund laughed.

The girls were climbing on the foundation stones. Their voices carried back to me. "I'll be the queen and you be the servant," instructed Ivy, typically.

"Right-o," agreed Sophie. Obviously she was going to be the perfect new pal for my sister.

I brushed fallen white blossoms off one of the wooden benches at the edge of the hill and settled myself gingerly onto the damp seat. The view was amazing, with the fields and woods on one side and the sea on the other, framing the whole of the village. I stared out at the panorama of Blackthorn below us, searching for the Old Mill House and our cottage. The features of Blackthorn were becoming familiar to me now. I located the Glendennings' house, Ivy and Edmund's school, the church, the village cemetery, Liza's studio, and the Pethering home in The Mews. I could see people down there, looking like beetles, making their way through the village on errands or whatever. Most were probably very friendly people I would like to meet, or had already met. One was the person who had left the rock on our doorstep.

There were as many people who had hated Liza as there were cobbled lanes in Blackthorn, I thought. All those twisting, narrow lanes and high stone walls . . . It was such a small town, and the architecture reflected the way people lived in it. A beautiful place, and full of charm, but also full of secrets.

Stop. Or be stopped.

My head ached. I pressed my fingers to my eyes, then to my forehead, massaging gently. The sounds of the children's play receded. When I opened my eyes, the low, wet clumps of heather and bare-branched blackthorns edging Castle Hill shimmered for a second, and then were gone. In their places were tall, dry beach grasses and scattered palm trees. Instead of the shouts of the Goops and their friends, two other voices—women's voices, I thought—low and intense, filtered through my head:

We made a deal and you're in on it. No backing out.

I'm not backing out—I'm just asking for a little more time to get the money . . .

You'd better come up with it. You have till tomorrow—

I can't leave my kid!

Oh, don't worry, I'll watch her . . .

I blinked, and the voices were gone—along with the palm trees and long grasses waving in the dry California air. I was sitting on a cold bench in a brisk English wind.

But . . . whose voices had I heard?

And . . . what was I remembering?

"HULLO, JULIANA!" MY reverie was broken by the sound of my name, shouted out by a group of people heading up the switchback trail below me. I blinked, then recognized Kate, followed by some of the kids I'd met at the Angel Cafe—Alina, Brian, and Will.

I stood up and waved to them. "Hi!" I called. Panting slightly, they arrived at the top. Kate had been leading the way but now hung back. Alina and the boys walked over to my bench.

"Marvelous view," said Brian.

"Yes, it is," I agreed.

Alina sank onto the bench next to me. "Do you come up here often? I come alone whenever I get the chance. It's a good place to think."

"Alina's our village poet," Will informed me. "She's always writing stuff. Won a poetry competition at school last week, she did."

"That's great," I said. "Congratulations, Alina!" Then I glanced over at the ruins. "But I'm not alone. My brother and sister and two other kids are chasing ghosts."

"Remember, Brian? How you and Harry and I used to chase all sorts of villains up here?" Will asked. "It was a great place to hang out when we were babies."

"Where's Harry now?" I asked, noticing that Will's brother wasn't with them.

"With Duncan MacBennet. Got a science project for school." Will crowded onto the bench next to Alina. "We've got projects, too, but we're procrastinating."

"And since there's nothing whatsoever to do in Blackthorn besides schoolwork," Brian added tersely, "we wander the streets and the hills."

"I don't blame old Veronica Pimms for leaving school," said Will. "Sensible girl."

"Don't be stupid." Alina frowned at him. "She's gotten into more trouble *out* of school than when she was *in* school. You know, I do worry about her. She's working two jobs now, and it's all very well, but how long will she last?"

"She's got a sort of talent for getting herself sacked," agreed Brian. "Skimming a few quid now and then out of the cash register . . . Poking her nose in everybody's business . . . Can't really blame people for firing her."

"No," agreed Will. "She'd better watch out that she doesn't get herself arrested. Liza Pethering once told my mum she'd caught Veronica red-handed, going through her handbag! Ronnie had taken Liza's wallet *and* her keys, just as cool as you please. And then returned them! Some nerve, that girl." He sounded faintly awed.

"Well, at least she returned them," Brian pointed out. "It shows she's not really dishonest at heart. But—what guts!"

Veronica's boastful words came back to me: *I copied 'em, didn't I . . . Silly cow.*

Alina was frowning at the boys. "Don't sound so impressed! And don't you two start hanging out with her."

"Aww, come on," drawled Brian. "It's just so *boring* being good."

Now Alina laughed. "You're not being very good today though, are you—trying to escape from having to chat with your auntie Mary!"

She turned to me. "Brian's aunt drove down from London. She's not his favorite person, so Kate and I came by to rescue him. Then we found Will sloping off from the library. It's that sort of day, I guess. Where you want to make an escape. Is that why you're up here, Juliana?"

"Not exactly. I'm just babysitting." I looked over where Kate was standing at the edge of the hill, gazing down. "Were you escaping from something, Kate?"

She didn't answer me directly, but just kept staring down at the village. "It's a lovely little place," she said dreamily. "And from up here it looks so peaceful. From up here there's no hint of all the turmoil. Funny, that."

I wondered if she were referring to the murder. I wondered if she had come up here to get away from her overbearing mother.

"No hint of gloomy Aunt Mary," added Brian with a grin.

"It looks so small," Alina observed, pointing down at the cluster of buildings framed by woods and ocean, "but there's a lot going on, really. A lot of people and a lot of stories. A lot of friendships and lives twined together. That's what's nice about a small village where everybody knows everybody." She laughed lightly. "I feel a poem coming on!"

"You should write one about all the angers and hostilities down there, too," I suggested drily. And then I told the kids about the warning rock left on our doorstep. Kate turned away from the view and looked at me with wide, surprised eyes. But she didn't say anything.

Brian did. "That's terrible!" he exclaimed. "I'm sorry, Juliana."

"You would think that in such a small town," Will said, "with everyone knowing everyone's business, we could figure out who would do such a thing."

"You'd think it would be obvious who murdered Liza Pethering, too," I said. "But it isn't."

"Of course it is," said Alina in surprise. And Brian nodded. "Simon Jukes did it," Will asserted. "And it's a relief to have him locked up."

I looked over at Kate, and she was staring down at the village again, silent.

THE OTHER KIDS chatted with me a while longer then continued their walk. I hung out until the cold wind was making me shiver, then rounded up the Goops and their friends and hiked back down to the village. It was good to get home, out of the wind. I hunkered down in the little bathtub and tried scrubbing the uncomfortable parts of the afternoon—the weird vision and voices, and Kate's hostility—out of my head while at the same time washing my hair. The bathroom was much colder than the rest of the cottage. And without a shower to sluice all the cream rinse out of my hair, I was having a hard time. My hair was long, my legs were long, there just didn't seem to be enough space in the tub, and the water from the silly rubber spray attachment was spraying all over the place. When I finally emerged from the tub, all clean but shivering, I still had to mop up the floor on hands and knees, using two towels, and wipe down the walls. By the time I finished, I felt exhausted. I thought of my private bathroom at home, tiled in sky blue with sea green accents, with the huge walk-in shower and adjustable showerhead with five different functions: *Massage. Waterfall. Gentle Rain. Mist. Pulse.* The bathroom had been designed and built by my dad, as had our whole house.

Dad, I thought, invoking his name as if he could banish all my troubles. I wrapped up in a towel and sidled out of the bathroom and through the kitchen, peering around corners to make sure the coast was clear before dashing up the stairs to my bedroom. I put on a black skirt and my fleecy sweatshirt, combed out my hair and braided it into one long tail while it was still wet, and stood there staring into the mirror, wondering whether Duncan thought I was pretty. Should I wear makeup?

Then came a knock on the front door and yodeling from the Goops as they welcomed Duncan. I smeared on a little lip gloss. That would have to be enough in the glamour department.

We walked across Blackthorn in the dark, in the cold. No rain so far tonight, but the air felt thick and smelled salty. Duncan didn't have much to say, but his shoulder jostled mine companionably as we walked. "Is Kate coming, too?" I asked as we arrived at his grandparents' house.

"No," Duncan told me shortly. "She couldn't be persuaded."

"Sorry."

"Not a problem," he said, and opened the Coopers' front door. "Come on in. Grandad and Granny are glad you're joining us."

I stepped inside and was immediately enveloped in stifling heat. The small sitting room had a fire lit in the grate *and* an electric space heater glowing in the center of the room. I shrugged out of my jacket as fast as I could.

Dudley Cooper, wearing a woolen vest over a long-sleeved flannel shirt, came to greet me. His wife, also dressed warmly in a wool skirt and sweater (*jumper,* Mom had told me it was called here), was right behind him. "We're so glad you could come, dear," she said to me in her sweet, quavery voice. "It's so good for Duncan to have someone new as his taste tester. It's all very well to learn to cook when you're just feeding family members, right, Dunk-o? But it's much more of a challenge, feeding a pretty girl!"

"Oh, Granny," Duncan said, reddening. "Well, we'll see if she likes it." Then to me he added, "I hope you're hungry!"

"Ravenous," I said, and it was the truth. But before I could be led into the dining room for the meal, Hazel Cooper patted the couch and smiled at me.

"Come sit here by me on the settee, dear," she said invitingly.

So I had to stay in that stifling room and chat with the Coopers while Duncan holed up in the kitchen making last-minute preparations. A large yellow cat leaped up onto my lap and settled down without any proper introductions. Hazel Cooper laughed.

"Well, now, that's Parsley. He's our old puss, and a good boy he is. We've had him since he was a kitten, and do you know? He's nearly eighteen years old, best we can figure. Eighteen! Have you ever heard of a cat living that long? And look how healthy he is! You're a lovely old puss, you are," she said, and reached over to pat the cat. I stroked his head and he started purring hard.

Dudley Cooper leaned toward me from his armchair. "Ah, a cat person. Cat people are always welcome here. Do you and your brother and sister have cats at home?"

"No," I said. "But we want a dog. So far our parents keep saying no."

"Try asking for a cat," advised Mrs. Cooper. "They're much cleaner."

Politely I said I might do that.

"So," said Mr. Cooper after a moment of silence during which I continued to stroke Parsley's head, "Dunk-o tells me you've received a threatening message. I'm sorry there's some anti-American sentiment in Britain, though you'll find most people don't share that feeling."

"I know," I said. "I don't really think the rock was left because we're American."

"Oh?" queried Mrs. Cooper.

"I think it's to do with the murder."

"Ah," said Mr. Cooper.

"That Simon Jukes is a bad 'un," Mrs. Cooper said comfortably. "I remember him as a lad—always had something up his sleeve. Always causing trouble, one way or t'other."

"But no doubt he'll be out on the streets of Blackthorn soon enough," added Mr. Cooper. "Soon as our American detective finds someone else to lock up in his place." He smiled slyly at his wife, then looked back at me. "Duncan tells us you're not convinced that Jukes is the murderer. Do you have a suspect in mind, dear girl?"

"Well, not really," I hedged. I could feel an air of suppressed excitement in the overheated room. "Do *you* have a suspect?"

Mr. Cooper shrugged. "I think enquiries into the case are best left to the professionals. The police are investigating, and in time all will become clear."

Mrs. Cooper coughed behind her hand. Her husband looked over at her with raised eyebrows. "I was just thinking," she told him softly, "about all the damage that Pethering woman did to our family. We're well rid of her, I don't mind saying."

"Now, Hazel," Mr. Cooper cautioned her. "All that happened a long time ago."

"It feels like yesterday," she said. I noticed her hands were never still. They moved in her lap, straining together, fingers wringing fingers. She turned to me. "One thing leads to another," she repeated. "You've got to watch out because any one little thing you do sets another in motion—and then you've got a chain of events unfolding."

"Like dominoes?" I ventured. I wasn't sure where this conversation was going. I hoped Duncan was nearly finished with his dinner preparations.

"Exactly!" Mrs. Cooper nodded at me. "The domino effect, exactly. You see, one day Liza Pethering met an Argentinian dancer in London and struck up a friendship. The woman was probably a stripper—and a prostitute—"

"Now, Hazel darling," Mr. Cooper interrupted. "Eliana was from Brazil, not Argentina. And we don't know she was a . . . lady of the evening. We don't know that for sure."

His wife ignored him. She reached over and put a trembling hand on my knee. "That meeting in London was the first domino tipping over," she whispered harshly. "And it led to the others falling, too. Because next thing anybody knew, Liza invited this 'lady of the evening' dancer friend here to Blackthorn. To have her portrait painted! And all hell broke loose."

"She took to sitting in the pub every evening," Mr. Cooper reported, leaning in closer to me. "And Ian—that was our Nora's husband, you know, and Duncan's dad— was a regular at the pub. So he met Eliana. And then—"

"More dominoes," said Mrs. Cooper. "Ian started

sneaking out to be with that tart! Sneaking out on our Nora, can you imagine!"

"But that can't be Liza's fault, really," I felt I had to protest.

"Perhaps not at first," Mrs. Cooper allowed, "but Liza helped them get together! She invited Ian to use her gallery as a trysting spot! Knowing all the while that her old friend Nora was thinking Ian was at work."

"She was always envious of Nora's talent as an artist," pronounced Mr. Cooper. "That's what it was. Liza was out to hurt our Nora because she was jealous. Nora was on her way up—her painting career was really taking off and the London critics were taking notice . . . Oh, yes indeed. Jealousy is a powerfully motivating force, I can tell you that."

Dudley Cooper was a fine one to talk about jealousy. I remembered his anger at not being given the lead in *Voyage of the Jumblies*.

But Mrs. Cooper was nodding in agreement with her husband. "People who are jealous will do anything. Anything at all." She met her husband's eye, and I saw a wordless communication pass between them.

What? I wondered, frowning. I was so hot now, I was sweating freely. The cat was like a hot water bottle in my lap, and my braid felt heavy on my back. *What are you saying to each other?*

"So, has *Voyage of the Jumblies* been canceled?" I asked abruptly. Speaking of jealousy.

They both turned round, blue gazes on me. "Not at all," Mr. Cooper said after a moment. "No need for that! Not after I stepped in as director. Reassigned a few parts, organized a group to do the set design . . ."

"Yes," added Mrs. Cooper with pride. "Dudley even

got some members of Girl Guides over here the other day after school for a meeting; they'll do the posters and advertising—"

"The show must go on!" bellowed Mr. Cooper, punching the air with one fist. He was grinning like a maniac. "Isn't that right, Dunk-o, my lad?"

I turned at the sound of a bell being rung from the doorway. There, thank goodness, stood Duncan, wearing one of his grandmother's frilly aprons over his jeans. He waved a little handbell. "Dinner is served," he announced. I stood up with a feeling of relief. Parsley jumped down and zoomed under the couch.

Hazel Cooper led the way out of the hot sitting room into a dining room that was cool by comparison. Duncan had set the table with his grandparents' best china. "I hope it's okay to use it, Granny," he said, helping her to her seat. "I just moved everything that was on the table over to the sideboard."

"Everything looks lovely, Dunk-o," she said, smiling at him. "I always say it's good to get the nice things out and use them often. Not only at Christmas."

"And serviettes, too," said Mr. Cooper approvingly. I looked around for a "serviette," and figured he must mean the napkins under each fork. "Now let's light these candles."

As Mrs. Cooper lit the white candles in the silver candleholders, Duncan held out a chair for me in true gentlemanly fashion. I sat down and unfolded my cloth napkin. As I did so, my elbow bumped the piece of furniture at my side. I glanced over. It was the sideboard, an antiquey-looking long dresser. The drawers probably held the Coopers' table linen and silverware. The top of the sideboard was piled high with sheets of poster board, papers, scissors, and glue. There was a basket holding markers in all colors. And then I saw something that made my eyes widen: a cluster of small paint pots. Yellow, blue, and red.

Bright red paint, next to a mug full of brushes.

15

I told myself I was being stupid. Anybody in this village of artists could have red paint. *But Mr. and Mrs. Cooper aren't artists!* I pushed the thought away. Pots of red paint were probably a dime a dozen—or in England, ten pence a dozen—and anybody was allowed to have them. I remembered they'd said the Girl Guides were making posters. The paint didn't mean a thing. I was being ridiculous.

Duncan's shepherd's pie was delicious. The concoction of beef and onions, tomatoes and peas topped with a thick layer of mashed potatoes quickly disappeared from my plate. I smiled and exclaimed over how good everything was, and answered the Coopers' questions about my home in California and about my dad and my school and my friends—still, I was super-aware of the red paint only an arm's length away.

At the end of the meal I offered to help Duncan clear the dishes, but he urged me to relax and wait while he brought in the dessert. The dessert was something called sticky toffee pudding, and it was luscious, and served with thick, hot custard poured over the top. It was so good, it took my mind off the paint for a while. I begged Duncan to come make this same meal for my mom and the Goops as soon as possible. He looked pleased and promised he would.

Mrs. Cooper seemed delighted at Duncan's success as a chef. "I always did say that boys need to know how to cook just as much as girls do," she told me heartily. "Our Nora was fabulous in the kitchen, I saw to that! But I would have made sure a son was just as good."

"My mum was a great cook," Duncan affirmed with a smile. "And Granny is, too."

Could I cook? they wondered. Was my mother a good cook? Talk turned to my family again. The Coopers asked what we'd already seen of the area. Had we gone to Hoarcute House, the stately home just two miles away in Lower Dillingham? "That's a must-see," said Mr. Cooper. "It's even grander than Quent Carrington's Mill House, if you can imagine. Owned by the National Trust since the war. Families just can't keep up a place like that—even wealthy families, not anymore. Dunk-o, you ought to take this young lady there! Do some sightseeing."

"I'd like to, Grandad. And also up Castle Hill. I was hoping we could have a picnic, Juliana. But now the weather's turned rotten again—we might need to wait till it's *truly* spring."

"It's the blackthorn winter," Mr. Cooper said gleefully. He pointed at me. "You know, my girl, that in the past the thorns of the blackthorn were made into ink? And the bark of the blackthorn was stripped and boiled to make a lovely red dye for linens and wool? A very useful bush is the blackthorn—and not only for predicting a false spring!"

"That's right," added Mrs. Cooper. "In fact, you can make all sorts of syrups and jellies from the blackthorn fruit. They ripen in late summer, but they're edible only if there's been a really good frost earlier in the year. Luscious blue black fruit, like plums."

"We have plum trees at home," I offered.

"My dad once tried to make sloe gin from the black-thorn fruit," Duncan told me. "It didn't turn out very well, but apparently it used to be made and drunk often around here."

"Just the thing for harsh winter weather!" cackled Mr. Cooper. "Have we got any sloe gin, Hazel? Or sloe wine for these children to take on their picnic?"

"Nonsense," said Mrs. Cooper cheerfully. "It'll be a real English picnic, Dunk-o. I'll pack you a nice basket, and you take along your umbrellas in case of rain. A little cold and damp never hurt a soul!"

"And there are benches up there," I offered. "We wouldn't have to sit on the ground."

"So you've been up Castle Hill already?" asked Mr. Cooper, approvingly.

"Just today," I told them. "But it would be nice to go again with Duncan."

Duncan winked at me. We decided we'd go the very next day. Then as we finished eating, Dudley Cooper re-galed us with facts and folklore about the ancient Castle Alnwick.

"There's a connection between this little house and that old castle, believe it or not," he told me. "But you'll never guess what it is!"

"No, you never will!" laughed Hazel Cooper. "Go on and guess, luv."

"Ummm, could it be that this house is built from the old castle stones?" I asked.

"Oh, probably," said Dudley Cooper dismissively. "Most buildings in Blackthorn are. But this special connec-tion is much more intriguing. Look, let me get the news clippings!" He shuffled over to the sideboard, moved aside the red pot of paint, and opened one of the drawers. From among a welter of papers, he managed to extract just the one he needed: a yellowing newspaper cutting. He brought it to the table and showed me. It was dated June 12, 1979.

"We were having a problem with our drains under the house back then," Mr. Cooper explained. "Remember that, dear?"

Mrs. Cooper nodded. "Yes, there was a foul smell coming out of the kitchen sink. So we had to call in the experts, and they said they were going to have to take up part of our kitchen floor and dig down under the house to clean out the old pipes and lay new pipes. Well, what can you do? I figured it would be a fine time to remodel the old kitchen as well. Get some new cabinets and nice lino on the floor. Well, you'll never guess! They ripped up the old floorboards, and went down under the house, digging a huge hole . . . and when they were fitting new pipes, you'll never guess what they uncovered!"

"A tunnel!" cried Mr. Cooper, his blue eyes bright with excitement. "Right next to our pipe system. Built of the ancient castle stones! Our repair crew contacted the newspaper, and the work on the sewage drains had to stop while historians and archaeologists were called in to figure out what the tunnel was and who had built it."

"Turns out to be an escape tunnel," Mrs. Cooper clarified. "Built back when Castle Alnwick was still standing. Probably built with the thought that there might be a siege someday, and if the enemy had the family trapped inside the castle walls, the poor family could escape right under their enemies' noses!"

I examined the newspaper article and accompanying

photo that showed a much younger Dudley and Hazel
Cooper standing with smiles on their faces, pointing down
into a huge hole.

"How exciting!" I said. Our own house back in California had been designed and built by my dad. It was airy and
big and modern, with beautiful landscaping and a hot tub
on the deck, but it had no history and contained no mysteries. Personally I liked the safety in that, but I knew some
people—like my sister, Ivy—preferred old houses *because*
of the secrets they might contain. "My little sister would
love to see this news clipping," I said. "She's really interested in history."

"Of course, the tunnel didn't end here at our house
back in castle times," Duncan said. "Our house wasn't even
here until the mid-1800s; this property was probably just a
field when the tunnel was built. But it's still interesting."

"Did you get to walk through the tunnel?" I asked the
Coopers.

They shook their heads. "No, although I did climb
down for a look," said Mr. Cooper. "Walked back about
fifty feet. Shone my torch around for a few minutes. But
nobody knows how stable the old stones are, so we didn't
go farther. Didn't want to risk a cave-in."

I pictured Mr. Cooper venturing into a black hole with
a fiery torch of burning grasses. "Why didn't you just take
a flashlight?" I asked.

When Duncan looked at me quizzically, I added,
"Wouldn't it have been easier?"

It took another minute of puzzlement for us all to work
out that we were talking about the same thing, and that in
England flashlights are called *torches*, and it was a *flashlight*
that Mr. Cooper had taken down into the tunnel with him

rather than a flaming stick. Obviously Mom hadn't completely covered my new English vocabulary.

"All right, all right," I said, laughing a little. "But what would people in castle times have used? They didn't have batteries then, of course. Would there be enough oxygen through the whole long tunnel for lanterns or fire-torches? It's a pretty long way up to the top of Castle Hill from here."

"Good point," said Duncan.

"Vents," said his grandfather. "The archaeologist found one out in our garden, covered by a metal grate, though it's pretty much covered now by earth. Probably there are others along the route. Must also be covered up now by gardens and houses."

"In California we sometimes hear of ancient Indian artifacts being found when a new house is being built," I said. "It always makes the evening news."

"Well, our tunnel was on the news for a few days," laughed Mr. Cooper. "Our moment in the sun, eh, Hazel?"

"Underground, dear. No sun there," she quipped. Then she started clearing the table, but Duncan jumped up to stop her.

"Oh, no, Granny," he said. "You and Grandad go have another chat with Juliana in the sitting room while I wash up."

No way was I going to be stuck back in that hot little room with the Coopers, chatting while I slow-roasted. "I'm great at washing dishes," I insisted. "And fast. We'll do them together."

I carried cups of tea into the sitting room for his grandparents, and then we were alone in the kitchen. He filled the dishpan with hot, sudsy water. I unfolded a clean dish towel and stood ready to dry.

He was in high spirits. "I'm glad you liked the shepherd's pie," he said, scrubbing the casserole dish. "But I hope you'll be hungry again for our picnic tomorrow because Granny packs enough for an army. I bet there will be at least half a roast chicken and a dozen sandwiches, not to mention an entire chocolate cake and some scones, too, for good measure!"

I laughed distractedly. He handed me the dish to dry and a rivulet of water ran out onto my sleeve.

"Oh, wait a minute—you need protection!" he said, taking one of his grandmother's aprons from the hook next to the back door. "Here—turn around." And when I did, he wrapped the apron around my waist. He tied the sash in a big bow, then let his hand trail slowly down my back.

Any other time I would have wanted to savor that touch and lean back into his arms. I'd want to turn up my face for the kiss that we both knew burned between us. But . . . there was a collection of round beach stones lined up on the window ledge above the sink.

I stiffened.

"What's wrong?" he asked me. "You're not an apron-wearing sort of woman?" His voice was warm and teasing. But I couldn't play along. "What is it?" He turned me around to face him.

I pointed back at the stone collection, silent. Then I glanced out the kitchen doorway into the dining room. "Look on the sideboard," I whispered.

"It's a mess," he acknowledged. "But—so what? Are you the sort of girl to get upset about a lapse in housekeeping? Or doesn't like rock collections?"

"Of course I'm not," I said wearily. "It's not about the

mess. It's about . . . the paint. And the rocks are *beach* rocks, Duncan."

He looked perplexed. I walked into the dining room and picked up the little red pot.

"What are you suggesting, Juliana?" His voice, deepening, told me I'd better not be suggesting anything. "This is paint I was using this afternoon for my science project."

I was relieved. "Oh, so you bought it yourself—just this afternoon?"

"No." He looked at me closely. "The Girl Guides were using it last week. Why?"

"Well," I hedged. "It's just . . . well, you know. And there are those stones by the sink."

"You can't be thinking my grandparents painted that warning on the beach rock."

"Well, of course not. I mean, not *really*. But, well, I'm just *wondering*—"

His frown was fierce. "You can't be thinking either of my grandparents would take one of their stones, and then paint it, and then carry it all the way across town to your cottage!"

"Look, I'm just trying to figure out—"

"You can't sit here and chat with this wonderful old couple, and eat their food and accept their hospitality, and then accuse them of *murder!*" Duncan's voice was cold.

"Well, I haven't actually accused them of anything, have I?" I said with asperity, "since you won't let me get a word out!"

"Why would they have killed Liza Pethering, anyway?"

"They hated her! They spent the whole time you were

getting the dinner ready telling me how much they despised her!"

"You're sick, Juliana."

"Oh—am I?" I untied the sash of the apron, my fingers fumbling in rage. Then I flung the apron onto a dining room chair.

"Yes, you are." He grabbed my shoulders. I felt his thumbs pressing hard.

Unhand me, I thought dramatically, trying to believe we were still friends, still somehow just playing. But I didn't say anything, because we both knew, really, that this was no game.

I took a deep, shuddering breath. "Listen, Duncan. I can't blame you for being loyal to your grandparents. But you can't blame *me* for wanting to know what's going on. Someone left a scary message on a rock at my door. Written in red paint. And your grandparents both sat there before dinner going on and on about how Liza Pethering ruined their daughter's life. Things start to add up, Duncan, that's all."

I wrenched myself out of his grip.

He laughed, but it wasn't a happy sound. "Just remember how bad you are at algebra. Adding up numbers isn't exactly your strong suit."

I walked into the hall and grabbed my coat off the hook. "Please tell your grandparents I had to leave."

"Are you going to the police about this stupid pot of paint?" He hurried after me to the front door. "And the stones?"

"I should." I opened the door.

"Anyone can buy red paint, Juliana! Lots of people pick

up stones from the beach. They'll just laugh you out of town."

"Good night, Duncan," I mumbled. My stomach was in knots. "Thanks for the meal."

"Wait—," I heard him say, but I turned and practically ran down Castle Street.

I'm losing friends just about as fast as I make them, I thought. *First Kate. Now Duncan.* I ran faster, needing the rush of cold air on my face, cold air in my lungs. I didn't know what I thought anymore. Nothing made sense. But every day I was finding new sources of unease.

As I neared the Old Ship, a hooded figure moved out of the old stone archway. The low-lying fog made it seem to glide down the street ahead of me—like a ghost. But when the person glanced back, almost furtively, the hood fell back and I saw it was Veronica Pimms. Before I could say anything or even lift my arm to wave, she ducked out of sight down an alleyway. I shivered, tucking my hands into my pockets.

Veronica Pimms looked guilty of something. Was it pilfering from the cash register of the Old Ship—or something far worse?

It would make everything so much easier if I could just believe, as everyone else did, that Simon Jukes was guilty as charged. If only it hadn't been for my encounter with Henry Jukes after the funeral—and his protest that his brother was innocent and the two brothers had been together the whole evening. The police discounted Henry's testimony. But I had seen something in his eyes that convinced me—another outsider looking in—that he was telling the truth. Yet if his brother Simon hadn't killed Liza—did that mean Veronica had? Or did I really suspect the Coopers of coming into our house and knocking Liza Pethering on the head, then dragging her to drown in the Shreen, then leaving that rock on our doorstep as a warning to me to stop asking questions? Did I really think Celia Glendenning could have done those things? Or Oliver Pethering? I remembered how the Coopers talked about Liza, how much they disliked her. I remembered Celia's fury over the ugly portrait. I remembered that Oliver's photograph stood on her bedside table, and Oliver had not seemed overly upset at his wife's funeral. But were these really reasons to kill?

Was *anything* a reason to kill?

The question reminded me of Dad. He and I would often have philosophical conversations during Saturday morning bike rides in the park, asking each other questions. If there were a fire and you could save only three things you own, what would they be and why? If you had to choose between drinking a cup of urine or drinking a cup of blood, which would it be? Would you ever want to travel in a spaceship to Mars? Would you still go if it meant you could never return to Earth? Would there be any reason you would kill another person? If so, why?

These questions roiled around in my head as I ran, muddling my thoughts and making my heart pound. And suddenly I wanted my dad desperately. As I turned the corner onto Dark Lane, I stumbled on the old cobblestones and had to put out my arms to keep from falling.

What kept me from falling was a person—a man.

"Dad?" I cried out.

But of course it wasn't Dad. The man held me up and we staggered together against a lamppost. "Whoa, girl!"

"Oh—sorry!" I said, catching my breath.

"No harm done," the man said, setting me back on my feet. He was tall, like my dad, but that was the only resemblance. He was wearing a black woolen coat and a jaunty striped red and purple scarf. His long hair was pulled back in a ponytail. "Oh—you're the American girl. What was your name again, duck?"

"I'm Juliana Martin-Drake," I told him. "And you're Rodney Whitsun. I remember now."

"Nice to see you again," he said with a grin. "Now, what's with all the rush through the cold, dark, foggy night? Are you on the lam? Running away from home? Or from the big bad wolf?"

"Sort of," I said, trying to laugh off my crazy flight through the streets of Blackthorn. "No, really, I'm just— um—jogging."

"You Yankees," he shook his head. "Always keeping fit! So, are you on your way home now in a desperate hurry? Or do you have time to pop in to our place for a moment? Andrew and I have just printed up some flyers about our glassblowing classes for children. If you wouldn't mind taking some, perhaps your little brother and sister might pass them around at school after the weekend, drum up some business for us."

Don't talk to strangers, Mom's voice whispered in my memory. *Don't ever go anywhere with a stranger . . .*

But then came Duncan's voice, cold and rough, just as I had heard it only minutes earlier: *You're sick, Juliana.*

Rodney Whitsun wasn't exactly a stranger. I had met him at Quent's party. He was a neighbor. I took a deep, calming breath.

"Oh, okay," I told him. "I can come for a minute."

He led the way to the end of Dark Lane and around the

corner onto a small, lamplit alley. The narrow passage was perhaps the width of a single car. The terraced cottages were very old and leaned toward each other from both sides of the lane. "This street—," I said. "It's right out of medieval times!"

"It is a lovely spot, isn't it?" asked Rodney. "But only for tourists, at least as far as we're concerned. It gets a bit claustrophobic in here, and there's hardly room to swing a cat. No room at all for running a business, a fact Oliver Pethering knew perfectly well when he decided to open his Emporium over on Castle Street instead!" His voice was jovial but held more than a hint of bitterness. "In fact, that's where I've just been—out to call upon our local grieving widower and feudal lord, Sir Oliver Pethering, Himself." He snorted. "Old Oliver is snatching up properties left and right, all through this village. Fancies himself some sort of superlandlord, I don't doubt. Wants to own the whole village, I daresay! Well, at least we've got our own little corner, for what it's worth. And . . . here it is," he said, stopping in front of a low stone cottage in the middle of the row. "Small and humble, but it's our own. Now come right in and I'll find those flyers for you." He pushed open the front door, ducking his head. "Andrew? We've got company!" Then he looked back over his shoulder at me. "You're tall, so watch your head on these low beams and doorways. This cottage is fifteenth century—parts of it, anyway—and people were shorter back then. When we first moved in I cracked myself on the head at least five times a day."

"Didn't knock much sense into you, though," said Andrew, appearing from the back of the cottage. He smiled at me. "Oh!—hello there—Juliana, isn't it? From America?"

"That's me," I said.

They showed me around their little place. They used the back rooms for their living space, and the front two rooms for their sales gallery and studio. Some of the glass sculptures were enormous, others smaller, delicately spun of glass that looked like sugar. Many hung suspended from wires in the ceiling beams like giant, luminous kites. Shelves lining the two front rooms were overflowing with bowls and goblets and vases, all handblown, Andrew told me proudly. He made the more utilitarian objects—things people could use in their homes—while Rodney made the more fanciful things: mobiles, sculptures, fountains, jewelry. At the back of the cottage were bedrooms, a minuscule kitchen the size of a closet, and a bathroom. Those rooms, too, were crowded with displays of glass and with boxes stacked in the corners.

"We don't have enough room to put out all of our glassware," Andrew said regretfully. "We hope we'll be moving again as soon as a more centrally located property becomes available. Castle Street would be ideal. Or over by St. Michael's."

"Liza Pethering's studio would be ideal," Rodney snapped. His face reddened. "I don't see why Oliver is being so *unreasonable*. You should have seen him, Drew! He just flat-out refused!"

"I *told* you—you approached him too soon, man. He's just lost his wife . . . I *told* you to wait awhile . . ." Andrew took Rodney's arm as if to calm him.

"He's just as grasping and greedy as she was," Rodney groused. "Two of a kind! Why he needs their big house *and* the Emporium *and* the portrait gallery, I don't know! All I can say is, he'd better watch himself—"

Andrew interrupted him hastily, thrusting a sheaf of

papers into my hands. "Here, young Juliana, these are the flyers advertising our Saturday classes for kids. Teens, too. I hope you'll join one of the two morning sessions. We'll start by making a simple vase—and move on from there. You'll love it!"

"I'll talk to my mom," I said. "I'd love to learn to make jewelry like the things you've got on display."

"Oh, absolutely," Andrew said cheerfully. "Jewelry's on the to-do list. Earrings! And perhaps your brother and sister can hand these flyers round to children at school?"

Rodney sank into an armchair in the corner of the gallery and stared broodingly out the window into the shadows of the alley. "Nobody will come to the classes," he said morosely. "They won't be able to find us back here."

"We'll be putting a big sign out in Dark Lane, Rod— you know that. With a big arrow pointing the way. Nobody will be able to miss it!" Andrew smiled at me. He headed into the studio room, motioning for me to follow. He pointed to the corner where a large freestanding signboard stood. He pulled it out from the wall with a flourish: "Look at this!"

GLASSBLOWING

Demonstrations and Classes for Children, Teenagers, and Adults of all ages!

Saturday mornings, 9:00 and 11:00 a.m.

COME and CREATE!

I looked at the carefully hand-painted sign. Painted in red. I looked at the red arrow pointing the way. I drew a deep breath and managed to smile at Andrew.

"Eye-catching," I said. "Did you paint it yourself or have it made for you?"

"Painted it myself," said Andrew easily. "Just the work of half an hour."

"It's great," I said weakly. "It'll really pull people in." I headed for the door, carrying the flyers. "Well, I've got to get home. My mother will be wondering where I am."

They waved me on my way. I heard the door of their cottage click behind me with relief. *That's the terrible thing about an unsolved murder,* I reflected, hurrying along the narrow alley and out onto Dark Lane where welcome light from the streetlamps made hazy circles in the night gloom. *Everyone seems suspicious.*

I was half laughing at my fears, but I still felt uneasy as I headed for Water Street. My footsteps sounded too loud in the quiet village. As I passed the clock tower in the center of town, I saw some dark figures leaning against the wall. I heard laughter and saw the glow of a cigarette. "Hey, Juliana," someone called, and one of the figures detached itself from the wall and became Brian. "Want to join us?" Alina's giggle coming out of the darkness sounded slightly demented, but I made myself answer pleasantly.

"No thanks," I said, waving in their general direction. "Not tonight. I've got to get home." And I hurried on. I could hear wind through the blackthorn branches and the crash of waves from the beach. All the way home I was looking over my shoulder, jumping at shadows.

It didn't help that Henry Jukes was passing outside our door just as I arrived at the wall. He was hunkered down against the wind and didn't look at me as he passed. But what was he doing near the Old Mill House?

Mom had taped a note on our cottage door saying that

she and Ivy and Edmund were with Quent, and that I should come over as soon as I returned home. So I walked back along the path to the Old Mill House and knocked. Quent let me inside, his smile warm and welcoming. "There you are! Isn't Duncan with you?"

I said he was still with his grandparents.

Quent shrugged. "We're in the middle of a rousing game of snooker—do you know it? It's a bit like pool, or billiards. You're welcome to join us." He led the way down a hallway, and I could hear Edmund's cackling laughter. "You probably remember this room from the house tour Duncan gave you," Quent said. "It was originally a 'smoking room,' where men would retire to after dinner to smoke and drink while the ladies went to another parlor. After the men had enjoyed their vices for a while, they would join the ladies again."

I did remember seeing the room on my house tour, but we had not gone inside. Now I stepped into the dark-paneled room and looked around. It was furnished with leather armchairs. There was the pool table—well, snooker table, I guess it was, and much bigger than a regular pool table—in the middle of the room. There was a fire roaring in the grate. My mom and Ivy and Edmund were all brandishing pool cues. "Hello, Jule!" cried Mom. "Come here and watch me win this game!"

"Your mum's got a steady arm and an eagle eye," Quent said appreciatively.

"You said I did, too!" Edmund grabbed his arm. Quent laughed down at him.

"You do, lad, but your mum seems to be the champ tonight." He and Mom exchanged a *look*. What did that look mean? I wondered.

"I'm good, too, Quent!" shrieked Ivy. "And so is Polar! Watch this!" My goofy sister had brought her stuffed friend to this gathering, and now held him up, paws attached to the cue. "He's a super shot."

Mom poured me a cup of tea from the pot on the low side table. "You look tired."

"Mom, I'm beyond tired," I said, accepting the cup, although I didn't really want anything. I was still stuffed from the shepherd's pie and sticky toffee pudding. "I'll drink this, but then I've got to go to bed."

I sat deep in the leather chair and watched the game and sipped my tea. My head was aching and I just wanted to clear out and go home and maybe sit in a hot bath for a while or something . . . because sooner or later Duncan would be returning, and if I stayed . . . then *what*? I didn't want to see him.

But the warmth from the fire and the sweetness of the milky tea lulled me. I had too many thoughts in my head, most of them uncomfortable, and too many images that made me uneasy: the red pot of paint at the Coopers' house, the red painted letters on the signboard at Rodney and Andrew's shop. Veronica Pimms slipping through the shadows on Castle Street. Henry Jukes walking along Water Street in the darkness. Celia Glendenning's eyes watching me. Celia's anger. Rodney's anger, Dudley Cooper's anger, Hazel's anger, Duncan's anger. Duncan's hands gripping my shoulders. My head was whirling. I set the teacup down on the table and closed my eyes for a minute. Then I stood up.

"Thanks for the tea," I said. "But I think I'll go on home now. I'm pretty tired."

"We'll be coming soon, too," Mom said. "Do you have your key?"

"Yes." I reached into my pocket and pulled it out.

"All right, then. Sleep tight!"

Quent walked me to the door. Low lights along the path illuminated the way across the lawn from the Old Mill House to our cottage door. "Good night," he said.

"You, too," I said. And hurried home.

I TURNED THE key in the lock, heard the *click*—but the door didn't open. Had Mom forgotten again to lock it? Had *I* just locked it? I took the key out of the door and stood looking at it in the palm of my hand. Then I tried again, turning the key hard, heard another *click,* and this time the door opened.

I stepped inside—and froze when I heard a soft shuffling sound. Mom and the Goops were at Quent's. So what was that noise?

The sitting room was lit with soft lamplight and looked inviting. I listened in the doorway and heard nothing. I knew I hadn't imagined the sound, but I also knew that I'd been spooking myself all evening with pots of red paint and whatever. I had alienated the nicest boy I knew. I was acting like a paranoid lunatic. And now—what? I was going to run back across the lawn and cry to my mom and Quent that I was afraid to come into our house alone and they should stop their game and hold my hand?

Shaking my head at my own cowardly lion act, I stepped into the sitting room and closed the cottage door. I looked around but didn't see anything wrong. I listened hard but heard nothing. Probably the noise I'd heard was simply one of those old house noises. We heard them all the time when we were all together and thought nothing of them. Even new houses like ours in California had noises. Water in the pipes. The humming of the fridge. A rattle in the heater. Whatever.

Still, there was a feeling in the air—a sense of something being different. Off-balance. The answering machine light was blinking. A message from Dad? I walked over to the phone with a smile and pushed the Play button. I had been thinking about him and our philosophical questions, and he had called me!

But no. Not Dad after all.

Hullo, Juliana, it's Duncan. I'm sorry about tonight, but—well, anyway, I am sorry, and I hope we can still go on our picnic as planned tomorrow. Up Castle Hill? Granny's going to make a cake. I'll ring you in the morning. All right . . . well, I'll see you tomorrow, I hope . . . Bye!

During the long beep at the end of this message I heard it again, the soft shuffle. I turned my head to the left, looking around. Nothing—only the sitting room. I turned my head to the right. Saw only the kitchen. But wait—what was that?

A creaking.

The closed bathroom door—creaking open.

16

I held my breath and heard my heart pounding. I watched the bathroom door. It was open just a crack. Had it been that way before?

There came the creaking sound again, and *yes*—the door opened wider. Then I heard the toilet flush.

I screamed.

The bathroom door flew open, and there was Celia Glendenning, holding a towel. "It's all right!" she said. "Really! Juliana, it's just me, dear."

I put the kitchen table between us. "What are you doing here? What the *hell* are you doing here?"

She dried her hands and laid the towel on our kitchen table. She was dressed in her usual artsy flowing clothes. Her purse—the tapestry tote bag—was looped over her shoulder. She didn't look the least bit scary, but I was terrified.

"What are you doing? What do you want? How did you get in here?" I fired off the questions like bullets aimed at her heart.

She laughed gaily, as if it were perfectly ludicrous that I should question her, but two bright spots of color appeared in her cheeks. "What was I doing in the *loo*? Well, the usual, I'm afraid. I just stopped by to bring back the key I've had for ages. No sense my having it anymore, now that you've moved in, right? But no one was home, so to save myself another trip, I thought I would just open the door and lay the key on the table. And then when I came in, well, I needed to use the toilet."

I looked pointedly at the table, bare except for Ivy's *Colouring Book of National Trust Properties,* her little box of markers, and now the towel. "Where's the key, then?"

Celia reached into her jacket pocket and drew out the key. She held it toward me, but I didn't move to take it. She laid it on the table. "Here you go. I'm sorry I frightened you, dear. But—nothing to worry about! It was only me." She laughed her trilling laugh and headed for the door. "I suppose I should be going now. Cheerio!"

I felt I should run after her and say, "Just a minute now!" and make her stay until . . . when? Till I'd called in the cops. Till Mom came home and yelled at her. How *dare* this woman just walk into our house and use the bathroom!

But I let her go without comment. I just stood there by the table and watched her leave. Then I sank into a chair and punched the answering machine button again, just to hear Duncan's friendly voice. Tears pricked at my eyes, but I felt too tired to cry.

Then there was another sound of a key in the door, and Mom and the Goops walked in. "We just bumped into Celia Glendenning on her way out," Mom told me. "She said she came by to return the key—wasn't that nice of her? I hope you offered her a cup of tea, Juliana."

And then I did start to cry, and it took fully five minutes for Mom and Ivy and Edmund to figure out what was wrong.

"She was *already* in here when you came home?" queried Mom.

"She was doing *what?*" demanded Edmund.

"What a *weirdo!*" yelled Ivy. And finally I was able to laugh.

"It's okay," I said. "But she totally scared me to death."

Mom hugged me. "No more deaths allowed around here."

But something about the whole thing was bothering me still. Celia frightened me. I didn't trust her.

"Mom," I said after the Goops had gone into the bathroom to brush their teeth, "I know what was wrong. Celia wasn't just using the bathroom when I came in, she was *hiding* behind the bathroom door. I saw it opening a crack and then closing, then opening again. And *then* I heard the toilet flush."

"What did you say?" asked Edmund, emerging from the bathroom.

"I think Celia ran into the bathroom when she heard me coming in, and then hid behind the door, watching me. And *then* she reached over and flushed the toilet to give herself an excuse for being in there."

"Let me try it," said Edmund, returning to the bathroom. He closed the door. Then opened it a crack and peeked out. "Like this?"

"Yes, but open it slowly, so it creaks."

"Let me try!" exclaimed Ivy.

Next Ivy closed the door and opened it very slowly. The same soft creak sounded, and I shivered. "That's it exactly," I told them.

"Now reach over and flush the toilet, Ivy," directed Edmund. "Can you reach?"

The toilet flushed. "Yup," called Ivy. The Goops came out of the bathroom, triumphant.

"Celia Glendenning's an odd duck," stated Mom. "But she probably didn't mean any harm. I might have a word with her, though, next time I see her."

"But why would she come here in the first place?" I asked.

"Probably to return the key, as she said. But maybe she snooped around a bit first. Some people are like that."

"She needs to learn her manners," said Ivy severely.

"Quent has good manners," Edmund announced. "When I fell asleep under the snooker table, he put me into the armchair. He said I could stay overnight if I wanted. Right there in the armchair!"

"I think he would have carried you up to a comfortable bed," Mom said, smiling.

The memory of Quent gently carrying drunken Liza along the upstairs corridor flashed in my mind. "But you decided not to sleep over?" I asked Edmund.

"Mom said not tonight." He yawned. "And I didn't have my toothbrush and stuff."

"I'd need my toothbrush and my pajamas *and* Polar—," Ivy began, then broke off and shouted, "Oh wait, Mom! I've left Polar Bear!"

Mom glanced at her watch. "Run back then," she told Ivy. "But hurry!"

I went into the bathroom to brush my teeth and wash my face and get ready for bed. It had been the longest day in the world. I said good night to Mom and Edmund and trudged upstairs.

After a while I heard Ivy return. "Polar Bear is spending the night at Quent's," she said forlornly to Mom. "I couldn't find him—but Quent said as soon as Polar turns

up, he'll bring him home. Duncan said he probably wanted
to have a sleepover with 'Normous."

"Did you check under the pool table?" I called
downstairs.

"*Snooker* table," Ivy yelled back. "Of course we looked
there. And in the kitchen, and the hallway, and also in the
conservatory because Edmund and I were playing explor-
ers in Africa, and Polar was one of the wild animals and—
oh! I didn't look in the bathroom. Mom, maybe I took
Polar into the bathroom! Can I go back and look in the
little bathroom in Quent's hallway? Maybe Polar is hiding—like Celia did."

"Not tonight, honey," Mom said. "It's very late now and
I'm sure Quent and Duncan are heading off to bed, too.
Polar will have a fine time with Duncan's old bear, and you
can run over first thing after breakfast."

Ivy fussed and fumed for a minute or two, and
slammed the bathroom door for emphasis.

I turned over, snuggled under my duvet, and closed my
heavy eyes. Sleep came promptly, but so did the dreams.

Disjointed images floated past me. My dad in the ocean,
treading water. The Goops on a ship, waving as they sailed
to Russia. My mother and Liza Pethering and a red-haired
woman I knew must be Nora climbing up a clothesline
onto a wrought-iron balcony.

Then the dreams shifted, and a tall, dark woman with
an angular jaw, sunken cheeks, and a frizzy afro intoning:
"*We'll be fine, just fine, you're perfectly safe with me. She's
not coming back, but she said she wanted you to stay with
me. We'll be fine, just fine. Now don't you worry about a
thing . . .*"

And the dreams of a child—was it me?—yelling *"No!
She wouldn't leave me, she never never would!"*

IN THE MORNING there was another child yelling—my sister Ivy, this time: "Mom—oh no! Oh no—look at Polar
Bear!" I struggled out of sleep. Was I still dreaming? I sat
up and grabbed my robe. The murmur of Mom's voice filtered up to me from downstairs, and the rumble of other
voices—*visitors? this early?*—and then I heard the awe in
Edmund's pronouncement: "Somebody is a real sicko
around here." As I headed out of the bedroom, I wanted to
grab the bedpost and hang on, and not have to go downstairs to learn what was wrong.

They were all standing by the open cottage door:
Mom, Ivy, Edmund, Duncan, and Veronica Pimms in all
her purple-headed glory. What was *she* doing here? What
was *Duncan* doing here? I grabbed my straggly hair and
wound it around my hand, wishing for a brush and hair
scrunchie. At the same time I knew that whatever had happened was so serious, nobody would notice or care what I
looked like.

Ivy ran to me, red-faced and tearful. "Polar is ruined!"

"Murdered," said Edmund. "Just plain murdered."

I looked at the pieces of stuffed animal Ivy held out in
her two hands and closed my eyes against the vision of that
beloved toy now savagely beheaded and smeared with red
paint. Further stab wounds rent the white fluffy fabric of
the headless body. "Who did this?" I whispered.

"And *why?*" wailed Ivy. "Why does somebody hate
Polar?"

"You know it's not really about Polar," Mom said gently,
coming over and taking the paint-stained remains from

Ivy's hands. "It's a message to us." She looked at me. "And there's another message on the doorstep."

I moved like a sleepwalker past Veronica and Duncan, expecting another beach stone. But outside of our cottage, Polar Bear's attacker had printed in red paint right on the stone step: *YANKEES GO HOME.*

"What are Yankees, anyway?" asked Edmund.

"We are," Ivy said sadly. "Americans."

I remembered Rodney Whitsun calling me a Yankee, teasing me about jogging. I rubbed my forehead as if I could delete the memory by pressing hard.

"Duncan and I saw it first," Veronica told me, her eyes gleaming with excitement. "Ooh, I can't believe anybody would be so nasty!"

"What were you doing here, anyway?" I asked abruptly.

"Veronica stopped by to see if I was interested in a job that's opening up at the Old Ship," Duncan clarified, frowning at me. "They're hiring part-time kitchen help— and she wanted me to have first crack at getting the position. I told her I couldn't do it because I can't get home from school early enough, but then we thought of you, Juliana. Because you don't go to school, I mean not in the regular way. And you're British as well as American, right? So you'd be able to work legally in this country, right?"

"I guess so," I said distractedly. "I mean, I do have dual citizenship. Ivy and Edmund and I all do, because of Mom." I was thinking it was very odd indeed that Veronica happened to stop by at the same time Polar had been found.

"The hours are weekdays from three till seven," Veronica added. "Starting tomorrow. It's dull, but the pay's not too bad . . ."

"Anyway, I thought we should come tell you about the

job," Duncan continued, "and then of course as soon as we got to your door we saw . . . it. So we knocked—"

"Ooh, it's just so *hateful!*" said Veronica, wide-eyed.

"But why would anybody hate us?" demanded Ivy. "What have we done?"

"Nothing," I said, giving Veronica a look. Why was she so excited? Was it because she knew a *lot* more about what had happened than she was letting on?

"Well, somebody's pretty mad about *something.*" Mom laid the bear on the wide window ledge, then closed the door. "I'm going to ring the police again." She crossed the sitting room to pick up the phone and started upstairs with it.

"Again?" Veronica jumped on the word. She was quick, that girl. Quick like a fox.

"Oh, yeah. We're getting to be really good friends with the local police," I told her. I could hear Mom walking down the hallway to the privacy of her studio.

"Yesterday there was a rock," Duncan informed Veronica, and then filled her in about the warning. Ivy and Edmund, who hadn't known about yesterday's message, listened with wide eyes.

"Wait a second," I interrupted. "How did the bear get on the doorstep? Last night Ivy left it over at your place. Quent said he'd look for it and bring it over when he found it."

"And he did." Duncan's voice was calming, smooth. Why did it grate on my nerves? "I was just going to bed late last night when Quent found Ivy's bear in our little downstairs bathroom off the front hallway. He told me he was going to stick it in a plastic bag—to keep it dry—and put it on your doorstep. He wanted Ivy to have her bear back as soon as she woke up."

"Where is Quent now?" Mom asked Duncan, turning to peer down at us from the stairs.

"He had to leave for London early—around six, I think. He'll be furious when he hears."

Mom nodded, then continued upstairs to phone the police.

"Was the bear in the plastic bag when you two found it?" I asked Duncan.

"No . . ." Duncan looked at Veronica. "Did you see a plastic bag, Ronnie?"

"Nope. I didn't see anything or anybody except for Henry Jukes—"

"Henry!" I exclaimed. "Where is he?"

"He arrived at the same time I did, didn't he, Dunk-o? What's he here for?"

"Quent hired him to chop down two dead walnut trees at the back of the garden. He came yesterday afternoon and was working until pretty late, and he's at it now—can't you hear him?"

When we all stopped talking and listened, we could hear the faint buzz of a chain saw at the back of the large garden. Would Henry Jukes have had time to murder an American polar bear before he started working? And—would he?

I just didn't believe this was a message from some anonymous anti-American lout, trying to scare us out of England. I had a feeling it was a message from Liza's murderer.

Liza's murderer was scared.

Somehow the murderer knew that I wasn't convinced Simon Jukes was guilty. The murderer wanted to stop me from talking about my suspicions, stop me from nosing around. The murderer was worried I was getting close to the truth.

"Oh—wait!" Veronica exclaimed. "Henry wasn't the only person I saw around here. I saw the Thurbers. They were just driving down Water Street, and they waved. Mrs. Thurber rolled down her window and said they were leaving early to get to an appointment with their adoption agency. She was so excited!"

"They don't live on Water Street," Duncan observed.

Veronica's eyes sparkled. "And I bumped into none other than Oliver Pethering just outside your front wall, Dunk-o. Just as I was arriving. We said good morning, and he told me he called round your place on his way to the shop to tell Quent about a new shipment of wines."

"So he did," said Duncan. "He stopped by just before you got here, Ronnie. But Quent had already gone off to London. I'll give him the message when I see him tonight."

My eyes darted from Duncan's face to Veronica's, trying to keep their account of things straight.

Questions tumbled over themselves in my head: Had Oliver left the beach stone on our doorstep yesterday, and then slipped into the garden again today, determined to leave another nasty message—and found Ivy's bear already on the step? Had Oliver destroyed the toy and painted the new message? Or was the stalker more likely to have been Henry Jukes, taking a break from tree cutting? Were those stab marks on the bear, as I'd thought—or chain-saw tracks? And the red paint—was it the same as the paint on yesterday's rock? Had it come from the Coopers' house, or from Rodney and Andrew's place? And those Thurbers! What were they doing taking a little detour off the main drag onto Water Street—when they were supposedly rushing off to their adoption agency? What about Celia Glendenning? She had left our house before we went to bed, and she could have hidden in the garden. She could have seen Quent leave the bear in the plastic bag. She could have come creeping back.

I looked over at Veronica, studied her face. Or . . . was the culprit right here, under my nose?

Duncan was looking at me intently. I scowled at him. "What?"

He shrugged. "You look so fierce, that's all."

"You'd look fierce, too," I told Duncan, "if you kept getting threatening messages!" *And if every single person in England seemed threatening,* I thought to myself.

"Well, at least you can't pin this one on my grandparents, can you?" His voice was mild.

"What?" yelped Veronica. "You mean she thinks your *grandparents* are going around defiling little girls' teddy bears? Come now, that's a low blow, Juliana—even for a Yank. Little old ladies and gentlemen don't *do* things like that. Maybe in California they do, but not in *England.*"

"Maybe it was Jean and Leo Thurber," Duncan suggested. "Just stopping by for a bit of criminal activity on their way to their adoption agency."

Both of them made me sick. I sat at the kitchen table ignoring them, my mind racing as I tried to piece the puzzle together. Henry Jukes could have beheaded the polar bear; so could Oliver Pethering. But what about Veronica herself? I had a bad feeling about that girl.

Or . . . even *Duncan* could have done it—to get back at me for suspecting his beloved grandparents!

Well . . . no. Even my paranoid brain had to reject that

possibility outright. I hadn't known Duncan long, but I couldn't picture him hurting Ivy that way. He was right: I was acting like a lunatic. But nothing made sense and so anything seemed possible, even things that couldn't be.

Something else wasn't making sense, but I wasn't sure what it was. Something seemed wrong—here, in our cottage, just like last night. But what? Celia Glendenning wasn't hiding anywhere this time, so what was it? I looked around the room, trying to figure out what felt off-balance.

"The police will be here soon," Mom said, coming downstairs and replacing the phone. "Veronica and Duncan, I'm afraid they said they want to speak to you, too. I hope you won't mind waiting."

"Ooh, not at all! At last—some excitement in my humdrum life!"

I couldn't tell if Veronica meant to be cute or if she was serious. Either way, she was so annoying, I couldn't bear it.

"Will they be able to fix Polar Bear, Mom?" asked Ivy.

Mom's voice was soothing. " I don't know, dear. But I'm sure they'll help clear this awful mystery up in no time. So don't you worry."

They all moved to the sitting room to wait for the police, but I stayed at the kitchen table, too angry and sick and afraid to move. The voice from my dream was back in my head, ringing hollow assurances: *We'll be fine, just fine. Now don't you worry about a thing . . .*

OFFICERS LINK AND Petersen arrived and took everyone's statement. Predictably, they told us the ruined stuffed toy was just a nasty prank. There was a lot of anti-American feeling in the world; perhaps someone in Blackthorn was making a political sort of statement. They would look into it. Mom nodded, reassured. But I shook my head in disbelief.

Still, there was no arguing with the police. They put the corpse of poor Polar into a plastic bag as evidence, promising to give it back so Mom could try to wash and repair it after they'd had the police photographer take pictures of it. Ivy ran to the mantel to get the photo from last year's birthday party—the photo of her and Edmund with their stuffed animals balanced on their heads—so they could see what Polar Bear had looked like before the attack. The officers studied the photo and made appropriately soothing comments.

And that's when I caught my breath—finally realizing what had been bothering me since the night before, finally seeing what was off-kilter. I hadn't seen it before—*because it wasn't there,* and that was the problem. My school photo was not on the mantel with the other framed pictures.

Had it fallen? I looked swiftly around the fireplace. Should I tell the police? But Mom was showing them out now. Veronica was leaving, too, thank goodness, needing to get to work at the Old Ship. That left Duncan at the kitchen table.

"Celia Glendenning was here last night," I told him, sitting in the chair across from him. I related how she'd been in the bathroom when I'd come home.

"Probably she was just returning the key, as she said." Duncan shrugged. His cheeks grew redder till they almost matched his fiery hair. Then his eyes flashed at me and his voice grew hard. "I'm getting really *sick* of the way you see danger in everything and everybody."

I glared back at him. "Well, Celia *did* sneak in here, and I think she stole my school picture, too. She was carrying a big tote bag. It would have fit!" Our angry eyes met and held for a long moment. Yes, he was gorgeous and caring and the only boy I knew who could make my pulse race, but he was also obstinate and thick-skulled and annoying. I could tell he felt the same way about me.

Mom came back to the table. "What's this about your picture?"

I pulled away from Duncan's gaze. "It's not on the mantel, Mom. I noticed just now. But I felt there was something wrong last night; I just didn't figure out what it was. I think Celia took the picture, Mom! But that's so weird. Why *would* she?"

Mom sank into a chair and scrubbed her fingers through her hair. "Who knows, Juliana. Who knows what's going on around here. I just don't know what to think anymore, and so it's probably best if we just try to forget it."

"*Forget* it?" My voice rose. "How can we just ignore what's happening?"

"Look, Celia is the least of my worries just now. She brought the key back and used the toilet. Or not . . . who cares? Your photo was on the mantel yesterday—that I know for sure, because I dusted it. But it's gone now. Maybe I moved it and don't remember. Who cares? I've got a mutilated polar bear and a very upset little girl, and I'm supposed to be getting ready for an art show and I don't have any time to paint because of all this weirdness!"

Mom's voice cracked. "I just wanted to come to a place that was peaceful and quiet, where I could focus on my work. I never expected . . . all this."

See? I wanted to say. *That's what happens if you walk out on Dad!* But this time I kept my mouth shut.

Mom sighed and smoothed her hair. "Okay, right. Let's

get organized. Yesterday Ivy and Edmund and I were invited to visit with Sophie and Charlie-Tom and their mum. There's a puppet show at the library, and then they've asked us back to their place for lunch and to spend the afternoon. So I think that's what we'll do. Something nice and normal." Mom looked at me. "Would you like to come, too, Jule? Or do you and Duncan have plans?"

I looked at Duncan.

"Are we still on for our picnic?" he asked me, taking a deep breath. "Because if we are, let's get going. Granny was last seen packing enough for an army. She'll be waiting for us. We can walk up to their house and collect the basket, and then head for Castle Hill."

"All right," I said reluctantly. "That does sound fun. But what if whoever is leaving these warnings comes back while we're gone—?"

"Better that we *are* gone, then, I think," said Mom firmly.

At least we've got Celia's key, I thought. Unless she'd made copies.

So Duncan and I set off, walking first to the Coopers to collect the humongous basket Duncan's granny had packed, and then along the winding switchback trail up Castle Hill. We didn't talk much at first. There was an unhappy tension between us and we both knew why. I didn't really believe that either of his grandparents had come to our house and destroyed Ivy's bear, and I had overreacted about the red paint, so I knew I owed him an apology.

"Listen," I mumbled. "I'm sorry, okay? I like your grandparents. And I know other people have red paint." I told him about how I'd met up with Rodney Whitsun and Andrew Parker. "Everybody seems like a suspect, and it feels awful not to trust anybody, and—"

"Not *anybody*?" he asked, reaching for my hand.

"Well," I said, "there's you. I mean, I *want* to trust you."

"But you don't?" He stopped walking and set down the heavy picnic basket. He put his hands on my shoulders and turned me to face him.

"No, I do," I said quietly. "I do trust you."

My heart was beating hard. We were standing there staring into each other's eyes again, just as we had at our kitchen table. But this time there was no anger, no annoyance. This time it was incredible. All my fears seemed to melt away. Bloodstains, beach stones, decimated polar bears, what were any of these to me? Weird voices and visions in my head, strange smells and half memories—what did any of these matter now? Old Tim-whatshisname back in California—who was he? There was only Duncan.

His kiss was sweeter than any cup of tea. We clung to each other there on the switchback path and just didn't want to let go.

A long time later, though, we did. We had to, because a man and his dog were coming toward us. The dog was bounding along, yipping happily as if delighted to have found us. The man, we saw as he drew closer, was the vicar. Outside on this brisk, cold day he seemed a very different sort of person from the long-faced, solemn person who had officiated at Liza's funeral. He greeted us and said what a lovely day for a picnic, then strode on, calling to his dog.

But it was as if the reminder of Liza had cast a shadow over us. Duncan picked up the picnic basket. Hand in hand, we trudged up the rest of the hill.

"I do trust you," I said again. "It's Celia I don't trust." I felt shivery just thinking of her.

"Let's try to forget her for now," Duncan said. "Try to

forget all this mess. It seems that ever since I met you, there's been only trouble." He paused. "That didn't come out right. I mean, because of the murder and all the suspicion and everything, you and I haven't ever just had time to get to know each other the way I . . . the way I hoped we would."

Now I felt a different sort of shiver. I squeezed his hand. "I know," I said.

The ground was damp so we sat on the wooden bench with the bird's-eye view of Blackthorn. We opened the basket to find, as Duncan had predicted, a mammoth feast. Chicken sandwiches and fat pickles (*gherkins*, Duncan called them) and chocolate cake and wedges of cheddar cheese and Scottish oatcakes to eat with the cheese. It was all delicious, every last bite.

"The entrance to that tunnel Granny and Grandad were telling you about," Duncan said through a mouthful of cheese, "is back there among the foundation stones somewhere. I remember Quent showed it to me once, when he and my mum brought me up here to fly my kite. It's been boarded over, though, because too many people wanted to go exploring." He stood up and wandered around the edge of the hill to the stand of black-branched blackthorn trees and remnants of the castle walls. "Let's try to find it."

Carrying the second half of my sandwich, I followed him. We climbed on the stones and poked in the crevices but couldn't find any sign of it. I didn't care in the least; I was just having a fine time being with Duncan and feeling for the first time in ages, it seemed, almost carefree.

Giving up on finding the entrance to the ancient tunnel, Duncan collapsed onto one of the low crumbled walls and started picking up fallen white blossoms. I watched him. He selected a long, thin reed of grass and used it as a string to thread the blossoms onto, making a sort of garland. Okay, I'd make a garland, too. But not his way. The only way I knew to make jewelry out of vegetation was to slit the stem of one flower to push another through . . . and so on. Like a daisy chain. There weren't any daisies on Castle Hill, though, so I picked dandelions. Their yellow heads weren't open yet, but the stems were nice and sturdy. Soon my necklace was ready, and I put it over Duncan's head. It wasn't big enough—so it rested on top of his bright hair like a crown.

"Now you," he said. "Come here."

"*All finished now! Come here, come try it on.*"

"*No, Buzzy wear it. Pitty necklace for Buzzy!*"

I knelt next to him, trying to ignore the voices in my head. He lifted my long braid out of the way, keeping hold of it for longer than he needed to—and I liked that. Then he fastened the blossom necklace around my neck—but I didn't like that. Somehow I felt a little ripple of unease.

"*All right, Toots. You win. I'll wear the necklace, and treasure it forever. It'll be my good luck charm because it's a present from my precious little Jewel-baby . . .*"

Those voices again! I reached up, wanting to pull the necklace off and dash it to the ground—but I couldn't do that to Duncan. He wouldn't understand.

I didn't really understand myself. I mean, how could I be uneasy about a lovely flower necklace, made for me by the nicest boy in the world? Why should having it around my neck bring on these fearful, half-formed memories?

"Thanks," I said weakly. "It's beautiful."

"Wear it for good luck," he said with a grin.

"It will be my good luck charm," I whispered, and then

felt a little dizzy. Why did the words make me feel I was being sucked into a whirlpool?

"Hey, are you all right?"

"Yes." I fought my way out of the dizzy spin and blinked at him. "Just tired, I guess. I didn't sleep very well last night after Celia's little visit. And then the thing with Ivy's polar bear."

"We aren't going to talk about Celia—or any of it," he reminded me with a lopsided smile.

"Oh, right, sorry!"

"How about that job offer, then. At the Old Ship?"

"I think I'll try it—if they don't mind that I'm not sixteen yet. At home you have to be sixteen to work—at least officially."

"Go talk to them, anyway. See what they say."

"I will." A chill sea wind blew up Castle Hill from the water, bringing with it a fine, stinging mist that wetted our faces. "It's good we had our picnic when we did," I said resignedly. "But I think we'd better go."

There was a dizziness in my head, and a sort of roaring in my ears—almost as if the ocean were rising in a tidal wave. Almost as if all the strange voices were babbling at once. I pressed my hands to my temples. I felt almost as if the dark shadows of my memory were pressing back.

Pitty necklace for Buzzy!

It'll be my good luck charm because it's a present from my precious little Jewel-baby . . .

"Picnicking in March is a rare delight," Duncan said, rather poetically. He laughed. "That's what my mum used to say."

I gave him a wan smile. "I think I need to go home, Duncan."

"Or back to my house? Quent's in London, still. We could watch a film. Or to my grandparents' house? We could sit by the fire and talk—"

I didn't want to watch a film. I just wanted—what? To take a nap. Get away from the voices in my head. The thought of having to chat with the Coopers was daunting. "No, I'm really sorry. I just feel really . . . tired. Not up to socializing."

"Well, I wish we could just hang out here," he said ruefully, "but I guess it isn't exactly cozy." The castle foundations would offer scant protection once the rain started. I stood up and reached out a hand to pull him up, too. He gave in gracefully. We packed our sandwich wrappings and leftovers into the picnic basket. He wore his dandelion crown all the way down the switchback path, looking like some sort of elfin king. I unhooked my necklace from around my neck, but held it safely in my hands all the way back to the cottage, bending forward to protect it from the wind and rain.

17

Mom and the Goops were still out when I unlocked the cottage door and stepped inside. I hung up my wet jacket on one of the hooks by the door. Across the room I could see the red light of the answering machine blinking. I peeked into the bathroom first, just to be sure no one was hiding there, then pushed the Play button and sank onto the couch in our sitting room to listen to the message. A wave of sadness engulfed me at the sound of my dad's voice. It was such a double whammy for adopted kids like me and Edmund, who had already lost one set of parents, to have our mom and dad separated like this. And awful for Ivy, too, of course, but in a different way. This was the first earthquake shaking up the security she'd always been able to take for granted. I hated that we weren't all together. I listened to the message twice, just to hear his voice.

"Hey, all my little ones and hello to Mommy, too! Greetings from sunny California, where everything is blooming like crazy, and if murders are happening, it's not to anyone I know. I'm worrying about all of you, having to deal with Liza's death. I was hoping to get a chance to chat with everyone for a while, but you're not home, so I guess I'll try again tomorrow, or soon. When are you getting e-mail, Hedda? What's with this

'back to the cave' stuff, with no Internet service? Oh well, guess I shouldn't complain; at least you've got a phone . . . Thanks for your letter, Ivy! I did figure out the code, but it took me about an hour. Love you, too, baby. Edmund, I have your amazing drawing of the pirate ship hanging in my office. It's super! And Jule, I miss you, too, honey. Very, very much.

Okay, kiddos, we'll talk soon. Bye!"

I went slowly up to my room. I had told Duncan I was tired, and so I would try to take a nap. I sank onto my bed, holding the blossom necklace in my lap. I stroked the soft petals. I couldn't wear it, but I didn't want to throw it away. Where could I put it to keep it safe?

I remembered that the necklace Nora had made was stored in the sunroom in that pretty little box inside the basket on the window ledge. I could keep my necklace there, too—and it would be a fitting place, since my necklace had been made by Nora's son.

O, very symbolic!

Smiling, I went down the hall to the sunroom, straight to the basket full of little boxes. I opened the first one and a small collection of tiny seashells spilled into my hand. "Oops, wrong box," I said to myself. I scooped up the shells and put the box back. I looked into the next little box. Dried flowers. The third held feathers. The fourth contained earrings made of shells and feathers. The fifth was empty—no, *almost* empty: One small blackthorn blossom lay in the corner of the box.

This was the box that had held Nora's necklace. I was certain of it. I checked through all the boxes again. No, this box had to be where the necklace had been. But it was gone now, with only the single blossom left behind.

Baffled, I stood holding the small box in one hand, and my necklace from Duncan in the other. Someone had taken Nora's necklace. But who?

Surely not Mom. Nor the Goops; they didn't even know it was there.

But the necklace had definitely been here when we first moved in. I stood as if in a trance, remembering how I had come up here that first day we'd arrived in Blackthorn, exploring the house, finding the sunroom, opening the box and lifting out the lovely necklace. Liza had come into the room then. She had seemed startled by the sight of me with the necklace, and had demanded to know where I'd found it. She told me then that it was Nora's special necklace.

Special necklace, special necklace . . .

I felt dizzy again, as I had on Castle Hill with Duncan, and I clutched the window ledge for support. I stared down at the green lawn and the Old Mill House but was not really seeing them. Instead I was seeing something else, someone else: a little girl crawling under a bed, reaching out to grasp what she found there, far back in the corner, dusty and tangled.

Buzzy's special necklace? What was it doing here? And if it was here—then where was Buzzy? Because Buzzy would never, never, never leave her magic charm behind!

I blinked and tried to focus, but the pressure of the shadows was enormous. I clutched my head.

"Buzzy . . . Buzzy," I whispered. The shadows shaped themselves into pictures, and I could almost see her now, my first mother, my birth mother. A very young woman, skinny and blond, with a big smile and a gap between her teeth. Probably a teenage mom with few resources and fewer parenting skills. Probably a drug addict. But sweet to me, I remembered that suddenly. Like a big kid herself. Oh yes, I remembered racing into the waves—back when the beach held no dizzy-making terrors. I remembered gathering shells on the beach. Making necklaces from the shells we found. One special necklace for good luck. A little insignificant sort of thing, but one Buzzy would never willingly have left behind.

I sucked in my breath. I felt I was looking through cloudy glass, trying to see clearly, trying to find my way. I closed my eyes and suddenly the blurriness was gone, and I was remembering Mrs. Thurber at the party, and hearing in my head, just as clearly as if she were speaking to me now, her chirpy voice. She had made a dramatic declaration at the party, something that hadn't really registered then, but now rang with significance: *Nothing short of death would keep me from wearing my stars!* We had all laughed and admired her jewelry.

And Liza said basically the same thing to me about Nora's necklace, right here in this sunroom on the day we'd arrived: *Only death would keep us from wearing our lucky charms!*

Nothing short of death . . .

Another voice was in my head—talking right over Mrs. Thurber's and Liza's: *I'll wear the necklace and treasure it forever. It'll be my good luck charm because it's a present from my precious little Jewel-baby . . .*

I was falling . . . falling . . . I released the window ledge and slid down the wall to sit huddled by the last of Mom's unpacked boxes, not far from the bloodstain. Instead of the stain I was seeing that dusty corner under the bed, reaching out my little-girl hand to pick up what lay there: a simple shell necklace strung on yarn.

Jewel? Jewel? You come on out from under there, now, girl.

I was falling into the shadows, but what did that matter? Darkness couldn't erase what was reshaping itself in my memory, fresh and nauseating, out of the long-buried past.

SHE WAS NAMED Jewel because her mama thought she was the most precious thing in the world. Her mama was called Buzzy because that was what people had called her in England, where she came from, and she wanted Jewel to call her Buzzy because "Mama" made her sound too old. "We're little girls together," Buzzy had told Jewel. "We're best friends forever."

Buzzy always told bedtime stories. She told Jewel about how she'd run away from home and met Jewel's daddy in San Jose, in California. He was called Petey because he was too young to be anybody's daddy, really. But they were super cool, the three of them. They traveled down the coast in the warm California sun, and Petey played the guitar and sang like an angel, and sometimes people paid him. He sang songs for Jewel. They lived on the beach or up in the woods

in the hills, or under bridges with other
people who were too cool to live in boring
houses and apartments. Sometimes Petey
went out to get more money, and when he
found some, he brought back the best food,
like sodas and hot nachos covered with
cheese sauce. Other times, when they didn't
have money, he taught Jewel how to fish.
She was good at it, because she could dangle
at the end of the rope like a little wiggle-
worm and pull all the best stuff out of the
Dumpsters. There was lots and lots of stuff
down there that people threw away that was
still perfectly good to eat! So they would
have slurpy drinks with the straws still in
them, and bits and pieces of hamburgers,
and even whole pickles that nobody had
wanted.

But then Petey went away. Buzzy cried a
lot and told Jewel that Petey had died. "It
was the drugs," she cried, "and fast driving
because of drugs. It's bad business, Jewel,
baby. Don't ever take drugs, you must
promise me that!" And Jewel promised,
but she didn't see why Buzzy wouldn't
promise, too.

Now Buzzy couldn't just hang out all day
with Jewel anymore because Buzzy had to
work. Now she couldn't play on the beach.
They had to look for shells and make

beautiful necklaces to sell to people who stopped at traffic lights when they saw Buzzy's sign that said PLEASE HELP ME FEED MY LITTLE GIRL. The people would take money out of their fat wallets and give the money to Buzzy and say how nice the jewelry was. But the one necklace they never, ever could buy was the one that Jewel had made for Buzzy all by herself! Buzzy wore that one around her neck whenever she went out to work. It was her good luck charm, she said. She took it off only to go to sleep.

Jewel and Buzzy moved in with a girl called Tiara. Tiara didn't play with Jewel. She lived in a little dark apartment and watched TV when she was home. Buzzy and Jewel watched TV, too. When Buzzy and Tiara weren't home, Jewel watched TV by herself, whatever was on. When Buzzy came back to the apartment, she always fell into bed right away and wouldn't get up all the next day. There was one real bed, where Tiara slept, and one mattress on the floor that Jewel and Buzzy shared.

Sometimes Tiara had people come over to visit, and those people slept on the couch or crowded into the bed with Tiara. When the friends came over, Buzzy said Jewel should watch TV in the bedroom and not come out, because some things weren't for

little girls. Once Jewel came sneaking out to
peek at what wasn't for little girls, but Tiara
saw her and shouted mean things and locked
her in the closet at the end of the hall. It was
dark in there, with a hard, concrete floor,
and Jewel cried so hard that Buzzy made
Tiara let Jewel out. But after that, Jewel
went running back to the bedroom and hid
under Tiara's bed whenever the people came
over.

One day there was a terrible big fight
after the people had gone, and Jewel could
hear Tiara and Buzzy shouting and yelling
about money. She could hear the crashing of
furniture, and the sound of breaking glass.
Jewel cradled her head on her arm under
the bed. She fell asleep to escape the noise.

Crashing music woke her up with a beat
that sounded like more fighting. Jewel
shifted on the dusty floor under Tiara's bed.
She heard doors opening and closing, and
water running—and finally silence. After the
silence had stretched out forever, Jewel came
sneaking out to see what was going on. But
nobody was there.

"Buzzy? Buzzy?" Jewel stepped over a
broken glass and curled up on the couch
to wait. She waited a very long time and
watched TV all night, but Buzzy didn't come
back, and Tiara didn't come back. When
Jewel got hungry, she opened Tiara's fridge

and found some cheese. It was hard, with greenish patches, but it tasted okay with the last of a box of crackers.

Jewel slept on the couch and finally Tiara came back the next day. She looked at Jewel as if she'd never seen her before. "Oh, Christ. I forgot about you!"

"Where's Buzzy?"

"Oh . . ." Tiara shrugged. "Buzzy? Oh yeah—Her Majesty had to buzz off for a while." Tiara collapsed onto the couch. "She's looking for work, and you're gonna be good and helpful around here, or you can't stay."

"Is Buzzy coming back soon?"

"Yeah, sure. Soon. When she finds a job."

"You mean she might be gone a long time? And she didn't take me?"

"Don't worry, you're perfectly safe with me. 'Her Royal Highness' ain't coming back for a long, long time, but she said she wanted you to stay with me. We'll be fine, just fine. Now help me clean up some of this mess, and don't you worry 'bout a thing . . ."

"No! Buzzy wouldn't leave me, she never never would!"

"Shut your trap and be a good girl or I'll be leaving you, too, so fast your head will spin!"

So Jewel tried to be as good as she could be and as helpful as she knew Buzzy would want her to be. She washed the dishes and she put them in the cupboard, she put out the cigarettes that Tiara dropped on the rug by mistake, and she waited obediently in the bedroom, watching TV, when Tiara had her friends coming over. One night the next week there was more shouting, and a man was yelling, and Jewel crawled under Tiara's bed. It was still daylight. And it looked different under the bed with light still coming in the window. The light lit long shafts of sun onto the floor, and the dust motes looked like fairies floating. In the light Jewel could see under the old dresser, too. More fairies darted here and there—and back in the corner something gleamed. Jewel edged her arm under the dresser to fish it out.

Buzzy's shell necklace! The beautiful one that Jewel had made for Buzzy all by herself! The one that Buzzy said was magic, and her good luck charm . . .

The one that Buzzy said she would never take off except when she went to bed.

So . . . if Buzzy was out looking for work, why hadn't she taken her good luck necklace? Jewel would ask Tiara. Maybe Tiara would know.

After the friends left and the shouting man left, Jewel came out of the bedroom and asked Tiara about the necklace. Tiara just shrugged and said that Buzzy obviously had forgotten the necklace when she left.

That's when Jewel knew that Tiara was a big fat liar.

Buzzy would never have gone away without her special necklace. Jewel had a bad feeling in her stomach. She started to look for Buzzy whenever Tiara was out of the apartment. She stood outside by the Dumpsters and wandered across the street at the Laundromat, calling for Buzzy at the top of her voice. She went to the big streets where there were lots of stop signs, checking to see if Buzzy was there selling her jewelry. She asked people if they had seen Buzzy. Nobody had.

But soon there was a bad smell in the apartment. Jewel asked Tiara what it was, and Tiara said there must be a dead rat in the walls and they were going to move as soon as she found another place. Rats scared Jewel, even dead ones, but she didn't want to move because how would Buzzy find her again?

The smell grew more terrible. After a few more days it was sweet and salty at the same time, and rotten through and through—much worse than the garbage in the overflowing Dumpster behind their building. Jewel sprayed Tiara's perfume in all the corners. The smell was especially bad by the closet at the end of the hall. The locked closet.

Jewel knew that Tiara kept her keys on a big ring inside her purse. She waited until she heard Tiara unlocking the apartment and coming home, then ran to the mattress and pretended to be asleep. After Tiara had a couple glasses of stuff to drink, plus some of the other stuff that she shot into her arms every day, she fell deeply asleep on the couch. So deeply she didn't even snore. That was when Jewel crept into the kitchen and took Tiara's purse off the counter. There were the keys!

She carried them to the stinking closet at the end of the hall. She tried first one and then another until she found one that made a click in the lock and the handle turned. The apartment was hot, stifling, but there was a fog rolling off the ocean. Jewel could smell the cooler salt air mixing with the other smell, the awful smell.

Just coats in the closet, and a stack of boxes. But there must be a hundred dead rats in there as well to make such a stink. Wait—what was that at the back? Jewel pushed past the storage boxes. She pushed past the coats. There was something on the floor under a blanket. The bad smell was so strong that Jewel gagged. She knew something was very wrong.

She reached out and pulled back the corner of the blanket. There was an edge of pink flamingo T-shirt. And on the closet floor, a dark stain.

Jewel gasped and backed out of the closet, calling for Tiara in a panic: "Help! Help! Come quick! Buzzy's here! I think she's hurt herself!" But Tiara did not come.

"See, see? I *told* you she wouldn't have gone away! I *knew* she wouldn't! Look, look . . . here she is! Oh, wake up, wake up—please wake up . . ."

But Tiara did not move off the couch, not even when Jewel pulled on her arms. Tiara would not wake up.

Jewel had to go back into the closet by herself. "Buzzy, my Buzzy?" she crooned softly, holding her hands over her nose to blot out the terrible, salty smell. "I knew you wouldn't leave without your necklace . . . Buzzy, wake up, oh please wake up . . ."

She pulled off the blanket.

And screamed.

Blindly she turned. She ran, ran, ran out of that place, away, away, away from . . . whatever she had seen that made her run and run and run away away away. A long time later she found herself wandering on the beach, where the fresh salty air breezed through her nose and banished the evil smell. She'd been running, sucking in the ocean air and kicking up sand, but now her legs gave out and then she couldn't remember why she'd been running in the first place and all she wanted to do was fall over in the sand and sleep forever.

I OPENED MY eyes and stared around me in confusion. I was slumped on the sunroom floor, right next to the stain, with the empty necklace box at my side. I looked around the sunroom, remembering everything. "Mom?" I called her name weakly. The memories had exhausted me. I needed Mom. I needed to tell her what I'd remembered—how I had broken through the shadows at last and *remembered*! I'd remembered *everything*.

Duncan said it had probably been some sort of trauma that made me lose my early memories—and he'd been right. He'd thought I'd need another trauma to break through the amnesia and restore the memories, but it hadn't happened that way. Why had I suddenly been able to remember what had happened to me?

I looked at the empty necklace box and felt a prickle at the back of my neck.

A sound from downstairs made me turn toward the door.

"Mom?" I called again, a little bit louder. I listened

hard, but no—all was silent. Probably just the creaking of an old house, I decided. Mom and the Goops must not be home yet.

I staggered to my feet, picking up Nora's necklace box. Then I realized that this box was what had finally triggered my memory: *Buzzy would never have left without the special necklace her little Jewel had made her.*

The empty box was triggering other memories now, more recent ones: Liza standing in this room telling me how exceedingly strange it was that Nora had left her necklace behind. Nora had not worn her own special necklace when she'd left for London for that big television appearance. She *should* have been wearing it—but she hadn't because it was right here in this box the day we'd arrived at the cottage.

Now it was gone. That fact had triggered my memories. But why did it also set an alarm bell ringing in my head?

What else had been here but was now gone?

My school photo . . .

Had Celia taken both?

I set the box down gently on the window ledge. I laid the necklace Duncan had made me next to it. I felt the prickle along the back of my neck again.

Liza had stood right here in this sunroom and told me about Nora's necklace.

And Liza had also been up here again—the night she died.

Liza must have come into our cottage the night of the party with someone else. And that person had conked her on the head. And taken Nora's necklace.

But *why?*

I stood leaning against the window ledge, looking around the sunroom, trying to think it through.

The police believed that Simon Jukes must have come upon Liza by surprise—and attacked her. But no one could figure out what Liza and Simon had been doing in *our* cottage that night. Had Simon seen her and followed, bent on revenge? But would he also have wanted to steal a necklace made of flowers?

It didn't make sense to me. So . . . what if it hadn't been Simon following Liza that night?

I turned back to the window ledge and stared down at the necklace Duncan had made for me, and at Nora's empty box. I felt the answer was bobbing at the edge of my understanding, just out of reach. I stared blankly out at the cold, gray afternoon. I was so close to figuring something out—I knew it. There were connections to be made here, and my mind just wasn't working fast enough. The five questions pounded into us by my journalism teacher fired in my head: *Who? What? Where? When? Why?* And I knew that if I could answer them, I would know what had happened to Liza that night.

Who? Someone had come here with Liza. Someone who hated her.

It could have been Celia. Or Veronica.

What? Someone had stolen Nora's necklace. That fact didn't seem to fit Veronica—or anyone else but Celia.

Celia had come sneaking in last night and hidden herself in the bathroom. Celia had stolen my school picture. Celia had mentioned she'd wanted a necklace but Nora had died before she could make one for her.

Where? The bloodstain proved the attack had happened right here in this sunroom. And at the restaurant Celia had dropped her menu when she'd heard we'd found the bloodstain. . . .

When? Celia had quarreled with Liza the night of the party. . . .

Why? This was the hard one.

What could the necklace mean to Celia? Why would she have attacked Liza for it? Why would she have taken it? That part didn't make sense. But why would Celia take my school photo? That didn't make sense, either.

I was still standing there in the sunroom, looking out the window, when I heard a faint noise downstairs. Mom must be home now. Maybe she could help me figure this out.

I turned to the door. "Mom?"

No answer. Just a queasy feeling leaping in my gut. Not Mom? Then . . . who?

Celia?

I listened hard—heard nothing—then turned back to stare out through the window, down at the green garden in the waning light. Beyond the well-kept lawn and dripping shrubs loomed the Old Mill House. I pictured Celia inside the Old Mill House the night of the party, quarreling with Liza, telling her she was a terrible painter, how she'd need a magic charm to stay in business. I remembered Liza muttering drunkenly in the kitchen, later. "I have my own strength," Liza had declared. "Not like Nora. She would never do *anything* without consulting her tea leaves or wearing that lucky necklace—" I remembered how Liza's voice had broken off suddenly, how she stared into space as if she had remembered something.

I sucked in my breath sharply. Had Liza remembered just then that Nora's lucky necklace was up in a box in our sunroom? It hadn't seemed important when she'd first seen it there, but at the party she suddenly made a connection between Nora's necklace and—what? My mind couldn't stretch that far.

But whatever she'd realized, Liza must have slipped out of the house soon after and gone to the cottage, using her copy of our key to enter. Someone must have followed her.

Celia?

But wait—it wasn't Celia who had been in the kitchen when Liza was talking about Nora's special necklace. Celia had not been there. . . .

There was another sound from downstairs: a quiet click. Then—were those slow footsteps?

My ears strained to listen. I heard measured footsteps coming up the stairs.

My mind raced, and I was seeing again that scene from the party with vivid clarity: Duncan and I watching from the doorway. The look on Liza's face as she realized that Nora's special necklace meant *something*. And Liza had not been alone, there in the kitchen. . . .

It couldn't be. Yet—

The footsteps padded down the hall. And I knew with utter clarity who must be standing outside the sunroom door.

Not Celia, after all.

How *could* it be true? How *could* it be true? The question pounded with my pulse. Stiffening, I turned slowly from the window.

"You," I whispered. "Yes, it was *you*."

PART 3

"For now we see through a glass, darkly;
but then face to face . . ."

—1 CORINTHIANS 13:12

❧ 18 ❧

Quent Carrington stepped into the sunroom. Two long strides brought him across the floor to stand over me. He reached out and grabbed my shoulder, spinning me away from the window. "You know too much," he said in a low, regretful voice. "And it really is too bad, Juliana. Because I like you. But you simply won't stop snooping around."

"It was you all along," I whispered. "*You* killed Liza."

"Liza drowned in the Shreen," he said firmly. "I just helped her on her way."

I tried to twist out of his grip, but he pressed his fingers tighter. "I can't believe this," I moaned. How could the evil murderer we'd all been afraid of turn out to be *Quent*? "Why would you do such a thing?"

He shook his head. "You'll quite likely figure it out sooner or later, and that's the problem."

"What do you mean?" I asked, desperately looking past him, thinking how I must get away. "Was Liza trying to steal Nora's necklace? Is that it? Did you follow her here that night and kill her because of that?"

"Not exactly, but never mind." He laughed, but it wasn't a happy sound. "That necklace," he muttered ruefully. "Such a little insignificant thing. How could I ever imagine it would come back to haunt me?"

"What do you mean?" I cried again. "*Haunt* you?"

Quent tightened his hold on me. "You ask too many questions," he snarled. "That's been the problem all along." With both hands hard on my shoulders, he propelled me across the sunroom and out into the hallway. I stumbled and tried to kick him. "Stop that!" he hissed into my ear.

"Leave me alone!" I shouted. "Let go of me!"

He released one of my shoulders only to clap his hand across my mouth. "Shut up!"

I struggled against him and tried to bite his hand. His skin was salty, cold.

He pressed me up against the wall at the top of the stairs. "Little Yankee girls who are too nosy for their own good end up going on . . . on a little journey."

I stared down the narrow steps. He held me pinned against him with one hand over my mouth. One push forward and I would fall. I could almost see how it would happen, how Mom and the Goops would arrive home to find me crumpled up on the floor at the foot of the stairs, dead of a broken neck. *What a terrible accident!* people would say.

I jabbed backward with my heel, hard and sharp, and caught his shin. When he gasped, I bit down on his hand. He swore and tried to slap me. I kicked out again, then raised my arms, elbows out like battering rams, and stabbed his stomach. He bent double, and I fled down those narrow stairs. I tore open the front door of the cottage, raced out into the drizzle, screaming my head off, howling for Mom, for Duncan, for Henry Jukes, for anyone. No one came. No one heard. I raced through the garden, toward the back wall where, maybe if I was lucky, I'd run into Henry Jukes—dear, innocent Henry Jukes—

pruning the walnut trees. My feet slipped on the rain-slick grass and I nearly fell.

Run, Toots! Run, run . . .

Buzzy's voice in my head?

Oh, wake up, wake up—please wake up . . . oh, help me, somebody!

A message from the shadows? I stumbled again as understanding stabbed me.

I had figured out that Quent killed Liza, but the *why* of it all had eluded me—until now. I gasped for air as I ran.

Quent Carrington killed Liza because she had figured out that he had also killed Nora.

I shook my head, even as I thought it. But everything fit. Liza knew that Nora would certainly, *definitely,* have worn her special talisman necklace to the big television interview. Superstitious Nora, who believed in luck and omens and talismans and magic, would never have gone to London without it.

So if Nora had not worn the necklace, that meant she had not gone off to London, either. Just as Buzzy had not worn the special necklace I'd made for her, and had never really gone away to look for work.

The necklaces. They were the link in my mind between then and now.

Tiara had lied to me. There had been that awful night of shouting about money and those awful sounds of a struggle. . . . Maybe Tiara had killed Buzzy over a drug deal gone wrong or some other sordid thing. Maybe Buzzy had simply died of an overdose and Tiara had panicked. But Tiara had stuffed Buzzy into that closet.

Quent must have been lying to everyone, too. To all of us. Because Nora had never really gone to London, and

Liza Pethering had figured that out—if not at first when she saw the necklace in the sunroom, then later, at Quent's party, in the kitchen.

Liza had figured it out. Or at least she had wondered about the necklace enough to ask Quent about it. And when Quent knew she was on to him, he struck.

I ran faster. I was passing the old stables where Quent had his studio. In the gloom I could see the shapes of his larger sculptures wrapped in blue plastic, waiting outside to be transported to the London exhibition. Had Quent killed Nora up in our sunroom? Or out here in his studio?

Behind me I heard wet footfalls. Quent was gaining on me. I yelled at the top of my voice—"It's Quent Carrington! He's trying to kill me! He killed Liza and Nora! Help me, help me, somebody!"—and reached the back gate. My fingers fumbled at the heavy iron latch . . . and although I was in Quent's green garden, with the salty sea air wrapping coldly around me and the rain in my face, I was also, somehow, fumbling at *another latch,* a latch on a locked door in *another place,* a dim, grungy place, and the salty sea air was there, too, but warm, with a touch of fog.

Would I ever break free from the shadows? I was gasping for breath from running and had to stop for a moment, leaning against the gate. Oh, yes, here was the trauma Duncan said maybe I'd need to restore my lost memory. Yes, now I remembered—in horrible detail. Oh, I remembered everything. Buzzy—in that closet. My mommy, my first mommy.

I remembered my little girl self pulling back that soiled blanket to reveal the decaying face of my birth mother, and then running, running, running—through the streets, across town, to the beach—as if by running away I could escape the nightmare vision.

For ten years now, I had.

But now I was running away from more than a terrible sight. I was running for my life. The two times—then and now—seemed superimposed, but this wasn't the wooden closet door of my memory. This was Quent's garden gate, made of solid iron. My fingers fumbled at the lock and panic welled up in me, and then I was slammed to the ground from behind. My breath whooshed out of me. Quent lay on top of me, pinning me to the wet grass. He kept his knee in my back as he dragged something over me, wrapping me tight. I recognized the blue plastic sheeting from his sculptures-in-progress. He pulled my braid hard, forcing my head back, then gagged me with his scarf. I struggled, throwing myself from side to side, grunting and straining against the woolen cloth that filled my mouth and the plastic wrapping that held me like a straitjacket.

Quent laughed roughly. "You're a fighter and you're quick, my girl. But not quick enough. Now we're going for a little ride, and I don't want any more trouble from you." He paused and held up another beach rock. "Or else."

Tears dribbled into my hair as he carried me over his shoulder to his car in the back alley. He tossed me into the backseat as if I were nothing more than a piece of sculpture and we drove off. "Of course I could kill you now," he said conversationally as we turned a corner. "But I'd rather not have any more bloodstains found on my property."

His words chilled me. Where were we going, and why? I strained against the plastic wrapping, fought to bite through the tight gag—uselessly. *Mom!* I shouted in my mind. *Dad! Help me, someone!*

And in my mind I heard another shout—from another time . . .

Buzzy, oh Buzzy, oh, wake up, wake up—please wake up . . . oh, help me, somebody!

With an effort I pushed the memories out of my head. *This* was real, this sickening gag and tight plastic sheet. This car was real as it raced through the dark and started climbing, gears grinding, up a steep road. But where was Quent taking me?

The car jerked to a stop and I fell against the seat backs. Quent hauled me out. He threw me unceremoniously over his shoulder again and started carrying me—where? I squirmed and bucked, but it was no use. I was desperate to see where we were, what he was doing, but now the blue plastic sheeting covered my face and head. A terrible sense of futility washed through me.

He stopped and slid me off his back. I hit the ground with a thud, and pain shot up my side. Where was I? What was he going to do to me?

I made frantic grunting noises behind my gag.

"I can't risk having the police find another body," he told me in the same low conversational tone he'd used earlier. "So you're going to have a nice new home up here, well out of the way." His words made no sense to me, but as he spoke he was trying to lift me. I made myself lie completely limp, a dead weight in the rain. I would make it hard for him—whatever he was trying to do.

He laughed coldly. "Brat," he said. "You don't make it easy, I have to hand it to you." But this was a man used to shifting huge pieces of metal, wood, and stone sculpture around. One scrawny teenaged girl was no match for him. As he dragged me, wrapped in my plastic, across the bumpy, rough surface, the blue sheeting fell away from my face and just for a second I glimpsed waning late-afternoon daylight through the steady drizzle—and a bird's-eye view of the village.

Then I knew where I was. That was Blackthorn down below, and I was up on Castle Hill. I was right back up where Duncan and I had been picnicking earlier. It seemed incredible that I should be back, lying among the ruined walls of the ancient castle foundations. Were there no other picnickers around here now? Were there no dog walkers? The vicar!

But no, not now, not in the rain.

Quent was dragging me toward a large hole in the underbrush nearby. "A nice, ancient, final resting place," he hissed, ignoring my panicky, frantic moans from behind the gag. He knelt at the entrance, looming over me, pressing me down hard with one hand. With the other he reached behind him, and in one fluid motion raised his arm to strike. With a desperate roll to one side, I narrowly missed being bashed on the head with the beach stone he held. He swore and reached for me. I pressed my heels into the ground and slid my body backward. Again he raised his arm to strike, then seemed to think better of it. "All right, then, die slowly if you'd prefer." I heard the scrape of stone against metal as he broke open an old grate.

He used his feet to shove me farther and farther into the tight, dark space. It was some sort of hole, a ready-made grave, and I was crying hard now, behind my gag, and trying not to because it only made me choke. His feet against my side kicked again, then moved away. Then he was pulling something across the entrance of the pit, and the faint remains of daylight died away. A new sheet of metal covering slid across the opening, and I heard the ring of metal on metal as he fastened some sort of latch into place.

With sickening certainty, I realized that this was surely the tunnel that Duncan had told me about. This was the tunnel built back in the time of the castle, to offer an escape to people under siege. It was meant to become my grave.

I lay there, tears coursing over my cheeks, my body bruised and aching, the gag in my mouth tasting of vomit. I was well and truly under siege, but this place offered no protection.

I moaned, imagining how I might be found someday—in a hundred years or more: a gruesome discovery by some teenagers on Castle Hill, sharing a kiss and a picnic. Nothing but bones left. Not even a real body anymore, just an old skeleton . . .

Memories reared up again like ghosts:

The body in the closet. Not quite a skeleton, but strips of flesh and soiled clothing . . . clothing I recognized. The pink T-shirt with the flamingo. A short blue-jean skirt with a ruffle.

Forget the visions, focus on the here and now. With effort I struggled off my side and wiggled into a sitting position. The wiggling loosened the tight plastic sheeting and I was able to squirm free of it. When my hands were free, I wrenched the woolen scarf out of my mouth. My lips were swollen, my hip was bruised, I was aching and shivering from the cold, and I was parched with thirst. But I was alive.

Unlike Buzzy.

Unlike Nora.

Unlike Liza.

I sat there shivering in the dark, walled up and alone and in terrible danger from a killer everyone had trusted.

There was a scraping sound on the sheet of metal Quent had locked over the tunnel. Rescuers? I called out to them. "Help! I'm in here!"

But then I heard a muttered curse, and realized it was Quent out there, changing his mind, coming back to finish me off.

Run, Toots! Run, run!

I struggled to my feet and crouched low so I didn't hit my head on the low stone ceiling of the tunnel. I started edging away from the opening, deeper into the tunnel. At the next sound from the metal covering, I was running, running, running—waving my arms ahead of me and above my head to determine where the walls were. Soon I found I could stand. I felt a cool gust of fresh air and reached out for it. There was a thin shaft of light coming from a very small metal grate above my head. I could poke my fingers out the grate and feel grass and dirt, but the opening was far too small to escape through. A thud behind me sent me moving deeper into the tunnel, away from that small grate.

"Juliana! Juliana—wait for me!" The voice, softly insistent, was borne along air currents and came to me clearly.

It was Quent's voice. It was Quent coming after me through the tunnel.

"Juliana, I'm sorry. I've changed my mind. I'll let you go. Come back here, dear." A rueful chuckle. "I can't think what came over me. Please—let me explain."

The calmness of Quent's tone unnerved me. I sagged sideways against the wall, scraping my hands. I took a deep breath and started moving again, more slowly this time, trying to put distance between myself and Quent.

"Wait for me, Juliana. I can explain everything." Quent's voice was a harsh whisper behind me in the darkness. "Who would have thought there'd end up being so many deaths? Who would have thought there'd even have to be one? If Nora had not started trying to overshadow me! If Liza had not been such a busybody! And if you had only been content to leave Simon Jukes in jail . . ."

I trailed my hand along one side of the tunnel wall as I jettisoned myself away from that friendly, fearsome voice. Suddenly I felt a current of air coming from the right side—and I reached out my arm toward it. Another shaft of the tunnel seemed to go off to the right. Should I take it? Or would Quent also take it? Would he follow the straight path or the one with the fresher air? Did the fresher air mean there was an end to this tunnel along the new path? Would Quent guess which way I had gone? Maybe I could fool him by staying on the main path, and he'd turn off on this one to the right?

"But stop running now, dear girl. I've decided to spare you. Stop running so we can have a little chat." A soft chuckle not too far behind me sent my adrenaline spiking, and I veered off to the right, gulping in the fresher air.

I must not make a sound. He wanted me to talk so he could find me in the dark. I remembered that Duncan had said the tunnel from the castle had once ended at the Coopers' house, but that exit had been concreted over ages ago. As I veered to the right, a couple notes of hysterical laughter bubbled out at the thought of digging myself out at the end of the tunnel and ending up in the Coopers' overheated kitchen. I pressed my lips together hard.

Now the tunnel was still slanting downhill, but at a gentler slope. That was good; that meant I was traveling down from Castle Hill. The air was chill and stagnant, but there was more light from small overhead gratings. I was so exhausted, I wanted to stop running and close my eyes and curl into a ball on that cold, dirt floor but I kept on going.

I had to keep going, had to keep running. In my head I heard voices. Young, puzzled, American voices.

"Hey, kid? Watcha doin' out here so late?"

"She's not alone, is she?"

"Looks like it. Hey, kid, where's your mom? Your dad?"

"What's your name, sweetie pie?"

"We'd better take her with us—take her to the police. We can't leave her out on the beach in the dark!"

"Come on, kiddo. Let's get you someplace safe."

"Jeez. You'd think people would take better care of their kids, wouldn't you?"

Yes, yes, I remembered them now, the young couple who had found me and taken me to the police. My next memory was of sitting in my foster home, working on the jigsaw puzzle.

Run, Toots. Run, run.

"Juliana, surely you can understand—a smart girl like you. It was all just too much for me! Nora was becoming a huge success in the art world, getting rather above herself. Thinking she was really something! I couldn't allow her to eclipse me, could I? Oh, sure, I celebrated with everybody else in town when Nora's paintings started attracting so much notice, but you can see how unfair it all was! And then when *her* work was selected to be exhibited in the London show—and *mine* was not—that was the last straw, surely anyone would understand that. Surely no one would blame me for what happened next. Do you blame me, dear? Tell me if you blame me."

His voice was a low murmur, the tone reasonable, and still close behind me. I kept my lips firmly shut. I must not make any noise at all.

I heard a grunt and a low curse. He'd probably banged

his head on the low ceiling. He was tall enough to have to stoop the whole way, whereas I could run easily if I just kept my head down. This was my only advantage. My heart knocked in my chest as I fumbled onward. The next turn in the tunnel took me into darkness again. The narrow air vents were unevenly spaced.

"I know you're a smart girl, but I bet you're wondering how it all happened, aren't you?" called Quent in a wheedling tone. I could hear him stumbling in the dark. "Slow down, dear, and let me tell you about it. I promise I won't hurt you!"

Run, run, run—I hoped fervently that there were no rats down here, or snakes, or spiders. But I was more willing to risk running into one of them than to let Quent catch me. . . .

"We were up in the cottage, in the sunroom, and I just did it. The work of a moment, that's all. And it was easy! Did you know that, Juliana? It is surprisingly easy to knock someone out cold. I bashed her on the head—with the very same beach rock I used later on Liza. Convenient, having the weapon just lying around, posing as art—don't you think?"

His laughter froze my blood, and I wanted to cover my ears as I picked my way farther into the endless tunnel. But now I needed my hands out in front of me, to feel my way and keep from crashing into the walls. With my ears uncovered, I couldn't help but hear everything Quent insisted on telling me. How he had stashed Nora's body in his car, covered it up with tarp just as he'd covered me, and driven toward London, taking back roads rather than the motorway.

"Up, up we went, up to the cliff road. I was clever, Juliana, dear. I skidded deliberately, making tire marks on the road. Then at the top of the cliff road I stopped the car, got out, and bundled Nora into the driver's seat. It was easy to release the brake and give the car a shove so it plunged down, down, over an old stone wall, and right into a farmer's stone shed. I stood and watched, then walked through the fields back to the village. When the police came on the scene, they found Nora apparently dead of a head injury ... watched over now by sheep ... with skid marks showing how recklessly she'd been driving before the crash. A very sad accident, but she never had been a very good driver. I made sure to tell them about her two speeding tickets the previous year!"

I wanted to shout at him that I couldn't believe anyone could be so evil—but he *wanted* me to respond, to be impressed by his cleverness. I wouldn't give him the satisfaction of a single word.

"I can hear your footsteps, my girl. Slow down so we can walk together."

I traveled as fast as I could, panting, waving my hands in front of me, fearful of running into something. The tunnel curved to the left and then to the right. *Who else had traveled through this tunnel?* I wondered bleakly. And on what frantic errand? There could be no casual reason to wander underground in the cold and dark. A person would hurry through these dank passages only in the direst danger.

I could almost see them materializing all around me now—the miserable, frightened ghosts of besieged castle dwellers or innocent prisoners desperately attempting escape. *Had* they escaped? Would *I*?

"The night of the party," Quent's voice continued relentlessly, "I was with Liza in the kitchen. You and Duncan came in to say you wanted to go on a house tour. After you left, I headed back to the party myself. But just as I was leaving the room, I looked back and saw Liza taking my ring of keys from the hook by the back door. She let herself out the back door and headed across the grass to the cottage. So of course I followed her. As she was letting herself into the cottage, Liza turned and saw me. She was strange, and started babbling about something Celia had said that had reminded her of something else that had been puzzling her. She took me up to the sunroom, wanted to show me something. I didn't know what she was on about at first. Thought it was just the drink. But then I realized it was something about Nora, something Liza had found, something that was not where it was supposed to be. When I finally realized what she was talking about—the necklace—I had no choice. Surely you can understand that, dear girl. You can understand that at a certain point, I had no choice but to do what I did—can't you?"

I understood only that I was in a dark tunnel with a madman. The smell of dank earth filled my nostrils. I tried to move faster, then tripped over something, and fell to my knees. What had tripped me? My hands scrabbled in the dirt as I struggled to my feet again. A tree root?

"Ah, there you are, my girl!" exulted Quent, bearing down on me around the bend. I screamed and limped away, my panting changing to sobbing. I increased my pace to a jog, lifting my knees high, trying to avoid any further obstacles. Sharp, stabbing pains shot up from my rib cage. I was crying in desperation now, though I knew he could hear me. I was terrified I was going to end up at a dead end, a blank wall, with no escape. Who would ever find my body down here?

Where was that proverbial light at the end of the tunnel?

Nowhere in sight.

But—wait.

Up ahead I could see another pale shaft of light— larger and brighter than those from the other small vents— filtering down from the roof of this tunnel. The low ceiling rose in height so that I could stand straight—so high that even Quent would be able to stand straight. I stumbled toward the light, holding my aching sides. When I stood directly under it, I could see the source was another metal grate set into the stone about three feet above my head. But this grate was larger—about two feet square.

Cursing myself for not having gone rock climbing with my dad more often—I'd tried it only twice at an indoor gym—I jammed my fingertips into the crevices in the rocks and started trying to scale the damp walls. Fortunately there were lots of good finger- and footholds. *Duncan would be able to do this,* I reminded myself, picturing his rock-climbing posters and stack of magazines. *I have to do it, too.* I hung on the side wall and reached out to grab the metal grid. It was rusty. Could I shift it? But with what?

I froze again, listening. There were footsteps in the darkness, coming closer. Another muttered curse. I hoped Quent would bang his head hard enough to knock himself out before he came to the high-ceilinged section.

What was that noise through the grate? A faint call in the distance. "Pars-leeeeeey!"

Adrenaline coursed through my body and gave me strength. I dropped to the ground, pulled off my shoe, clambered back up the wall, and started battering the grate with my shoe. "Help!" I screamed at the top of my lungs. "Help! Help! Help! I'm down here in the tunnel! Hurry! Hurry! *Help!*"

Behind me I heard a muttered curse. I tensed, ready to—to what? To throw my shoe at Quent if he appeared around the bend? "Help! Help me!" I yelled in desperation. "I'm down here with Quent Carrington! He killed Liza! And he killed his wife—" I screamed this over and over again. I heard a shout behind me. I couldn't hold on to the rocks any longer and dropped back down to the packed earthen floor. But I kept on screaming. "He's a murderer! Hurry!"

When I stopped for breath, I was sure I heard faint footfalls, but no one emerged around the bend in the tunnel. And then a querulous voice right above me rang down through the grating: "Who's that down there? Whatever is going on?"

"Mrs. Cooper! Oh, Mrs. Cooper, it's me, Juliana. Juliana Martin-Drake! Oh, thank you for finding me!" My voice broke. "Help me!"

"What are you doing in there, young lady? What in the *world* are you up to? You gave me the fright of my life! Imagine! A voice coming up out of the ground—"

"Please!" I cut her off. "Hurry! Call the police!" This was my chance—my only chance—to save my life. I took a deep breath to hold back the sobs, then spoke rapidly, desperately. "Mrs. Cooper, listen. I'm in terrible danger. It's Quent Carrington. He forced me into this tunnel—he's trying to kill me!"

"I was just coming out here to the garden to call for Parsley—he *will* insist on staying out in the rain, but it can't be good for him, not at his age—and I heard this awful wailing," continued Mrs. Cooper, just as if she hadn't heard me. "As loud as a caterwauling cat fight, and I thought it was Parsley again, tangling with the neighbor's cat—wait a minute, *what?* What did you say? Quent put you into the tunnel? Why in the world? I've never heard such nonsense—"

"Mrs. Cooper—Quent killed Liza! And he killed your daughter, too!"

Mrs. Cooper let out a shriek, then all was silence. For once Mrs. Cooper had nothing to say. And in the silence I heard footsteps again, but this time they were moving away from me, thank God, growing fainter.

Then I heard a different voice—a very welcome voice. "Granny? What's going on?"

I shouted for Duncan, and he was soon peering down the grate at me in disbelief. "Hurry," I panted. "Can you open this grate? But first call the police. Tell them to get up to the ruins on Castle Hill. Quent must be running back through the tunnel and he'll escape in a few minutes if nobody stops him. He killed Liza and he killed your mum, too—oh, don't just stare down at me! He admitted it all. He *bragged* about it, Duncan! Go get the police!"

For a moment Duncan just frowned at me, and I half expected him to tell me again that I was a crazy girl with an overactive imagination and that I'd watched too many lurid Hollywood films. But then without a word to me, Duncan was gone. I heard him calling in a frantic voice, "Grandad, Grandad, do you have a crowbar? Take it out to Granny; she's out in the garden! Hurry!" Then I heard the back door to the house slam shut.

"What in the world?" Now Mr. Cooper's face was looking down at me. "Finding yourself in a spot of bother, luv?" he asked.

"Worse than bother, Dudley," said his wife as her face came into view beside his at the grate. "The girl says Quent put her down there. Says he killed our Nora *and* that Pethering woman."

"*And* he's trying to kill me," I cried. "Did Duncan phone for the police?"

"He's ringing them now," said Mr. Cooper. "Now let me see if I do have a crowbar. And my metal saw should help. We've got to get you out of there."

I had broken through my shadows and now had memories that filled in all the gaps, though still left a lingering horror—I was a prisoner underground in an ancient tunnel; I was wet and shivering and bruised; and Quent Carrington had killed two women and tried to kill me. All this, and yet I relaxed and smiled up at the pairs of faded blue eyes in lined faces peering down at me. I heard sirens in the distance.

19

Two policemen I hadn't seen before sawed through the metal grating with a special saw, then hauled me up and out. Emerging into the chill, damp air felt like being born into a new world. I babbled my story incoherently, and the two officers who were rescuing me understood enough to radio for help. Soon we heard more sirens in the distance—other police heading up Castle Hill to capture Quent at the other end. Mrs. Cooper brought me inside and sat me down in her kitchen and made me a cup of sweet, milky tea. "Best thing for shock," she said, adding another heaping spoonful of sugar. "I'd better have a cup myself . . ."

Duncan wanted to go up to Castle Hill where the action was and talk to Quent himself. He did not doubt my story, he said, but he thought there just had to be some mistake . . . somewhere. This was *Quent*, after all. His stepfather. The officers said we were all to stay put. They phoned Mom, and drank cups of tea with us while we waited for her. Detective Inspector Link arrived, with Constable Petersen right behind. Parsley came in with wet paws and was cuddled and kissed by Mrs. Cooper. Then he settled down on my lap, a comforting bulk. I was shaking. Duncan sat across the table from me with his head bowed. When Mom and the Goops also arrived, out of breath from having run all the way from Water Street, Mrs. Cooper ushered them into the kitchen, too, and put the water on for still more cups of tea.

"I couldn't take the car," Mom told everyone, "because police are swarming around the Old Mill House. They've got a cop at every door and gate into the property, looking for Quent. I can't believe any of this!" She reached for me and hugged me, hard. "Juliana—are you hurt? Tell me what's happening!"

I licked my swollen lips, felt the throb of my scrapes and bruises. "I'm okay, Mom," I said softly.

The officers standing in the kitchen holding their cups of tea made the room seem very small. There were the two men who had rescued me—one very tall, and the other seeming very short by comparison. Constable Petersen opened a notepad, and Detective Inspector Link asked for my statement. "If you're ready, dear girl, we'll want you to tell us everything—from the beginning," she said. "What made you suspect Mr. Carrington?"

I took a deep breath, suddenly unsure where to start. "Well," I said hesitantly, "when I was three or four years old, I made a necklace out of little shells . . ."

The kitchen was quiet. The Coopers looked puzzled. The police constable was writing everything down. Mom sucked in her breath sharply, then reached out to take my hand. "Jule," she whispered. "Have you remembered—?"

At my sudden, sharp movement, Parsley jumped off my lap with a loud meow. "I remember *everything*," I said raggedly, and then—right there in front of all those people—I broke down crying like a baby in Mom's arms. It took a long time before I could get the whole story out.

I told them what I'd remembered about Buzzy and Tiara, and then I told them how Liza had insisted Nora would have worn her special necklace when she set off for her big London television interview. I told them how I'd suspected Celia Glendenning and Oliver Pethering. (I didn't mention all the others I'd suspected; as Duncan said, I *had* been acting paranoid.) I told them how Quent had come into the sunroom and forced me down the stairs. I told them everything.

When I was finished, Mom was crying. Duncan was sitting there, glaring down at the table, shaking his head like maybe he didn't believe a word. Mrs. Cooper bustled over to put the kettle on again. Mr. Cooper kept clearing his throat. The Goops sidled up and wrapped their sticky arms around me. I hugged them back, hard.

Constable Petersen closed his notebook. "Thank you for your statement," Detective Inspector Link said. "We'll have it typed up, and we'll need you to come to the station tomorrow and sign it."

I nodded. "Okay."

"And perhaps you'll want a medical exam—for the record. To check out any damage—"

"No," I said. "I'm fine. Just a few scrapes."

"You've had quite an ordeal, young lady," the inspector said. "But it seems to me you've solved not one but two murders for us today. Well done."

"Three," said Duncan suddenly, "if you count Buzzy's."

"I don't even know for sure how she died," I murmured. "Just that Tiara must have stuffed her into that closet." I wiped my eyes. "Do *you* know, Mom?"

"Honey, your dad and I were told only that a woman

who was thought to be your birth mother had been found dead of a drug overdose. A second woman was also dead in the same apartment."

Two women? Tiara dead, too? I remembered her lying on the couch, unmoving, and my little girl self desperately trying to wake her. Not sleeping then, after all?

I shuddered.

"It might be that your birth mother died of an overdose, and her friend panicked and hid the body," said Duncan. "And then later overdosed as well."

"Or Buzzy could have been murdered," I whispered.

Mom stroked my hair. "There was a white woman and a black woman. Someone the police interviewed reported that the two lived together, and the white one had a little girl, he thought, and once somebody had mentioned a boyfriend or husband who had been killed in a motorcycle accident. The police guessed that the white woman might have been your mother. But there were no records of anything—no driver's licenses or passports or marriage records or death certificates. No papers identifying either woman."

Mom spread her hands on the table. "I never even heard anything about *how* the women were found. There was no mention of possible murder. Or a body locked in a closet. And I don't think anyone knew that you had found the bodies first, honey. You were discovered walking alone on the beach—you know this part already—and you gave your name as Jewel Moonbeam." She shook her head. "My poor baby. You must have been running away from the terrible shock of finding your birth mother. No wonder you blocked it out."

"And no one checked into the child's background?" inquired Mrs. Cooper, frowning. "The police, I mean. Or the social welfare workers?"

"Of course they tried. But nobody by that name had been registered in the state." Mom shrugged lightly. "Probably Juliana was born at home—wherever home was for her then." She reached over and hugged me.

"I want to call Dad—," I began, still feeling dazed, still half in the past, half in the present. "I want to ask him to check with the police whether it was murder—"

"We'll call him," promised Mom. "But right now, I think we've got enough going on right here."

As if to prove the truth of Mom's statement, the radio strapped to the taller officer's belt crackled, and he moved into the other room to listen to it and reply. We all waited without speaking until he returned.

"Well, folks, looks like Carrington's got away. He reached his car and zoomed off before anyone could stop him. Heading for the motorway. There's a chase going on right now."

We heard this news in silence. We just looked around at each other, shocked.

"We'll get him," the shorter officer predicted. "He might try to hide out in London, but we'll track him down."

"He'll find it hard to live in hiding," Duncan said softly. "Loves the limelight too much."

Mr. Cooper snorted. "That's right, lad. You've got him pegged, and you know him better than most! Sooner or later those sculptures of his will start appearing again— and then the coppers will be onto him like a shot." He turned to the police officers. "You'll let us know when that happens, eh?"

"Yes sir, absolutely," promised Constable Petersen.

Mr. Cooper accompanied the police officers to the door. Detective Inspector Link promised to be in touch as soon as they had any further information. She also promised to station someone outside our house as an extra precaution. Until Quent was in police custody, I could still be in danger.

In the kitchen, Mrs. Cooper sank into a seat at the table. She had been bustling around ever since I was pulled out of the tunnel, but now she lowered her head into her hands and sat quietly. After a second I saw her shoulders shaking with sobs. "It's starting to sink in," she choked out. "Did he really kill our Nora? Can you believe it, Dunk-o? That he killed your mum?"

"I always thought it was strange that she left without me," Duncan said softly. "I was supposed to go to London, too. We were supposed to go together." He stood at his grandmother's side, but he was looking at me. His eyes were wet. I sensed he was feeling a lot like I was just then: hollow, leaden, weighted down with an ocean of sorrow. But in some small way also mightily relieved that truth had floated to the surface at last.

20

The police called the station for an officer to escort us home. We were happy to linger. The Coopers' kitchen was warm and cheerful, and the village outside was gray and cold. I had the shivers, and had to keep wrapping my arms around myself, squeezing hard. Duncan's expression was blank, his mouth set. When Mr. Cooper invited us all upstairs to see his model train set, the Goops leaped up in excitement, ready to be diverted. But Mom shook her head, smiling, and stayed at the table with Mrs. Cooper. Duncan and I followed the others upstairs to the top-floor attic where Mr. Cooper had an electric train and village set up on a big table in the center of the room. We watched for a few minutes as the trains whizzed around the tracks, past the miniature farms and towns. The Goops were enchanted.

I imagined for a moment that there were people in those little trains, traveling through villages and countryside, gliding through tunnels. Little people with their secret lives.

Just as Mr. Cooper let Ivy and Edmund take over the controls, I felt Duncan's hand close around mine. He squeezed my fingers gently. We slipped out of the room together and went down the little hallway to the small room that was his whenever he stayed at his grandparents' house. It would probably be his room all the time now, I thought.

Because how could Duncan go back to living at the Old Mill House with Quent in prison or living somewhere as a fugitive?

As if he had read my thoughts, Duncan slumped down onto his bed and said, "Guess I'd better move all my stuff over here now."

"Yeah," I said, sitting on the bed next to him. It was a narrow bed, like my own. The room was simply furnished with a dresser, desk and chair, and a faded blue rag rug on the floor. The curtains at the window hung limp. They were white lace, yellowed from age but clean. The walls were bare, nothing like the bright walls hung with posters in Duncan's room at the Mill House. "I guess you'll be living here now. But what will happen to all Quent's stuff?"

He shrugged. "I don't know. Don't know much about anything, it seems. I mean—damn it, Juliana, *how* could I not have known?" He punched the mattress. "How could I live with a murderer for two years and never have a clue?"

"Nobody suspected him," I said. "How *could* you have known?"

"You'd think there would have been *something*. Some clue."

"But there wasn't?"

"Not so I noticed. I mean—nothing that made me think *murder*! Still . . ." He hesitated. "I knew he was jealous of her. I'd known that for a long time."

"How did you know that?" I asked.

Duncan stared up at the ceiling. "Well, every time Mum won a local prize for her paintings, Quent would cheer and celebrate. But then he'd work extra long and hard in his studio. And the day she got the call that her work had been selected to be exhibited in that prestigious London show, he was furious. I could see it in his face. Furious that hers had been chosen and his had not. Because he had submitted work, too."

"Did he say anything?"

"Not to Mum and me. No, he was all congratulations and big hugs and a bouquet of flowers. But I heard him out in the studio later that same day, crashing around. Through the window I saw him hurling pieces of wood against the walls. Letting off steam, I thought."

"You didn't realize then that all her successes were like knives twisting in his gut," I murmured.

Duncan reached over and lifted my braid. He wrapped it gently around his hand, then unwound it. He closed his eyes. "No, I didn't realize," he whispered.

"But even if you had, what could you have done? Lots of people might be upset about not winning an award," I reasoned. "A lot of people might stomp around and throw things in private to let off steam. But it wouldn't go any further than that. It wouldn't lead to murder."

"I wonder how he did it," Duncan said, eyes still closed. "You told the officers that Quent confessed to my mum's murder. But you didn't give details, really. Did he tell you? How could he be sure she would have the accident? Did he fix the brakes somehow, so they wouldn't work? What did he say to convince her to leave so early, while I was still at school, when she knew I was planning to go with her?"

"No," I said. "Duncan, she *didn't* leave willingly. She wouldn't have gone without you—and she wouldn't have left her special necklace behind. That's the whole point. That's how I figured it out. And then—in the tunnel—he told me more. He said he knocked her on the head with the same beach stone he used on Liza. He put her in the car and arranged the accident."

Duncan sat up, groaning, and put his head in his hands.

I rubbed his back, silent. I couldn't think of anything to say to make things better. I could just picture it happening. Quent knocking Nora out, carrying her to the car, wrapped up in blue plastic just as I had been. He would have bundled her into the back, and set off for the coast road, heading toward London. He would have positioned the car at the edge of the cliff, sat Nora in the driver's seat, seat belt properly fastened. And then he would have released the brake so the car plunged down the cliff.

Had he walked all the way home? Or did he have a bike in the back of his car, so he could ride home on the back lanes, unseen? In any case, he was back in Blackthorn in time to play the part of the grieving widower when the police found the wreck.

Mom's voice called to me up the stairs. It was time to round up the Goops, she said, and head home. An officer had come to escort us. Reluctantly I stood up. Duncan stood up, too, and we embraced in the darkness of his little room. Then I moved away. I went back to the model train room where the Goops were happily acting as engineers. Mr. Cooper sat in an armchair, staring blankly out at the dark windows. He was in shock, too, I realized. It was his daughter Quent had murdered.

The police officer waiting to escort us was the tall one who had helped lift me out of the tunnel. Since the main road was blocked in an attempt to catch Quent, he would walk with us to our cottage. We left Duncan and his grandparents standing silently at their front door, and traveled swiftly across the quiet village. The Goops were subdued and clung to Mom's hands. The chilly sea wind buffeted our bodies as we hurried through the night.

I kept my eyes on the broad back of the officer, fearful that any shadow might conceal Quent. He might leap out at me, arm raised, hand wielding a beach stone.

As we unlocked the door in the stone wall of the Old Mill House and stepped through, I looked over to the big house. All the windows were dark. *Quent will never live there again,* I thought, as we followed the path across the lawn to our place. Despite all that had happened that afternoon, despite my conversation with Duncan in his room, I still wasn't used to thinking of Quent Carrington, our trusted landlord, as the bad guy. And what if Quent had eluded the police and somehow doubled back, and was hiding inside his house in one of the dark rooms? I looked over my shoulder as we passed the house.

He will never live there again. Again, this thought came to me with certainty. Prison would be home to Quent from now on, unless he evaded the police and maybe escaped to another country and lived as a fugitive. How long would he be able to manage that, when he so loved being in the center of the art world?

I tried to shake Quent out of my head as we went inside our cottage. The place looked strange to me, as if I had been away from it a very long time instead of only a few hours. The police officer checked every room, then smiled and left to take up guard outside the cottage. Mom ran me a full tub of hot water, drizzled in some of her special daphne-scented foam bath, and insisted I have a nice, long soak. I eased into the bath, wincing as the bubbles closed over my scrapes and bruises. For once I was allowed to use

up all the hot water, and I didn't have to hurry out so someone else could use the bath after me, while it was still hot.
I lay back, eyes closed, breathing shallowly. I was comforted
at the thought of the policeman stationed outside, watch-
ful in the dark. Quent would not find me now.

My arms floated. Images, too, floated through my
mind: Liza, smiling at us on our arrival in Blackthorn, her
witchy black hair blowing in the wind off the sea. And Liza
again, carried in Quent's arms through the upstairs hallway
of the Old Mill House. Buzzy, smiling at me as we walked
on the beach together, collecting shells. And Buzzy again,
crumpled up in that dark closet, partially hidden by blankets. *Buzzy* . . .

My eyes popped open and I focused hard on the bottle
of bubble bath on the ledge. I tried to force the images of
dead people out of my head, tried to keep my mind a
blank.

I heard Edmund's voice from the kitchen. "Let me talk
to him, Mom!"

And Ivy's voice: "Me, too!"

I heard Mom's voice muttering and realized that she
must have phoned someone. There were few silences. Mom
was doing all the talking, but I couldn't make out what she
was saying. I closed my eyes again and drifted. I don't know
how long. I nearly fell asleep.

Then the phone rang. I sat up in the tub and listened.
Heard Mom's surprised yelp. "*What?*" she cried loud and
clear. "Oh, no, are you *sure?* Oh, no!"

The water was still enticingly hot, but I sloshed my way
out of the tub and grabbed a towel. I stood on the mat and
dried myself hurriedly, reached for my bathrobe, and
jerked open the bathroom door.

Mom stood by the kitchen sink, wide-eyed. When she saw me, she turned away and hunched over the phone. Her voice grew softer but still I heard: "That's just awful. So sad . . . I can't believe it . . . but maybe it's for the best? I just don't know . . ."

Ivy and Edmund sat at the table with mugs of cocoa. They both looked at me and shrugged, mystified by Mom's phone conversation. I pulled out a chair and sat with them, waiting for Mom to hang up. The room seemed full of shadows.

After another moment she laid the phone down and turned slowly to us. Two bright spots of color stained her cheeks. "That was Detective Inspector Link."

I think I had already known as much.

"There was an accident," she continued softly. "On the motorway to London. The police were chasing Quent's car at high speed. Quent spun off the road suddenly, trying to take an exit, and his car rammed into a concrete post."

The shadows receded. I pictured Quent as I'd first seen him, driving wildly with Duncan in his sports car. And then later that day, smiling and genial, taking us off to the Old Ship for our welcome-to-Blackthorn meal. And then I pictured him as I'd last seen him on Castle Hill: face contorted, voice hissing in fury as he shoved me into the ancient tunnel. *"In you go."*

"Did the police catch him, then?" Edmund demanded. "Did they take him to jail?"

"They caught him," Mom said, then fell silent for a moment before adding, "he was in bad shape."

I caught my breath. *Oh, Quent.*

"While they waited for the ambulance, Quent confessed to both murders," Mom continued. "A full confession, and one of the officers wrote it all down, everything Quent was saying. He kept talking all the way to the hospital. The officer said it was as if a floodgate had opened and he had to get everything off his chest before—" She stopped.

"Before what, Mom?" pressed Ivy. But I knew.

"Before he died, honey," said Mom quietly. "Quent died before he got into surgery." She looked at us for a moment, and her lips quivered. She lowered her head into her hands and started to sob.

We all started to cry then, right there around the table, but whether I was crying for Quent, or for Liza, for Nora, for my own poor Buzzy, or for *all* of them—I just didn't know.

The phone rang again and it was Dudley Cooper. Mom stood up and went over to the kitchen counter to talk to him. He and his wife and Duncan had also been informed by the police of Quent's death—and his confession. Mr. Cooper was apparently doing all the talking, because for a long time Mom just stood there nodding and murmuring and taking notes on a pad of paper. When Mom got off the phone again, she was calm and composed. The bright spots of color had faded. She sat down at the table, took a deep breath, and told us the details of Quent's confession.

Although he was gravely injured, he seemed determined to relate everything, Mom told us. He told the police what he had revealed to me in the tunnel, plus more—maybe because his conscience was troubling him, but maybe just wanting the police to know how clever he had been. Mom shook her head. "Quent staged it all very thoroughly," she said with a twist of her lips. "Showed real artistic flair."

"And he nearly got away with it," I added.

"Yes, he thought he had," said Mom. "Until the night of

his welcome party in our honor." Quent had told the police how Liza grabbed the ring of keys off the hook by the door, and set off for the cottage. He followed, asking her what she was doing. She babbled something about Nora's necklace and he realized Liza would never keep quiet about her suspicions even if she couldn't prove anything. He grabbed the same rock he'd used on Nora, and bashed Liza on the head. When she was unconscious, he stopped the flow of blood with one of Mom's painting rags, then took a few more minutes to stack our boxes over the blood that had stained the floorboards. "Then he carried Liza's body back to the house," concluded Mom, "pretending she was so drunk she had to sleep it off."

"That's when we saw him in the hallway," I said, picturing it again. It made me queasy to think that Liza was pretty much dead at this point, yet Quent passed it off blithely as a drunken stupor. And we'd all believed him.

"Yes." Mom nodded. "He was obviously a good actor as well as a gifted artist." She wrapped her arms around herself with a sudden shiver. "He was clever—and ruthless. He returned to the party and rejoined his guests as if nothing had happened! Sometime a bit later he slipped out again and carried Liza down the back stairs, out to the Shreen, where he left her to die." She shook her head with the horror of it.

"But Jule figured it out!" Ivy said.

"And he nearly got away with murder again!" Edmund added.

"That heartless bastard!" Mom seldom swore, but as she reached across the table and grabbed my hands, I could feel the intensity of her rage. "Messing with my baby."

Mom had never known me as a baby, but I loved when

she called me that. Now the thought of somebody else's baby was bothering me. Nora's baby. "Poor Duncan," I whispered. "He finds out his mum was *murdered* by Quent—and now he's lost Quent, too. Now he doesn't have anybody."

"He has his grandparents," Mom reminded me.

We continued to sit at the table together for a while longer, none of us wanting to break up the family circle and go off to bed. Too much had happened today. I didn't think I was alone in wondering how life would ever feel normal again.

When the phone rang for a third time that night, I stiffened. It was late; who would be calling now?

But Mom smiled at me before getting up to answer. "Hello?" she said into the phone. "Oh, good, it's you. I was hoping . . . Yes, that's great. Yes, perfect. Thank you so much. I really appreciate it. No, really, I do. You didn't have to—well, all right. Of course." She listened for a long moment, then nodded, as if the person on the phone could see her. She wrote something on the notepad. "We'll be there, right on time."

Then she hung up and smiled at us.

"We'll be *where*, right on time?" I asked, bewildered.

"At the airport, day after tomorrow," Mom said. "To meet your dad's plane."

21

Dad's coming? He's coming *here*?" Of course that announcement had us all cheering, but when we calmed down, I had to ask. "Are you two getting back together again? Is that why he's coming?"

"No, honey," Mom replied. "He's coming for you. He was horrified to hear about all that has happened—and when I talked to him while you were in the tub, we hadn't even heard yet about Quent . . ."

"But *why* is he coming?" I pressed. "I mean, I'm not hurt . . ."

"He needs to see you. Wants to be with you. I told him about how Quent tried to—" She hesitated. I think it was all still so hard for us to believe. "How Quent tried to *kill* you, and how that fright cut through the amnesia about your life before you came to us. When Dad heard that you'd remembered what had happened to your poor birth mother, he said, 'I'm on the next plane.' And so he will be." She reached over and stroked my cheek. "He hates to think of your remembering a traumatic death by suffering through another trauma. What you've been through is something no parent wants a child to experience. I think he needs to see you just as much as you need him. He's your dad. He loves you very much."

"We do, too!" declared Ivy loyally.

Edmund was nodding vigorously. "Yeah! We don't want you dead."

"I think there's been enough dead people around here," Mom said. And then she herded us all up the stairs to bed.

Sleep didn't come quickly, despite my exhaustion. I lay in my little room in the narrow bed and tested my memories. Yes, I remembered finding Buzzy's body. I remembered running to the beach. . . . But I remembered other things— little snapshot moments. Collecting shells with Buzzy. Filling a sand pail and turning it over to make a castle. Riding on the back of a motorcycle, wearing a helmet that was much too big and heavy, zooming on city streets. Clutching the driver—was it my birth father?—around the middle. His leather jacket soft on my cheek and smelling of cigarette smoke. Sleeping in blankets outside—were we homeless? I recalled only the coziness of being cocooned between two people—my parents? A dark-skinned, very tall woman— was that Tiara?—teaching me to dance, loud music filling a smoke-filled room, the two of us bopping to the beat and laughing.

"DAD'S FLIGHT WILL actually be leaving California late this afternoon, California time," Mom told us the next morning at breakfast. "It's an eleven-hour flight, so with the time difference, it'll be tomorrow morning here when the plane lands."

"I don't get it," complained Edmund, so Ivy, who understood such things, started trying to explain. Mom slid a mound of fluffy scrambled eggs onto my plate. I poured myself a glass of black currant juice, and poured some for Mom and the Goops as well. We were back at the kitchen table, just where we had been sitting last night. I still felt I was in some sort of dream. Everything seemed different, somehow new and unreal.

The knocking on the cottage door was very real. Loud and peremptory, as if the person on the other side had no time for nonsense and did not want to be kept waiting. *Probably the police again,* I thought, going to answer.

But it was Celia Glendenning standing there, with Kate hovering like a shadow behind her. "Good morning!" boomed Celia. "I've heard the most incredible account of events from Hazel Cooper. She came into the Emporium this morning and was talking to Oliver, and I was there, too. What a horrifying ordeal for you, my dear!"

"Yes," I said, not quite sure what Celia had heard. About Quent, no doubt. But had Hazel also passed on the news that I'd remembered finding my dead birth mother? Did all of Blackthorn know things about me now that I barely knew myself?

"And then I saw that unsavory Simon Jukes walking down Castle Street with his equally awful brother. Heading straight for the pub, no doubt, even at this time of day."

Celia was dressed impeccably as usual, wearing a dark blue skirt and sweater, a colorful silk scarf at her neck, navy blue pumps with sensible heels. She carried her tapestry bag over one shoulder. "May we come in for a minute?" asked Celia when I just stood there, staring at her. I was thinking that I was glad Simon Jukes was free, unsavory or not.

"Oh, I'm sorry—of course." I stood aside and smiled like a good hostess, though she was one of the last people I felt like seeing. Celia sailed in, with Kate slipping in quietly behind her. "We're still having breakfast, but—um—would you like a cup of tea?"

Mom came into the sitting room and welcomed our

unexpected visitors more warmly than I ever could. She invited Celia to sit down at the table, and Celia did. I stayed back, close to Kate, near the door. I was still remembering how frightened I had been when Celia Glendenning was hiding behind our bathroom door, still remembering how even as recently as yesterday afternoon, I was thinking she could have been the one who killed Liza Pethering. Celia Glendenning was a very strange person, and I doubted I would ever feel comfortable around her, even now that she hadn't turned out to be a murderer.

I glanced over at Kate. She was standing with her arms wrapped around herself as if for warmth, though the room didn't seem cold to me. "I can't believe Mr. Carrington killed his wife and Liza," Kate whispered to me. "It's such a shock. Poor Duncan!"

"I know. It's a tragedy, really."

"Come here, Juliana," Celia summoned me imperiously. "I have something for you."

Kate and I went to sit at the table with the others. I looked at Celia with raised eyebrows.

Celia rummaged in her large tapestry bag. I let out a little yelp as she withdrew my framed school photograph and set it on the table in front of her. "I've come to return this, Hedda," she said to Mom, although she kept looking straight at me.

I knew it! I knew you'd stolen it! My thoughts were triumphant, but only puzzlement must have shown in my face because Celia reached over and patted my hand. "I owe you an apology, and an explanation, of course."

"Yes," said Mom drily. "I rather think you do."

Kate was looking mortified. She would probably rather

be anywhere than here with her obnoxious mother who went around breaking into people's homes and stealing their pictures off the mantel and hiding in their bathrooms. I looked at my own normal mom and felt proud of her, and grateful. What if someone like Celia had adopted me instead of my own mom and dad? It didn't bear thinking about, really. I'd be dead from embarrassment a hundred times over. Poor Kate!

"The other evening I stopped by to return your key—just as I've already told you. No one was at home, and since I had the key with me, I thought I would leave it inside on your table rather than outside under the doormat or something. So I opened the door—"

"You could have put it through the mail slot," Edmund pointed out. "I mean the post slot, or whatever."

I nodded and gave my little brother the thumbs-up sign. But Mom frowned at us both. "Let Mrs. Glendenning tell her story, please," she said to Edmund.

"I could have dropped it through the post slot, indeed," Celia agreed, nodding at Edmund. "You're quite right, young man. But I must admit to having another reason for coming to your house that evening. I wanted to look again at the photos I'd seen earlier on your mantel." Her gaze shifted back to me. "You see, ever since I first met you, my girl, you reminded me of someone. Someone I knew when I was a child, living in Norwich. Her name was Barbara-Elizabeth Ellis and she was jolly good fun to be with, but rather wild with it, all the same. She was always seeking attention and coming up with the most daredevil sorts of schemes. She was an incredible risk taker, too, and I was not encouraged to play with her. We never did become real friends, but I watched her escapades from afar, with a kind of envy. Our mothers had once been friends, but her mother died of cancer when Barbara-Elizabeth was only about three or four, and I remember her father as a remote man who left Barbara-Elizabeth on her own most of the time. She grew wilder as she got older, always seeking attention of the most outrageous sort and messing up at school. Her father couldn't handle her."

Ivy's eyes met mine across the table, and when she rolled them at me, I knew my little sister was thinking *so what?* But I found I was holding my breath as I listened. Somehow this obnoxious woman's seemingly random story was going to matter. I listened hard.

"When we were teenagers," Celia continued, "Barbara-Elizabeth was sent off to live with her aunt and uncle in Hethel, a tiny village outside Norwich. But she soon ran off, taking all the cash they'd had on hand in their house. The aunt and uncle did make enquiries, and her father was quite upset, but the girl was nearly eighteen, and no one had any idea where she'd gone. When I met you, I was immediately reminded of her. Same eyes, same hair. Same shape of the face. You'll remember I asked you, Hedda, whether you had relatives in the Norwich area. You told me you didn't, and I knew your husband was from America, so I was stumped. I thought it must just be coincidence, after all, that your daughter should look so much like this girl I remembered from my childhood."

I shifted in my chair. "So . . . where does my school photo come in to the story?" Despite my nonchalant tone, I was feeling a little tremor of possibility.

"I'm getting there, dear. But I must tell the story in my own way, so you'll see I'm not really a thief!" She chuckled.

"Poor dear girl, you had such a fright when you found me in the toilet."

I still didn't see what was funny about that, so I sat staring at her until she cleared her throat and continued her story.

"I rang my mother, who still lives in Norwich, though she's in a retirement home now. I asked her whatever had happened to Barbara-Elizabeth Ellis. Mum recalled that Barbara-Elizabeth did send her aunt and uncle a post-card—just one—about a month after she'd left, promising to pay back the money someday. But first, she said, she needed to get rich! Silly girl. But the exciting part about this news from my mum was that the postcard had been sent *from America.* From *California,* in fact. There was no return address on the postcard.

"Now I knew *you* all were from California, so I still thought there might be some connection. And then later, learning you had been adopted, Juliana, I felt even more certain there must be. The resemblance is too striking! My mum suggested I send a photo of you to her, and then she would show it to the aunt and uncle, and to Barbara-Elizabeth's father, who is still living in the same house in Norwich. I wanted to proceed cautiously, and not get their hopes up if there were no connection. I didn't want to tell you about what I was doing for the same reason. And, well, maybe you'd say it was none of my business! You'll remember I asked Kate to snap a photo of you and develop it quickly. That was so I could send it to my mum." She cast an irritated glance at Kate. "But her camera was broken—"

"It still is! Because *you* dropped it, Mother!" Kate snapped so unexpectedly that we all stared at her. "You don't think my camera is of any value, so you treat it like it's just some old plastic toy—and now it's broken!"

"It got knocked off the counter in the kitchen," Celia said icily. "And if you would put your belongings away properly in your bedroom instead of leaving them lying around, things wouldn't get broken."

"So you decided to get a photograph another way." Mom tried to get the conversation back on track.

"That's right," Celia nodded. "I let myself in with your key, took Juliana's school photo off the mantel, and put it in my bag. And then—what a fright I had!"

"Not as much a fright as Juliana had," Edmund, my staunch little protector, said severely.

"Well, perhaps not, dear," Celia said vaguely. Then she continued, "I heard someone fumbling at the door, trying to open it with a key! Of course, it was already open, so the person just locked it, trying to open it. That gave me the few extra seconds I needed to bolt into the loo. When I came out, I had the photo hidden in my bag, and I took it home and scanned it, and e-mailed it straight off to my mum in Norwich."

"What did she find out?" Mom asked.

"It is rather interesting," Kate murmured. "She sent us something—through the post. Something she got from her neighbor."

Celia drank deeply from her teacup, making us wait. I was holding my breath. Then she fished deep in her tote bag and withdrew another, smaller photograph. It was un- framed. She turned back to me, and winked. "Barbara- Elizabeth's old dad gave this to my mum to send to you. It was taken the last year she lived at home with him, right before she was sent off to Hethel. What do you think of it?" She handed me the photo.

It was a formal school photograph, faded now, of a girl looking so much like me that I gasped. I could see now why Celia Glendenning had remarked on my hair when she first met me—because the girl in the photo had the same single blond braid, lying over one shoulder like a thin yellow rope. She was wearing a sort of school uniform with a blue sweater and a white collar; a red, blue, and green plaid jacket; and a necktie, worn crooked. It was nothing like anything I'd ever worn to school, but she had the same gray eyes and the same wide smile and the same exact gap between her front teeth that I had had—until my braces came off last year.

It wasn't like this girl was my twin; you could see differences, too. Her face was rounder, and she had freckles. The shape of our noses was different—hers was smaller, sort of pert, while mine was longer. "An aristocratic Roman nose," Dad used to call mine.

"Amazing, rather!" said Celia Glendenning, pleased with the results of her meddling in our affairs. But I really couldn't blame her.

"*Wow*" was all I could say.

Mom and the Goops pushed back their chairs and came around the table to look over my shoulder.

"Hey, cool!" shouted Edmund. "It's like Juliana's alien clone!"

"Do we know this girl?" asked Ivy, looking puzzled. "She must be your sister or something, Jule."

Mom drew in a quick breath. "Oh, Jule," she whispered. She reached for the photo and examined it closer, looking from it to me, and back again. Then she turned it over. "Oh, my, Juliana—*look*."

I leaned over and then blinked at what was written

there. I didn't see stars—no, nothing so dramatic—but I felt a kind of wave wash over me, a fresh, clean, invigorating wave, and I felt I'd somehow come to the end of a long journey, or was maybe just setting off on another. On the back of the photograph, written in faded blue ink, were these words, and the date: *Buzzy Ellis, aged sixteen years. 1981.*

22

So I guess we have to forgive Celia Glendenning for being such a snoop," I told Duncan over dinner at the Coopers' house. "After all, if it hadn't been for her, I'd still have the awful memory of Buzzy in the closet as my only way of picturing her. And now I know I really am part English. My birth mother was from England! Not Australia, not New Zealand."

We had all been invited to dinner—Mom, the Goops, and me. Hazel and Dudley Cooper needed company, Duncan felt, and he'd pushed them to phone Mom and ask us to come. Mom had insisted that she would bring the dessert and salad, and Hazel was only to boil up spaghetti and open a couple bottles of tomato sauce. Nothing fancy.

It wasn't fancy, though of course Mrs. Cooper did much more than boil up spaghetti. She'd made two succulent steak-and-kidney pies with flaky pastry crusts, and a rich chocolate cake. "I'm so glad you're here," Duncan whispered to me when we first arrived. "Granny spent half the day cooking up a storm, and the second half lying on her bed, staring at the cracks on the ceiling."

I'd been lying on my bed much of the day, too. But not staring at cracks. Staring instead at the photo of Barbara-Elizabeth (Buzzy!) Ellis. Staring and wondering and shivering sometimes with the amazement that I should be holding that photo in my hands.

Hazel and Dudley Cooper had a dazed air about them, and I wondered if the shock of learning that Quent had killed their Nora was really only just beginning to sink in. Everyone seemed glad to have the photograph of Buzzy to talk about instead of the events of yesterday. That got us through dinner. We also discussed how Simon Jukes had been let out of jail and was planning to sue for false imprisonment, police brutality, and deliberate food poisoning. I couldn't help but laugh, though I thought he might have a case with the false imprisonment charge. It seemed to me the police had been very quick to lock him up.

We talked about the new glassblowing class that Mom had signed the Goops up to take with Rodney Whitsun and Andrew Parker. Edmund told everyone how he wanted to learn how to make a ship inside a bottle. Duncan told me that Kate and Veronica Pimms had signed up for the class, too. "Maybe we should take the class as well," he said. "Give them a little healthy competition."

I said absolutely. Even a class with Goops in it would be fun with Duncan there, too. And though I thought I'd been sensing that Kate's feelings for Duncan really were more sisterly than anything else, it wouldn't hurt to stay on the scene. Veronica Pimms I was not worrying about.

After dinner Mom helped Mrs. Cooper wash up the dishes in the kitchen. Mr. Cooper invited the Goops out into the back garden to see the ancient grating into the tunnel. Edmund declared that there should be a plaque installed, with the date of my rescue. I ruffled his hair. When they were all out of the way, Duncan and I sat in the sitting room together, and I was glad to be alone with him.

We held hands, but we didn't have a whole lot to say, all of a sudden. The silence stretched between us, a good kind of silence. I loved the feeling of our fingers twined together, but my thoughts were not on romance just then. I was wondering so many things, like what would happen when my dad arrived the next day, and what would happen to the Old Mill House now that Quent was dead, and whether we would still be able to live in our cottage now that our land-lord was gone—or whether we'd stay in England at all. But these were not concerns to bring up to Duncan. These were things my mom would handle.

After a while I asked Duncan something I thought he *would* know the answer to. "Will you stay here with your grandparents? Or go to live with your father in South America?"

Duncan snorted. "If I didn't go live with him when my mum died, why would I go now that my *evil stepfather* has died?"

I winced. "I just wondered. I'm *glad* you won't be going away."

"The bloody murderer," Duncan muttered under his breath. I squeezed his hand.

He squeezed back. "So, how soon are you going to Nor-wich?" he asked. "I mean, I'm assuming you'll want to go to Norwich to meet Barbara-Elizabeth's family. You might have *piles* of relatives! More family than you can handle! But they'll be family, and that's the important thing, right?"

"Well," I said, "of course I want to go to Norwich and meet them. Sometime. But—I've already got my family right here, and Ivy and Edmund are already more relatives than I can handle. Besides," I added, "my dad is coming tomorrow. *That's* the important thing."

BEFORE WE LEFT the Coopers that evening there was a surprise visit from Oliver Pethering. When the knock sounded on the front door, Dudley Cooper twitched the white lace curtain aside and peered out from the sitting room window.

"Now what is *he* wanting?" groaned Mr. Cooper. "Probably come to say *he's* now the director of the *Jumblies.* His wife maybe left him the position in her will."

"Grandad!" chided Duncan. "Aren't you going to let him in?"

Mrs. Cooper was bustling to the door. "Of course we are," she was saying at the same time her husband was grousing to Mom, "No—just ignore him and maybe he'll go away!"

Oliver came in carrying a painting wrapped in white sheeting. He stepped awkwardly into the sitting room, holding it out in front of him like a shield.

"Oh? And what would this be?" asked Mrs. Cooper.

"A painting. My wife's." Oliver nodded to Mom and then to me and the Goops. "Hello, Hedda. Youngsters. Excuse the interruption." His staccato voice boomed out.

Oliver unveiled the painting of Nora holding baby Duncan. I was watching Mr. Cooper, and for once he was silent. Mrs. Cooper reached out her arms as if to embrace the painting, or to embrace her daughter and the red-haired baby in the picture. Then she took a shaky breath.

"Are you offering this for sale, Oliver?" she asked tremulously. "Oh, we must buy this!"

"You may not," he barked, and immediately Mr. Cooper reared up off the couch, muttering threateningly.

"You may not buy it," repeated Oliver Pethering firmly. "It's a gift. For the boy. For your Duncan."

"A gift!" cried Mrs. Cooper.

"Liza would want him to have it," Oliver said. "I'm sure."

Duncan seemed unable to speak for a long moment. He just stood staring at the painting that Oliver had leaned against the armchair. Then he stepped forward and pumped Oliver's hand. "Thank you so much," he said. "It's really— it's just . . . It's great. It's perfect." He stopped, probably kicking himself for stammering all over the place, but I knew how he felt. It was like a gift from his mum, or a message from her—just when he needed one.

Mr. Cooper recovered his manners and asked Oliver to stay for a cup of tea, or even something stronger, but Oliver declined. "Must be going," he said, jovial now. "Doesn't do to keep the ladies waiting!"

Mrs. Cooper shut the door, shaking her head. "*Tsk, tsk.* And his wife not in her grave more than two weeks."

"At least some of Oliver's instincts are right," Mom murmured to me, nodding in the direction of Duncan, who sat on the floor in front of his painting, rapt, studying it inch by inch.

It was time for us to go, too, and we soon said good night and walked back across the village to our cottage. The Old Mill House stood like a silent sentry as we passed it.

IN THE MORNING we left early for the airport, arriving in good time to meet Dad's plane. Ivy and Edmund were in high spirits, and therefore very annoying, singing all sorts of raucous camp songs in the car until we got there. My ears rang with bottles of pop on the wall, fires in the shed, and holes in the bottom of the sea. It was a relief to park and walk into the airport.

Dad's plane was on time. Dad came through customs quickly, waving his arms when he saw us, and scooping both Goops up into a huge hug (did I mention that our dad is a large, strong bear of a man?). Then he hugged Mom, and last he turned to me.

He didn't say anything for a moment, just studied my face, and then reached out and crushed me to him. "You amazing kid," he murmured into my hair. "I'm so thankful you're safe."

Tears pricked my eyes as I hugged him back, and I thought how I'd missed him, and how phone messages just hadn't been enough.

On the drive back to Blackthorn, I watched Dad and Mom closely to see how they would be with each other now. I couldn't see that they acted any differently at all. They were friendly and polite, chatting together in the front seat; but they never had been the kind to yell and throw things. I wasn't sure how to gauge their relationship or predict what would happen in their marriage. But I was more sure than ever, though I'd never doubted it, that even if they didn't love each other, they loved their kids. They loved *me*.

Ivy chattered nonstop, relating historic details of Britain, starting with the Druids, and then somehow moving on to *mongers*—iron and fish in particular. Edmund pointed to passing cars and made jokes about dogs in the drivers' seats. I was mostly silent.

At last, we were exiting the motorway and heading along the narrow lane lined with the hedgerows—the lane where we'd first seen Quent Carrington and Duncan racing past. Then we were heading over the hill toward Blackthorn. The now-familiar scent of salt air overlaid with woodsmoke held no added terror today—though my memories were tender, sad, and sore. I would take Dad on a walk tomorrow, on the beach. We would cross the field of beach stones down to the rim of sand, and as we walked along the ocean's edge, I would tell him everything that had been happening. I would tell him everything I'd learned about Barbara-Elizabeth Ellis and everything I remembered about Buzzy—every last detail that had been hidden in my mind all these years.

And then, out of the past, I would take him into the village and introduce him to everybody we'd met since we'd been here. We would stop at the Angel Cafe and the Old Ship. The Goops and I would take him up Castle Hill to see the view. And the ruins.

I made my plans as we drove down Castle Street. And as we passed the thicket of blackthorn bushes, their dark branches spreading like lace, I had a feeling that my blackthorn winter was over. It seemed to me there was a hint of springtime in the air.